MW00773168

FRIEDRICHSBURG

NUMBER THIRTY-TWO

Jack and Doris Smothers Series in Texas History, Life, and Culture

FRIEDRICHSBURG

A Novel

Colony of the German *Fürstenverein*

by

FRIEDRICH ARMAND STRUBBERG

Translated, Annotated, and
Illustrated by James C. Kearney

UNIVERSITY OF TEXAS PRESS ᐱ AUSTIN

Publication of this work was made possible in part by support from the J. E. Smothers, Sr., Memorial Foundation and the National Endowment for the Humanities.

The paper used in this book meets the minimum requirements of ANSI/NISO Z39.48-1992 (R1997) (Permanence of Paper). ∞

Design by Lindsay Starr

LIBRARY OF CONGRESS CATALOGING-IN-PUBLICATION DATA

Armand, 1806–1889.
[Friedrichsburg. English]
Friedrichsburg : colony of the German Fürstenverein : a novel / by Friedrich Armand Strubberg ; translated, annotated, and illustrated by James C. Kearney. — 1st ed.
p.   cm. — (Jack and Doris Smothers series in Texas history, life, and culture ; no. 32)
Includes bibliographical references and index.
ISBN 978-0-292-73769-3 (cloth : alk. paper)
ISBN 978-0-292-73770-9 (e-book)
1. Armand, 1806–1889—Fiction. 2. Texas—History—1846–1950—Fiction.
3. Fredericksburg (Tex.)—Fiction. I. Kearney, James C. II. Title.
PT2532.S3F75I3 2012
833'.7—dc23
2011041454

Dedicated in love and respect to my wife of
thirty-seven years, Paulina van Bavel

Contents

———————— ★ ————————

FRIEDRICHSBURG
Colony of the German *Fürstenverein*

★

Translator's Note

FRIEDRICH ARMAND STRUBBERG figured prominently in my first book, *Nassau Plantation: The Evolution of a Texas German Slave Plantation.* In October 1847 Strubberg (or Dr. Schubbert, as he was known at the time) was involved in a gun battle for control of the plantation in which two men were killed. My research into this dramatic episode led me to a wider interest in Strubberg, both as man and author. I felt it necessary to acquaint myself with his literary works, most of which are based on his experiences on the Texas frontier in the 1840s. It became clear that the Friedrichsburg novel, especially, has great historical value, for Strubberg/Schubbert served as the first colonial director of Fredericksburg, Texas, during its foundation years (1846–1847). Additionally, the novel offers an entertaining read in its own right—an old-fashioned melodrama, very much within the sensibilities and conventions of the period. I thought it worthy of translation and resolved to do so. The translation, along with introduction and annotations, also served as my dissertation, which I successfully defended in December 2010.

James C. Kearney

Acknowledgments

*S*PECIAL THANKS TO Dr. Janet Swaffar of the Department of Germanic Studies at the University of Texas, who spent many hours editing and commenting on the introduction, the text of the translation, and the annotations. Also special thanks to Ulf Debelius, MA, of Marburg, Germany, who offered valuable insights into the life and works of Friedrich Armand Strubberg based on his own extensive research. Herr Debelius also graciously shared a new and accurate bibliography of Strubberg of which I made use. Finally, my thanks to Jean Howze, whose keen eye caught many embarrassing mistakes in the manuscript.

FRIEDRICHSBURG

Friedrich Armand Strubberg. Courtesy Stadtarchiv Kassel.

Introduction

*F*RIEDRICH ARMAND STRUBBERG's novel *Friedrichsburg*, published in Germany in 1867, is a fountain of information about the German settlements in the Hill Country of Texas, which were established in 1845, 1846, and 1847 by the Society for the Protection of German Emigrants in Texas. As the first colonial director of Fredericksburg, Strubberg was not only an observer, but also an important participant in this story. Strubberg places himself in the novel as Dr. Schubbert, the name he used at the time, and the background of the novel as well as most of the people named are historical. Thus the novel has a strong autobiographical contour.

Thousands of German emigrants began to arrive in Texas during the period between 1844 and 1848 under the auspices of the *Adelsverein*, a consortium of German nobles.[1] These immigrants came without adequate survival skills or provisions for coping with the dangers and rigors of settling on the Texas frontier in areas devoid of infrastructure and still inhabited by warlike Indians, most notably the Southern, or Penateka, Comanche bands.[2] Here they attempted to make the transition to new home and community without ready access to manufactured tools or self-sustaining industry or agriculture.

The noblemen safely ensconced in their comfortable estates in Germany attempted to live up to their responsibilities and supply the settlers with basic needs, but their efforts fell woefully short.[3] In consequence, the immigrants often were thrown upon their own devices and compelled to live from what they could learn to grow or hunt in a new land with unfamiliar climate, plants, and animals. Many hundreds perished from disease, exposure, and malnutrition.[4] But after a painful period the German settlements took root and began to prosper, lending a Germanic stamp to the Hill Country area of Texas that endures to the present day.

Any catalog of the factors that allowed the town of Fredericksburg to survive despite all arrayed against it would have to begin first and foremost with the admirable resilience and resourcefulness demonstrated by the German settlers themselves. To this we must add their pronounced communal spirit, which contrasted markedly with the more individualistic approach of the average Anglo settler. But beyond this, several fortuitous factors helped Fredericksburg to survive, to wit: (1) the peace treaty with the Penateka Comanche Indians in the spring of 1847; (2) the establishment of the Mormon community of Zodiac four miles southeast of Fredericksburg on the Pedernales River in 1847; and (3) the assistance and guidance provided by the Delaware and Shawnee Indians, who traded for valuable bear oil, wild game, and animal skins, and who acted as intermediaries with other Indian tribes, particularly with the Comanche tribes; (4) logistical support supplied (largely) by Nassau Plantation in Fayette County; and (5) the opening of the road to Austin.

Friedrichsburg presents all these situations vividly and entertainingly, and although the book offers a romanticized and, in this sense, a sanitized version of the immigrants' travails, I maintain that it contains historically accurate depictions of people and events that have been largely overlooked in other accounts of the period.

The novel also invites us to reevaluate the role of Dr. Schubbert, as Friedrich Armand Strubberg was known at the time in Texas. Dr. Schubbert has come to be regarded as a scoundrel, a swindler, or worse; his positive contributions have been essentially excised from history books and public consciousness.[5] I would argue that a reinterpretation is in order. To be sure, Dr. Schubbert had his faults: he was clearly an extremely narcissistic individual who could play fast and loose with the facts when it suited his purposes or when it supported his own self-image. These shortcomings, however, should not obscure his significant accomplishments and the important role he played as the colonial director of Fredericksburg during the foundation years of 1846 and 1847.

Before substantiating these assertions, I will first briefly outline the historical conditions that motivated German immigration to Texas, the hopes entertained by their sponsors, and the lack of information and preparation that led to near disaster for the immigrants themselves. I will also present an overview of the life of Friedrich Armand Strubberg and his historical connection to the Society for the Protection of German Emigrants in Texas and to the town of Fredericksburg. This will be followed by a short discussion of Strubberg's life, post-Fredericksburg, and his subsequent career in Germany as an author of adventure novels based largely on his experiences on the Texas frontier. I will conclude with a discussion of the historically significant events depicted in the novel.

WHY GERMANS EMIGRATED

The root cause of German emigration in the nineteenth century was overpopulation, which in turn exacerbated other emerging stresses of a political, economic, and religious nature. A clear upward trend in population growth

Meusebach/Comanche Treaty. Courtesy of the Texas State Library.

began in 1750 and continued throughout the nineteenth century.[6] In 1816 about 25 million people inhabited the areas that became the German Reich after 1871.[7] By 1914, this figure had grown to almost 68 million. This astounding increase was due in part to improved sanitation practices and the introduction of childhood vaccination; Germans now lived longer, married earlier, and had larger families.[8] About three-quarters of the population still lived on the land at the beginning of the nineteenth century, but the agrarian way of life was becoming more difficult to sustain since in many regions primogeniture left younger siblings with little or no property.[9] Even where laws enabling equal division between heirs prevailed, each succeeding generation had less land to divide among ever more descendants. In most areas of Germany, land ownership and tenure continued to be governed by a system of late-feudal privileges, which compounded these problems. After 1815, agrarian reforms were introduced and hereditary bondage (*Leibeigenschaft*) was phased out, but this often had the short-term effect of converting subsistence *Häusler*—cottagers—into contract laborers on aristocratic estates.[10]

Because Central Europe lagged fully fifty years behind England in industrial development, virtually no new jobs or occupations were created by modern industrialism to absorb the excess population.[11] Craftsmen continued to produce shoes, clothing, and other artifacts of life and trade within a system regulated by closed guilds (*Zunftwesen*) rooted in practices dating from the Middle Ages even as cheaper, mass-produced items from England began to flood the continent and render these products less competitive.

Given these conditions, it is not surprising that many hundreds of thousands of Germans chose emigration to the New World as a solution to the lack of opportunity in their homeland. Of the 18.75 million immigrants who came to the United States during the nineteenth century, approximately 5 million, or 27 percent, came from the German-speaking areas of Europe.[12] It is not possible to provide such detailed statistics for Texas, since the port of entry records for Texas disappeared in the great Galveston hurricane of 1900, but much can be inferred from the 1850 census and other sources. From the 1850 census, it appears that about 20 percent of the white population of Texas was of German descent, and two Texas towns were of almost exclusive German citizenry, New Braunfels and Fredericksburg, ranked fourth and seventh in population, respectively.[13]

GERMAN INTEREST IN TEXAS

Texas began to attract attention as a possible goal for emigrants while still a province of Mexico. A glowing letter written by a German immigrant in 1831 who had settled in Texas created a sensation after it was passed along among friends and relatives in the Grand Duchy of Oldenburg. Friedrich Ernst moved to the Mexican state of Coahuila y Tejas in 1828, where he applied for and was granted a league of land (4,428 acres) in the rolling hills of South-Central Texas. He and his family then settled on the banks of Mill Creek in a region that was still essentially frontier. His letter portrayed Texas as a veritable paradise.

> The meadows have the most sumptuous stands of grass. . . . The soil is so rich it never requires fertilizing. . . . The climate resembles that of lower Italy during the summer . . . a persistent fresh east breeze cools the air. . . . The sun and air are always bright and clear; bees and butterflies are seen year round, birds are singing in the shrubs, some of which are evergreen; and in winter as well as in summer, the cattle find their own feed. The cows calve without assistance.[14]

The letter also stated that, by comparison, the rest of the United States no longer offered the opportunities that it had in the past. In his new home, Ernst was owner of an entire league of land, an awesome treasure to behold. Moreover, the land had virtually been given to him for the asking by the Mexican government. His life in Texas, as Ernst reported it, was unproblematic and pastoral, indeed idyllic. Other than perhaps Archduke August himself, did any man in Oldenburg own that much land?

Ownership of such magnitude was invariably associated with social status, privilege, and nobility—not with ordinary people. Consequently, his letter struck a chord that would in time motivate scores of Germans to seek a new life in what was soon to become the Republic of Texas.

FIRST GERMAN SETTLEMENTS IN TEXAS

One of the first to respond to the Ernst invitation was the extended von Roeder family. Father, mother, and five grown sons with wives made the move in 1835. They settled on the sandy plain near the San Bernard River and named their community Katzenquelle, later anglicized to Cat Spring.[15] It became a magnet for others who filtered in singly or as family groups. The disruptions caused by the Texas war of independence from Mexico, which broke out in October 1835, only temporarily halted the influx of new arrivals. After the defeat of Santa Anna and the Mexican army at the Battle of San Jacinto April 21, 1836, the trickle became a flood,[16] and soon several distinctly German communities coalesced in South-Central Texas; these were little islands of transplanted German culture and language in a sea of predominantly Anglo settlement, places with names like Cat Spring, Millheim, Cummins Creek, Biegel's Settlement, and Industry.[17]

The struggle for independence and the aggressive and expensive Indian policies of the republic's second president, Mirabeau B. Lamar, had left the Republic of Texas teetering on the brink of financial collapse.[18] Above all, the young republic needed settlers to infuse new cash and increase the tax base. In recognition of this reality, President Sam Houston, upon assuming the presidency for the second time in 1841, sought to encourage European emigration as a means to hasten the development of Texas. In January 1842 the Texas Congress empowered the president to offer conditional title to vast tracts of land as an inducement to entrepreneurs who would agree to settle specified numbers of colonists within a set time on vacant lands.[19] The law echoed the empresario system by which Stephen F. Austin had established the original Anglo colony in Texas. Under this arrangement, empresarios entered into a contract with the Mexican government to introduce certain numbers of settlers in a given period of time. Mexican authorities issued land titles to the settlers directly and upon satisfaction of the terms of the contract rewarded the empresarios for their time, effort, and expense with enormous tracts of land proportionate to the number of settlers introduced. This time, however, three of the four grants were issued to European entrepreneurs.[20] Resurrection of the land grant system held out the possibility of enormous financial gain for those who could secure a colonization contract and who had the energy and resources to fulfill its terms, a fact quickly noted by entrepreneurs on both sides of the Atlantic.

GERMANY IN TEXAS: THE *ADELSVEREIN'S* ASPIRATIONS AND FOIBLES

One group in Germany was quick to respond to the republic's offer. In the spring of 1842, twenty German noblemen and one noblewoman convened at the residence of Adolph, duke of Nassau, in Biebrich on the Rhine in response to an invitation from Christian, count of Leiningen.[21] The corporation they formed was convinced it had the means and will to fashion a program of important national significance whereby the opportunities of Texas could supply an answer to the frustrations of Germany. They also hoped to enhance the prestige of that particular class of German noblemen to which nearly all of them belonged, namely the *Standesherren*,[22] and also to increase their personal wealth by speculating in inexpensive Texas land. They adopted the official name *Der Verein zum Schutze deutscher Einwanderer in Texas*, which is usually shortened to *Adelsverein*, or Society of Noblemen.[23] In scope and audacity, the plan they adopted holds a unique and dramatic position in the history of immigration to the New World in the nineteenth century.[24]

The *Adelsverein* proposed to settle German emigrants in the Fischer-Miller grant, one of the four land grant contracts issued under the Colonization Act of 1842. This grant was defined as the confluence of the Llano and Colorado Rivers to their sources with a line drawn between these two points to form the western boundary.[25] It was an enormous area encompassing many millions of acres. Except for a few hardy adventurers, few Anglos had laid eyes upon it. Certainly, none of the officials of the *Adelsverein* had visited the area.[26] They had relied on hearsay and anecdotal accounts, which, like Ernst's letter, painted the region as the most beautiful and fertile area of the republic—accounts that, sadly, turned out to be utterly false.[27] The area, moreover, was the winter hunting grounds of the Penateka, or Southern Comanche, the most warlike of the Texas Indians and a tribe determined to resist encroachments into their hereditary hunting grounds.[28]

In 1844 the *Adelsverein* advertised for emigrants throughout Germany, promising 320 acres of free land and agreeing to provide food, shelter, and tools to the settlers for the first year in Texas or until the first crop was harvested.[29] Thousands responded, and soon the main arteries leading to the North Sea, the Rhine, and the Weser and Elbe Rivers saw boatloads of emigrants making their way to the port cities of Amsterdam, Bremerhaven, and Hamburg. In the fall of 1844, the first chartered sailing ships began arriving in Galveston and at Indianola on Lavaca Bay, the vanguard of what was to amount to over eight thousand individuals.[30] In chapter 2 of *Friedrichsburg*, Strubberg gives a nice synopsis of the origins of the *Adelsverein* and the causes of German emigration. He is careful never to directly criticize the noblemen in Germany directly, averring instead that they were misled by Henry Francis Fischer, who had sold them his land grant contract with the Republic of Texas.

NEW BRAUNFELS ESTABLISHED

Carl, prince of Solms-Braunfels, had been sent over in the summer of 1844 to make preparations for the first shiploads of emigrants, which began arriving in the late summer and fall of that year. The prince quickly realized the practical impossibility of transporting and settling the new settlers into the Fischer-Miller grant, which lay beyond the north bank of the Llano River about two hundred miles to the north. Consequently, in the spring of 1845, he bought from the estate of Juan Martin de Veramendi, former Mexican governor of Coahuila y Tejas, two leagues of land in a beautiful valley east of San Antonio at the confluence of the Comal and Guadalupe Rivers. He named the town after his own family. The idea was to form a home base and staging area away from the coast and closer to the grant area, where the settlers could assemble and await the next move into the grant the following year.[31]

Above: Seth Eastman, above Dutch House, Fredericksburg, Texas, January 1849 *from* Sketch-book, *1848–1849. Graphite on paper, #1961.5.108. Collection of the McNay Art Museum, Gift of the Pearl Brewing Company. Below: Seth Eastman,* Dutch Church, Fredericksburg, Texas, 70 Miles North of San Antonio, Texas, January 1849 *from* Sketchbook, *1848–1849. Graphite on paper, #1961.5.102. Collection of the McNay Art Museum, Gift of the Pearl Brewing Company.*

New Braunfels was also the headquarters for the *Adelsverein*'s bureaucracy in Texas, which had grown to over twenty individuals by 1847.[32] Strubberg is very deferential to Prince Solms-Braunfels in *Friedrichsburg* and praises him for the wonderful location of the town he established. In the novel, Strubberg often refers to the town as simply "Braunfels" rather than the more common "Neu [New] Braunfels," and the translation retains this convention, when used. In the novel, Strubberg often refers to the *Direktion*, or bureaucracy, in Braunfels, and the opening scene begins with the young German hero, Rudolph, carrying dispatches from Braunfels to Fredericksburg.

FRIEDRICHSBURG [FREDERICKSBURG] ESTABLISHED

In 1845, Johann Otfried Freiherr von Meusebach succeeded Prince Solms as commissioner-general of the *Adelsverein* in Texas.[33] Meusebach considered it his first duty to fulfill the terms of the Fischer-Miller contract, which required that the grant area be surveyed by September 1, 1847, and six hundred emigrants settled by January 1, 1848.[34] To facilitate the movement of emigrants into this area, he purchased ten thousand acres four miles north of the Pedernales River on the old La Pinta Trail in the spring of 1846.[35] The first wagon train of 120 settlers arrived from New Braunfels on May 8, 1846, after a sixteen-day journey, accompanied by an eight-man military escort provided by the *Adelsverein* and under the command of a former Prussian officer, Lieutenant Bené. For this reason Bené is often considered to be the "father" of Fredericksburg. Bené continued as the nominal head of Fredericksburg until he was replaced by Dr. Schubbert. Named for Friedrich, prince of Prussia, one of the charter members of the society, the new town was situated about seventy miles to the northwest of New Braunfels, but still lay forty-five miles below the southern boundary of the Fischer-Miller grant in present-day Gillespie County.

DR. SCHUBBERT ENGAGED AS COLONIAL DIRECTOR

Meusebach needed a director for his new colony on the Pedernales, someone who combined force of personality and administrative skills with experience on the Texas frontier. In the spring of 1846, he made the acquaintance of Friedrich Armand Strubberg, aka Dr. Schubbert, and offered him the position.

WHO WAS DR. SCHUBBERT?

The three published biographies of Friedrich Armand Strubberg contain much that is either unsubstantiated or out-and-out false. Preston Barba, Arnim Huber, and Gunter Sehm have all written about Strubberg's life. The second two authors clearly relied heavily on Barba, whose study served as his dissertation and later was serialized in a scholarly publication in 1912 and 1913 in

Pennsylvania. Barba traveled to Germany, where he interviewed several people who had known Strubberg personally, and he was granted access to some of Strubberg's personal papers. He did not, however, dig deeply into newspaper articles, official records, or police reports of the period to verify many of the dramatic claims made by Strubberg concerning his life. Instead, he appeared to accept at face value much of what Strubberg had written in his early, semi-autobiographical novel, *Bis in die Wildniß* [As Far as the Wilderness]. Barba combined this material with the anecdotal accounts he obtained in Germany.

A synopsis of Barba's account would read as follows: Strubberg was born in Kassel, Germany, in 1806. He hailed from a prominent tobacco merchant's family and came from an extremely cosmopolitan background. His father was from Holland, his mother from France, and he was related to the king of Sweden through a morganatic marriage of his grandmother on his father's side. He was the recipient of a good education, with an emphasis on business. A good shot, but quick to anger, Strubberg seriously wounded a man in a lover's duel in Germany, which prompted his first journey to the United States in 1826, where he served for several years as the agent of European firms in New York and the East Coast.[36] In 1829 he returned to Germany to help in his father's business, which had suffered reverses. After ten years, Strubberg once again returned to the United States. His itinerary took him first to New Orleans and then on a long journey through the South. Eventually he arrived in New York to resume a career as a commission agent. In 1842, a duel in New York City led to a murder warrant and Strubberg was forced to flee. Since Texas was not part of the Union, it provided a likely haven from the hangman's noose. Along the way, near Louisville, Kentucky, the riverboat he was on ran aground and sank.[37] While waiting to retrieve his luggage, he met a German doctor who ran a medical academy. Strubberg enrolled in the medical academy, and after two years of study emerged with a medical degree and a new name, Dr. Schubbert. Thereafter, he continued on his journey to Texas, arriving in or about 1844.

Once in Texas, the account continues, he headed for the frontier. Arriving at the headwaters of the Leona River in South Texas, at the base of the Edwards Plateau, he and three companions erected a log fort far from the nearest white settlements, in the heart of Indian country. Here they lived an idyllic existence, sustaining themselves mainly from the plentiful buffalo and other game that inhabited the area in abundance. The thrill of the hunt and occasional Indian encounters served to break the monotony of their lives. Here, so Strubberg claimed, he first came into contact with many different tribes and chiefs, forging many lasting friendships among the Indians, which he alludes to in all his Texas novels.

Ulf Debellius, the leading contemporary scholar of Strubberg in Germany and also the editor of a new edition of Strubberg's collected works, provides counterpoint to the Barba-Sehm-Huber version of Strubberg's life. Herr Debelius writes:

1. As to the duel in Bremen, there is not one shred of evidence outside of Strubberg's own claim, which he continued to repeat his whole life long. Neither police documents, nor court documents, nor newspaper reports of the period exist that would substantiate such an occurrence.
2. The same applies to the supposed duel in New York. Still, I hold this one for possible, but I would only mention it in his biography with appropriate qualifiers.
3. The putative morganatic descent from the royal Hessian family was convincingly shown to be false as early as 1913 and again in greater detail in 1927 by Phillip Losch.[38]
4. I am likewise unfamiliar with any documents that would substantiate the study of medicine in Louisville and the conferral of a medical degree. That Strubberg, in fact, had amassed a large store of medical knowledge appears indisputable in light of his medical successes during his engagement by the *Adelsverein*. But in respect to a doctor's title, at the very least we have to consider that such a title in Germany would have brought with it a certain social standing and deference. Karl May, in the style of a classical con man, also assumed for himself the title of doctor. Given Strubberg's pronounced narcissistic tendencies, he surely would not have allowed such documentation to slip from his possession, and he would have been quick to display it—but no one ever laid eyes on such a document.[39]

Strubberg's claims about the fort located on the headwaters of the Leona River are also doubtful, though Barba et al. accept this claim at face value. His description of the landscape does not match the region. He claims the Leona was a tributary of the Rio Grande. It is not; the Leona debouches into the Frio River, which in turn empties into the Nueces River, which finally spills into the Gulf of Mexico. He claims that one could see the mountains of Mexico in the distance. One cannot see any part of Mexico from any given stretch of the Leona River. He claims magnolia trees grew along the river. Magnolia trees are not native to South Texas and would not have been introduced until a later date.

Yet, for all this fabrication, Strubberg most likely did spend some time on the Texas frontier in 1844–1845. Several cryptic allusions of the period suggest he settled for a while, perhaps with one or two partners, somewhere on the San Gabriel River, north of Austin rather than in South Texas.[40] In this venture, he might have been connected to Henry Francis Fischer and the San Saba Colonization Company,[41] or he might have been acting on his own. Fischer also hailed from Kassel, and the two may well have known each other from this period. In either case, Strubberg would have had ample opportunity to come into contact with the Indian tribes and chiefs he claims to have met on the Leona and experienced many of the adventures he wrote about in his books.[42]

We can only speculate why Strubberg spun a fictitious tale about a fort on the Leona, which becomes a kind of touchstone in his Texas adventure novels. Perhaps he considered the Leona in South Texas to be more exotic and to have a greater appeal to his readers in Germany. In respect to his own life, it is clear that Strubberg's works offer a complicated blend of fiction and truth, while gaps remain in his biography that we may never be able to fill.[43]

DR. SCHUBBERT BECOMES COLONIAL DIRECTOR OF FREDERICKSBURG

It can be documented with certainty that Henry Francis Fischer introduced Dr. Schubbert to John Meusebach, commissioner-general of the *Adelsverein* in Texas, in March 1846. The two traveled together from Houston to Nassau Plantation, the *Adelsverein*'s slave plantation in northern Fayette County, where Meusebach was staying at the time.[44] Impressed with Schubbert's medical credentials, apparent knowledge of the frontier, and imposing presence, Meusebach offered his new acquaintance the position of colonial director of the new settlement on the Pedernales.[45]

DR. SCHUBBERT AND THE EPIDEMIC IN NEW BRAUNFELS

Dr. Schubbert arrived with Meusebach in New Braunfels from Nassau Plantation July 14, 1846.[46] Hermann Seele, a Texas-German commentator of the period, has left us with his first impression of the doctor upon his arrival in New Braunfels:

> His regal figure with fiery eyes, dark beard and hair on which he jauntily wore a dark hat, his gallant manner, as well as his fluent, assured way of speaking, created an imposing first impression.[47]

Meusebach and Schubbert arrived to find the new settlement in the grip of a very serious epidemic. Curiously, none of the standard works of the German settlements in Texas—Biesele's *The History of the German Settlements in Texas*, Tiling's *The History of the German Element*, Benjamin's *The Germans in Texas*—

mentions Dr. Schubbert in this connection. Preston Barba's *Life and Works of Friedrich Armand Strubberg* even casts doubt on Schubbert's presence in New Braunfels.[48] Documents in the Solms-Braunfels Archives, the official records of the *Adelsverein*, however, show conclusively that Schubbert was present from July until October 1846, and that he labored day and night to minister to the sick and to prepare their medicines.[49]

There is controversy to this day as to the exact cause of the epidemic.[50] Dr. Schubbert diagnosed the disease as advanced scurvy and treated it accordingly, and, just as he claims in the novel, he used native plants and herbs as remedies, with some success.[51]

The epidemic finally abated in the fall of 1846 and Schubbert was able to depart for Fredericksburg in October to take up his position as director of the new colony. The initial contingent of settlers had already made the trek, but new arrivals came in a steady stream. By January 1847, five hundred families had been settled in the town and 189 houses had been erected.[52]

FREDERICKSBURG: A UNIQUE TOWN IN TEXAS

Fredericksburg was unusual if not unique in Texas because it was, in a sense, completely artificial. Far from any established trading routes, in the heart of *comanchería*, it lacked any history of natural, organic development. Where one

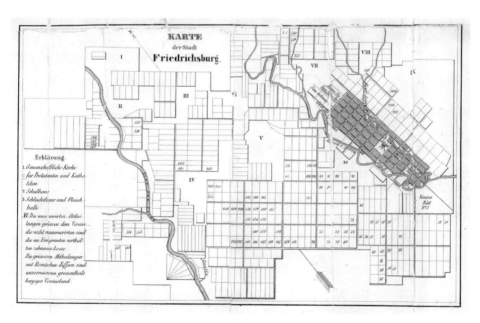

City map of Fredericksburg (Karte von Friedrichsburg), 1850, #2182.
Courtesy of the Texas General Land Office, Austin.

year only raw frontier existed, six months later a town of nearly one thousand inhabitants had taken shape, the seventh largest town in Texas by the 1850 census.

New Braunfels, also, was in a sense an artificial town, but due to its proximity to San Antonio and its location on the old and established trade route, El Camino Real, the town found itself much better positioned for success and less artificial in its existence. Fredericksburg, on the other hand, was remote, isolated, and incapable of feeding itself during its first year of existence. Its fate hung in the balance for two years, and the settlement came close to complete collapse because of the factors just mentioned, which were exacerbated by the outbreak of another epidemic. Had Fredericksburg failed, it is clear that there would have been a general retrenchment in respect to the German settlements in the Hill Country, and the demography of this part of Texas would be very different today.

DR. SCHUBBERT: A CONTROVERSIAL FIGURE

The people of Fredericksburg, as much as any other Texas town, are knowledgeable about and proud of their heritage. But when one mentions Dr. Schubbert, one is likely to hear a version of the following: "Dr. Schubbert, that swindler; we don't talk about him." How did Schubbert come to get such a reputation? How is it that on the town square in Fredericksburg, not one plaque or marker can be found commemorating Dr. Schubbert? Behind the reconstructed *Vereinskirche*,[53] the symbol of Fredericksburg, and, ironically, a structure built originally on orders of Dr. Schubbert, one finds a bronze statue of Meusebach passing the pipe of peace to an Indian chief. One also finds a replica of an overshot mill wheel to acknowledge the assistance of the nearby Mormon settlement of Zodiac. But no mention is to be found of the man who served as colonial director during the most critical period of Fredericksburg's existence, 1846 and 1847. He is not acknowledged as part of the town's heritage; he is remembered only as a swindler.

An examination of original documents and letters from the period, however, paint quite a different picture: Dr. Schubbert had his detractors, but he also had many friends and a host of sympathetic supporters. Indeed, when word reached Fredericksburg in the summer of 1847 that Dr. Schubbert might be replaced, seventy-seven prominent citizens signed a letter to Dr. Schubbert expressing unqualified support and gratitude for his leadership. A quote from this letter is in order:

> Our modesty prevents us, most honorable Sir, from listing all the services which you have rendered us in your short stay here. It was you who appeared among us to offer assistance when our need and suffering were at

their greatest. You were the saving angel who through personal dedication and sacrifice restored life and health to many of us as well as our children. Through your boundless energy and ceaseless activity on our behalf, you procured the bare necessities of existence, which earlier, prior to your appearance, were so often woefully short or non-existent—in short, you were the one who restored hope in us that we might, despite all, have a secure future.[54]

These are not the words of a community unified in dislike for their leader. When Schubbert was finally dismissed in August 1847, there was even fear of an open revolt on his behalf among the townspeople of Fredericksburg, so strong was his support and, concomitantly, so pronounced their antipathy to Meusebach.[55] How, then, did the judgment against Dr. Schubbert come to be so rigidly one-sided in the contemporary public consciousness? First, Schubbert and Meusebach came to despise each other, and because there is a consensus that Meusebach was a great man, it follows that Dr. Schubbert must have been a scoundrel. Second, Dr. Schubbert was involved in a deadly shoot-out at Nassau Plantation in October 1847 after his dismissal as colonial director, which further discredited him. Third, and most importantly, when Fredericksburg celebrated its fiftieth anniversary in 1896, Robert Penninger, a local publisher, brought out a commemorative book of reminiscences by old pioneers.[56] By luck or design, the men who contributed, especially Julius Splittgerber, were unified in their dislike of Dr. Schubbert. Nearly all subsequent articles and accounts of the doctor hark back to the Penninger book, while ignoring documents that give a more balanced interpretation.[57] Thus, to use a wonderful German word, a *Deutungshoheit*—a sovereign interpretation—emerged to eclipse all others.

SCHUBBERT CONTRA MEUSEBACH

The archivally substantiated facts about the Schubbert/Meusebach dispute are as follows: On January 1, 1847, a major disturbance took place in New Braunfels.[58] A mob marched on the *Sophienburg*, the official compound of the *Adelsverein*, where Meusebach was staying. Fifty or so men gathered outside and talk of violence was directed at the commissioner-general. Rumors that the settlers would not receive title or access to the 320 acres of land promised to each head of household had fueled the ugly mood of the crowd. Meusebach bravely confronted the mob and defused the situation. The following day Meusebach departed on an expedition to explore the grant north of the Llano River and make contact with the Comanche Indians.

Meusebach seems to have held Schubbert partially responsible for the uprising in New Braunfels and for otherwise undermining his authority.[59] Among other infractions, Schubbert had mounted his own foray into the grant area in December 1846, a month before Meusebach's expedition. His party returned without ever crossing the Llano River into the grant or accomplishing anything noteworthy. Upon returning to Fredericksburg, Schubbert reportedly claimed that there were up to forty thousand hostile Comanches in the area.[60] This rumor, apparently, fueled the mob's anger in New Braunfels, for, if true, any realistic program of settlement in the grant area would be rendered unfeasible and the 320 acres promised, even if granted, would be worthless.

The novel *Friedrichsburg* throws light on this controversy. In one scene, Dr. Schubbert explains to his companions his case for scrapping in total the plans for settlements in the Fischer-Miller grant. Instead, he argues, it makes more sense as a first priority to buy and fill in the fertile river valleys and other arable lands between New Braunfels and Fredericksburg. He suggests a series of interlocking settlements between the two places that could quickly be summoned to one another's mutual defense if attacked by hostile Indians. Dr. Schubbert continues that he tried to persuade the *Direktion* in New Braunfels (i.e., Meusebach) to adopt this stance, but to no avail. Meusebach had made it clear that he was dead set against this approach because in addition to being expensive it would undermine his determination to satisfy the terms of the Fischer-Miller land grant contract.[61]

Thus the novel confirms what Meusebach wrote at the time: that Dr. Schubbert opposed his program and authority. In hindsight, Schubbert's position appears to represent a rational approach to the altered circumstances and the real dangers facing the German settlers. It must be said, also, that what Schubbert called for is largely what happened: on their own initiative, German immigrants settled the fertile creek and river valleys between New Braunfels and Fredericksburg, making this region, rather than the Fischer-Miller grant proper, the concentrated center of German settlement in the Hill Country.

In fairness to Meusebach, failure to survey and settle the territory in the Fischer-Miller grant would have nullified the terms of the land grant contract. The result: the *Adelsverein* would have relinquished its claim to hundreds of thousands of acres of bonus lands and broken faith with the promise it had made to the emigrants. Because of Meusebach's stubborn determination, over 4,200 settlers (by one account) eventually did receive certificates to land in the counties that made up the Fischer-Miller grant, though only a limited number actually chose to settle there.[62]

Meusebach's displeasure led to further accusations. Prior to dismissing Schubbert from his post in Fredericksburg, Meusebach charged him with extravagant use of supplies he had purchased and deficiencies in the accounting of their use.[63] He also intimated that Dr. Schubbert had profited personally from the sale of alcoholic spirits, which he had shipped in at the *Adelsverein*'s expense, in generous quantities.

In a long letter of defense, Schubbert answered both these charges convincingly.[64] Yes, he conceded, he had sold the *Adelsverein*'s liquor provisions, but only to Americans who were passing through; and with the profit from these sales, he had bought badly needed medicines and other provisions for the colonists in Fredericksburg, which, according to Schubbert, Meusebach had withheld even after an epidemic broke out.

Meusebach was also opposed to the communal approach that Dr. Schubbert initiated. He argued that it made the settlers too reliant on one another and on the *Adelsverein*. The settlers needed to wean themselves from dependency on *Obrigkeit* [authority] and become more like the Anglo pioneers, self-sufficient and independently resourceful. It was also very expensive.[65] Schubbert countered that material support was the least the *Adelsverein* could do considering that the settlers had yet to receive their promised land in the grant area.

Meusebach had also criticized the communal church, the *Vereinskirche*, which Dr. Schubbert ordered built in the spring of 1847, although he appears to have acquiesced to its construction.[66] As many intellectuals in Germany were at the time (and as quite a few transplanted intellectuals on the Texas frontier continued to be), Meusebach was an unapologetic *Freidenker*, or freethinker.[67] Meusebach claimed that the *Vereinskirche* violated the principle of separation of church and state, and that Schubbert had exceeded his authority by ordering it to be constructed at *Verein* expense. Dr. Schubbert, on the other hand, took offense at what he perceived as Meusebach's atheism, as did many others at the time.[68] Near the end of *Friedrichsburg*, Schubbert provides a vivid and moving description of the laying of the cornerstone of the communal church. His depiction of this event, resplendent with ceremony and dedication speeches, conveys the role of the church in filling a glaring void in the communal life of the town.

DR. SCHUBBERT DISMISSED

Dr. Schubbert's letter of defense, cited above, was the last straw for Meusebach. On July 12, 1847, he replied tersely to Schubbert that he was "either incapable of understanding the orders given to [him] or unwilling to follow them," that his "actions and words amount[ed] to insubordination," and that it was "not [his] role to lecture [his] superiors, but rather to follow their instructions."[69] Meusebach informed Schubbert that he henceforth was relieved of all duties and he was to be replaced by the accountant von Coll.

Sometime in the summer of 1847, Meusebach also discovered Dr. Schubbert's true identity. This misrepresentation was for Meusebach "unredlich," a grave and unpardonable moral defect.[70] Meusebach resigned in August 1847, but his last official act was to fire Dr. Schubbert as colonial director of Fredericksburg and to revoke the lease on Nassau Plantation, which he had originally offered under very favorable terms as inducement for Dr. Schubbert to become colonial director of Fredericksburg.[71]

THE CATASTROPHE

This turn of events set the stage for one of the most sordid affairs connected with the *Adelsverein* in Texas, and a situation that helped to further discredit Dr. Schubbert (henceforth Strubberg). In the fall of 1847, Strubberg was involved in a gun battle in which two men were killed at the *Adelverein*'s plantation in northern Fayette County.[72] Because the event had such dire consequences for the *Adelsverein*, financial and otherwise, the episode came to be termed *Die Katastrophe* [the catastrophe] by the officials of the *Adelsverein* in their reports.

Strubberg was convinced that Meusebach was behind the whole episode. The following year, he wrote Meusebach a parting letter from New Orleans, extraordinarily frank and aggressive in tone, wherein he defended himself against the charges that had led to his dismissal, and he challenged the abrogation of his lease to Nassau Plantation that had provoked the shoot-out. He also leveled some serious charges against Meusebach. He stated that nothing but jealousy had been behind Meusebach's hostility; that he, unlike Meusebach, was a man of numerous talents, greater energy, and of an engaging and sympathetic nature, all of which had rendered him more effective as a leader. His most damning charge was that the shoot-out at Nassau was in reality a planned assassination (*Meuchelmord*), which had been conceived and orchestrated by Meusebach behind the scenes. As a final insult, Strubberg averred that he had researched their respective family backgrounds and had discovered that Meusebach's ancestors once were servants to his family. Strubberg closed by saying that their paths were destined to cross again, at which time Meusebach would receive his just desserts.[73]

Happily, their paths did not cross again, but Strubberg did take a civilized revenge: in *Friedrichsburg* he expunged Meusebach from the story, as if he had never existed.

STRUBBERG AFTER 1847

The shoot-out at Nassau Plantation resulted in a flood of litigation that clogged two terms of the district court in Fayette County. Strubberg eventually received a sizeable settlement from the *Adelsverein*, by one account $3,000,[74] as part of an overall deal in which each party agreed to drop his civil suit against the other. According to one of his biographers, Strubberg then moved to Arkansas, where he resumed his profession as a medical doctor.[75] He is said to have become engaged to the daughter of a wealthy plantation owner, but, once again, an accident occurred that altered the course of his life. He was stung in the left eye by an insect, and the wound refused to heal.

By this account, in 1854 Strubberg broke off the engagement and decided to return to Europe in the hope of finding relief from his malady. He was never successful in fully restoring the eye, and consequently often appeared with a patch over it.[76]

Strubberg eventually moved in with a spinster sister who still lived in Kassel. He was in the habit of spending part of each day at a local coffeehouse in the Hotel Schombardt. Here, he entertained acquaintances and strangers alike with tales of adventures on the Texas frontier. According to Preston Barba:

> Dr. Strubberg, with his remarkable tales of adventures, ever new, varied and endless, never wanted for an attentive circle of listeners. *Oberststallmeister* [master equerry] von Eschwege one day asked Strubberg to put his adventures into literary form, so that they could be circulated among his friends as a memorial of the many pleasant hours which had been afforded them.[77]

Strubberg took his advice and, with the assistance of his sister, produced his first manuscript, which he offered to a publisher. In 1858, his first novel appeared, *Amerikanische Jagd- und Reiseabenteuer* [American Hunting and Travel Adventures].

Thus Strubberg embarked on a new phase in his life as an author of adventure novels based on both firsthand experience and hearsay from his years in the United States and on the Texas frontier. He was remarkably productive. In the next ten years he penned over forty volumes, about half of which related to the Texas frontier. A bibliography of his first editions has been provided as an appendix to give a sense of the scope and thematic focus of his oeuvre. His literary output gained for him a certain prominence during his lifetime and provided a comfortable living. Preston Barba summed up Strubberg's literary career as follows:

> Strubberg occupies a unique position in the history of German letters. He was led to a literary career by the merest accident, but for the intervention of which he might have ended his days as a planter in Arkansas. Far from being a literary man, not even widely read in his own literature, much less in a foreign, we see him publishing his first book in his fifty-second year. Influenced by no literary tendency, a member of no literary school, he

wrote, so to speak, "frei von der Leber." . . . He sought to express what he had seen, heard, and experienced in a simple, straightforward manner. There are but few literary allusions and little conformity to the ascribed forms of art.[78]

The novel *Friedrichsburg* was published in 1867, toward the end of Strubberg's career as an author. It is arguably his best novel. The earlier works suffer from being overly episodic and much too long, with little sense of balance and flow in plot structure. In *Friedrichsburg*, however, Strubberg has constructed a good love story, albeit one mirroring the elevated discourse and sensibilities of nineteenth-century popular literature.

> "You sweet, you heavenly creature, how should I, how could I ever thank you for your love that blesses every hour, every minute of my life!" exclaimed the young man as he pressed the maid to his heart. "With your love, Rudolph, you put me in your debt," answered Ludwina as they walked into the entrance of the alcove, arm in arm. (1:12)[79]

Yet, consistently, Strubberg depicts the natural landscape of Central Texas in a way that can still be recognized today. The degree of detail, the deep appreciation for natural beauty, and the narrative itself convey the atmosphere and experience of the Texas frontier:

> A deathly silence lay upon the countryside; only the crash of the waves cascading over mighty boulders below the ford and the distant howls of a pack of wolves celebrating a kill interrupted the sacred serenity of the night. The darkness had lessened and a man could make out the slender trunks of the towering pecan trees along the banks, through whose crowns, inclining over the river, the stars shone down into the dark torrent with a reflection of a thousand lights. (1:6)

Despite the tendency toward elegiac raptures, as typified in this passage, anyone who has experienced isolated countryside near or in a place like Enchanted Rock by night can appreciate the veracity of Strubberg's observations about the impact of this landscape on the viewer.

FRIEDRICHSBURG: SEPARATING FACT FROM FICTION

From the first pages of the novel, the reader is confronted with an admixture of truth and fantasy. Rudolph von Wildhorst and Ludwina Nimanski are almost certainly Strubberg's literary creations, but their sentimental love story plays out against the actual founding of Fredericksburg and the impending peace treaty between the German settlers and Comanche Indians, who had called the area on the upper reaches of the Pedernales, Llano, and San Saba Rivers their winter home for as far back as their wise men could recall.

As has already been indicated, a startling omission occurs throughout the novel. The man who had engaged Strubberg to be the colonial director of Friedrichsburg, the man whose bold initiative led to the historic treaty with the Comanches, John Meusebach,[80] commissioner-general of the *Adelsverein* in Texas, is not mentioned at any point in the book.

In the case of the Delaware chief Youngbear, most likely based on the historical Jim Shaw (his English name), the reader encounters the opposite problem: Strubberg elevates and amplifies Shaw's persona beyond anything that is historically verifiable. Youngbear becomes a hero of the novel, even surpassing the role of the young German hero, Rudolph von Wildhorst, with whom he becomes a blood brother. In the end, after a botched shot by Rudolph, Youngbear's well-placed shot saves Ludwina from the murderous intentions of the

John Mix Stanley, Jim Shaw, Delaware, *1843. Oil on cardboard.*
Courtesy, the Bridgeman Art Library Limited.

villainous Kateumsi. In the final scene of the book, Youngbear is allowed to have the dance of honor at the wedding celebration of Rudolph and Ludwina, a remarkably suggestive and taboo-breaking scene.

In Kateumsi, Strubberg develops the most complex character of the novel, and here he blends fact and fiction in a startling way. Kateumsi, an important historical war chief of the Penateka (Southern) Comanches, is portrayed in the novel as a die-hard renegade who refuses to sign the peace treaty. Corroboration for this depiction can be found in newspaper accounts of the period, where Kateumsi is portrayed as wily and treacherous.[81] At a later stage, however, the historical Kateumsi apparently became a voice of restraint and moderation in his tribe, counseling reconciliation and even taking up residence in a house on a reservation.[82]

Although Kateumsi is cast as a villain, Strubberg provides him with several moving speeches that suggest the author's sympathy for the existential plight of American Indians and his recognition of the unjust treatment they had received, as in this passage:

> Like the raging grey bear, who kills and dismembers solely from bloodlust, so have the palefaces driven the red children from the shores of the Big Water and exterminated entire tribes, and now they are seeking them out in these far-removed mountains in order to trick them into venturing out where, defenseless, they can be killed. (1:62)

Strubberg acknowledges the truth in Kateumsi's words, but counters his accusations with a question:

> Was this part of the world created for the sole purpose that a small number of original inhabitants could wander over the countryside hunting in perpetuity? (1:158)

The tension between these two points of view is never resolved, and it functions as the dramatic mainspring of the novel.

STRUBBERG AS COLONIAL DIRECTOR AND EVERYDAY LIFE IN FREDERICKSBURG

One of the more entertaining and significant aspects of the novel is the portrayal of the everyday life of the citizens of Fredericksburg and the interaction of Strubberg as "Direktor Schubbert" with the settlers and the other officials of the *Verein* during the foundation year. These descriptions offer a glimpse into Strubberg's leadership style, into the authority he exercised, and into the enormity of the responsibility on his shoulders. They also provide insight into the energetic and creative solutions he often initiated.

Some of the many corroborated events that Strubberg depicted include the strange case of the parsimonious Herr Küster from Frankfurt, "who died from his own miserliness," the layout of the *Verein* compound in Fredericksburg and the organization of its bureaucracy, the communal cornfield, slaughterhouse, the magazine, the laying of the cornerstone of the *Vereinskirche*, the Sunday afternoon dances, the surveying of a new road to Austin, the successful treatment of snakebite using Indian remedies, trade with the Delaware and Shawnee Indians for venison and bear oil, treatment of scurvy through the gathering of native plants, the story of how Chief Old Owl fled the town in a panic because of a bad dream, festivities attendant to the signing of the peace treaty in 1847, and the important symbiotic relationship that developed between the citizens of Fredericksburg and the nearby Mormon community of Zodiac.

THE ETHNOGRAPHIC COMPONENT

Strubberg stated in the preface to his novel that one of the purposes of the book was to offer real pictures of the American Indians he had encountered. True to this intent, *Friedrichsburg* offers detailed and exquisite descriptions of costumes, habits, and ceremonies of various tribes of frontier Texas Indians. Strubberg takes pains to draw contrasts between the various tribes. The first description the reader encounters is of the Delaware and Shawnee tribes, two bands of displaced or so-called immigrant tribes who had allied themselves with Anglo settlers. The grand entrance of the Comanche chiefs into Fredericksburg for the signing of the treaty is a marvelous and touching scene, the descriptive high point of the novel.

STRUBBERG'S PLACE IN GERMAN LITERATURE ABOUT TEXAS

In the nineteenth century, literally scores of books, pamphlets, and reports were published in Germany about Texas—an extraordinary and largely forgotten output. These were by a wide margin nonfiction travelogues and firsthand reports designed to quench an almost insatiable thirst for facts and figures by those contemplating emigration to Texas. This output began with Detlev Dunt's important little book, *Reise nach Texas* [Journey to Texas] (1835), and reached its highpoint in 1848, when there was a steady increase in production of nonfictional works that parallels the curve of German emigration to Texas under the auspices of the *Adelsverein*. After 1848, the number of nonliterary works written in German about Texas fell off rather dramatically.

Two important books, however, stand apart from this trend and deserve mention. In 1841, Charles Sealsfield (Karl Postl) published *Das Kajütenbuch oder nationale Charakteristiken* [The Cabin Book or National Characteristics]. This work went through many editions and is still in print today. Controversy raged from that day until this as to where to place this book in German literature.[83] Sealsfield, unlike Strubberg, was consciously literary and claimed to have invented a new type of novel, a kind of psychological work. In the book, as the title suggests, Sealsfield offers insights into those characteristics that enabled the Anglo settlers in Texas to successfully revolt and secede from Mexico, a country with a population twenty times their number.

The other noteworthy work is a memoir by Herman Ehrenberg that was published in 1843 under the title *Texas und seine Revolution* [Texas and Its Revolution]. The book found a large audience in Germany and enjoyed several reprints under different titles.[84] As a young man and fresh immigrant from Germany, Ehrenberg joined the New Orleans Greys in 1835 and marched with the volunteers across Texas to help the Texans in their revolt against Mexico. He participated in the Battle of Bexar (December 1835) and subsequently was among the handful to escape the Goliad massacre. Ehrenberg emerges as an extraordinary *Glückskind* [darling of fortune] who escapes one hair-raising adventure after another, always with an infectious joie de vivre. His powers of description are formidable, not only of battle scenes and individuals but also of the charming natural landscapes he encounters on his travels through Texas.

Ehrenberg's memoir has garnered a tremendous amount of attention, not only as an entertaining historical document but also for the controversies it has generated in its own right. The prevailing interpretation of Sam Houston during the so-called Runaway Scrape rests heavily on an early translation of Ehrenberg, which, it turns out, is fundamentally flawed.[85]

Strubberg's work differs from that of both of these other men. Unlike Karl Postl, Strubberg was an eyewitness to the history he wrote about, thus offering an element of authenticity absent in *Das Kajütenbuch*. And by weaving a fictitious love story into his personal story, Strubberg's *Friedrichsburg* offers a melodramatic quality missing in Ehrenberg.

After 1858, Strubberg's Texas novels began to edge out *Reiseführer* [travelogues] and other nonfictional writings as the works most published in Germany about Texas. This clearly represents a shift in the public's appetite from factual curiosity about Texas as a possible destination for emigration to a new awareness of Texas as a mythical landscape where America's heroes on the frontier become Germany's heroes. In this, Strubberg clearly points the way toward the new genre of *Abenteuerliteratur* [exotic literature], which was in its infancy in the 1850s and 1860s. The genre developed an enormous popularity among the German public that continues to the present day. Many scholars now see in

Strubberg a direct precursor to Karl May, the author of the wildly successful Winnetou/Old Shatterhand novels that appeared in the 1880s and 1890s and the author who represents the most admired exponent of the genre. Jeffrey Sammons, for example, wrote the following in his influential *Ideology, Mimesis, Fantasy: Charles Sealsfield, Karl May, and Other German Novelists of America*:

> Strubberg . . . reminds us forcibly of Karl May, who undoubtedly drew extensively from him. . . . Strubberg is a kind of proto-Karl May, the predecessor who resembles the later writer most.[86]

A thorough comparison between Strubberg and May could be a study in itself, and is well beyond the scope of this discussion. For present purposes, it should be noted that despite obvious similarities, substantial differences also exist between the two authors. Strubberg, unlike Karl May, remains thoroughly grounded in reality. Karl May amplifies his heroes to superhuman status; Strubberg does not. Rather than concentrating on one or two superheroes, Strubberg offers a whole range of heroes: German settlers, Indians, women, and even entire communities, and they always remain recognizable as human. Karl May offers his readers a mythical landscape; Strubberg portrays his landscapes accurately, intimately, and with a painter's eye for detail, for he was an accomplished amateur artist as well. In short, Karl May imagined the American West; Strubberg experienced it. In conjunction with this point, Preston Barba sums up the importance of *Friedrichsburg* as follows:

> Strubberg has never received due recognition for having given to the world the most faithful account of the German colonies, New Braunfels and Fredericksburg. Though these accounts are in literary form, a comparison with later histories will show how conscientiously the author endeavored to give historical accuracy to his work. In *Friedrichsburg* the author has devoted himself in particular to that colony in whose early history he himself played no unimportant role as colonial-director.[87]

To this assessment, I would add that *Friedrichsburg* bears up well as the literary equivalent to the work of three well-known German artists of the Texas frontier: Richard Petri, Hermann Lungkwitz, and Theodor Gentri. These men have provided posterity with a marvelous visual record of early Hill Country landscapes and of the German settlements. These artists came out of the tradition of Northern Romantic landscape painting, yet their work is surprisingly faithful to the subjects they portrayed.[88]

Next Page: Hermann Lungkwitz, Friedrichsburg. *Lithograph, 1859. Courtesy of the Dolph Briscoe Center for American History, University of Texas at Austin.*

N.d. Nat. v. H Lungkwitz

FRIED

BURG.

Lith. Anst. v. Kau & Sohn, Dresden.

My research in the long-neglected and underutilized reports of the Solms-Braunfels Archives, as well as in contemporary newspaper reports of the period, largely corroborate what Strubberg asserts in his preface, namely that most of the episodes portrayed in the novel, aside from the abduction and subsequent rescue of the heroine Ludwina, are rooted in factual occurrences. On the other hand, in *Friedrichsburg*, readers come away with a picture of the town as it should have been rather than the way it was. The same might be said of the author's depiction of himself.

Strubberg/Schubbert emerges from these pages as someone whose leadership qualities always shine forth; as a great father figure, universally beloved and respected by those in his charge; as a leader sympathetic but resolute in all his decisions; as a man whose mental alertness and physical prowess make him equal to any challenge he encounters on the Texas frontier; and as a man whose European sensibilities lift him above the narrow prejudices he encounters in Texas and make him an admirer and friend of the American Indians, a man who recognizes their humanity and sees value in their way of life even as he acknowledges, regretfully, that it appears doomed to disappear in the face of advancing "civilization."

In truth, Strubberg/Schubbert was not the paragon depicted in the novel, but neither was he a complete scoundrel whose memory should be expunged from public consciousness. Narcissistic, yes; undermining of Meusebach's authority, probably. Arguably, though, without Strubberg's leadership in those first two years, Fredericksburg might not have survived.

In post-unified Germany, Strubberg has recently enjoyed a mini-revival. His collected works are being reissued,[89] and in 2008 he was the subject of a radio reading by Michael Quast.[90] None of Strubberg's Texas stories, however, have ever been translated into English. Thus, Strubberg's works have remained largely inaccessible to the communities whose legacy they bring vividly to life. My hope is that this annotated English version of *Friedrichsburg* will enhance our understanding and appreciation of this legacy even as it offers the reader an entertaining adventure and love story.

FRIEDRICHSBURG

A Novel

Colony of the German *Fürstenverein*

by

FRIEDRICH ARMAND STRUBBERG

*a.k.a. Dr. Schubbert, First Colonial Director
of Fredericksburg, Texas*

*T*HOUGH I HAVE WOVEN THE THREADS of a novel into this story as a kind of seasoning, this in no way interferes with or distorts the historical aspect of the story, for all the various episodes rest on real happenings. This approach serves rather to lend more color and contrast to the picture which has been presented.

Because so many ties of kinship, friendship, and love were established at that time with the far-away wonderland; because so many fervent wishes and hopes accompanied the people as they journeyed across the wide expanses of the ocean to the Promised Land; and because so many heartfelt well-wishes still extend from the old German homeland across the trackless expanse to the happy, sunny, perpetually green Texas—for all these reasons I allow myself the modest hope that my esteemed readers will still find interest in a true and accurate depiction of the circumstances and conditions of the German colonies in Texas, of the land and country, and of the native peoples and their various customs and rituals.

CHAPTER 1

The Solitary Rider • The Wild Ones • Friedrichsburg • Early Morning Hour
The Lovers • The Major • The Two War Comrades

MOONLESS NIGHT LAY OVER TEXAS, but the sky was cloud-free and the stars sparkled with unusual majesty. It was already past midnight as a rider traveled along the road connecting the German town of Braunfels with the second German settlement, the newly founded Friedrichsburg, which lay a hundred miles farther to the north beyond a stretch of barren limestone hills and a completely uninhabited wilderness.[1] Here the road ended. The rider had given his horse plenty of time to make his way up the steep hill, but after reaching the top, he spurred him to a fast trot, for the road continued along the smooth back of the high hill for almost a mile. The stallion's hooves clattered noisily on the hard stone trail through the tomblike stillness of night while man and horse, silhouettes on the ridge line, hurried along in an unbroken trot. The rider reached the top of the ridge, where the road once again wound its way steeply into the valley below, and, as he let his mount settle into a walk, offered him an affectionate pat on his taut neck. He laid the reins on the horse's neck, took off his wide-brimmed felt hat, and ran his right hand

Rudolph on horse pursued by Indians. Drawing by James C. Kearney.

through his hair, for it was quite warm and only along the top of the hill was a light, refreshing breeze perceptible. Then he took out his small pipe, filled it with tobacco, and halted his horse in order to light the pipe. He had laid the tender on the stone and made several hits with the striker when suddenly he froze and listened intently for several moments with bated breath for sounds from the valley beneath him, and then, quickly, as if sure of his decision, put away his pipe and striker, shortened the reins, and at the same time gripped his double-barreled shotgun, which lay across his thighs behind the saddle horn. Giving his stallion the spur, he urged his horse forward toward the valley below.

Ever clearer now, in front and to his right, he could make out the sound of rapid hoof beats. Many swift horses were heading steadily for the road from the direction of a side valley. When he had reached the bottom where the road led into a wide plain for many miles between the hills, he spurred his fleet-footed horse on at a full run in order to get ahead of the oncoming riders, who, with each passing moment, came ever closer to the road. All the while he searched the darkness for the unseen riders, and it appeared more and more doubtful whether he or they would be the first to reach the point where the paths intersected.

Under spur and quirt, the stallion shot ahead; then the rider recognized the dark shapes, surging forward in quick bounds to cut him off. Once again he put the spurs to the flanks of his steed and in the same instant yanked a pistol from its holster. At just that moment the foreign host met the road a short distance behind and, letting out the fearsome war whoop of the Indians, released a hail of arrows in the direction of the fleeing rider. He, however, had gained the advantage over the savages,[2] and as he stormed past, fired off two shots to the rear from his revolver. The thunderous procession pressed on in this manner: the single rider in the lead, the band of savages behind.

The fleeing rider demonstrated the quality of his horsemanship, for no sooner had he increased the distance between himself and his pursuers by over the length of an arrow's shot than he reassured his steed with soothing tones and a gentle pat to the neck while lifting himself up lightly in the saddle to relieve the burden on his animal. Although his horse was accustomed to perilous night rides, the rider did not want to overtax him as he navigated a sure path along the road. Nonetheless, the speed of the stallion was such that he put distance between his pursuers from minute to minute. His master seemed less interested in them than in what lay before him, as if he expected that the unbroken war whoops, echoing from the hills, might be answered by others to the front. But up ahead, all remained quiet and still, with only echoes reflecting the savage yells coming from behind.

He reached the spot where the road once again climbed steeply. Here he slowed his horse to a walk and turned calmly in his saddle to listen for his pursuers, who were still a full half-mile behind him.

"Poor Carlos, to get you so lathered up," he said quietly to the noble animal, while patting him lovingly on the neck and rump. "Lucky that none of the arrows struck you."

As he said this, he urged his horse to a livelier gait with his legs, a command the horse willingly obeyed, while snorting loudly.

"Well, look here," said the rider suddenly. "The scoundrels really did strike me with an arrow, but only in my pistol holster." And as he spoke he removed with some difficulty the projectile which had lodged sideways in the bearskin saddle blanket.

"I'll keep it as a souvenir," he continued, while looking around simultaneously in the direction of his pursuers, who were attempting to close in on him once again. But by the time they reached the base of the hill, the rider was only a short distance from the top.

"Come on, Carlos," he repeated to his horse, while slackening the reins. His horse immediately sprang into a gallop and, in a short time, gained the crest of the hill. From then on it was top speed.

The rider arrived in the next valley without another sign of the savages. He then followed the road with the utmost calmness, which led to a broad, dense stretch of woods lining the churning Pedernales River. Here he dismounted, letting the horse slake his thirst and refreshing himself as well with a drink from the cool, clear mountain water.

A deathly silence lay upon the countryside; only the crash of the waves cascading over mighty boulders below the ford and the distant howls of a pack of wolves celebrating a kill interrupted the sacred serenity of the night. The darkness had lessened and a man could make out the slender trunks of the towering pecan trees along the banks, through whose crowns, inclining over the river, the stars shone down into the dark torrent with a reflection of a thousand lights.

Once again the rider listened intently to the rear. Then he swung into the saddle, forded the stream at its shallow part, and urged his spirited horse forward at a calm trot, for he now felt himself at home, as the town of Friedrichsburg lay only a half-hour's ride farther down the road.

The path now led over hill and dale. Soon it passed through a stretch of solitary blackjack oaks, covered underneath by a lush mat of thick grass. In all directions the startled steps of fleeing game signaled his approach.

The stallion quickened his gait so much—as if he knew this was the path home—that the rider had to rein him in from time to time; yet the way to the town was quickly traversed and the creek[3] crossed near where the slaughter-house[4] of Friedrichsburg stood.

The rider now turned into the main street of the city, into San Saba *Straße*,[5] on whose left side, in the first house, one built of sandstone,[6] the colonial director, Dr. Schubbert,[7] lived. Next to it stood the *Verein* compound, at the end of which a cannon[8] had been set up like a menacing watchman over the street.

In passing, the rider cast a glance at the house of the director while following the long, straight street between the small wooden houses which stood behind their fenced-in yards until he reached the *Marktplatz*[9] in the center of town. Then he turned to the right, crossed Austin *Straße*, and turned left into Schubbert *Straße*, following this one to its end. In this, the western quarter of the city, the houses stood singly and between them stretched wide, open fields of grass.

The rider turned at a fenced-in yard and rode to the back door of a wooden house. Here he dismounted, removed saddle and bridle, and, patting his horse affectionately on the rump, said, "So now you can rest, my brave steed; once again you have saved my scalp."

The stallion shook himself, rolled over in the grass, and took off across the field while the rider placed saddle and gear on the porch behind the house and stepped inside. In a few minutes, though, he reemerged from the building with a mandolin in his hand and, treading lightly over the grass, hurried toward a solitary log house on the outskirts of town.

The angry barking of a deep-throated watchdog greeted his approach to the stake fence surrounding the house, but when he reached the entrance and opened the gate, the powerful animal welcomed him with happy bounds and received, in turn, an affectionate pat.

The dawn broke, the sliver of light on the eastern horizon began to turn red, and daylight spread over the land. Silently the young man stepped up to the side of the house beneath a small window and began playing his mandolin, sending up soothing, melodious chords from its resonating strings.

The young man's name was Rudolph von Wildhorst.[10] He was eighteen years old, a portrait of powerful, youthful vitality. His close-fitting leather suit revealed a muscular frame that was compact and well proportioned. The light of the gathering morn highlighted his lush brown locks, accented his features, and reflected brightly from his large brown eyes.

The race for life or death that he had just won left no mark on his countenance. He faced the window, flush with joy, and in a rich, manly voice began singing a morning song to his beloved.

Hardly had the first tones passed over his lips than the window budged slightly. But only after the song was finished and the sound of the mandolin's strings had faded did it open up, suddenly revealing the angelic countenance of a charmingly beautiful young lady with dark hair and deep blue eyes.

"My Rudolph!" cried the maid with blissful surprise. "Thank God that you are here again!" she said as she bent over, stretching out her arms to the young man below, while he, raising himself with one hand on the window sill and with the other grasping the back of her snow-white neck, pressed his lips to her beautiful mouth in a passionate kiss.

"My Ludwina—my own—my precious!" he said, his joy overflowing, as he caressed, embraced, and kissed the young maid tenderly and blissfully.

"Will you forgive me for disturbing your sweet sleep?" he asked playfully after a while, taking her chin in his right hand and gazing into her deep violet-blue eyes.

"Oh, my good, sweet Rudolph, how thankful I am for every moment I am blessed by your presence," answered Ludwina, drawing her beloved even closer to her. "I couldn't sleep; I was thinking of you. Leo's barking woke me, and my first thought when I opened my eyes was of you, you, my life!"

"Oh, dear angel, you are so good, so sweet, and how indescribably happy your love makes me," whispered the young man fervently, giving words to his overwhelming feeling of joy, after which he fell silent and snuggled once again in the arms of his beloved. After a short, blissful pause, he continued, "Come out to the arbor, Ludwina. Listen how the mocking bird is already singing in the live oak; the morning is so delightful. Come outside, but don't wake your good father!"

"I'll be right there, Rudolph," replied the maid quickly and happily, as she disappeared from the window. In the meantime, the young man walked over to the alcove, which was completely shadowed by a large live oak tree on the side next to the fence. There he placed his mandolin on the table, made of rough-hewn boards, and began to weave the shoots of the vine into the living wall of the alcove.

Then the door of the blockhouse opened and Ludwina hurried out, light of foot. Her tall, lithe figure was clothed in an airy, silver-grey morning dress, which was held loosely on her slender body by a red ribbon made of silk while her slim, delicate feet were adorned with red slippers, stitched in gold.

"My Rudolph, my beloved," she cried tenderly, hastening toward him with open arms and cleaving to his breast. "Thanks be to God!"

"You sweet, you heavenly creature, how should I, how could I ever thank you for your love that blesses every hour, every minute of my life!" exclaimed the young man as he pressed the maid to his heart.

"With your love, Rudolph, you put me in your debt," answered Ludwina as they walked into the entrance of the alcove, arm in arm.

"Oh, my hair!" she suddenly exclaimed, grasping laughingly for that mag-nificent adornment given to her by nature. The shining black hair fell down in wavy locks over her shoulder as far as her knees, for in her haste she had only rolled it up loosely, fastening it to her head, and a branch at the entrance had set it free.

"It is a real nuisance because when I leave it braided, I can't sleep," she continued, wanting to quickly twist her hair together and put it up. But Rudolph held both her hands firmly and said, "Oh please, just for a moment . . . it's too, too beautiful!" In so doing he gazed upon the silky soft fullness of her locks, pleasantly taken aback, while running his hand through them.

"Oh, you beautiful creature," he said, admiring her hair. But Ludwina pulled it back from his hand and quick as lightning bound it up on her head with the words, "It is not pretty at all. I look like a squaw!"

Then she sat down on the bench with her lover and said, "Now tell me how things went for you for the long time we were apart—you have been gone for ten days." Rudolph then gave an accurate report about his ride to Braunfels and back, and as he closed with an account of his escape from the Indians, Ludwina threw her arms around his neck anxiously and said, "No, no, my Rudolph, you cannot make these dangerous rides anymore, even though you might earn a lot doing so."

"But someone has to deliver and pick up the dispatches. The well-being, yes, even the existence of our settlement depends on it. Without our connection with Braunfels we would soon be at our end. We receive all our supplies from there,"[11] replied Rudolph.

"Someone else will step forward who will risk it; you shouldn't do it anymore. Think about it! If the savages had killed you, what would have become of your Ludwina?"

"Don't worry, sweet maid. The danger will soon cease because the government of the United States wants to make peace with the Indians.[12] I have already brought instructions about this to our director from the executive committee in Braunfels. A Treaty of Friendship is supposed to be concluded here in Friedrichsburg this August."

"May God allow it!" Ludwina added quickly. "Like most of the people living here, I am having a hard time getting used to the constant danger surrounding us, and I am amazed that the savages have not taken advantage of our complete vulnerability. Tell me, Rudolph, what resistance could we, my father and I, hope to offer if they attacked us at night? We live so far out on the outskirts; our cries for help would go unheeded."

"You are right, Ludwina, and the thought of it has caused me many a sleepless night. How many times already have I left my quarters and hurried over here in order to assure myself that no danger threatens you? But, as we say in Germany, "Fear is the best deterrent![13]

"It is the moral superiority of the white man that holds back the Indians from being a more serious and direct threat," replied Rudolph reassuringly, adding after a short pause these words: "And our firearms have something to say in the matter. Since the Indians can't maintain and repair rifles and since they can't get ammunition for them in any case, all of these hostile Indians here in the Southern Plains are outfitted with weapons they make themselves.[14] From a short distance, their arrows are certainly dangerous enough, but our musket balls reach farther and have a much different effect. Truly, if the savages were conscious of their own strength and were to concentrate it, they would surely prevail. The Comanches alone, the ones to whom the land really belongs, count over twenty thousand souls.[15] Would the wild stallion submit to a flimsy bridle or the lion stay cooped up in a wooden cage if either were truly aware of his strength?"

"What they can't accomplish through force they get through deception," interrupted Ludwina. "Think about it, Rudolph, how many settlers in Friedrichsburg have already fallen victim to them?"

"Victims of their own carelessness and lack of vigilance," replied Rudolph. "Each time, following the murder of a settler from Friedrichsburg by the Indians, the men refuse to leave their houses unless armed to the teeth. They pack muskets, shotguns, pistols, swords, and axes, and only venture out of the city in packs, during which time not a single sign of Indians is to be seen. Soon, however, the fright is once again forgotten; the weapons become burdensome to carry; the danger something ordinary, something commonplace, and once again you encounter people a mile or so out from the city without a shot to fire. How often has the director called the people together and implored them urgently never to go about unarmed, and to what effect? No, the people themselves are to blame when such a misfortune befalls them."

"Well, the same applies to you, dear Rudolph; you also place yourself unnecessarily in harm's way. How easily the savages could have cut you off; how easily your horse could have stumbled and fallen," cried out Ludwina to her beloved, while gently brushing aside the shining locks from her forehead.

"In the exercise of my duty I am in God's hands, Ludwina; he will not forsake me," answered the young man. He then looked for several moments through the fence to the south and continued, "Look over there. During my absence another neighbor has moved in. The little twig hut is certainly small enough. Who built that palace?"

"A *Herr* Küster from Frankfurt am Main. He arrived with the last caravan of emigrants and is said to be a rich man. He owned, so I heard, a coffee business in Frankfurt, and his wife, who ran the business, supposedly forced him to emigrate to Texas alone. It must not have been a very good marriage—so much unhappiness in the world—the man looks so sad and downcast," replied Ludwina in a sympathetic tone.

"Who knows what circumstances brought them together, but apparently their hearts weren't part of the bargain," said Rudolph, and laughingly added, "Hopefully you will never have me emigrate?"

"My Rudolph," interjected the maid imploringly, throwing herself on the young man's breast, "if you were to leave, would not the life of your Ludwina depart too?"

As the young lovers exchanged their heartfelt sentiments, the time slipped by unnoticed. The valley of Friedrichsburg, so far removed from the civilized world, filled in with the day's cheer, and the rising sun's first rays gilded the rocky contours of the hills which surrounded the town on all sides. High above on the steepest crown, a mile north of the city, illuminated by the golden light, a huge white flag flapped in the morning breeze, a landmark in the distance for the citizens of the settlement, should they lose their way in the hills.[16] Director Schubbert had ordered the flag to be planted there for that purpose.

By now the town had come to life. Beginning the day's work, a large part of the male population had left for the communal cornfield,[17] situated on the eastern edge of town. The women and children were already busy in the gardens surrounding their houses, and here and there the sounds of an ax could be heard constructing blockhouses or felling trees.

"I have to go now, my dear Ludwina," said Rudolph as he arose. "I need to bring the director the dispatches right away. He has most likely been up and about for a while already and is probably outside with the workers in the cornfield. As soon as I can, I will be back with you again."

"See if you can come and have lunch with us, Rudolph. That would make father happy," interjected the young lady as they stepped outside of the alcove together. She added, smiling at him lovingly, "And your Ludwina will make it well worth your while."

With this she pressed herself to the heart of her beloved and offered him her fresh mouth for a morning kiss. Just at this moment the door of the house opened and out stepped old Major Nimanski, the father of Ludwina.

"Good morning, Rudolph. Welcome back," he said as he approached Wildhorst and offered him his hand. Leo was the first to announce your arrival, and then your song confirmed it, but it was still a little too early for me to greet."

Then he shook the right hand of the young man heartily with the words, "It went well for you, then; you look refreshed." Turning to his daughter, he kissed her and said: "And nothing is missing for my Ludwina's happiness except perhaps some of the household belongings we had to leave behind in Lemberg."[18]

"No, dear father, she is wanting for nothing. For she has you and her Rudolph, and in you two all her happiness is contained," Ludwina said, interrupting the old man happily while putting her arms around him and stretching out her hand to her beloved. He, however, quickly took his leave, and Ludwina called after him from the gate, "If you can, Rudolph, lunch! There will be a fine venison roast!"

"An upright, true German lad, your Rudolph," said the father as he watched the young man leave. "He makes it clear why a good providence allowed an old man like myself to succumb to the Texas fever,[19] causing me to emigrate here together with you, my great joy, my only child. You were meant to find Rudolph here! To be sure, the circumstances in our old beloved Galicia were unsettled and discouraging. And we were only able to get by on my pension in Lemberg with difficulty, while here it is more than sufficient for our simple life. Still, we pulled up stakes for a new world for basically shaky reasons."

"And a beautiful world too, dear father," interrupted Ludwina, raising her hand to her lips. "Think about the dreadful winters in Galicia and what a paradise we exchanged for it here; we are living in a perpetual springtime."

"Yes, it is nice here, but mainly because you found Rudolph," answered the old man. "And how curious that his father, retired and pensioned like me, together with his son, also succumbed to the Texas temptation. It had to be divine intervention, and, therefore, things will also work out well for you, Ludwina."

"God has stood by us with His grace so far, and will continue to do so," she replied, basking in her happiness while going back to the house arm-in-arm with her father. After a short pause she continued, "Wouldn't you like to invite Rudolph's father to our table? We have the nice roast!"

"Yes, certainly, I will go right over. He might be intending to take a walk or to ride to the Pedernales to do some fishing," answered the major as he entered the house with his daughter. Soon thereafter he reemerged, armed with a long pipe, and strolled across the grass pasture to the house of the retired Prussian colonel, von Wildhorst.

Both had been widowers for a long time and both had responded to the invitation to emigrate to Texas, which the *Fürstenverein*[20] had advertised throughout Germany, and upon becoming acquainted here in Friedrichsburg, they had become fast friends, a connection made stronger by the heartfelt alliance of their children.

After only a few minutes' walk with long but measured steps, the tall, angular figure of the major arrived at the house of his friend, whom he found sitting comfortably on the porch in his nightshirt, smoking his morning pipe.

"Hey there, Major Nimanski, so early out and about?" the colonel called out to him, pleasantly surprised, and walked toward the garden gate. There

Wildhorst welcomed his guest, shook his hand heartily, and, as he strode with him back to the porch, said, "Rudolph already informed me that you had your boots on; come, have a seat next to me, and let's chat a while."

The colonel spread out his nightgown, sat down next to his friend on the wooden bench, and continued, "Rudolph once again was pursued by those damned Indians last night in a life-or-death chase. This plague should be torn out by the roots. I don't understand the government: they are the one enemy, and actually an impotent one at that, standing in the way of civilization. The United States has the means at hand to exterminate these useless tribes and yet they continue to pander to them, as if they were beholden to them for God knows what reason. Now they are supposed to conclude a great peace treaty with this rabble. Rudolph has brought instructions for the director."[21]

"My daughter has already told me about it," the major answered. "I must confess to you, Wildhorst, these hair-raising rides of Rudolph cause me a lot of concern; the Indians appear to have sworn an oath of death on him. How often have they been behind him now?"

"Yeah, but think how, despite this, the youngster comes to their defense and maintains that they were within their rights and were doing nothing but defending their property from the white man. He says he wouldn't so much as disturb a hair of an Indian if he weren't forced to defend his life, and all the while he laughs after they have chased him over hill and dale."

With these words the colonel became agitated and, clenching his fist, continued, "If I run into these dogs, I'll shoot them down as long as I can still load my rifle. They are rabble—with one Prussian cavalry regiment I could run the entire Indian nation into the Pacific Ocean."

"Well, old comrade, you would have a bit of trouble there; the Comanches alone count over twenty thousand souls," interjected Nimanski. "We are lucky that they are split up into so many small bands and live disunited among themselves.[22] Incidentally, many of these bands are already friendly toward the white people, and obligated in friendship especially to our director, Dr. Schubbert, since they bring their sick to him from far and wide and put up their tepees next to his house so that he can tend to them. Just in the last week the band of the head chief of the Comanches, Santa Anna, who named himself after the Mexican general, was here. He also left behind several sick members for treatment."

"Yes, Schubbert is said to have been acquainted with these Indians before he took over the directorship,"[23] observed the colonel.

"Entirely correct. He lived for many years in the far west in a wooden fort among the savages and battled on and off with them until they found out that he was a doctor, at which time they began a friendship with him. In time they will all come around to understand that they are better off living in peace with us and trading with us."

"I don't trust the scoundrels. They look like devils, and in spite of their assurances of friendship I am convinced that when they catch a white person alone in the wild, they will make short work of him," interjected the colonel as he stroked his white mustache.

"Well, let's leave the Indians alone for a minute and talk about something else. Ludwina passes on a request for you to enjoy a delicious venison roast with us today. Rudolph will also be there if the director doesn't detain him."

"I certainly will not turn that down," answered the colonel. "And I'm glad that you came over early, because I wanted to ride downstream along the Pedernales a bit and catch some fish. Please tell Ludwina that I have some tender lettuce here in the garden; I want to send her some. A good salad along with wild game is something exquisite."

"She will accept that with thanks. We also planted lettuce, but it didn't turn out. The two of us, Ludwina and I, are poor gardeners," said the major.

"I don't understand why you didn't, as I did, bring along an old trusted soldier as a servant," continued the colonel. "My old Anton, who has already served me for twenty years, and my old Liese, who has been in my service as cook even longer, keep my garden in first-class shape, and since things grow here in the winter and the summer, it is ever a puzzle to me why in all of Friedrichsburg there are no vegetable gardens, except for mine and Weltge's."

"Certainly I considered bringing an attendant along, but I was concerned by reports that the servants here throw off authority quickly and so one would have wasted the expense," replied the major.

"One would not expect that from a real soldier; nothing trumps having been a real soldier, and in my opinion, it would have been a great help to have had an old comrade around."

CHAPTER 2

The *Fürstenverein* • Prince Carl Solms • The New Braunfels Colony
The Colonial Director Dr. Schubbert • The Cornfield • The Town
The Man from Frankfurt • The Quartermaster • The Cannons of the *Verein*
The Shawnee Indians • Supper

*F*RIEDRICHSBURG WAS THE SECOND established colony of the *Fürsten-verein*, the group of German noblemen who constituted the Society for the Protection of German Emigrants in Texas.

By the 1830s the continued emigration of Germans to North America had already caught the attention of the German princes, and the many reports of dashed hopes of the emigrants and of the shameless deceptions and misdeeds perpetrated upon them in their new chosen home, where, instead of happiness and joy, they had found only misery and despair. These facts led the German princes to contemplate reshaping the emigration system in such a way that they might be able to guide the destiny of the emigrants and insure a happy future for them.

Friedrich Strubberg, Trust, Czar, and Armand. *From first edition of*
Amerikanische *Jagd- und* Reiseabenteuer, *1848.*

Their attention was drawn to Texas, a country that seemed to meet all the requirements for reaching this goal. It was the single southern region in North America that appeared suitable. It possessed the richest, most fertile soil; it was ideally suited by nature for livestock production; and immeasurable tracts of land were to be had for fire-sale prices. The princes sent a delegation[1] to Texas in order to gather more detailed information about the circumstances and conditions in Texas; should the reports be favorable, they decided, they would organize their emigration endeavor as a stock company.

During this period, the western part of Texas was very troubled by hostile Indians. The frontier settlements were continually under attack. Even the most intrepid settlers felt compelled to pull back and seek protection in the more heavily settled regions. The eastern bank of the Colorado River in the vicinity of Austin and Bastrop was especially vulnerable to the depredations of the plains tribes because on the west bank trackless, inaccessible hills arose from which the Indians could approach the river undetected. They could carry out raids with lightning speed, murdering and plundering on the other side, and just as quickly as they came, once again disappear without it being possible for the white settlers to pursue them.[2] The government of Texas came to the conclusion, quite correctly, that once the upper, fertile areas of the Hill Country were settled by white people, the warlike tribes would no longer feel so secure and could no longer reach the settlements on the Colorado River undetected and unmolested. Two Germans, a Mr. Fischer and a Mr. Müller,[3] who had already been living in Texas for many years, had learned about the intentions of the German princes, and recognized a welcome opportunity to set up a promising business venture. They persuaded the Congress of Texas to grant them ownership of the land north of the Llano River on the high plateau of the Hill Country as far as the bend described by the Colorado River from west to east under the condition that in a set number of years they would be required to settle a specific number of colonists in the region. The government agreed willingly to the proposal, and the documents were drawn up granting Fischer and Müller conditional title to the lands in question.

They then sold this contract for the sum of $200,000[4] to the German princes, who then founded a stock company, the "Society for the Protection of German Emigrants in Texas," this being the official name appearing on the *Verein*'s stock certificates.

The conditions under which those interested in emigrating would be transported and settled in Texas by the society were advertised throughout all of Germany, and they were so favorable, so inviting, that people streamed forward from all sides. Thousands gave up house and hearth, business and home, in order to emigrate to that paradise on earth, Texas.

His Majesty, Prince Carl of Solms-Braunfels, undertook to found the first colony in the lands purchased by the *Verein* and arrived with the first two shiploads of emigrants in Texas. It became clear to him only too quickly, however, that the distinguished gentleman in their dealings with the *Verein* had not mentioned virtually insurmountable difficulties standing in the way of the enterprise and had sold a tract of land unknown and unseen by any white man with the chance exception of a few adventuresome hunters. To be sure, toward the end of 1600, the Spanish government had founded a *presidio* in the territory on the San Saba River and set up a military colony there.[5] This, however, had been destroyed by the Indians, and in Texas one spoke of the old fortress on the San Saba as if it were an ancient myth. From the Gulf Coast, where the emigrants landed, the nearest border of the grant area was close to three hundred miles farther north, but the existing American settlements reached barely eighty miles inland. From there, neither road nor trail led to the grant area, and only un-arable, desolate hills stood in between, populated solely by wild animals and wild humans.

Prince Solms soon recognized the complete impossibility of leading the emigrants to their destination and quickly decided to establish his first colony as far as possible along the way toward the grant area. In a prudent choice, which cannot be praised highly enough, he purchased a sizeable tract of land in the wonderfully beautiful Guadalupe River valley, land the likes of which, in terms of fertility and charm, is not to be found anywhere else in North America. In a word, this tract was a paradise whose appeal the *Verein* would be unable to exaggerate in its advertisements to attract emigrants. Prince Solms led the emigrants entrusted to his care to a place where the one-of-a-kind Comal River[6] empties into the Guadalupe River, the Comal being only a few miles from its source, where it bursts forth from the earth in a hundred colossal springs. Between these two rivers, he founded the promised home.

The town of Neu Braunfels was laid out, in the beginning with just tents and huts. The plot of arable land contractually promised to each immigrant by the *Verein* could not be parceled out here by the prince since the land purchased was not nearly sufficient to this purpose. He did, however, assign to each a so-called city lot, big enough to put up a dwelling and lay out a garden.

This vanguard of the great German exodus, which had gathered along the coasts of Europe in order to move to a new home on the other side of the ocean, was easily transportable, because it consisted for the most part of several hundred young unmarried men and so, in proportion to the number of persons, considerable stocks of supplies from Germany had been brought along. Therefore, the founding of the first settlement progressed quite quickly.

Soon, however, a much larger group of eight thousand emigrants under the protection of the *Verein* approached the coast and landed there.[7]

Prince Solms had done his job; he had founded the first colony, even though not in the grant area proper, for there was no possibility of being able to do this. He returned to Germany with the full thanks and blessings of those who had been in his charge. He was replaced by a director-general, who set up office in Neu Braunfels with his staff.

From this point on, the affairs of the *Verein* took a different turn. Neither transportation nor provisions for the second wave of emigrants had been pre-arranged; no one in charge had the ability, or even the good will, to lead and offer assistance. A terrible epidemic[8] broke out among the emigrants as a consequence of this neglect, and neither doctor nor medicines were present to prevent its spread.

ALREADY SEVERAL THOUSAND unfortunate[9] souls had fallen victim to this situation before the *Verein* authorities called on Dr. Schubbert for help and turned over the position of director to him.[10] He immediately took over the care and treatment of all the sick. He had them moved out in the open air, away from the dense woods along the Guadalupe, where they lay crowded together, hut on hut and tent on tent. Quickly, the disease shed its nasty, epidemic-like character. Soon it lifted completely with only occasional and temporary symptoms which manifested themselves benignly as a slight, intermittent fever.

Dr. Schubbert then saw to it that those under the care of the *Verein* received better nourishment, and he also facilitated the transport of those still stranded on the coast. He founded an orphan's home[11] and placed the many parentless children in it. He mediated between the emigrants and the *Verein* authorities in a way that was both accommodating and reconciling. After the conditions in Neu Braunfels had once again taken on a more promising aspect, he led about fifty families a hundred miles farther north into the hills, where, on the far bank of the Pedernales River, the second settlement, the town of Friedrichsburg, was established.

Over a year had now passed since the founding of this colony, during which time all the citizens had been continually supplied with provisions from Neu Braunfels. The number of inhabitants in the new town had swollen to more than a thousand souls, and newly arrived emigrants from the Gulf Coast were still being sent up by way of Neu Braunfels. With the exception of an insignificant yield from their gardens, the citizens of Friedrichsburg still had not produced a harvest, and it was no longer possible to transport from Neu Braunfels even the cornmeal needed to make bread for so many people. It became, therefore, a matter of life or death for the colony that enough corn be harvested that year to correspond to the number of souls in the settlement. Without it, the settlement would have to be abandoned and a move made back to a more settled region.

Director Schubbert knew only too well, however, that little or no harvest would be left over if he allowed families to cultivate, fence, and plant the corn individually on those plots that had been given to the settlers by the *Verein*. For this reason he ordered that a communal field be prepared for cultivation, to be divided by lottery among the participants only after the corn had ripened.

And it was to this field that the larger part of the male population of Friedrichsburg walked this early morning.

The director was always one of the first to greet the new day. As a rule, he stood in front of his house with his faithful companion, Joe, an enormous old bloodhound, while the townspeople passed by on their way to work. He usually went to the field to supervise the work himself, and so it was the morning Rudolph von Wildhorst hurried to his house to deliver the new dispatches.

Because the cornfield was not the only claim on the director's attention, Rudolph had had to look for Dr. Schubbert at several places around the town. He was occupied with putting up a mill, building an apothecary, and preparing a ten-acre field for a garden in order to produce vegetables for the citizens. And, notably, he had also put up an orphanage and brought up all the orphans from Neu Braunfels so that he could care for them himself.[12] For the present, he had also ordered that several often-flooded streams on the way to Neu Braunfels be bridged. He rode out daily to check on the progress of these projects. And, in addition to all of this, his medical skills were daily more in demand because scurvy had made an appearance among the settlers several weeks before.

When Rudolph climbed the fence into the cornfield, the director spotted him and hurried over.

"Welcome, Wildhorst," he called to him, reaching out his hand with a smile, "You stayed away longer than I expected. I was beginning to worry about you."

At this, he took the dispatches from Rudolph, opened them up, and scanned them quickly. After reading for a few minutes, he folded the papers together again and placed them in the breast pocket of his leather jacket, saying, apparently still preoccupied with the content of the letters, "Well, nothing new, then, Wildhorst?"

"Nothing, *Herr Direktor*, except what is written," answered Rudolph. "The administration in Neu Braunfels has no more corn on hand even for themselves. They have to have more shipped from Austin before they can send any to us. There are also difficulties with the transportation of cattle for slaughter.

"Too bad, too bad," said Schubbert impatiently. "This dependency on Neu Braunfels in respect to provisions must and should cease or Friedrichsburg will collapse. It is really stupid to transport corn here by way of Neu Braunfels when the distance from Austin to here is less than the distance to Neu Braunfels, and therefore the freight expenses for the extra hundred miles from there to here are completely unnecessary. Granted, between here and Austin are found some of the most rugged hills, places where a white man has probably never set foot. Still, as the crow flies, it cannot be more than eighty miles. And besides, these hills can't be any more of an obstacle than those between here and Braunfels. I will at least make the attempt to scout a road through the wilderness to Austin.[13] I want you to come along, Wildhorst."

"Gladly, *Herr Direktor*," responded Rudolph with a slight bow. "I think, however, we would do well to take along several others, because the Indians are pure devils."

With this he related to Schubbert the episode with the Indians the previous night.

"Certainly others shall accompany us; I will need in any case to have the surveyor Döbler along, and Burg and Kracke will not want to be left behind—they are our best hunters. We want to begin early tomorrow, at the crack of dawn."

"I think it would be a great pleasure for my father to ride along and see Austin, the seat of the Texas government," said Rudolph.

"The old gentleman is welcome to come along, if it's not too hard on him," the director responded.

"Certainly not; he is, thank God, still quite robust. A hardier rider you're not likely to find; it would please him a lot to go along," interjected Rudolph enthusiastically.

Followed by Rudolph, the director then strode along the furrow between the cornstalks, which had already grown a foot high, in the direction of the workers, who were busy at the other end of the field piling loose dirt around the plants with their hoes. There he gave several instructions with respect to the task and then turned to Rudolph with these words:

"Let's go back to town now; I need to speak to quartermaster Bickel. He has to be careful with the distribution of the corn; otherwise, we will find ourselves in an embarrassing situation. Then I will go with you to your father because I need to visit a new arrival who lives close by."

"Will Joe come along tomorrow?" asked Rudolph as they strode along, patting the powerful yellow dog on the back.

"Sadly no, the faithful animal is already quite old and I don't want to put him through any more stress than he can handle," replied the director as he smiled at his dog. "He has saved my life too many times not to enjoy a peaceful old age."

At this, he snapped his fingers at the dog, who, with a deep-throated bark, took off in giant bounds for his master's house.

After the director had taken care of several necessary items at the business office of the *Verein*, he walked with Rudolph up San Saba *Straße*, along which, now here, now there, people would call out to him, if only to offer a morning greeting.

The street presented an extremely lovely and picturesque view. Rows of gardens lined both sides of the street; all were fenced in neatly with stakes, and behind each stood a wooden house. Grapevines, roses, and blooming vines adorned the walls of the buildings, and several of them were so thickly over-grown with them that one could hardly discern anything except the door and windows. The street was half a mile long, and in front of it, not too far away, the hills rose to their craggy heights while lush, green groves of trees covered the ravines.

But, above all, the personalities animating this scene imparted to it a most unusual character. Here, in front of her door at her wash bucket, stood *Frau* von Rawitzsch, a born Duchess B., a small, charming lady from the highest social circles in Vienna, who, smiling, called out to the director her most cheerful greeting while her two young children tugged at her dress. Over there, a lady from Berlin was standing in her fire-red corset with a short, black, sleeveless dress, all trimmed in red, waving her morning greetings with a potato hoe. And over here, a proper German *Frau*, with bonnet and apron, busy with the peeling of a beet. In the garden next to her a petit *Fräulein* with gloves on was planting flowers, while next to her, sawing on a heavy log, stood a haggard looking woman with long black locks and dressed in a white dress.

Director Schubbert returned all the greetings in the friendliest manner, and added to every "Guten Morgen" he proffered a few words of hope, cheer, and consolation.

In such a manner, he arrived with Rudolph at his home, where both old gentlemen, the colonel and the major, were still sitting together chatting on the porch. They received the two warmly and asked Dr. Schubbert to have a seat next to them, a request he declined with the remark that he still had business to take care of.

After he had invited the colonel to take part in the expedition to Austin, an offer he eagerly accepted, the director took his leave with the remark:

"I need to see who this *Herr* Küster[14] is who arrived here last week and moved onto a town lot on the far outskirts. I wasn't present when he showed up and he hasn't paid me a visit yet."

"Quite right," said Nimanski. "His stake house, which he paid to have erected, is not too far from my place, but I, too, have seen nothing of him except when he heads for the creek with his bucket to fetch water; he appears to shy away from human contact. If you will permit it, I will go along with you; a man needs, after all, to know his neighbors!"

With this, the major offered his hand to the colonel with the words: "*Auf Wiedersehen!*" The director asked Rudolph to pay him a visit again around sundown and then, after a hearty farewell, the two headed off in the direction of Nimanski's home.

"The cornfield looks very good, *Herr Direktor*," remarked the major as they walked along.

"Thank God, the corn has sprouted nicely even though it was planted unusually early. I was afraid, however, that we wouldn't finish in time," replied Schubbert.

"If the administrators in Braunfels would only pay attention to my suggestion that it would be better to cluster newly arrived emigrants in small settlements along the way instead of sending them all up here. In this way, a kind of natural connection between the two towns could develop. As it is now, there is not a single house between us and wayfarers are completely helpless and defenseless. And even though they can't even supply this town with the most basic needs, the administration is now speaking of establishing another town in the grant area proper, whose border lies a further hundred miles to the north. If, on the other hand, one were to proceed with small settlements which reinforce one another, food could be produced all along the way, and the towns would arise naturally and from necessity as they do with the Americans. They will not listen to me, however, and are beginning with that which, by rights, ought to be the last step. Instead of acquiring for ourselves those fertile, well-watered valleys along the way, we are giving the American land speculators[15] time to snap them up even as we make them more valuable for them."

The two were now approaching the major's dwelling, and the pretty Ludwina emerged from the garden gate to receive them. The director, however, declined to enter since they were expecting him before lunchtime at the *Verein* business office.

"I can't let you just pass by, *Herr Direktor*; you are so seldom a guest here," said Ludwina in her lovely, melodious voice. She stepped to the side to allow him to pass through the gate, smiling and fixing her beautiful eyes on him as she spoke.

"You mustn't interpret the infrequency of my visits as neglect, *Fräulein* Ludwina," answered the director pleasantly. "My time doesn't often allow me the pleasure of following my wishes. But I will pay a visit in the near future, and then I will bring you a nice present rather than announcing myself empty-handed."

"A present for me, *Herr Direktor?*" asked Ludwina, laughing. "And may one be permitted to inquire of what it might consist?"

"Of the finest she-goat from a flock of several hundred head," replied Schubbert. "I have put in a special order for the goats from a Mexican trader, because it takes so long to get cattle delivered and because the lack of milk is one of the reasons for the outbreak of scurvy."[16]

"Oh, you could not make me happier, and I thank you in advance from the bottom of my heart," said Ludwina happily.

"But in exchange I need to take away your bridegroom, once again, tomorrow," continued the director, smiling.

"Rudolph?" asked Ludwina, taken aback.

"Yes, *Fräulein*, but this time I am going along and his father is coming too," answered Schubbert.

"Well then, if you are going along, I will allow it, but under no other circumstances," inserted Ludwina, half in jest and half seriously.

"I will deliver him back to you unharmed, *Fräulein*," said the director. He excused himself most graciously and headed with the major in the direction of the hut of *Herr* Küster from Frankfurt, which stood a couple of hundred yards away.

Through the open door they spotted the inhabitant of this miserable shack sitting on the edge of the bed, which was made of four poles driven into the ground, with twigs and sticks attached to these for a support, upon which a feather mattress had been spread.

As soon as Küster spotted the approaching men, he jumped up and came out of the hut.

"Oh, my God, *Herr Direktor*, how can I excuse myself for not having paid you a visit to express my sincere respect? I was so overwhelmed with the task of setting up my household that with the best of intentions, I couldn't find the time," said Küster. He was a small, thin, nervously agitated man, who accompanied each of his words with quick movements of his arms and hands and who imparted to his features a different look from one minute to the next. As if struck by lightning, his face twitched, his black eyebrows shot up, his dark blue eyes opened up widely, and his breath seemed to stick on his thin lips. In the next moment, however, his mouth parted in laughter, his long, white teeth stood out, and his eyes shone as if animated by a hilarious joke; then suddenly he looked up imploringly with a humped back, the corners of his mouth drooping, and with an expression of such distress in his dull eyes that one half expected him to break out in tears.

The director looked at him astonished since he couldn't form a clear-cut picture of the man. Finally, in order to say something, he said:

"You have made progress, then, in setting up your household, *Herr* Küster?"

"Charming, charming, isn't it, *Herr Direktor!*" the man answered, rubbing his hands together.

"That is to say, nothing has been done, and I hope you won't be living in this stall for much longer and will soon build for yourself a real house, or pay to have one built," continued Schubbert in a more serious tone.

"Oh, *Herr Direktor*, how could one contemplate living in such a place!" exclaimed Küster, putting on an expression of utter horror and waving his hands around defensively.

"My thoughts exactly," interjected the director flatteringly. "A gentleman like yourself, a man of your education, could never be satisfied to live like that."

"Yes, yes, yes, how would that be possible?" repeated the man, striking his breast. With a proud look, he continued, "No, no, *Herr Direktor*, you will see how Küster is used to living!"

"I hope that you set a good example for the others and that your property will be a plus for the city; you are a rich man," the director continued cheerfully. But with these last words Küster shrunk suddenly into himself, folded his hands, and said in a sniveling, weepy tone, "What rich? You mean poor, honorable *Herr Direktor*, not far from the beggar's staff?"

"Well, I wish that all the people here in Friedrichsburg were such beggars, *Herr* Küster, and could carry around $4,000 in cash," interrupted Schubbert quite seriously. "I hope that you will fence in your plot soon and build a house on it; this is the requirement for receiving the land."

"Certainly, certainly, as soon as possible," answered Küster, now quite embarrassed, but maintaining a normal expression on his face.

"If I can be of service to you in any way, then come right over to me, *Herr* Küster," the director continued reassuringly. "I always prefer it when my charges come directly to me with any complaints, requests, or questions. If you want to put up a simple blockhouse, then you can call on the brothers Leidecke; if you prefer, however, a nicer, more comfortable structure, then I can recommend the carpenter Schandau, who will give you satisfaction in every way."

"Very good of you; so thankful, *Herr Direktor*," answered Küster, overcoming his embarrassment, rubbing his hands together and adopting once again a cheerful and engaging expression.

Director Schubbert took his leave then with friendly well-wishings and said as he departed, "I will visit you again next week to see if your workers are doing their job." Küster answered with only a smile and a deep bow.

That evening, after darkness had already settled over the city, the director stepped out of the workroom of the *Verein*'s headquarters with the quartermaster Bickel, an unusually tall, large man of an extraordinarily jovial and friendly disposition.[17] They entered the gateway through the building leading from the street in the direction of the smoky courtyard behind.

At the far end of this courtyard a cheerful bonfire cast its flames upward and illuminated all the surrounding buildings, especially the long shed that was supported by rough log uprights, in which the horses of the *Verein* were sheltered and held in readiness to protect the settlers and their property from hostile Indians. About twenty men in number, illuminated brightly by the fire and clad in their red woolen jackets, were lying stretched out on their saddle blankets. They appeared to be in a good mood, for their lively conversation was punctuated by repeated laughter.

"Keep a close watch on everything during my absence, my dear *Herr* Bickel," Schubbert said to him, "and keep the guards nicely at home, so that if you need them they will be close at hand. Likewise, should the Indians show themselves in a hostile way, do not forget to fire the cannons as a signal for all the men of the city to grab their weapons."

"Do not worry, *Herr Direktor*, everything will go according to the guidelines," replied Bickel with that brand of equanimity that was peculiar to him. "And if the Indians come in friendship, I will present them with several pounds of tobacco, some iron stock for arrowheads, mirrors and cinnabar to paint their faces with, and little things like that. I will be done with them quickly enough."

This conversation carried them into the courtyard, and they walked up to the campfire as the guards raised themselves from their blankets. All greeted the director in a most friendly manner. While shaking many by the hand, the director said, "I will be riding out early tomorrow to scout for a road to Austin and will rely on you during my absence, gentlemen, to be ready and available by day and night." At this, the entire group reiterated their willingness and readiness to serve.

"Two of you, Burg and Kracke, will accompany me, even though I know that you will be reluctant to do this," continued Schubbert in a joking tone, whereupon an expression of general merriment followed. Burg, however, spoke up, his countenance flushed. "The bear-hounds, Leo, Pluto, and Weiko, will come along, won't they?"

"No, unfortunately not this time, Burg. We want to leave the bears unmolested, and the dogs might possibly get in the way," the director answered. Suddenly, the clatter of horse hooves became perceptible and they strode quickly back to the doorway with Bickel. Before they reached it, an Indian stepped into the court and bid them good evening in perfect English.

It was a Shawnee Indian,[18] a man from a tribe that had been living at peace with white people for many years.

"Well, Kalhahi,[19] it is you," answered the director, as he warmly shook his hand. "You are here, as if summoned. You will ride with me tomorrow. I need to scout out a road from here to Austin that is just as good as the one from here to Braunfels."

"Right good," answered the Indian. "Kalhahi could lay it out through the hills in the dark of night. However, he has brought along lots of horses, mules, tanned deer hides, and bearskin blankets, and wants to trade for tobacco, powder, and lead, and many other nice things from the whites."

"You didn't come alone?" asked the director.

"No, Kalhahi's brother, Minitori, came along in order to share with me."

"Well, he can take care of the negotiations until we return. *Herr* Bickel here will help him and even trade for a lot himself. We can always use deer hides, and you will be able to dispose of all your horses and mules right here in the town, if they are decent."

The Indian appeared quite happy and said, "Kalhahi will go light his fire and then bring his drinking horn back to Schubba (as he called the director) so that he can fill it."

"No, you are going to eat with me, Kalhahi. Go and set up your camp, and when you are finished, come back," answered Schubbert, whereupon the Indian took a hasty leave.

The director was still standing with the quartermaster next to the *Verein* compound, giving him instructions related to the various projects to be executed by the *Verein* during his absence, when Rudolph von Wildhorst walked up to them.

"It was a lucky coincidence that brought Kalhahi, the Shawnee, to us. He came to trade, and I have decided that he will ride with us tomorrow. He believes it will not be difficult to lay out a road to Austin," the director told Rudolph.

"He will be a great help to us in any case, because the Shawnees, together with the Delawares, have been carrying out all the negotiations of the government with the wild Indians in this country, and they are familiar with every pass through these hills. In addition, he will be of use to us in case we should encounter hostile tribes, because the area between here and Austin has a bad reputation," remarked Rudolph.

"Good, it will be the eight of us, then, and we won't have anything to fear," replied the director.

At this time, two more officials of the *Verein* walked up, and a little later Kalhahi also returned, at which point the assembled group retired to the dining room for supper. The director took his place at the head of the table and bid the Indian to have a seat to his left; to his right sat the quartermaster, with Rudolph to his side. (Rudolph was also fully employed by the *Verein*, although he only made occasional use of his right to sit at the *Verein*'s table.)

The Indian had put on a heavily fringed hunting shirt of tanned deerskin, sewn and embellished with colorful silk stitching. In addition, he wore moccasins and leggings that reached over his knees that were similarly fringed and adorned. He had already taken many meals with the director, but the use of knives and forks was still uncomfortable for him, and after he had unsuccessfully hacked at a wild turkey thigh placed on his plate by the director, he laid the fork down, took the leg in his hand, and used his nice white teeth to separate the meat from the bone.

"What do you think, Kalhahi?" asked the director after a while. "Do you think the Comanches will bother us on our ride?"

"Kalhahi will keep a sharp lookout by day and sleep with one eye open at night," answered the Indian.

"The majority of the Comanche bands have already concluded peace with me," continued the director.

"The war chief Kateumsi,[20] however, has not offered you his hand in peace and will not slacken his bow as long as a single white man inhabits these hills. He calls these hills his own," replied the Indian.

"Santa Anna[21] told me Kateumsi's band is not very large, numbering barely fifty warriors," said Schubbert.

"The name Kateumsi means archer, and his arrow flies as straight as a rifle ball. He is the best shot among the Comanches, and each of his warriors can bring down a buffalo with one shot. Our rifle balls will have to keep him at a good distance from us. He has never made a present of his scalp to a white man," replied the Indian.

"Hopefully even this enemy of the white man will come to his senses and make peace with us," continued the director deftly, "because as I am informed from Braunfels, the government of the United States has sent Delaware Indians to all the bands of the Comanche Indians as peace negotiators and has set a time when they should meet here in Friedrichsburg to sign a peace treaty and to receive gifts. Kateumsi won't hold out alone."

"Kateumsi will not come. All the gold and all the enticing gifts of the whites will not turn his heart toward peace. He will take his hatred with him to the eternal hunting grounds of his fathers," interjected Kalhahi. He added with a dark look, "He also sees the scalps of the Shawnees with a false eye, but he fears their rifle balls."

"Well, let him hold back, then, and after peace is concluded, I will let several of our guards pay him a visit. They will gladly spoil his stay in the realm of his fathers," remarked Schubbert. Turning then to Bickel, he said, "If the missing piece for the iron millworks arrives from Braunfels during my absence, have the mill smith Wurzbach[22] have a look to see if everything is there. Otherwise, he can ride down with the teamsters and see to it himself that we finally get possession of them.

"The lack of a mill has impeded the construction of our homes here. Every board has to be cut by hand, and when our corn crop is ripe, I don't know how we are going to grind the corn for meal without a mill. The people can't waste their precious time grinding corn with hand mills."

"I have laid the matter urgently before the officials in Braunfels once again and asked them to load the very first wagons carrying up supplies with the necessary parts, and they have given me a firm promise," noted Rudolph.

"Yes, yes, promised," interrupted the director. "They pack all the wagons with the chests and luggage of the newly arrived emigrants and send these up to us here, so as not to have to listen anymore to their endless grumbling and complaining that they cannot yet move to land promised them in the grant area. So they would like to see how we deal with them here."

CHAPTER 3

Kateumsi (the Archer) · Call for Peace · The Path through the Wilderness
The Beautiful Valley · Laying Out the Road · Ambush by the Comanches
The Saving Shot · The Night Camp · The Buffalo

WHILE THE OFFICIALS SAT AROUND the bear oil lamp on wooden stools, discussing the pressing problems of the town, a narrow valley lying between them and Austin was brightly lit by many fires. They were the campfires of the Comanche band whose chief called himself Kateumsi (the Archer).

Forty or so white, round tepees with pointed tops, made of tanned buffalo hides, stood on the banks of a rushing Hill Country stream that flowed through the valley. Before each one burned a large fire whose flickering flames illuminated the naked, red bodies of the wild ones,[1] who lay stretched out on animal hides, or squatted on their heels, or stood.

In front of the roomiest of these tepees, the chief Kateumsi rested on a colossal, colorfully spotted jaguar skin. He was a tall and handsome man, somewhere in his thirties. His slender, sinewy limbs revealed an unusual muscular development, especially evident in his arms, which he had doubtless strengthened through his use of the bow. His reddish-brown facial features were noble,

Ambush by the Comanches. Drawing by James C. Kearney.

his eagle nose as well as his dark eyes gave him an expression of unbending will and decisiveness; his raven-black hair fell in two heavy braids on both sides of his head onto his powerful copper-colored breast. His wide, dark brows cast a shadow over his countenance.

A dozen women, all his wives,[2] were busy in front of the tent and around the fire, several with the roasting of meat and marrowbones, others with the repair of saddle gear, or with preparation of animal pelts. The youngest and prettiest of the squaws[3] sat next to the chief and worked on an arrow, of which she had already completed several, which lay on the ground between her and Kateumsi.

"Choose strong sinews for fastening the arrowheads onto the shaft, Mona, so that they don't give way when the arrow hits a bone; it needs to shatter the bone," said the chief to the squaw, while he rested upon his elbows and observed her work.

Soon thereafter, she handed him the finished arrow, and after he had inspected it for a while, he placed it next to the others with the words, "It is good; may the Great Spirit allow that Kateumsi be able to shoot it at the heart of a paleface."

Suddenly, however, he turned his head, and quickly sitting up, looked and listened up the valley, and after a few moments, he called out harshly toward the closest fire, "Kateumsi hears horses' hooves; have you no ears?"

The men, who were lying around the fire, jumped up, shocked, likewise listening, and then quickly fetched bows and arrows from their tents.

Now the hoofbeats of the approaching horses grew louder, and soon thereafter a rider appeared in the far light of the fire, a rider who directed his horse down the stream toward the camp.

"One of the betrayers of the red children,[4] a Delaware," said Kateumsi, fixing his dark gaze upon the approaching rider, who, after several minutes reached the tent and dismounted his horse.

"Youngbear,[5] my chief, wishes you luck on the hunt and in your tent," said the Delaware, as he stepped up to Kateumsi and offered him his hand.

In the meantime, while one of the squaws fetched a buffalo hide from the tent and laid it by the fire for the stranger, the chief said to him, "You are welcome at my fire; rest yourself." He pointed with his hand at the buffalo hide.

While one of the squaws removed saddle and gear from his horse, the Delaware leaned his long, simple musket against a nearby tree, and following the invitation of the Comanche, took a place next to him on the buffalo hide.

Then one of the women spread out a deerskin between the two men and placed cooked meat and split marrowbones that had been roasted over the coals of the fire in front of them.

"You are welcome at my meal," Kateumsi repeated, and pointed toward the food. As he raised himself up, he took an enormous split bone and consumed the marrow within it.

The Delaware followed the invitation quietly, and his appetite indicated that he had ridden a long way without eating.

After both had satisfied their hunger, one of the wives handed the chief a pipe. He lit it at the fire and then quickly inhaled several draws of tobacco smoke. Then he handed the pipe to the Delaware, who did the same. Both stared a while into the fire once again, as if lost in thought, until Kateumsi sat up straight and puffed out a cloud of the inhaled smoke. Then he leaned forward on his elbows again and said in an indifferent tone, "Now speak; why have you come to Kateumsi?"

After the Delaware had also blown a cloud of smoke from his mouth, he turned his equally indifferent gaze upon the Comanche and began, "Our Great Father in Washington has instructed my chief to invite all the Comanche bands to Friedrichsburg in order to conclude an eternal peace and friendship treaty with the whites, and to receive valuable presents. They have set the time for the month of August when the moon is full. Youngbear has sent me to bring you the invitation."

At this the Delaware fell silent and fastened his unchanging gaze upon the Comanche, whose features had grown darker.

"Where are Youngbear's tepees?" he asked after a while.

"Upon the ever-green meadows on the banks of the beautiful, clear Medina," answered the Indian.

"And why did he have you tire your horse for nothing? Or doesn't he know Kateumsi yet, and believes he too will close his eyes to the treachery of the palefaces and open his ears to their forked tongues? Youngbear is no friend to his red brothers. Otherwise he would not have sent you to Kateumsi."

Turning toward the Delaware scornfully, his face even darker than before, the chief listened as the other replied, "Youngbear is a friend of his red brothers, and just for this reason he hopes that you will accept the invitation of the Great White Father and make peace so that you too can rest calmly by their fires." The eyes of the chief lit up brightly at these words of the emissary.

"And wasn't it also the Delawares," he called out in an angry voice, "who invited old Mapotuska[6] and some forty other Comanche chieftains to San Antonio to a peace conference with the palefaces, who fell upon the Comanches, who had been tricked into giving up their weapons, and slaughtered them all with the sole exception of Sanacho,[7] who managed to save himself through flight?[8] Oh, you Delawares—you are friends of the red children for the gold of their enemies, the palefaces."

With this, the chief threw himself back on his elbows and held out his hand to the other Indian in a gesture of derisive dismissal.

"This time you are mistaken, Kateumsi; the whites are sincere in their desire to live in peace with you and to trade with you."

"Like the raging grey bear, who kills and dismembers solely from bloodlust, so have the palefaces driven the red children from the shores of the Big Water and exterminated entire tribes, and now they are seeking them out in these far-removed hills in order to trick them into venturing out where, defenseless, they can be killed," interjected Kateumsi in a sober voice. "What remains of the great nation of the Delawares, who once ruled over the entire land where the sun rises? Your friends, the palefaces, have ground you down to a few small bands, which they now make use of for gold in order to betray the still strong, free races of red children so as to drive them from the face of the earth.[9] Tell your chief you have sat with me at my fire, that my wives have served you food, and that you have slept peacefully in my tent; but let them know that I am an enemy of the Delawares, and when we meet, my arrows will take the measure of their musket balls. Now find a place in my tent or sleep here by my fire, as you wish, so that when the sun rises, you can leave refreshed and nourished. I have spoken."

With this, Kateumsi made a gesture with his hand, as if in farewell, turned over, and closed his eyes.

BY THE TIME THE STAR-FILLED NIGHT had passed and the faint glow of the approaching day had begun to fill the sky, the *Verein* compound in Friedrichsburg was already filled with lively activity. In the courtyard, the home guard[10] was busy at the fire preparing their breakfast. There was cooking and heating of water in the kitchen, while the *Verein* officials[11] gathered in the business office in order to receive last-minute instructions from the director.[12]

The dawn had barely penetrated the morning fog, which rolled through the valley toward the hills as a delicate cloud, when the director strode with his companions through the gateway to the waiting horses, there to be heartily greeted by Colonel von Wildhorst and his son, who had just ridden up. He mounted his horse and the others quickly did the same. Schubert gave the quartermaster his hand in departure, entreating him once again to remain ever vigilant and careful. The eight riders then departed at a trot in an easterly direction, with Kalhahi in the lead and the director and both Wildhorsts close behind.

The town was quickly behind them and the forest of oaks soon took the riders under its protective canopy.

Neither bush nor shrub impeded the horses. The lush, thin-stemmed grass under the mighty trees, fresh, green, and low, shone like a silver plane in the heavy dew. The fog hung in small patches here and there as the view from under the oaks into the distance became ever clearer. In all directions, the fields and meadows were full of life. Here a flock of several hundred wild turkeys fled, half-flying, half-running; over there stood a herd of deer nervously watching the riders before taking to the distance in graceful leaps and bounds. And soon enough a herd of enormous buffalo thundered off in a heavy gallop, while now and then the dark shape of a bear loped away in long bounds through the trees.

The sun climbed over the high hills, sending its warming rays through the high foliage above the forest floor, and, like a blanket of diamonds, the pearls of dew shimmered in its light. All of nature was alive: the birds sang, the hawks screeched, while the buzzards lifted themselves by the hundreds from their perches in the branches, swooping and circling, as if performing a morning dance above the treetops.

Soon the forest thinned out; the old live oaks with their massive outstretched arms became scarcer; large rocks broke up the fields of grass more and more; the rushing waters of the Pedernales became ever more perceptible; and soon the last cliff-like banks of the roiling, swirling river were reached. The horses had to pick their way through the boulder-strewn path and tall grasses, and large plants hindered their progress. Here, the hills had closed in and steep cliff faces bordered the narrow valley on both sides of the river, so that from time to time there was barely enough room for one rider to pass. But soon the stony heights widened and a fertile, lushly grassed and at times heavily forested valley opened up on both sides of the river. Its banks were once again adorned with majestic trees which concealed the waters of the river for long stretches.

"It is incomprehensible to me," said Schubert to the colonel, who was riding next to him, "why the home office didn't choose this valley to establish Friedrichsburg. If I had been with the commission, I certainly would not have cast my vote in favor of putting the town several miles from the river, and I would have examined the banks of the river for several miles both upstream and downstream. The more often I come to this place, the clearer this mistake becomes to me. And what an enormous amount of force the water has there above at the gorge."

"It is truly charming here," noted the colonel, as he looked around the valley. "Couldn't a settlement be laid out here for the newly arrived emigrants?"

"That is impossible on several grounds. It would be difficult to supply the people so far off to the side from the predetermined route into the grant area, and also to advise them and offer them assistance," explained the director.

"Wouldn't this also be the case with isolated settlements between Braunfels and Friedrichsburg? What would the people live on?" asked Wildhorst. "They wouldn't be able to make the trip into either of the two cities twice a week in order to get fresh meat, cornmeal, beans, peas, and coffee from the *Verein*'s warehouse. And they are entitled to provisions, since they turned over their money to the *Verein* in Germany in order to draw it here in cash, provisions, or other necessary supplies."[13]

"You are entirely correct, Colonel," replied Schubbert. "But to the extent that we keep the emigrants together in towns and feed them like children, we keep them locked in that peculiar condition of German dependency, in the unfortunate habit of relying on others, of being watched over and taken care of by others. They are content to stay in the towns and let others satisfy their needs as long as they will do it, and as soon as they stop, they are clueless and hapless and complain that they have been mistreated. But yet they came here in the first place in order to gain a measure of self-sufficiency and to be able to take care of themselves. If it had been possible for the *Verein* to send them right away into the grant area and to assign them their land there, then they would have settled in a more isolated and dispersed manner than would have been the case with a string of small settlements that could offer interlocking assistance and protection. Certainly, it is more comfortable to live in town and to wake up every morning with the reassuring awareness that someone else is taking care of your food, shelter, and amenities. But who takes care of the American who, along with wife and child, moves twenty miles into the wilderness beyond the nearest border settlement, and there, relying on himself alone, with no assistance from anyone, begins the process of building a hearth and home?"

"Entirely correct, *Herr Direktor*," acknowledged the colonel, joining in the conversation once again. "But the fact of the matter is that the *Verein* has assumed the responsibility for the care of the emigrants, and they came over under this arrangement."

"And with the best intentions and after enormous effort, the *Verein* up until now has fulfilled the obligations it took on. It is unfortunately the case, however, that the officials in Texas have not chosen the right path to attain the proposed goal," replied the director. "If they had begun with a program to establish small settlements in all the beautiful and attractive valleys between here and Braunfels, the financial outlays to the *Verein* would have been significantly less, the settlers would have become self-sufficient, would have learned to feed themselves, and their resources in hard cash could have been better employed for their own benefit. And, if they had finally reached the grant area with such settlements, each settler would receive his parcel of land to do with as he pleased."

"I see that clearly enough," interrupted the colonel. "It's just that I don't see how a man with a wife and four children, for example, would have been able to exist in that first appealing valley he came upon, four hours or so from Braunfels."

"I will explain it to you, Colonel," answered the director. "I would never have sent just one family, but rather five or six. I would have assisted them in building blockhouses with log palisades around them, and also in helping them to plant small gardens. They would have needed to be supplied with corn and a hand mill in order to grind cornmeal, with a cow or some goats, with a couple of sows, with chickens, and with seeds for their gardens. Then they would be in a situation to provide for their own needs in a very short period of time without any outside assistance. The cows, sows, and chickens need little attention; they take care of themselves and reproduce faster here than in any other country in the world. After just a few weeks, the settler's garden would provide for vegetables and fruits, continuing for the rest of the year. Even if the *Verein* had to offer them assistance for this or that need, after they harvested their first corn crop, it would be able to leave them to their own resources completely. Towns will arise on their own; tradesmen of all sorts will naturally move into the settlements; businessmen will set up shop; and a lively traffic in goods and services will spring up along the entire route into the grant area.

"For the establishment of such a settlement, the *Verein* would need to engage a man with practical knowledge, preferably an American planter, and make him available to the people for a while, so that they could learn the manner and means of how an American approaches the wilderness, how he lives and works. But let me be clear, our Germans do not yield a whit in enterprise, tenacity, and skill to the American; in fact, they are superior in all these traits; it's just that they need an example. They must learn to gain confidence in their own abilities, something not possible for them to do in their adolescent life in Germany. Do you know, Colonel, that I lived along with three other Germans for many years in the midst of the Indians, even more removed from the whites than ever an American, before or since, so that it took more than two days' ride to get to the closest settlement?"

"Yes sir, I have heard about that, and I have also read reports on several occasions in American newspapers of your life in the wilderness," replied Wildhorst. "And certainly, because of this, you have delivered the best proof that Germans can make good colonists."

For over an hour now the riders had continued along through the valley at a quick trot, when Kalhahi struck a course away from the river and toward a passage between two high, barren hills, which they reached after traversing several miles.

Here the country took on a wilder character, less suitable for agriculture. The naked tops of the hills lifted themselves as ragged cliff faces. Steep, dizzyingly deep abysses opened up between them in a series of broken-up chasms, while the narrow side canyons were forested, especially with cedar. From the crest, one's gaze ranged into the faraway hazy distance over a sea of hills whose tops arose like blue clouds.

Immediately after departing the Pedernales River valley, the *Verein*'s surveyor, Döbler, began to mark the route by having his two helpers notch trees clearly with an ax on the east and west sides so that they could be seen from a distance. Where no trees were present, he had them set up stone pyramids, in which anyone would recognize the hand of man.

Even though the work was quick and crude, it nevertheless slowed the progress of the riders considerably. By the time the sun set and they had unpacked their horses to spend the night on a lush meadow next to a rushing mountain stream, they had followed their guide only about half the distance that otherwise would have been possible.

The horses were hobbled and put out to graze in the tall grass, and before darkness had settled over the land, the sojourners were settled around a large campfire, busy with brewing coffee and roasting wild game on sticks over the fire. Burg had shot a fat deer and two wild turkeys. The night was warm and still. Only after midnight did the resting men wrap themselves in their woolen blankets.

With the first graying of the following morning, all were busy with the preparation of breakfast, and before the sun had gilded the hilltops, the riders were once again in their saddles, following the Indian up and down the mountains.

It was astounding how effortlessly and with seemingly little thought this Indian found his way through the labyrinth of hills, and, yes, found a path that a wagon would be able to traverse and, with a little effort, a road could be constructed.[14]

The region did not change much as they proceeded that day; the riders still surveyed an endless sea of hilltops from each crest, and the same dark cedar forests looked up from the canyons below. The sky also remained cloud-free and clear, and fresh breezes softened the sun's hot rays. But today the riders were able to cover a substantial distance before sunset. Excited by the prospect that the undertaking would be crowned with success, they spent a relaxed night under a heavenly, star-covered tent.

Again they saddled up before sunrise to begin their work. Many rocks had been piled up and many trees notched by the time they reached the saddle of a high hill around noon, from which they could survey a valley stretching from north to south. A stream, most likely a tributary of the Pedernales, snaked across its grassy floor.

Back and forth the Shawnee led them down the steep hillside, and man and horse welcomed the meadow below and the refreshing drink it promised. But they had barely covered half the distance across the meadow to the stream when suddenly from farther up the valley, the war cry of the Comanche sounded and a band of riders came storming down the valley toward them in a flying formation.

"Forward!" cried Kalhahi to his followers, spurring his horse in the flanks and racing ahead, as if carried by the wind, straight for the creek. Close behind, the others followed, urging their horses to a flying run with whip and spur.

The Shawnee had already reached the high elderberry bushes overshadowing the stream, sprung from his saddle, led his horse down into the stream, and tied him to a bush when his companions arrived and hastily followed his example.

Hardly had the horses been safely secured and the riders scrambled back up the bank with their weapons than the swarm of Indians, some forty in number, came straight at them in a full charge with the obvious intention of overrunning them and forcing them back into the stream. Then the rifles of the Germans barked back at them and five of the savages fell from their saddles. A hail of arrows flew over the shooters at the same moment, landing behind the stream bank—all missing their targets.

With a wild cry, the entire swarm wheeled around and fell back while a tall, powerful rider on a black steed tried in vain to hold them back. With a raging voice of thunder, he galloped after them, bringing them to a halt and leading them once again in an attack upon the whites. Hardly had they come in range of the rifles than a new round of rifle balls flew in their direction, and once again several of the savages fell from their horses.

"Kateumsi!" cried the Shawnee Indian to his companions, who were frantically attempting to reload their weapons. But Kateumsi did not want to give them opportunity to do so, for in the next minute he came charging once again with his warriors, encouraging them with his lion's voice to follow in the attack.

"Doesn't anyone have a shot ready for the chief?" the director yelled out to his companions, as he threw down his ramrod and jerked his revolver from his belt, for the wild pack had already charged to within forty paces of the stream.[15] Then Rudolph sprang up the bank, took aim, and fired; the chief tumbled from his black steed to the ground.

With a cry, as if the spirits of hell had been set loose, the mass of savages surrounded their chief and lifted him to one of their horses and off the whole swarm surged, disappearing behind the bend of the stream.

"You have saved all of our lives, Rudolph," said the director, picking up his ramrod. "This time they would have overrun us for sure, and their arrows would not have spared a single one of us. How was it that you still had a round left in your rifle?"

"I nailed one of the poor devils with one barrel, but when they approached again, I was reluctant to take the life of another, since they are only fighting for what's rightfully theirs," Rudolph answered, laughing, as he tamped down a fresh load into his rifle barrel.

"And because of your humanity we all could easily have lost our lives," the colonel interjected.

"Not at all, Colonel; this time 'humanity' came to our rescue, because if your son, like us, had not held back a shot, then none of us would have escaped with his life."

"Thank God the devils are gone," said the colonel. "Truly, the grape-shot cannonade of the French at Waterloo didn't cause my blood to run as hot and cold as the sight of these devils. They paint their faces as if they came straight from the underworld. And how powerfully they fire their arrows! Just have a look at this three-inch-thick elderberry trunk, split and splintered—the arrow would have gone completely through any of us."

"No question about it," added Schubbert. "They shoot their arrows through the strongest buffaloes so that they come out the other side and end up no telling where."

Then the director turned again to Rudolph and said, "But you did more than just save our lives. With the death of this notorious, irreconcilable foe, you have performed a great service for the entire population of Friedrichsburg."

"If he really is hit that badly," remarked the colonel, still flush with excitement.

"I'm afraid I hit him in the chest a little off from the heart," Rudolph noted ruefully.

"You're afraid? Please, what are you saying here? You should be glad that you have dispatched such a monster from the world," interjected the senior Wildhorst indignantly. "I really don't understand you at times, Rudolph!"

"If the truth be known, dear Colonel, it was the same with me in my earlier and frequent fights with the Indians, as if right were not entirely on my side," observed Schubbert. "I never fired my weapon at them unless compelled by self-defense. They are in their domain and we are the ones who want to drive them from it, and, in the end, to cause them to disappear from the face of the earth," said the director as he set a new percussion cap to his rifle. With these words he walked from the stream bank over to his horse.

"Good enough, then. Let us continue. We have nothing more to fear from these enemies, and as soon as we have left, they will return to tend to their wounded. Though none is moving, they will not all be dead."

In a few minutes the riders were all on horseback and hurrying forward in the direction of a nearby rise on the other side of the stream. Here, they erected another large pile of rocks and rode away, leaving the valley behind.

The sun was still fairly high above the horizon when they reached a rolling grassland savanna upon which here and there groves of enormous live oak trees stood at great distance from one another, and through which an insignificant stream meandered. The same originated in a thorny thicket which stood in the middle of this expansive grassland. Barely fifty steps from this thicket many old oaks stood on a hill, and as the party neared the hill, the colonel said to the director, "Look at this. This would be a splendid place to set up camp: water is close by, dry wood is in abundance, there is lush grass for the horses and a clear view all the way around."[16]

"Nevertheless, I would never spend the night here," replied the director. "Do you see the thicket over there? Who could know? A hundred Indians might be lying concealed in it, waiting to ambush us after we fall asleep. Still, I propose that we stay here in the area. We can't ride much farther in any case, and it's far from certain that we will be able to find grass and water again. We will want to water our horses, refill our gourd canteens, and then ride over to that oak grove at the top of the hill. We cannot be surprised there."

"Ah, there aren't any Indians hidden in the thicket," interjected the colonel, pointing laughingly at the thicket. But once his decision was made, the director stood by it. They watered the horses, filled their canteens with water, and rode to the hilltop, where under the ancient, magnificent oaks they lit a campfire, while Döbler erected another stone pyramid on the highest rise.

It was a charming site for a camp, where the view far off to the west scanned the line of hills and the crests over which they had ridden. The sun sank behind the purple-blue heights while the sky above them turned a more glowing, fiery red from one moment to the next.

A silence settled over the wayfarers. Mother Nature cast her magic spell over the men, the magnificence of the setting overcame them, and withdrawing in unspoken awe, they kept their gazes fastened on the wonderful, beautifully illuminated picture before them, when Burg suddenly cried out, "Buffalo!"

Immediately he jumped up and grabbed his rifle, and both hunters stood there motionless, looking intently in the valley where a herd of buffalo, some fifty in number, wandered toward the thicket where the colonel had wanted to set up camp. The enormous beasts had barely disappeared behind the crown of the oaks near the thicket when the two hunters took off in a fast run over and down the hill toward the valley and soon reached the clump of trees and brush.

"Look, Colonel," said the director. "The same thing could have happened to us as with the buffalo had we set up our camp there. An entire band of Indians could have approached undetected from the other side of the thicket, crept up through the undergrowth, and overwhelmed us in a hail of arrows before we had ever thought about an enemy in the vicinity."

In the meantime, the two sharpshooters had crept up the left side of the thicket, where the springs disgorged their waters, and hardly had they taken up position behind some bushes when the buffalo sauntered up quietly and without care from the other side to quench their thirst.

Then fire shot out from the bushes; a mighty buffalo sank to his knees and the thunder of the two shots rolled down the valley. The hunters, however, did not move. Thunderstruck, the herd stood still. When they noticed their companion collapsing to the ground, they trotted around him in a circle, attempting to get him back on his feet by nudging him with their horns.

"It is thus with the hunter," said the director. "He doesn't kill from bloodlust. What would we do with more than one buffalo, from which we only need a few pounds of flesh, when he weighs close to two thousand pounds? But our hunters will shoot another one without delay. They will be looking for only the best."

In the same instant two more shots rang out from the bushes, and a second of the colossal animals fell to the ground.

At this, the two hunters sprang shouting and waving their rifles from their place of concealment, and the entire herd took flight in a heavy gallop, leaving their two fallen comrades behind.

"We need to send them a horse, a hatchet, and some rope so that they can field-dress the animals and bring up the meat, tongues, and marrowbones. Burg will not leave the best behind," the director said, whereupon Rudolph fetched his horse from the meadow, saddled him, and, accompanied by Döbler's two helpers, hurried down the hill.

CHAPTER 4

The City of Austin · The Delegates · The Wild Horsemen · Scurvy
The Gathering of Herbs · The Rattlesnake · The Sick One
The Convalescence · The Nanny

T HE NIGHT PASSED UNEVENTFULLY, and the riders continued their
journey the next day similarly undisturbed. They reached their goal in
the evening, arriving in the city of Austin on the opposite side of the
Colorado River. The water was very low, so the horses could easily ford the
stream, and before night had fallen, the director and his fellow travelers found
lodging in the Washington Hotel.

Schubert paid a visit to several businessmen soon after his arrival and
shared with them his plan to use the newly surveyed route to transport supplies directly to Friedrichsburg. So that the teamsters could mutually support
one another, he put in an order for five or six wagonloads at once. In addition,
he offered to supply them with an additional twelve men for protection of the
wagon train and to help clear the path when necessary.

The hotel was overflowing with guests because the Texas Legislature had
just begun its session. Strangers from all over the state had gathered in the city.
The director and both Wildhorsts received a room with beds; their companions, however, were assigned pallets on the floor in the dining room.

Rattlesnake. Drawing by James C. Kearney.

By seven o'clock the next morning the tom-tom was already announcing breakfast, and soon enough the table, which could accommodate eighty seats, was entirely filled. The guests ate and drank with such haste that after a scant fifteen minutes those guests who did not take a seat in the first rush could find a place at the table.

The director and his companion counted among the later arrivals and passed their time enjoying their morning bread with typical German *Gemütlichkeit*, spicing it with lively conversation.

After breakfast, Schubbert and the two Wildhorsts left the hotel in order to tour the city and also to keep appointments with several businessmen concerning the intended shipments. At about eleven o'clock, they stepped out of a place of business at the same time a crowd of Texas legislators and spectators were streaming out of the capitol building to take a short recess from the work at hand and also to fortify themselves for the work yet to come with some stout brandy mixed with water. To this end, a large number of men headed in the direction of the several saloons and bars in the vicinity, which soon grew very loud.

Schubbert and the two Wildhorsts had stopped at the plaza in front of the capitol to have a look at the scene when suddenly wild, angry voices echoed from one of the nearby bars. Two bodies came crashing out through the mass of men standing around: the one backing up, with his hands raised in defense; the other following him and striking at him with a cane.

The man backing up was a lawyer by the name of Marsdon, generally acknowledged as a notorious and dangerous drunk, while the man who was attacking him so violently, likewise a lawyer, was a widely respected and honored older gentleman by the name of Franklin.

"You are a despicable crook," said Marsdon to his attacker as he parried the blow of the cane with his hand, withdrawing hastily back toward a wall. "A liar, a thief, a swindler, a scoundrel," he continued, and each word seemed to heighten the anger of the old gentleman, leading him to strike out with ever more fury.

But no sooner had Marsdon reached the wall than he cried out for help as loudly as he could. In the same moment, he drew a pistol from his breast pocket and, uttering words that only his assailant could hear, fired at the old man, "Look at this, you old fool; now you die!"

With the shot, Franklin turned, his hand pressed to his breast, and sank, mortally wounded, to the ground. In a moment, hundreds had gathered around him. But his opponent, Marsdon, remained standing quietly next to his victim, explaining to the shocked and agitated crowd that all of his good words to Franklin had been for naught, and when driven against the wall where escape was no longer possible, he had been forced to defend his life and make use of his weapon.

Franklin was carried to a doctor's house and put under his care. Here he gave a decidedly different version concerning the chain of events before expiring a couple of hours later, to whit, that he had been the unwitting victim of well-calculated nefariousness. Nevertheless, a court of law later pronounced his murderer innocent.

This unhappy event caused a large uproar among the population in Austin. Two parties formed: one for and the other against the murderer, and on every corner the matter became an occasion for lively discussion the following day.

Also, in the evening, after the work of the day had been done, but before the supper bell had sounded in the taverns, the streets were full of life. People stood around in groups, discussing the excitement of the morning.

Suddenly a loud cry went up from among the crowd along the sandy street leading up from the river. A swirling cloud of dust came flying up the street, with the people parting frantically to the right and left. In the dust cloud, three Indians rode abreast with their long lances, spearing anyone they could reach.[1]

In a wild panic, the crowd scattered, trying to reach the safety of a door, but the attack of the Indians took place so quickly that any attempt at flight was useless. In the plaza in front of the capitol, the warriors made several widening circles in pursuit of the fleeing throng. In the batting of an eye, one of the Indians grabbed a twelve-year-old girl, lifted her in front of him on his horse, and, with a victory yell, the three made their escape down a side street toward the river and were soon safely across and secure in the hills beyond.

The horror, the panic of the people was boundless. The death and wounding of some twenty people enraged and disheartened them. The objects of their anger, however, found themselves by this time far beyond their reach, and they could do nothing but take precautions against a future, similar occurrence. The following morning no one appeared on the street unarmed and all swore eternal revenge on the Indians.

The men from Friedrichsburg mounted their horses right after breakfast, said goodbye to Austin, and struck a path for home. Although they took time on the way back to add more trail markers, they were still able to make good time and arrive in Friedrichsburg by noon the third day, where they received a warm and enthusiastic reception. Nothing out of the ordinary had taken place during their absence, and the news that the road to Austin had been laid out and a direct connection would soon be reality was greeted with general approbation.

Unfortunately, during this brief interlude, many new cases of scurvy had appeared, and the malady now seemed to have a much more serious character. Dr. Schubert was well aware of the cause of the disease, which lay in a deficient diet, but without being able to improve and expand on the nutrition of the people, any sort of medicine would have little benefit. The corn as well as the cornmeal had suffered in transit, but even corn of the highest quality supplemented only with dry peas and beans, and a modest about of meat thrown in from time to time, would not count as a healthy diet. Fresh vegetables, fruit, and milk were missing, and these would be needed to improve the general level of health. But how could he obtain these things in sufficient quantities to supply all the people? Vinegar from fruit was also somewhat effective in the treatment of scurvy, and several barrels were on hand in the warehouse. The director thought to himself, "If there were only some leafy green vegetables available, which could be dressed with the vinegar for the people to enjoy." It then occurred to him that many herbs that could be used in salads grew next to the streams and in the meadows of Friedrichsburg.

On the evening of his return, the doctor issued a challenge, calling on the young ladies of the town to gather at the *Verein* headquarters the following morning with baskets and sacks. The director would then lead them himself out into the fields to collect greens and herbs for salads. The summons resulted in a good thirty young ladies and wives showing up at the appointed time, and at their head stood Ludwina Nimanski, who had personally visited with the others and asked them to go along.

Ludwina and Rudolph, her fiancé, counted among the most beloved personalities in the settlement. Everyone was well disposed toward them and was glad to accord them the esteem they deserved. But truly, there was good reason for this, for the two never missed the opportunity to advise when asked to do so, to help out, and to offer their services in whatever capacity would benefit the community. Where want and misfortune befell, there you could find Ludwina to soften it; where pain and distress appeared, there was Ludwina to relieve it; but also where joy prevailed, Ludwina was not missing, enhancing it by her presence.

It was the same with Rudolph. He was the favorite, the friend and advisor for the whole town. No one was shy about approaching him with a favor because they knew he would willingly comply. His strong sense of justice also brought him high regard, as well as the extraordinary energy with which he tackled even the most menial tasks.

For all these reasons, people eagerly looked forward to the approaching marriage, which was to take place the following year. The two were still quite young, and the fathers intended to have a large house constructed in the winter where they could all live together.

"Well, well, *Fräulein* Nimanski, so you intend to go out yourself and help gather greens," the director remarked, as he greeted her warmly. "I am both mistress and servant, and when there is suffering to take care of, it is always the role of the mistress to be the first to step forward," replied the charming young lady half-seriously. "But," she continued in a lighter tone, "still, if the truth be known, it's a great pleasure for me to go out barefoot into the tall grass and just wander among the beautiful flowers as the fancy strikes me, but my basket shows that I intend to be productive at the same time."

"Well, you must have considered, at least a little bit, that I could be of help there," Rudolph interjected happily, "because it wouldn't be much fun to fill the basket with all these little plants and herbs by yourself. I'll be there to help you every step of the way."

"I am confident we will find another, larger plant, which is to be found in big stands. It is valuable both as a source of nourishment and as a plant with medicinal benefit. It is portulaca,[2] which is so carefully cultivated in hotbeds in Germany, but seems to thrive here as a prolific weed in the poorest soil. It serves as a delicious vegetable and if we can find some, you will quickly fill your baskets," the director noted. Then he quickly cautioned, "Over forty are sick and not a few are seriously ill and in grave danger. I am hoping there is still time to help them; we want to do our best in any case."

"And I promise to do all I can to help you," added Ludwina happily. "I will go out every morning."

With this, the director gave the nod to proceed. Rudolph took the basket from his future bride. The two of them, arm in arm, followed by the other women, led the procession outside the town limits to the place where the two creeks merged into one and then followed it for a mile or so downstream to a place where the banks were covered with grass, not very high, but fresh and lush. Here the director pointed out to his followers the plants that they were to gather. Soon they spread out over the banks and could be seen bent over, busily engaged in the task at hand. In Rudolph, Ludwina had an active assistant. Still, the work proceeded slowly, for the plants were only scattered singly amid the other vegetation.

The director had gone up the bank to a rise to look for portulaca. He soon returned with the good news that he had found a stand. Ludwina and a few of the other women who had large baskets accompanied him back to the place where the plants were found in great abundance. After a half-hour's time, they had filled their baskets to overflowing. They then returned to help their companions; all arrived back in town by eleven o'clock with a full load.

The leafy green plants, as well as vegetables, were then distributed with special deference to the sick. At the same time, vinegar was generously apportioned as an additive to the vegetables.

The following morning twice as many women ventured out, mainly to gather portulaca for cooking, but other herbs were collected as well, and, in this way, they were able to generously supply the needs of the sick.

Ludwina was never missing even though the grass often was covered with heavy dew and her basket (with Rudolph's help) was always the heaviest. The work was not in vain: the sick recuperated rapidly, and the general level of health of the settlement rose markedly.

One morning, when Ludwina and her companions met in front of the *Verein* headquarters and went out to collect salad greens, the director accompanied them as far as the town limits, where he left them in order to visit the cornfield. He promised, however, that he would soon rejoin them.

"I found a place yesterday, before we returned to town, where the plants are so thick, you can gather them by the handful," Ludwina said cheerfully to Rudolph. "You will see how quickly we can fill our basket."

They soon reached the meadow where as a rule the herb collectors were wont to spread out. Ludwina then led Rudolph a little bit farther to a place with a stand of tall reeds along the bank of the stream.

"Look over there at the reeds," she said. "Close by is some grass covered with the plants we want." With this, she sprang happily in the lead and stopped near the reeds, waving to Rudolph to catch up.

"Look, Rudolph, see how much!" But no sooner had she taken a step forward than she jumped back with a loud cry. In front of her, a huge rattlesnake raised himself from the grass, the fearsome sound of his rattling clearly evident.

"For God's sake," cried Rudolph, lunging forward at the rattler and striking at it with the basket so that it turned around and quickly retreated into the canebrake.

Ludwina, however, had turned a deathly pale, and said in a quivering voice, "He bit me, Rudolph!"

"My God, is it possible?" he said, frightened to death. "Where did it strike you?"

"Here, on the foot," answered Ludwina, even more pale, and sank unconscious into Rudolph's arms.

Rudolph cried out for help with all his strength while placing his beloved on the grass. He tore the shoe and sock from her foot and saw to his horror the two bloody marks left behind by the poisonous fangs of the snake.

He had heard once that it is sometimes possible to suck the poison from the wound. He threw himself down, pressed his lips to the wound, and sucked the blood from the wound with all the force he could muster. In the meantime, the others had hurried to the place. They stood helpless and horrified.

But Rudolph pulled himself together and called on one of the girls to run as fast as her feet could take her to the director and tell him what had happened. He then hurried down the bank to a stand of young crabapple[3] trees and with his hunting knife quickly cut down two and trimmed away their branches. He carried the poles to Ludwina and in an amazingly short time fashioned a litter by tying and covering the poles with branches, twigs, and cane stalks. He placed her upon it, took one end himself, and with four young women at the other end, proceeded to carry her back to the town as fast as the situation would allow.

In the meantime, Ludwina had regained consciousness completely, but the thought that she was facing death held her speechless in terror. She took no heed of the growing pain caused by the wound. "Rudolph! Father!" were her only words. She kept her hands folded on her breast. Rudolph, however, sought to comfort her with encouraging words even as he implored the girls not to slow down.

They were just approaching the town when the director came running from the field to meet them. Without a word, he signaled the bearers to lower the litter to the ground and quickly examined the wounded foot. He then gave the command, "Carry her to my house!" and ran swiftly ahead. He met the procession again as they came by his house, where he cauterized the wound with silver nitrate[4] and wrapped it in a bandage soaked with disinfectant. He then placed a piece of onion in Ludwina's mouth with the request that she chew it and swallow the juice. As he did this, several members of the *Verein* militia took Rudolph's and the girls' place on the litter, and they continued at a rapid pace down the long street.

People came running from all sides to discover with horror and grief what had transpired. They crowded around the stretcher, looking anxiously at the poor girl, and many a "May God be with her!" could be heard, and many a word of sympathy and consolation was cast her way as the party proceeded along.

With every step, the size of the throng increased, and as the crowd neared the house of the elder Wildhorst, he came rushing out to greet them with a bewildered look, for this was the far edge of the town, with only one house further out than his, and that was the Nimanski household. He got the sad news only too quickly. Stricken to the core, he followed the litter at the side of the director.

They had barely reached the meadow in front of Ludwina's house when her father stormed out with the words, "Good God, my child, my Ludwina!" Anxiously, he gripped her hand.

"Nothing will happen to me, dear father," she said in a low voice, forcing a smile to her lips, but it was a painful smile, and there were tears in her eyes.

In silent terror, the old man accompanied his afflicted child to the house. Here, Rudolph took the victim in his arms, carried her into the house, and laid her upon her bed.

The director again examined the foot, which had already begun to swell noticeably. Her foot had turned reddish-blue, while the inflammation and pain increased from minute to minute.

A friend of Ludwina's, the wife of former Austrian captain von Rawitsch, also came inside and offered to take over the care of the patient. The director gave her instructions.

He placed a large bottle on the table with which to moisten the bandages. From another bottle he had placed on the table, he ordered a certain number of drops to be administered at intervals. Finally, he once again took a wild onion from his pocket, which he cut into two pieces. He smashed one half on the table and laid it on the wound; the other half he ordered Ludwina to nibble from time to time and swallow the juice.

"This is how the Indians treat snakebite, a remedy known to every frontiersman in America as the 'rattlesnake master,'" said the director. "The wild onion has a leek-like, pale-green leaf with brown spots on it, quite similar in fact to the markings and colors of the snake itself. It grows in marshy bottomlands; I discovered it three miles from here. Luckily for our beloved patient, I still had some in my hunting knapsack, but I will quickly ride out and gather a fresh supply; what I had on hand is used up."

With this, he handed the other half of the onion to *Frau* von Rawitsch, encouraged Ludwina to keep her spirits up, and left the house.

With a mixture of hope and fear, the elder Nimanski, Rudolph, and his father all now stood around the bed. The prospects for happiness in this life hung in the balance for all. With a mighty effort, they tried to conceal the anxiety oppressing them. For her part, Ludwina wanted to appear strong and not betray the fact that her situation was quickly worsening, that the pain in her foot was pulsing through her body, and that she was rapidly sinking into a nauseous state of unconsciousness. Still, she repeated to them over and over that she was feeling better, although the hoarse and listless tone of her voice conveyed rather the opposite message.

Friends and acquaintances of Ludwina's gathered on the porch to inquire about how she was doing. All offered to help if there was anything they could do. An hour had passed before the director returned to the house on his sweating horse, and with the greatest concern reentered Ludwina's room.

She was much sicker now than when he had left her. The swelling had increased noticeably and feeling had gone out of the wound. The patient's physical and mental strength was deteriorating quickly, and she had succumbed to a state of feverish restlessness and anxiety. Dr. Schubbert was shocked and frightened by her appearance, but he didn't reveal his deep concern for the recovery of the young woman to the bystanders; to do so would have filled them with an inconsolable sense of helplessness.

From the onions, he quickly prepared a new compress and applied it to the wound. He also gave Ludwina a fresh portion to eat and had *Frau* von Rawitsch rub the afflicted limb with bear oil. All the while, he reassured everyone by predicting a quick recovery, words which he himself could manage to believe only by sheer willpower. Soon, however, he felt compelled to leave the room because a longer presence would betray his worst fears to the others.

He came and went from hour to hour. But no matter how fervently he hoped for some change for the better, all indications pointed to the contrary, to a worsening of the patient. By evening, she no longer recognized anyone. She lay there motionless, her pulse barely detectable.

Nevertheless, Dr. Schubbert was of the opinion that the swelling had not increased at all in an hour; it even seemed to him that it might have gone down a bit. But then he reproached himself for being delusionary and had to concede the possibility that recovery was now impossible.

The inconsolability, the pure despair of the father and the betrothed increased from one hour to the next. Silently, without tears, they sat on her bed and watched every breath of air she drew, as if counting down the seconds left for her young life. Dr. Schubbert endeavored in vain to keep up their hopes, but the image which lay before them was a picture of death.

The director came back into the room after midnight, took the lamp from the table, and walked to Ludwina's bed. No sooner had he put his finger on an artery to check her pulse than he received an unexpected and welcome shock. No longer did he feel the weakening pulse of a dying person. The pulse was once again regular and strong. He quickly checked the wound. The swelling had definitely gone down and the coloration was more natural. When he let the light fall on Ludwina's face, the paleness of death had left and a deep sleep appeared to have overtaken her. In that moment, he fought the urge to shout for joy and yell "Victory!" to the distraught father and future son-in-law. Instead, he stepped softly back from the bed, turned the light away from her and said, "Thank God, she is saved!"

Those in the room in the presence of Ludwina who had sunk so deeply into despair and grief could not have been affected more had these words come from heaven on high. They stared speechless at the director for a short moment, as if they could not trust their ears. But then they shot up to him, grabbed him by the hand, trembling, and asked him with tears in their eyes if it were truly the case that they could now allow themselves to hope.

"Yes, yes, she is saved; heaven has been with her," answered Dr. Schubbert with heartfelt emotion. "The deep sleep into which she has sunk is good for her and she will come out of it physically and mentally invigorated. We mustn't disturb her."

Then he quietly instructed *Frau* von Rawitsch to do nothing more for the patient other than leave her to rest. He also convinced the old colonel to return to his house and get some rest since his presence was no longer required. Beside themselves with joy and happiness, the two old warriors shook hands heartily and then the colonel quietly left the room with the director, who accompanied him to his house.

With the first light of day, the director was once again at the side of the patient, where he saw his expectations fulfilled. Ludwina was not completely conscious, but her vitality had been restored. Although the swelling and tightness were still considerable, the fever had disappeared, and her aspect was that of a person to whom life had returned.

The good news spread like wildfire through the town, and the morning found the porch at Ludwina's house anything but empty; everyone wanted to go and see for themselves how Ludwina was doing and express personally their joy at her recovery.

The inhabitants of Friedrichsburg received another bit of good news this same morning, namely that several hundred goats were close by and would soon arrive. Old and young alike took to the Braunfels road in the direction of the animals, and shortly before noon the herd was driven into the city with great fanfare. Standing in front of the *Verein* headquarters, the director distributed the valuable and long-hoped-for animals among the population, and each led his prized possession, like a valuable treasure, to his own household.

Held back, however, was a fine white nanny, which the director had led over to the house of Nimanski, but not before he had first gone ahead, where he found Ludwina of good cheer and engaged in a lively discussion with her father and Rudolph. He sat down with them and when the goat was in front of the house, he opened the door and said:

"I will now keep my word, *Fräulein* Nimanski, and give you the present I promised." With that, he had the large white nanny brought into the room and led up to Ludwina's bed so that she could pet the animal and run her hand through its coat of silky-soft hair.

Her joy was boundless and she thanked the director from the bottom of her heart. Her sole regret was that she would not be able to take over the care of the animal immediately. In a few days, however, she was so far along on the road to recovery that she could again face her household chores. She named her pretty white nanny Lili and adorned her with a red collar. She tethered her on a long rope in the best grass, and she did the milking herself. The nanny became so accustomed to her that it followed her around through the town like a pet.

CHAPTER 5

The Slacker • The Stranger • The Mormons • The Three Happy Ones • The Miser
The Rats • The Invalid • Imagination • Death • The Gruesome Apparition
Ready Money • No Peace in the Grave • The Rat King

*O*NE MORNING THE DIRECTOR passed by the house while Ludwina was sitting at her window offering a treat to her nanny goat, which was standing outside on her hind legs to receive it. The director gave a warm greeting to the pretty young lady. The elder Nimanski, who had seen the director approaching, hurried out the door and invited him in. The director declined the invitation, however, saying he wanted to pay another visit to *Herr* Küster from Frankfurt, because he had heard that the newcomer had taken no steps to improve the city lot that had been assigned to him.

Nimanski offered to accompany him. Schubert excused himself to Ludwina and then walked with her father in the direction of *Herr* Küster's hut. As they approached, Küster emerged to greet them in the doorway, just as he had done on the previous occasion. He bowed deeply and while rubbing his hands together, said with a nervous smile, "You will find things little changed here, *Herr Direktor.* It is so difficult to find workers."

The miser. Drawing by James C. Kearney.

"That surprises me. There are so many people here who would be more than willing to earn some cash money. Whom did you approach about it? I'll look into this matter right away," replied the director angrily.

"Actually I didn't approach anyone. It wouldn't be a good idea to let people know right from the start that you are in need of their services. Otherwise, they will make unreasonable demands," continued Küster, even more nervously, and with an expression of great concern on his face.

"And so, because you don't want to let anybody know about it, the property given to you by the *Verein* has remained in this lovely condition," said the director, quite annoyed. "Now let me tell you something, *Herr* Küster; I will give you eight days' time. If by that time you have done nothing about building a house or putting a fence around your property, I will have it done for you at your expense, or you will have to surrender ownership of this property. If others had behaved like you, what would Friedrichsburg look like?"

"Yes, Yes, *Herr Direktor*, you are completely right. But I have not been well, and, please, forgive my procrastination. I will get right on it with all my energy," answered Küster with the look of an eager entrepreneur, as he straightened himself into a proud posture.

"That would make me very happy, *Herr* Küster. Until next week, then," replied Schubbert gravely. He then offered his hand to Küster in a friendly gesture and departed.

Walking back, Schubbert turned to Nimanski and remarked, "What on earth possessed a man like him to want to emigrate? He is a nervous weakling with neither the will nor the energy to do anything for himself. I really don't know what will become of him. Why didn't they keep him in Braunfels? With his cash money he could have at least started some sort of business venture there. Here in Friedrichsburg, we need hands willing to work."

After a short pause, the director continued, "And another thing that has caused me a lot of aggravation: consider the fact that some of the parts for millworks have come up along with the belongings of the emigrants, but the main gear is missing, and the *Verein* sends word that that is everything they have. So, the mill project, which is so important for us, is at a standstill. I have to see if the missing gear might be available in the eastern states."

That afternoon the director sat at his window enjoying a cup of coffee and occupying himself with all the many decisions and responsibilities for which he was answerable and upon which the well-being of the colony depended. He spied an unknown rider approaching the town. In a little while the rider reached the house of the director, where he halted his horse and called out a greeting.

"I would like to speak to the director, Dr. Schubbert," he said in English, whereupon Dr. Schubbert indicated that he was the person in question. He then invited the rider to dismount and come inside.

The stranger was a man between fifty and sixty years of age with grey hair and of a tall, powerful build. He had black, bushy eyebrows and lively grey eyes. He sported a grey, wide-brimmed felt hat, and he wore a grey linen suit. He had on brown leather shoes, on one of which was buckled an old, rusty spur. Instead of the usual riding quirt, he held in his hand a large knurled walking stick.

"My name is Grey,"[1] he said as he entered the room and offered his hand to the director in greeting.

"Please be seated, Mr. Grey," the director answered, pointing to a chair at the window. Taking a seat himself, he then addressed the stranger. "How can I be of help?"

"I would like to be your neighbor and I would also like to be of service to your town," Mr. Grey continued. "I am camped with my family four miles from here on the Pedernales, where I would like to settle. The manpower at my disposal is not inconsiderable, and I am willing to put up a saw- and gristmill in order to provide your town with sawed lumber and cornmeal, two items that will not be unwelcome to you."

"Definitely not unwelcome," the director interjected happily. "You have shown up at just the right time. I was about to write a letter inquiring about an iron part we need for our millworks."

"That will not be necessary. Before you could even receive a response to your inquiry, my mill will be up and running," continued the stranger, and then he added after a few moments, somewhat awkwardly, "I also wanted to secure your permission for my settlement."[2]

"My permission?" replied Schubbert, somewhat taken aback at hearing this request from an American. Although they often took into consideration the rights of their neighbors, the Americans usually did as they pleased without bothering to ask for permission. "I can't stop you from settling anywhere you wish as long as it is outside the grant area, but as the builder of a mill, you are doubly welcome, and I will do everything in my power to support you in your undertaking."

"Well, you will find me to be a good and peace-loving neighbor," said Mr. Grey as he touched the end of his walking stick to his nose.

After a short pause, he continued, "I would be obliged if you would ride back with me to my camp. Together we could then scout out the best place for the mill. In six weeks, it will be delivering daily four thousand board feet of lumber and as much cornmeal as you would like. I also intend to put in a field right away to supply you with corn by the end of the summer. By the looks of the field I rode by, you will not be able to harvest enough to supply the city."

The director listened to the man with ever more amazement, and finally said, "Well, you must have a big family indeed if you intend to undertake such large projects all at once. And it is getting late in the year to plant corn."

"I have planted even later with good results. Moreover, the soil where I have located a field along the Pedernales is well suited for corn: loose, fertile, and easy to work."

"I will have my horse saddled right away, but first you can have a cup of coffee, Mr. Grey," said the director in a tone of happy excitement.

"No thank you, Doctor," he answered, "but if you have a spot of brandy, I'll take a little of that."

Dr. Schubbert then poured him the drink he desired. Soon thereafter, both were seated on their horses on their way out of the city. Instead of following the usual road to the Pedernales, however, Mr. Grey took the path which the director had marked a few weeks before on the way to Austin.

"Where did you come from, then, Mr. Grey?" asked the director, somewhat puzzled.

"We came here along the route from Austin which you yourself surveyed. They told me about it in Austin, and because it was a shortcut, I took it," replied Mr. Grey.

"Then you must be camped in that first pretty valley along the Pedernales."

"Yes, that's right, on this side of the river next to the chute, where the force of the water is the greatest."

"Then you have located at a better place than Friedrichsburg itself," noted the director, "but I don't begrudge it at all, since you have promised to be so helpful to our town. But how were you and your family able to blaze a path through the wilderness without any help? Surely you have wagons with you."

"Where it was necessary, we put bridges over the streams and gorges or cleared a path through the hills. Now any wagon will easily be able to make the journey," replied Mr. Grey, but he directed the conversation back to the mill and the many benefits the city would enjoy as a result of his family's settlement.

With this, they reached the point where the canyon along the Pedernales narrowed. At the other end, it opened out into the beautiful valley, revealing to the director a whole city of tents, among which were to be found many heavy wagons. Many hundreds of horses, mules, cattle, and oxen were also grazing in the valley.[3]

"My God, what is that?" he cried out, dumbfounded. "You spoke to me only about your family, Mr. Grey!"

"And so it is, Sir. We call ourselves a family because we work together for the benefit of all. We are truly one family."

"You mean that you are organized in an association similar to our *Verein*," remarked the director with astonishment.

"That is right, but with the difference that we all work and contribute to a common account from which one and all derive benefit equally. Because complete equality prevails among us, we can easily take on large projects and see them through to completion,"[4] said Mr. Grey. With that, the two approached the large camp, which consisted of more than fifty tents,[5] set up in four long rows, like streets.

In the middle, a very roomy tent, similar to a house, had been erected in a larger space. Its sides had been rolled up to allow the breeze to pass through. Mr. Grey headed his horse toward this tent.

As they rode along, the director began to take note of the fact that there appeared to be an inordinate number of women present, and he noticed the same thing in Mr. Grey's tent. They dismounted in front of the same and were met by eight women of all ages, the oldest of whom appeared to be in her fifties while the youngest was barely sixteen.

Mr. Grey invited the director to step inside the tent. The director bowed to the female crew in passing, though no one offered to give her name, which was odd because to do so was standard practice among Americans. Consequently, the director turned to Mr. Grey with the request that he be introduced to the ladies.

Mr. Grey appeared to be flustered for a second, but quickly regained his composure, and with a gesture of the hand toward Schubbert, said, "The director, Dr. Schubbert." And then turning to Dr. Schubbert and pointing at the collection of ladies, he said, "My wives."[6]

"Your wives—what do you mean by that, Mr. Grey?" replied the director, truly astonished at what had been said.

"It is easy enough to explain," replied Mr. Grey resolutely. "We are Mormons, and, as will be known to you, our belief allows us to take as many wives as we would like."

"Mormons," repeated Schubbert, quite taken aback. "Then I cannot promise you my protection, Mr. Grey. You have been banned from the United States because your religious and social beliefs are contrary to the laws of the land, and we still find ourselves here within the boundaries of the United States."

"I am not asking for protection, Sir. My only hope is that you not undertake any moves against us and my promise to you will be that we will in no way be a disturbance or bother to the citizens of Friedrichsburg; on the contrary, we want to be useful and helpful neighbors. If you will leave us in peace, you will have every reason to be satisfied with our presence. Outside of necessary business contacts, which you will find desirable and helpful, we will have no traffic with those under your care and protection. As for the government of the United States, they will find no cause whatsoever in intensifying their persecution of us by following us here into the wilderness. Once this area has become more populated, we intend to move on. Our final home lies beyond the Rocky Mountains, along the Great Salt Lake."

Schubbert listened to the man in silence, and then, after a short pause, remarked, "I can find nothing objectionable in your proposals. It is not up to me to pass judgment. I will do nothing against you as long as you are not a disturbance in our own affairs. I certainly welcome the advantages which your presence offers to our colony. And, likewise, if we can be of help to you, we will gladly be of service."

"So we find ourselves in complete agreement," continued Mr. Grey," and soon you will be amazed by what we Mormons, who have been so maligned, can accomplish and by what an exemplary life we lead. Can I offer you a glass of milk for refreshment? Brandy is something we never keep, even though it is not contrary to our laws to partake occasionally."

The director accepted this offer, at which point the youngest of Mr. Grey's wives, a charming young lady in the full glow of youth, opened the lid of a container, poured a glass of milk, and graciously offered it to the director.

The eight wives seemed to enjoy a sincerely amicable relationship, which was clearly evident from their conversations and interactions, but the oldest was obviously dominant, and all the commands came from her.

The tent was orderly and clean. The floor was made of wide boards that had been laid over one another, and the tent itself out of dyed cotton canvas that had been stretched over a frame of long poles. The furniture consisted of a large folding chair and several large chests that had been placed in a circle around the walls and were covered with white cotton cloths and embroidery work so that they could double as seats and even, possibly, as beds during the night. The wives were all dressed very plainly, but tastefully, and above all in fresh, clean garments, with their hair carefully and nicely done up.

The director had taken notice of these things as he enjoyed his milk and quietly admired old Mr. Grey as he rose and made the suggestion that they view possible sites for locating the proposed mill.

The director said good-bye to the wives in a friendly and courteous manner and mounted his horse. Mr. Grey did the same, and they rode off along one of the rows of tents toward the river below.

Numerous charming and lovely female faces peered out from the tents as they passed by, and all appeared to be in the best of moods and in good cheer. The men Schubbert saw were all in the bloom of youth: strong, energetic, and of a cast and temperament to get things done. It struck the director that such a cooperative society could accomplish great things and had a bright future in front of them. Also, the whole compound was alive with children, younger and older, but all nice looking and healthy.

In the last tent the director noticed a young man with black, curly hair and dressed in a clean, white, long-sleeved shirt, a veritable picture of male attractiveness. He sat on a chest covered with a colorful throw. On one knee he held a charming blonde, and on the other a voluptuous brunette, both of whom were hanging tenderly on his neck and playing happily with his locks.

Mr. Grey, noticing that the three had caught the director's eye, commented that the young man was one of the society's most energetic and valuable workers. "He is a jack of all trades: a blacksmith, mechanic, cabinetmaker, carpenter, and an experienced mill builder. By all rights, he deserves a dozen wives, but the two he has count for more in terms of tenderness, accomplishment, and pluck than any other dozen."

As much as this last scene had touched the director, it still remained a puzzle to him how true love could thrive in such a divided and shared manner.

"These three are the happiest in our camp," added Mr. Grey.

In a little while, the two riders reached the river at the point where it cascaded in a rapidly flowing stream over colossal falls, thundering into the depths below. Here, they decided, would be the best place to locate the mill.

After they had considered all the points in a realistic and thoughtful manner, they parted company on the friendliest of terms. The director headed for town with the promise that he would soon pay a return visit to Mr. Grey.

Having previously heard so much about the Mormons and their way of life, he had come away pleasantly surprised by his own observations concerning their social and domestic arrangements, and he could not suppress the thought as to what the result would be if the same customs were introduced among the settlers of Friedrichsburg. But almost immediately, the less appealing thought of Sodom and Gomorrah occurred and dampened these reflections.

A week later the director sat at the noon conference table and asked about *Herr* Küster, whether he had made any move toward starting a house. No one was able to offer any information. "I feel sorry for the man," commented the director, "but I can't and won't tolerate his indolence any longer. The city lot was given to him under the condition that he would fence it in and erect a house on it. What does the man live on, after all? No one ever sees him?"

"He lives on cornbread and coffee. He brought a large quantity of both along," answered the quartermaster. "He is such a miser he wouldn't eat anything at all if hunger didn't drive him to do so. He withdrew his entire deposit with the *Verein* in cash from the business office in Braunfels,[7] so he can receive nothing from us on credit. On one occasion only, he paid cash for some cornmeal. Presumably, he has calculated that he can live out his days in this manner from the $4,000 he brought along."

"It is astounding how often a miser can end up acting contrary to his own best interest," added the director, once again seizing the word. "This $4,000 would earn him $200 a year in interest, money which, under his present circumstances, he would be able to put a good part of back into principal. Such avarice is foolishness, and not without reason is it called the root of all evil. But I can't help the man. Either he acts like a citizen of Friedrichsburg or he forgoes his right to a city lot."

At that moment an assistant of the director entered the room to say that *Herr* Küster from Frankfurt had sent a messenger with the humble request for some arsenic; the rats would not leave him in peace in his hut, and he needed to put out some poison.

The announcement provoked laughter all around, and after the assistant had departed, the director remarked in amazement, "Rats—rats in the open field. I have never heard of a rat in Friedrichsburg before. Truly, the man appears to be a bit unbalanced."

"Should I tell the messenger we can't give him any arsenic?" asked the pharmacist, as he rose from his seat.

"I'll tell you what. Give him some cream of tartar instead. He will be able to drive off the bothersome rats with it, but he won't be able to do any other mischief, and so we will have satisfied his request."

Smiling, the pharmacist took his leave, and the entire group at the table broke out in laughter afresh, which occasioned the following remark from the quartermaster, *Herr* Bickel: "He must be afraid that the rats might be able to snitch on the whereabouts of his cash!"

The incident was quickly forgotten, but Küster soon earned the nickname "Rat King" as a result.

One morning several days later, the director found himself on the western side of town, where he took the opportunity to pay Küster a visit and remind him of his responsibilities.

This time Küster did not come out to greet him, and the door to his hut stood half open.

Schubbert opened it up fully and to his regret noticed Küster in his wretched bed, obviously sick.

"My God, are you ill, *Herr* Küster?" he asked, concerned. "Why didn't you send for me?"

"I have nobody who could do it for me, and I thought it would most likely pass," answered Küster in a weak voice as he made an effort to sit up in bed.

Schubbert questioned him about his ailment but was able to diagnose only anemia and heightened nervousness.

"You need to improve your diet, *Herr* Küster. You need meat and soup and now and then a glass of wine. With only cornbread and coffee your health will go downhill quickly," said the director as he checked the pulse of the sick man.

"I will send you a bottle of Rhine wine as medicine, which will improve the situation. Then you need to engage someone who can get you some food supplies from the *Verein* warehouse, or even better, you need to take your meals with a family; you can't continue with this Cossack existence. What good is all your money then? Do you intend to take it to the grave with you?"

"Yes, yes, honorable *Herr Direktor*, you are entirely correct. I will make other arrangements," interjected Küster, quite agitated, even as his thoughts appeared to be elsewhere. "I will stop by your nearest neighbor, Major Nimanski, and ask him to look in on you and offer you assistance until you are on your feet again. After that, you will have to take care of your own needs," stated the director. He offered Küster his hand and departed the hut with the words, "Until tomorrow!"

Just as he had anticipated, his request for assistance from Nimanski was met with greatest willingness. Ludwina gathered together some foodstuffs right away and packed them in a basket with a pitcher of milk. Then, as soon as the director had left, she went over to the hut of the sick man, accompanied by her father.

The next morning the director met the major and Ludwina in Küster's hut; they had just brought him breakfast. He found Küster in the same state as the previous day: very agitated, unsettled, and weak.

"I could not have sent better care your way, *Herr* Küster," said the director, "and you will need to be a very good neighbor of the *Herr* Major in order to repay his kindness and show your gratitude."

"Oh no, *Herr* Küster, such a service is not worthy of any special thanks; it would be a requirement of anyone toward his fellow man; we will help you gladly," said the major sympathetically. Pressing the sick man's hand in reassurance, he added, "I will come by often and see if you need anything."

"And I will cook up a rich, tasty meat stew, *Herr* Küster; it will give you strength for sure," said Ludwina optimistically.

"You are much too good, my dearest *Fräulein*," answered Küster very anxiously, while fidgeting with the corner of the woolen blanket spread out over him.

At this Nimanski and Ludwina left the hut with the director, and as they walked along, Schubbert said, "The man has settled into a most peculiar state. He has no fever, his digestion is not disturbed, he complains of no pains, yet he is still sick and has lost all his strength. But under your care, *Fräulein* Nimanski, he shall soon recover."

Around ten o'clock the next morning the director received an urgent message from the major with the news that Küster had taken a turn for the worse and was perhaps in need of immediate attention.

As quickly as the situation would permit, Schubbert made his way to the hut, where he found Küster extremely agitated and anxious. He had barely laid eyes on him when he sat up in bed, held out both hands to the director, and with a shaky voice and a forced smile, said, "Please God, *Herr Direktor*, isn't it the case that you find me very sick?"

With these words, his features assumed an expression of horror, but in the next moment they altered into an expression of forced cheerfulness, and he said, "But what is sickness to you, but something to try to cure?"

With this he jerked around in his bed, fixed his gaze on the director, and let his head sink into his chest.

Suddenly, then, as if he had come to a firm decision, he fastened his wide-open eyes on the director and said, "What's the use? I have to confess to you; otherwise even with the best of intentions you have no chance of helping me. Yes, I have to tell you—I have been poisoned!"

With these words his eyes opened so wide that the whites of his eyes could be seen all around; his lips parted, baring his teeth completely, an expression of utter fear filled his being, and with both hands stretched out, he cried, "Save me, *Herr Direktor*, save me, somebody has poisoned me!"

"My dear *Herr* Küster," replied the director quite calmly, "How can you, a reasonable man, come to such a thought? Who in the world would want to threaten your life?"

With this he patted the sick man on the shoulder reassuringly and continued, "You have worked yourself into a nervous pitch. You need to calm down and try to get some sleep."

"*Herr Direktor*, I am poisoned, believe me," said Küster, even more frightened, "and most likely with the arsenic that you sent me. Wait, we need to have a look—I put it here underneath the pigskin of this old chest."

With this he looked up to Schubbert, turned quickly to the side for the chest that stood next to his bed, and raised the torn flap of leather with which the chest was upholstered.

"Have a look! The powder is gone. Somebody used it to poison me!"

"But my dear Küster, who is supposed to have poisoned you? Nobody has been here in the hut with you except the major and his daughter," interjected the director.

"Yes, yes, entirely correct, and because nobody else has been here, nobody else could have done it. I was asleep this morning and when I awoke, he stood with a pot of coffee at my bedside. Please believe me, most honorable director, but only between us, strictly between you and me, he did it and definitely with the powder that you gave me."

"*Herr* Küster, have you taken complete leave of your senses? Otherwise, how could you dare make such an accusation about a man of honor such as *Herr* Major Nimanski?" replied Schubbert angrily. "But to prove to you that you could not have been poisoned by this powder, I am telling you it was not arsenic at all, but rather a harmless concoction of cream of tartar that I sent you."

"Oh, *Herr Direktor*, I can feel it; it was arsenic," answered Küster with an indescribably woeful smirk.

"No, no, I swear to you, and all my officials will back me up; it was nothing more than cream of tartar," Schubbert assured him again.

But Küster shook his head, sinking into himself and pressing his trembling hands together. Suddenly he arose again with a start, an expression of complete hopelessness on his face, stared at the director with outstretched arms, and said in a pleading voice, "Save me—give me an antidote, *Herr Direktor*! I have been poisoned with arsenic!"

"That is not true, *Herr* Küster!" the director cried out, beside himself.

"Yes, yes, it is true, as true as my belief in God; I have been poisoned with arsenic! They wanted to rob me!" Küster added in a stuttering and horror-stricken voice as he let his head sink once again to his breast.

With this last definite assertion on the part of Küster, it suddenly became very clear to the director, as if a light had illuminated the matter: the man had intended to poison himself. He had taken the powder and now he regretted the act and did not want to confess his own culpability at the transgression. Therefore, another had to be to blame.

The entire chain of events was now obvious and comprehensible to the director, and after considering the matter briefly, he continued in the following vein:

"You have accused the *Herr* Major Nimanski of attempted murder, *Herr* Küster, and it is my duty to turn him in to the court. I will immediately summon twenty-four men from the city in order to place him on trial. But I serve notice to you that you are committing a grave crime if you knowingly accuse someone who is innocent. You will have the loss of his honor and reputation, perhaps even the loss of his life, on your conscience. And, once again, I say to you, the powder that I sent over to you was not a poison, but rather cream of tartar."

Küster appeared to have been shocked out of his state of self-pity by this decision on the part of the director. He began to shake and stared at the director with his mouth half open, as if he wanted to withdraw his accusation.

The director, wanting to hear such a confession, continued, "Isn't it true, *Herr* Küster, that you have done an injustice to the major and that the truth of the matter is quite different?"

The man, however, drew back from a confession and said with a quivering voice, "I have been poisoned—who else could have done it? Besides the *Herr* Major and his daughter, nobody has been with me."

"Very well, then, *Herr* Küster, we will stay with my decision, but think about your conscience," said the director. After a short pause, he added, "I will have some medicine brought over right away by the pharmacist and have your meals prepared at the *Verein* kitchen."

He quickly left the hut, closed the door, and hurried to Nimanski, where he reported what had taken place with Küster.

"The poor fellow is mentally disturbed; I feel sorry for him," remarked the major sympathetically. "But I share your opinion. He wanted to take his own life but now he is afraid to admit the deed to you."

"As soon as he sees that he hasn't been poisoned, he will need to own up to it and apologize to you. But for now, he is so overwrought and full of anxiety that we shouldn't excite him any more," the director remarked, and asked the major not to visit Küster any more since the town would take over his care.

Toward evening, the director returned from the cornfield, where he had visited the workers. Just as he was about to enter the *Verein* headquarters, the pharmacist came hurrying up the street and announced to him that Küster's condition had deteriorated noticeably.

"He is calling for you like a wild man and says he has something important to share with you because he senses that death is near and he wants to clear his conscience," the pharmacist reported.

The director hurried at a double-quick pace through the town with the pharmacist at his side. The two reached the sick man just as the glowing evening sky cast the last fading rays of day into the recesses of the hut. His eyes stared intently at the director as if they were about to spring out of their sockets; his mouth opened to speak and he attempted to raise himself but fell back on his bed. Once again, he made the attempt to lift himself on an arm as the director stepped next to his bed. It was not possible, and he motioned for the director to bend down.

Taken aback by the sight, however, the director gripped the sick man's hand to check his pulse, and said, "Calm yourself, *Herr* Küster, I will help you."

Küster, however, made one last mighty effort to elevate himself while moving his mouth to and fro, but he was only able to bring forth frightfully anxious, unintelligible sounds.

"Yes, yes, I understand you, *Herr* Küster; just be quiet," the director implored. But the man sank back on his bed. His eyes turned up so that only the whites were visible. A few quick, cramped gasps followed, and he was a corpse.

The director looked down with horror at this unfortunate victim of greed and stinginess. Again and again he felt for a pulse, but his life had left him and the ashen color of death settled over his features.

With an inner regret, Schubbert pressed his eyes shut, closed his mouth, and asked the pharmacist to hurry back to the *Verein* compound and request of *Herr* Bickel that he come over right away with the *Verein* seal and to bring along one of the guards to post a watch.

The pharmacist hurried away. The director closed the door to the hut and went straight to the Nimanski household. With a few short words he was able to report to the major the sad end of Küster, and he asked him to accompany him back to the hut, since he wanted to lock and seal it. The major made himself ready right away and slowly the two took the path, arriving at the house of the deceased at the same time as the quartermaster, the pharmacist, and the guard.

Although the sky had not yet lost its red evening glow completely, it had already become quite dark. Bickel needed to strike a match and light Küster's oil lamp.

Küster lay just as the director had left him, on his back, with his eyes and mouth closed. His limbs had become cold and stiff.

"We want to leave everything as it is until tomorrow morning. At that time we will undertake an inventory in order to send his belongings back to the authorities in Braunfels," said the director. He stepped out with the others, closed the door, and the quartermaster then sealed the same.

Schubbert placed the guard so that he could keep watch; he told him that he would be relieved in a few hours, thanked the major for accompanying him, and departed for his house.

The following morning after breakfast the director appeared with several officials and a few curious citizens in front of the dwelling of the deceased, removed the seal, and opened the door.

Bickel stepped into the hut, but after the first step the giant frame of the quartermaster rushed back out with a cry of horror.

With the words, "What is it?" the director went back in.

There Küster lay bent over on his side, his face turned toward the director with wide open eyes and mouth ajar, staring at the director.

"My God, the man is not dead!" exclaimed the director in shock as he looked into the live eyes staring back at him. He gripped the man's hand. It was cold as ice. He moved his arms. His limbs were stiff, but yet his eye was alive and followed his movement.

A small mirror hung on the wall. The director quickly took it down and held it to the mouth of the deceased to see if it revealed a trace of breath—the glass remained unchanged: clear and unmarked.

"He is dead, but still his soul appears not to be able to leave the body completely, as if it had one final account with this world to close," observed the director as he stepped back with a shudder. Meanwhile, his companions stood around the bed, transfixed by the eyes of the corpse.

Little by little, however, the eyes lost their luster; the lids sank; the mouth closed slowly, and once again death took full possession of the body.

A fairly long period of time passed before the witnesses to this horror scene were able to overcome their shock and get on with the business of completing the inventory. The trunk was opened. It contained old articles of clothing, but the $4,000 was missing.

"He probably hid it in his bed," said the director, so the bed was thoroughly examined. But, with the exception of a small purse with a few gold and silver coins which lay under the pillow, no cash was evident. Then they examined the entire hut, the floor, all the pockets in coats, pants, and vests; the money was nowhere to be found.

"Incomprehensible!" exclaimed the director. "Surely he had to be in possession of the money. Where can it be? He definitely had it at the time of his death; otherwise he would have complained of robbery."

Once again everything was thoroughly searched, but the result remained the same: the money was not there.

"We can't do anything more but gather up what we have found," the director finally said. The inventory was closed, signed, and the door once again sealed.

By the second morning thereafter, the grave had been dug and the director was present at the hut when the corpse was laid in the flimsy board coffin which had been nailed together. He was then carried through the streets of the city to his eternal resting place in the cemetery.

The procession was small and was made up entirely of officials of the *Verein*, Major Nimanski, and the pastor. Although the deceased was almost completely unknown to the pastor, he nevertheless pronounced several pious wishes for his benefit at the graveside.

Afterward, the officials gathered at the noon table, and the conversation turned once again to the deceased and specifically to the baffling disappearance of the money.

"Maybe toward the end the man sewed the bank notes into his clothes," remarked the director.

"Yes, indeed, that would be quite possible," replied Bickel. "Nobody thought of that."

"I really believe we ought to exhume him in order to be sure," added the director.

"I will go straightaway with the grave digger after lunch and see to it," interjected Bickel. After a while he added, "It looks like the rogue can't even find peace in the grave."

"Yes, do it if you don't mind, *Herr* Bickel," said the director. "We owe it to his heirs in Frankfurt; otherwise, the money will disappear."

No sooner said than done. After lunch, the quartermaster strode with several guards and the grave digger out to the cemetery. The grave was opened, the coffin taken out, and the lid pried off. The garment of the deceased was examined, and to the great astonishment of those present, the banknotes were found wrapped in waxed cloth and sewn into the inner side of the back of the shirt.

Bickel was happy to take possession of the packet. The deceased, robbed of his money, was returned to his grave and again covered with dirt. The quartermaster hurried back to the *Verein* compound with his newly revealed treasure, which he turned over to the director.

"Thanks be to God that the money was there," said the director. "Heaven will now be able to give him peace in the grave."

The strange and morbid tale of the "Rat King" was the topic of discussion throughout the whole town of Friedrichsburg that evening. But the story was not over, and received yet another disturbing twist the following morning: the grave digger came rushing up to the *Verein* compound with the horrific news that wolves had dug up *Herr* Küster in the night and completely devoured him.

CHAPTER 6

The Delaware Indians • The Chief • Believed to Be Dead • The Request
The Hunting Horse • The Trial Shot • The Irreconcilable Enemy
The Ride through the Forest • Welcome • The Presents • The Wild Friend

*T*HIS SAME MORNING, a new, more pleasing picture replaced the dreadful memory of the eccentric miser, for a band of Delawares came into the city, a group that, under their chief, Youngbear, had demonstrated their friendship on many occasions.

This band, one of the few remaining from the once mighty Delaware Nation, only numbered between five and six hundred souls, among which only about one hundred were warriors. Nevertheless, it was a band that all the other tribes up to the far north feared and with whom they would go to great lengths to avoid conflict. All the men carried firearms and were renowned for their marksmanship. Their friendship with the government of the United States added to the respect in which they were held by the other tribes.

Chief Youngbear, a handsome, knightly young man, had been personally befriended by the director years ago.[1] Whenever he and his tribe were in the vicinity, he would take the opportunity to visit the director. His home territory was much farther to the north, along the Kansas River, where the old men and

The Delaware Indian. Drawing by James C. Kearney.

women of the tribe lived and engaged in farming and the breeding of livestock. Chief Youngbear, however, spent a good part of the year roaming and hunting between the Rocky Mountains and the Gulf of Mexico with his younger and more vigorous tribesmen, only returning to visit his kinsmen on the Kansas from time to time and to supply them with tallow, honey, bear fat, dried meat, and animal skins.

Each time the Delawares appeared it meant a festival for the people of Friedrichsburg. Because of their knowledge of English, which they all spoke to some degree, it was much easier to communicate with them than with other Indians, and the common knowledge of their proven friendship helped to remove all wariness. Also, the Delawares always brought along many items of fine workmanship, such as decoratively stitched and beaded leather bags, moccasins of deer leather, extremely tasteful feather fans, leather leggings for riding, and many other items of this nature, which they traded for tobacco, gunpowder and lead, knives and axes, needles and thread, and similar objects. Also, these Indians always brought with them the best and healthiest horses and mules to trade, and the buyer did not have to fear being deceived.

For the first few days, the Indians camped as a rule next to a creek a short distance from the town. After they had finished with their trading, the Delawares moved their camp to the Pedernales because their animals found better pasturage there and the braves a more successful hunt.

On this morning, as the parade of Delawares arrived in front of the *Verein* compound, hundreds of townspeople followed them and soon mingled with them to welcome and greet them.

The men dismounted from their horses and shook hands with the townspeople on all sides. The chief stood among the town officials and expressed his pleasure at seeing them again. Soon the director emerged and they shook hands heartily.

"Well, you finally show your face again, Youngbear. Where have you been keeping yourself for so long?" the director asked the Indian happily.

"On the always green banks of the Medina, Nueces, and Frio Rivers,[2] where the flowers always bloom, where the birds always sing, and where the deer never get poor. The tender, lush grass, the green leaves, and the warm breeze of the Gulf need to go ahead of Youngbear on his journey to the north," answered the chieftain, a slender young man of extraordinarily noble appearance and with a naturally refined and gracious demeanor.

"Well, it is good that we have you with us again," said the director as he patted the Indian on the shoulder. "You can let the green grass and the warm breezes get well ahead of you while you and your people rest yourselves among us. You know that there is always a place for you at my table."

"Youngbear and Schubba old friends," answered the Indian with a happy, sincere smile, grabbing the hand of the director and pressing it to his heart.

Then he turned quickly to Rudolph, who had just walked up, opened his arms to him, and cried, "The heart of Youngbear rejoices once again to see the young eagle (a name he had given Rudolph earlier). Your wings are still powerful and your eye is still clear."

With this, he pressed Rudolph to his breast and shook his hand happily. When he suddenly spied the quartermaster Bickel coming out of the *Verein* building, he cried out joyfully, "Big Buffalo! Youngbear feels himself lucky to see him again; he is a good, dear friend." He then gave Bickel a hug, giving expression of his esteem through word and gesture.

Many similar scenes of happy reunion between the Delawares and the citizens of Friedrichsburg took place as the procession of Indians once again resumed their march, moving toward the outskirts of the city, where their camp was to be made.[3]

A large number of Germans followed; each wanted to be the first to trade with the Indians. Soon a large number of people gathered at the *Verein* warehouse in order to procure the necessary goods with which to do business with the Delawares. Youngbear also mounted his horse and followed his people in order to be present when the tents were erected.

The Delawares did not go about half-naked, as did most of the wild Indians. The men wore blouses of colorful calico or leather shirts that were fringed and stitched very tastefully, and knee-high leather leggings. They were not used to covering their heads and only occasionally did one see a colorful silk cloth wound like a turban around an individual's head.

The women wore four-cornered, painted, and beaded leather blouses of tanned deerskin with long fringes and an opening in the middle for their heads so that the skins covered both breasts and shoulders. The leather fringes hung as far down as their hips. A shorter dress decorated in a similar fashion and fringed in the same way covered their bodies, while leggings reached from their delicate, moccasin-clad feet to their knees.

For the noon meal Youngbear was with the director and took a place beside him at the table. "On instruction from the government, you have invited the Comanches here for a peace conference. Will many of the bands come?" the director inquired of the Delaware.

"More than forty want to come and plant the lance of peace between the Comanches and the whites; also many bands of their cousins, the Mescaleros,[4] intend to come," answered Youngbear. After a short pause, he continued: "My messengers have not located all the bands of the Comanches as of yet, but only a few have refused so far to make peace and friendship. Kateumsi is at fault for this; he turns their hearts to hatred, and his own heart will continue to hate as long as it beats."

"Kateumsi's heart has stopped beating," observed the director, laughing. "Our friend Wildhorst here extinguished his life-light."

"Kateumsi dead!" the chieftain called out in surprise. "And the young eagle sank his talons into him. So, the Delaware has no need to mold any shot for him."

The director then told the story of the fight in which he and his companions had taken part on their trip to Austin and in which Rudolph had shot the chieftain Kateumsi from his horse.

"Then you have killed my worst enemy," continued Youngbear to Rudolph. "But still I would have preferred that he had come to the peace conference, for his friends will hold back and seek revenge on the whites. If a ball from Youngbear's rifle had sent him to the Eternal Hunting Grounds, his friends would have made peace with the whites."

"You speak of the Mescaleros," the director said to Youngbear. "When I was living on the Leona[5] and a young member of your tribe, Tiger,[6] lived with me, a band of Mescaleros visited me and made peace with me. Their chief was named Wasa."[7]

"A powerful and good chief, this Wasa. He will come to the peace conference, and he will bring other bands of Mescaleros along with him."

"Does he know, then, that I live here?" asked the director.

"When I mentioned your name to him, he asked if you had lived in the fort on the Leona, and then called you his good friend. His heart yearns to see you again. I will be moving from here shortly far to the north, where the lands are still white and the buffalo still make their way in the snow, and along the way I will speak with many tribes and place friendship for the whites in their hearts. There should be peace between the whites and the red children," said the chief, with sincere conviction. "The well-being of the Indians depends upon it."

At the end of the meal, as Youngbear started back to his camp, the director ordered bread, coffee, raw sugar, tobacco, salt and pepper, and other such items to be packed in a basket, and directed a servant to carry them along with the chief.

For several days the Delawares camped a short distance from the town, and their camp was continually visited by the citizens of Friedrichsburg. This was in part to conduct trade but it was also partially to satisfy their curiosity and delight in the unusual and exotic. As soon as the trading was over, however, the Indians broke camp and moved to the point where the road crossed the Pedernales and set up their camp not far from the ford on the river, here to await the advance of spring so they would be able to continue their migration farther north.

The road from Friedrichsburg to the Pedernales made a broad curve. Consequently, the director, using a compass, had a path cut through an oak thicket standing between the town and the river, and, by so doing, cut the distance almost in two. He often rode over to the camp of the Delawares along this straight path, and Youngbear also used it almost daily to take his place at the noon table in the headquarters building of the *Verein*.

One day the chieftain did not show up for lunch and the director decided to ride over toward evening to see why he had not appeared.

He stepped out of the gate with the quartermaster and Rudolph when suddenly an Indian on a black horse stopped in front of him on the street.

"Kateumsi!" cried the director and Rudolph as with the same breath, and looked at the wild Indian in front of them as if a ghost had appeared before them. But Kateumsi sat as if cast from iron ore on his magnificent steed, motionless, and returned their stares.

"How dare you come here after you attacked me with your warriors on my way to Austin?" asked the director angrily. He looked around, for in the same moment the guards, whom Bickel had summoned, came rushing up from the courtyard with their weapons.

Their appearance, however, seemed to make little impression on the chief. He stared down at them with the same steely calm, and said to the director, "Kateumsi no make peace with the whitefaces, but now he has come to do so." With this he crossed his arms and laid his hands on his shoulders.

The director overcame his anger and the complete surprise brought on by the sudden appearance of a sworn enemy he thought was dead and, in consideration of what the chief had said, replied, "If you really intend to be our friend, then I will welcome you, and do everything in my power to maintain our friendship. Step down."

"Kateumsi wants to see a sign of friendship," countered the savage.

"And what should that be? I am willing to offer it," replied the director.

"The Delawares have Kateumsi's best hunting horse; you get back my horse for me. Kateumsi and Delawares no good friends," the wild Indian said with a dark expression on his face.

"I will do this as a sign of my friendship, and I am sure Youngbear will agree to return the horse," said the director. "Do you want to ride along with me? No Delaware will do you any harm."

"Kateumsi's heart bigger than Delaware heart," said the wild one as his expression lit up his brown features. He added in a cold tone, "I ride with you to get horse."

"Good. Burg, go saddle my grey horse," the director said to the guard, and made it known to the chief that he would return momentarily. He then hurried to his house to get his weapons.

When the director disappeared, the wild Indian turned to gaze at Rudolph, who sensed clearly that the chief recognized him as the one who had shot him off his horse, but resolved to say nothing so as not to derail the promising peace initiative with the Comanche.

"You have a nice horse," he remarked deftly, and stepped somewhat to the side in order to gain a better view of the magnificent animal.

"You have seen him better than he stands before you here," said the savage with an animated look. "You have seen him broadside as he lunged forward, have seen him with flashing eyes, flared nostrils, and a flowing mane, and have seen him as he tore away riderless. Your eye was good, but your ball was bad; it was too weak for Kateumsi."

With this he lifted the quiver from the leopard skin he wore over his shoulder and pointed to a small reddish spot on his chest. It was the scar which the ball from Rudolph's weapon had left.

"Kateumsi's arrow through two white men," he added proudly, turning to the director, who had just emerged from his house.

A few minutes later the director was mounted and on his way to the Pedernales with the chief. They had ridden along a good while next to each other without either one breaking the silence. Finally the director said, "You know that in August all the Comanches and some Mescaleros are coming to Friedrichsburg to conclude an eternal peace treaty with us and to receive many valuable gifts. I hope that you will not be missing."

The savage hesitated a second and then said, "Kateumsi will be with his friends."

After a while, the director resumed the conversation with an offer: "You need to visit me sometime in the town with your people just as Santa Anna, Sanacho, Pahajuka,[8] and many other big chiefs of the Comanches do, and you will always receive gifts from me."

"What can Kateumsi give you in return? You take his land from him without asking," answered the savage, his eyebrows furrowed.

"Do not believe that, Kateumsi. We do not want to take your land; we only want to establish here and there small settlements; and we want to trade with you, which will be a great benefit to you."

"When you first came over the big water in your winged canoes and stepped onto the shores here, you founded small settlements and as time went on traded us out of all the land up to the place where we now stand, and still you want to trade for more until we shall perish at the foot of the mountains along with the buffalo. That is what we have gained from your settlements and your trade," the chief answered, even darker.[9]

The director felt the truth of the wild one's words only too well, but had this part of the world been created for the sole purpose that a small number of original inhabitants could wander over the countryside hunting in perpetuity?

"You will see, Kateumsi, we will be good friends to you, and we will bring no harm to you in your land. But you must also show us that you are our friend, because you will do the most harm to yourself as our enemy."

The wild one gave no answer, looking ahead as if trying to catch sight of the camp of the Delawares.

They rode quietly until they reached a high point at the foot of which the tents of the Delawares had been pitched along the Pedernales.

"Kateumsi here wait on horse," he said upon spying the camp, and reined in his horse.

"Very well," replied the director, "I will bring the horse back to you here."

With this he gave him a nod and rode down the hill to the camp.

No sooner had the Delawares noticed the director than they also spotted the Comanche, and with their hands shading their eyes, they stared hard at him.

Youngbear rushed forward to the director and exclaimed, "Isn't that Kateumsi, whom the young eagle shot from his horse?"

"It is he; the ball didn't do anything to him. Now he wants to make peace with us. He just arrived with a demand. You Delawares have one of his horses in your possession and I am supposed to get it back for him. As a favor to me, I will ask you to return the horse," the director said, reaching out his hand to Youngbear.

"The horse is in our hands, but I have to ask my warriors before I turn him over to you. Come along to our camp; I will speak with my people. If you hadn't come with Kateumsi, then there would have been a race between him and the Delaware where he could have lost not only his horse, but also his life. He is a real scoundrel."

Schubbert handed the reins of his horse to one of Youngbear's people and accompanied the chief to his camp. There he gathered together his warriors and explained to them the director's purpose and advised them to surrender the horse.

The council was short, with the quick result that they agreed to turn over the horse as a gesture of goodwill to the director. One of the young men then went to the pasture where the horses were grazing. The horse was a sorrel with a white mane and white tail. He put a rope around the horse's neck, led it to the group, and turned it over to Schubbert. The director expressed his thanks and explained that he intended to repay the value of the horse.

"Why haven't you been coming to our meals, Youngbear?" asked the director.

"Buffalo have turned up in the area. We have gone on the hunt and have bagged ten animals. They were very fat," answered the chief, promising to return to the director's table the following day.

The director thanked the chief heartily and then took his leave. He mounted his horse and, taking the sorrel by its halter rope, led the horse to the top of the rise, where Kateumsi was waiting like a dark ornamental column under the shadow of the last oak.

Schubbert expected to see some sign of joy and to receive some word of gratitude for the service he had rendered. Kateumsi, however, with a totally impassive and unchanged expression on his face and without uttering a word, took possession of the horse and headed his steed back to town on the path over which they had come.

The director made several attempts to strike up a conversation with his companion, but the Indian persisted in his silence. The two had covered nearly half the distance back to town when the director spotted three fat deer to the side, about two hundred steps distant, who were looking at them warily.

He was happy for the opportunity to demonstrate to the wild one how superior firearms were to the bow and arrow. He tapped him on the arm, pointed out the deer, and then dismounted from his horse. A few seconds later, he took his shot. One of the deer sprang high in the air and then fell dead to the ground. Schubbert was happy that his shot had been successful. He cast a quick look in the direction of the wild one to see if there was any register of surprise or wonder on his face. No change in expression could be seen; he seemed lost in thought on his horse, as if the shot had been nothing at all out of the ordinary.

The director led his horse to the slain deer, quickly split the animal into parts with the hatchet he carried tied to his saddle, fastened the hams and backstrap to his horse, and rode back to the Comanche to resume the path back to town.

They had not ridden very far, however, when Kateumsi took the bow and an arrow from his quiver, strung the bow, and tapped the director on the arm. He then pointed to a large oak tree a far distance away, from which a piece of the bark the size of a man's hand had been chopped away to serve as a guidepost. A split second later, without stopping his horse, he fired an arrow at the hand-sized mark on the tree and hit it squarely in the middle. When they reached the tree, the director could see that the iron arrowhead had buried itself completely in the hard wood, which had been splintered by the force of the shot.

He looked with amazement at the arrow which had hit the bull's-eye perfectly and had to silently concede that this shot, taken from a moving horse at a distance of eighty steps, was much superior to the one he had made to bring down the deer.

In a little while they came to the outskirts of the town. Here the chief brought his horse to a halt and said, "Kateumsi's camp over there." With this he pointed to the east and turned the head of his horse in that direction.

"Don't you want to come with me and rest up a bit? You told me you wanted to be friends," added the director.

"The tent of Kateumsi is a long way from here," answered the wild one, without bothering to pause. Schubbert started to give him a piece of his mind, but he overcame his aggravation as he watched the Comanche ride off. He then rode on into town himself.

The following morning the Delaware chief took his place at the dinner table of the director. Upon hearing an account of the abrupt and disrespectful manner with which the Comanche had taken his leave, Youngbear commented, "I have often told you that he has an evil heart and that he will take his hatred of you whites with him to the grave. You had better hold a shot in reserve for him always. Too bad you didn't let me sic my Delawares on him. Our horses are faster than the black stallion he was riding."

Soon after the noon meal, Youngbear took his leave, since he had arranged to hold a counsel with his warriors in his tent. Rudolph walked out with him to his horse, which stood next to the water in the meadow behind the *Verein* compound. As they parted, Rudolph said, "Perhaps I will visit you this evening and bring along my bride; she would like to get to know you."

"You have a bride? Well, carry the torch of marriage[10] to her door so that Youngbear can come to the celebration," answered Youngbear happily.

"She will not become my wife until springtime; first we want to build a big house," replied Rudolph. The Delaware departed with the request that Rudolph bring Ludwina to the camp.

The sun already stood fairly low when Rudolph strode through the gate of the Nimanski house, where he found his bride-to-be and her father sitting on the porch. At their feet lay the large, black hound and in front of them in the grass stood the goat, looking at her mistress as if awaiting her attention. Ludwina was reading a newspaper from the old homeland aloud to her father, a paper which *Frau* von Rawitzsch had recently received and lent them.

When Rudolph appeared, she quickly put the newspaper down and jumped up to greet him, offering her mouth for a kiss.

"You have come early, my Rudolph. Did you long for your sweetheart?" she asked him with a cheerful, sunny smile while looking deep into his large, trusting eyes.

"Do you think I could stay away from you without yearning to be back, my dearest? Do you not hold tight to my soul when I am away from you, my beloved?" answered the young man as he put his arm tenderly around her and led her back to the porch, where he greeted the major heartily.

"You have often expressed the wish to visit the Delawares in their camp," continued Rudolph while facing Ludwina. "It is a pretty, still evening and the road to the Pedernales leads through the marvelous oak forest. Let's ride down together. I have half-promised it to the chief, and he is looking forward to meeting my bride-to-be. He said I ought to carry the marriage torch to your door right away so that he could come to the festivities."

"Oh yes, we should make it possible for him to enjoy the wedding," Ludwina replied, picking up the thread lightheartedly. "What do you say to that, Papa?"

The old man smiled benignly, took a couple of draws from his pipe, and then replied, "It is all right by me, my dear; your happiness can never come too soon for me, because my happiness is tied directly to yours. But ride with Rudolph to the camp. You need to get out of the house. It will do you good."

"Why don't you come along with us, dear father?" asked Ludwina.

"That will not work. I promised the pastor a visit this evening. Ride with God's protection!" replied Nimanski, and after a couple of moments added, "You two should take the opportunity for a nice ride in the cool of the night since the moon is shining so brightly."

"The moon wouldn't help us. We need to return with the last daylight; otherwise we would be compelled to take the regular road, which is half an hour around. We could easily lose our way in the oak forest since even with moonlight we wouldn't be able to make out the marks on the trees," added Rudolph. Ludwina declared herself ready to ride as soon as Rudolph wanted to start.

He quickly went to fetch the major's pony, which was grazing hobbled in the pasture behind the house. He led the golden brown animal to the fence and then hurried to his own house to saddle his horse. Soon he returned mounted. In the meantime, the major had put a lady's sidesaddle on the pony. Rudolph lifted her up into it, swung himself into the saddle of his red steed, and with the blessing of the father the pair of lovers rode away.

Soon they reached the forest and the fresh, cool air settled over them in a way that was both pleasant and stimulating.

"These are pleasures unknown in our lovely old homeland," observed Ludwina as she drew in a deep breath. Their horses carried the couple forward noiselessly along the grass carpet under the magnificent old oaks. Only now and then did a ray of light make its way brilliantly through the thick crowns of the treetops.

"Yes, it is pretty under these perpetually blue skies," Rudolph added enthusiastically. "Still, my dear Ludwina, it bothers me that life here, with all its deprivations, will be bad for you in the long run; your environment is so restricted, and all the work and activity you have thrown yourself into—these are not really the ones for which your education and station in life have prepared you."

"But how much more natural and rewarding these activities are, dear Rudolph. No, no, even if I didn't have you to call my own, I would not like to exchange my life here for the stale, useless routine of a young lady in Germany.

And now, since I have you, and can live and do for you, and the good, loving God has permitted me to bring happiness to you, oh, dear Rudolph, then this magnificent nature, this wonderful land has become all the more a paradise." Reaching out her right hand to her loved one in a gesture of indescribable charm, she continued, "No, Rudolph, with your love the only thing that is wanting for my complete happiness is to live in peace and harmony with the wild Indians, and that, they say, is coming."

"And you are the one who gives me heaven on earth in this place, Ludwina. I can't find the words to express this feeling of total happiness I have in your presence; it is as if I should lie prostrate at your feet for the rest of my life, giving thanks for the joy your love blesses me with," replied Rudolph while guiding his horse next to Ludwina's pony and laying his arm over her shoulder.

The two horses had fallen in step, and, caught up in the wonderment of their love, the two made their way, arm in arm, through the balsamic forest air without noticing that they were nearing their destination until they had reached the last oaks and were able to look down upon the many white tents of the Delawares.

"Here we are already, Rudolph," cried Ludwina in surprise. "I really don't know how we got here so quickly; my, it was so lovely in the forest."

"And it was so lovely to be at your side, my angel," answered Rudolph, intoxicated with bliss, as the horses trod slowly downhill through the grass.

The chief emerged from among the tents to greet and welcome the couple with a loud shout of joy. But no sooner had he approached Ludwina than he fell silent, staring at her in wonder and amazement.

Rudolph jumped from his horse, lifted Ludwina from the saddle, and turned over both animals to a waiting Indian. He took the hand of the chief, shook it heartily, and declared, "You see, Youngbear, I have kept my word and brought my bride-to-be, Ludwina, here to meet you. She has looked forward to meeting you, my friend, for a long time now."

"Also her friend—Youngbear's heart must also belong to your bride," answered the Delaware solemnly, and one could see that he had not completely overcome his astonishment at the beauty of the young lady.

"And Ludwina is also your friend because you are such a good friend of my future husband," interjected Ludwina, speaking in a most natural manner while looking into the dark eyes of the chief in a friendly way and extending her hand to him in a gesture of trust and confidence.

"The young eagle the truest lover of Ludwina; Youngbear truest friend of her," answered the chief seriously, as if swearing a holy oath.

Then he strode in front of them toward the tepees until he reached his own, which stood under the shadow of a mighty oak overlooking a roaring waterfall on the river. At his appearance, several pretty and tastefully clad young Indian women hurried to spread out magnificent jaguar- and bearskins for the guests. Youngbear welcomed his guests to his camp and bade them take seats on the soft hides, whereupon he took a seat opposite them.

"You haven't told me yet if you are pleased with my bride, Youngbear," continued Rudolph jokingly, trying to lighten the air of earnest solemnity enveloping the normally talkative Delaware.

"Who can say that he likes the sun—its rays blind," answered the chief in a heightened tone while fixing his thoughtful gaze upon Ludwina's beautiful countenance. After a short pause he continued and said in an expression of overflowing emotion, "You are the moon that shines between dark clouds before whose light the darkness flees; your eye resembles the blue lake of the mountains, surrounded and shadowed by the dense forest, and your skin is whiter than the plumage of the white turtle dove at the ocean's edge, where the sun is now bending low—you are the most beautiful maiden ever seen by the eye of Youngbear!"

These words, which welled up from his deepest soul, were accompanied by corresponding gestures and movement of his arms and hands, and indeed with a grace and dignity which would have done honor to the highest level of sophistication.

And words that Ludwina would not have listened to from any white man, with the exception of Rudolph, did her well to hear from the Indian, because it was pure nature which spoke to her.

"You are so kind to me, Youngbear, because you are our friend, but just as I please you, so too do you please me, because I am your friend," answered Ludwina, tearing herself from her semi-embarrassed state and casting a hidden glance at Rudolph to ask him whether or not her answer met with his approval.

He, however, looked at her in a friendly way and then said to the chief, "You must be sure and be here in a year so that you can be present at our wedding."

"As sure as the spring arrives will Youngbear's presence be assured, and the Delawares will do their best work for the bride," answered the chief as he turned quickly toward his tent and spoke several words in his language. Soon an Indian girl appeared with a lovely beaded leather purse of the finest workmanship. Another girl appeared with an enormous and wonderfully soft tanned bearskin and also a magnificent jaguar pelt, which she handed to the chief, who stood up and placed the skins before Ludwina, saying, "And so that the bride will remember Youngbear until next spring, so he gives her these mementos."

"And so that our friend Youngbear remembers us, so Ludwina gives him this memento," said the girl decisively, as she took the red shawl from around her neck and handed it to the Delaware in a most congenial manner.

"Youngbear's heart is now filled with happiness," he said, laying the shawl around his neck, and casting a proud look in the direction of the people in his tent. He then took a seat next to Ludwina.

Now he once again became very talkative and told of his stay during the past winter in the beautiful southwestern part of the state. Then he related other experiences during his peregrinations following the hunt into the far north, emphasizing the natural wonders of the Rocky Mountains. He also mentioned his first encounter with Director Schubbert, and in all of this he painted such lively, imaginative, and poetic pictures with words that Ludwina listened transfixed to his stories in wonder and admiration.

The time passed quickly, and the sun had sunk low when Rudolph commented that the couple must ride home before nightfall, whereupon Youngbear had his guests' horses brought up and his own as well, because, as he said, he needed to insure a safe escort on the ride home for the white dove, his lovely new friend.

A squaw led the chief's proud, thoroughbred steed, decorated with bright feathers and colorful ribbons, the saddle covered with a magnificent leopard skin. Youngbear swung effortlessly and skillfully into the saddle and then rode at Ludwina's side along the row of tepees with the red shawl spread full over his breast.

The night overtook them on their ride through the oak forest, and the moonlight shown through the canopy only here and there. Yet Youngbear followed the path without ever pausing to think, and, engaging in the most cheerful conversation, they arrived at the outskirts of Friedrichsburg.

Here Ludwina and Rudolph intended to take their leave from their half-wild comrade, but he insisted that he wanted to accompany the white dove to her house. Together they entered the city and soon reached Ludwina's dwelling, where the major greeted them happily and added his thanks for the escort of his children. Ludwina reiterated her thanks, especially for the beautiful mementos, which Rudolph had carried on the front of his saddle. In reply, Youngbear pointed to the shawl that he had received from the bride.

So parted the Indian with a feeling of friendship in his heart that could not have been more true and pure in any human's breast.

CHAPTER 7

The Settlement of the Mormons · The Bloodhound · The Bear · The Jaguar
The Fandango House · The Arrow Shots · The Hunt

*W*ITH THE PRESS OF EVERYDAY BUSINESS, several weeks had passed by without it being possible for the director to visit his new neighbors, the Mormons, and nothing had been seen or heard from them. As soon as his busy schedule allowed, the director mounted his horse right after breakfast, and accompanied by his bloodhound, Joe, determined to see for himself what the Mormons had undertaken and completed in the interim.

He could hardly believe his eyes when he first glanced into the valley where the tents of the newly arrived stood. To his right, the mill arose as a solid stone building over the banks of the wildly foaming waves below, and farther to the left of the tents, an enormous field had taken shape, which the eye could scarcely survey in a single glance. At the mill, some thirty or so young men and women were occupied in tasks, while a hundred or so appeared to be at work in the field. About twenty teams of oxen with heavy plows were turning the soft sod under, working it this way and that, while teams of mules followed with disks to break up and loosen the soil. Men were at work in all parts of the

Jaguar hunt, Mormon tent city, and Fandango House. Drawing by James C. Kearney.

field, felling trees or transporting rails for fencing that had already been split, and wherever one looked, one saw busy hands at work. The women were not themselves engaged in heavy work; rather, they were only assisting and helping the men, and it appeared that the many pretty young wives were doing it out of their own joy and satisfaction. It was all taking place in a surprising calm: there was no shouting, no calling, no orders, no cursing, and one could see that each person knew exactly what to do.

Full of wonder, the director was approaching the field when the leader of the Mormons, Mr. Grey, noticed him and strode his way. After exchanging greetings, Mr. Grey remarked that they had made a good start and that he hoped to be finished with the work soon. "For you, Mr. Grey, the saying that the beginning is always the hard part[1] hardly applies; the work seems to be flowing from your hands. I have never seen anything like it," the director declared in amazement.

"This is because we are joined by one common interest, which we collectively work toward: all for one and one for all. You see how complete unity of purpose prevails among us and how efficiently the various tasks dovetail; and you will never hear an overly loud, hard, or vulgar word among us, either at work or at rest. Strife and discord go against our laws, and whoever starts it has to leave."

As he said this, Mr. Grey was pleased to notice the admiration in the face of the director, which he was not able to conceal.

"Our mill is also coming along," continued the leader of the Mormons. "It has an excellent location and I will keep my word: on the sixth Monday, I will deliver sawed lumber and flour."[2]

"I must confess to you, Mr. Grey, that I was very prejudiced against you in the beginning, about your chances for keeping your promises to us, but now I can find no words to express my respect and acknowledgment for your diligence and enterprise," said the director in a surfeit of admiration, as he made a courteous bow.

"And after you have become more closely acquainted with our circumstances and our institutions, you will find occasion to recognize not only our enterprise, but also our entire way of life; a stricter morality will not prevail in Friedrichsburg than among us."

The director did not reply to this, but rather tied the reins to his horse's head in such a way as to allow him to graze freely in the lush grass, signaled his dog to stay with him, and accompanied the Mormon-King[3] to his tent, where, as with the first visit, he was offered a drink of milk.

"I am hoping for a rich corn harvest because the soil is unusually rich and not tight as is the case with most prairies. It is naturally loose; and with a good and thorough cultivation, it will be productive as early as the first year. You will be able to cover any shortfall from your own harvest from me instead of drawing on supplies from Braunfels or Austin," said the Mormon.

"I will gladly take advantage of this," replied the director. "As already stated, I will do everything to be obliging and useful."

"Very well, perhaps we can also do business in other areas," Mr. Grey continued. "I see to my great surprise that you have no pigs in Friedrichsburg, a circumstance that any American on the frontier would notice right away. Pigs will take care of themselves, and they will quickly reward their master with a large increase without costing either money or effort. Shortly, I will have several hundred of these valuable creatures driven up from Braunfels in order to fatten them for slaughter in the fall; if you wish, I will bring along a number of sows for your use."

After they had discussed many business matters, the director stood up in order to fetch his horse and start the return trip. At this, Joe, the bloodhound, greeted him from the distance with his deep voice, and Mr. Grey remarked, "You have a fine hound there; do you use him for hunting?"

"He is the best bloodhound ever found on the frontier; he will follow the trail of a wounded animal even though it is twenty-four hours old," answered the director as he signaled Joe, who eagerly came running and barking toward his master.

"Well, perhaps he could find a bear which one of our young men, a good hunter, shot near the crossing of the river yesterday evening. He said he hit him well. The bear crossed back over the river and early this morning the hunter looked a long time in vain for his quarry; he said that the animal had stopped bleeding."

"Well, let's go find him," the director said, his hunting instinct revived. "Call the young man so he can show us where he shot the bear."

"He is working at the mill; he is the same young man with the two young wives who made such a strong impression on you during your earlier visit; let's go over to him."

They walked over to the director's horse, which then followed him and Mr. Grey to the mill. Mr. Grey called for the hunter Strabbo and explained that the director had offered to help him find the bear with the assistance of his dog.

The young man quickly threw down his ax, Schubbert mounted his horse, and the two headed for the shallow ford on the river where Strabbo had shot the bear. He went to the front, crossed the river to the far bank, and pointed out a clear trail of tracks left by the animal in the soft soil.

Schubbert then showed his hound the trail. The dog put his nose down, looked up at his master, and with a nod from him, quickly followed the trail up a rocky rise, not far away.

"What if the bear is not yet dead? We don't have a rifle," noted Strabbo as he strode along.

"I have a revolver," replied Schubbert, opening the flap of his holster.

They continued to follow the dog, who adjusted his pace to that of his master, advancing no more than thirty paces ahead of him, until after a half-hour they reached the base of the hills bordering the valley of the Pedernales. A ravine covered with thorn bushes and brush rose up to split two precipices, and the hound headed up this draw.

"He will be sitting there in the thicket," the director said as he drew his revolver from the holster. Joe, in the meantime, had reached the first bushes and stood there looking back for his master.

"We should stop here and let the bear leave the thicket, because it will choose the opposite side from where I ride, and I won't be able to follow," said the director as he signaled the hound to go into the thicket.

Like an arrow, the hound shot up the ravine, and, a few moments later, cut loose with his angry baying. Soon thereafter a colossal black bear appeared on the right side of the ravine at a heavy gallop, heading for the treeless heights. The bear had, however, only managed a few bounds before Joe caught up with it in powerful strides and grabbed the animal by the haunch.

The bear wheeled around and tried to swat the hound, but Joe avoided the deadly claws, retreating a short distance, where he remained waiting for his master, who was galloping forward.

The bear turned to look at the rider and started to flee once again, but in this instant Joe bit him again from behind and then sprang nimbly to the side to avoid the bear's deadly paws.

Then the bear sat upright and looked with bared fangs first at the hound and then at the rider, who had approached within twenty feet and halted his horse.

Schubbert took aim at the head of the bear and shot. The bear collapsed.

"Back, Joe!" he called out to his dog, waving him behind his horse. He then rode up to the bear, which, in the throes of death, was thrashing around with its paws, and shot it once again in the head.

The bear was dead. Schubbert dismounted and approached him in order to ascertain how fat he was.

In this moment, Strabbo ran up, yelling excitedly and eagerly preparing to renew his fleeting acquaintance with his black quarry from the previous evening.

As he checked the bear and felt it from all sides, the director said, laughing, "You looked for his heart too far to the rear. You hit him in the haunch, and your slug did no damage—it didn't even lame him. The director then took his hunting knife out from under his coat, opened up the bear, and cut off a piece of his liver, which he presented to Joe while petting him affectionately.

After Joe had finished his victory meal, Schubbert mounted his horse again, offered his hand to the young Mormon, and rode off with the promise to send assistance to help transport the bear back to the camp.

Back at the river crossing, Mr. Grey approached him and signaled happily with his handkerchief, as he had followed the hunt from a distance.

Once back at the tents, Mr. Grey quickly had a two-wheeled cart hitched up to a mule and set out with two men to bring back the quarry. He invited the director to have lunch with him, but Schubbert declined and rode back to Friedrichsburg.

The following day was a Sunday, and a serene, sacred calm lay over the town. All work rested. The townspeople sat contentedly on the porches in front of their houses or weeded their gardens, and here and there one saw men ambling along the streets in a comfortable and relaxed way with long pipes in their mouths, out to visit friends and acquaintances.

Around nine o'clock, however, the city became livelier as the wives and young ladies, accompanied by their husbands and young men, headed for the church.

It was an authentic German picture because even though the settlers had come to resemble the Americans during the weekdays, come Sunday, they outfitted themselves in their finest German attire, which they had brought over with them from the old fatherland. One could see in their demeanor and bearing that the Old Country was on their minds. With hymnals in hand, the family groups strode silently along and entered reverently into the roomy wooden building that served as a church.[4]

After the service was over, people lingered at the entrance, greeting one another and swapping stories. The men then retired to the tavern while the women used the time before lunch to visit.

In the afternoon, many took walks; the young men went out to hunt or to fish; the wives and young women came together for coffee, and in this way the day passed—a proper German Sunday. In the evening, however, many people looked forward to the pleasure of a dance, or "fandango," as they termed it, the name being adopted from not-so-distant Mexico, even though the fandango[5] was not danced, but rather a real German waltz, or "Galopp."[6]

After lunch that Sunday, Ludwina went on a horseback ride with her father, Rudolph, and Colonel von Wildhorst into the nearby hills. Rudolph intended to do some hunting there, and the others chose to accompany him part of the way.

Shortly before sundown the three returned to the town. The major went over to *Herr* Wildhorst's house to enjoy a pipe together, while Ludwina occupied herself with a sewing project on the porch, where she could enjoy the wonderfully refreshing evening breezes.

Leo, their large, black hound, lay in front of the house in the pathway, and Lili, the goat, grazed a few paces away on the grass, munching here and there on the juicy stems.

It was so quiet all around, as if Mother Nature were also taking a Sunday rest. Ludwina had let her work fall to her lap; it had become too dark to continue, and contemplating the great happiness which the Almighty had bestowed upon her in this place, she looked out at the golden red sky and the fiery cast it imparted over the whole landscape. Suddenly a shape, an enormous jaguar, sailed over the fence and landed in the yard. With his next bound, he fell upon the goat, gripping her firmly by the back in his jaws and then springing back over the fence.[7]

The hound, normally so brave, flew howling for safety to Ludwina, who, horrified, had jumped up for the door, but after the brightly spotted predator had escaped with his quarry still bleating pathetically for her mistress, she broke out in a loud wail, and, wringing her hands in distress, looked, crying and whimpering, in the direction of her unfortunate pet.

Then she called for Leo to follow her out of the enclosure so the hound could chase the robber. Leo, however, wanted nothing to do with the jaguar and sought refuge behind Ludwina. The jaguar, in the meantime, trotted proudly across the meadow toward the hills in the distance with his by now dead trophy in his mouth and soon disappeared from view of the distraught young lady into the darkness of the evening.

Ludwina was beside herself with grief. She had no idea what she should do. She ran this way and that, into the house and then out again. Finally, she closed the door and rushed over to the Wildhorst house to tell her father her woeful tale.

She was barely half finished when Rudolph called to her from a distance and came riding up with a large deer on his horse.

"Oh Rudolph, Rudolph—my Lili—a tiger stole her away from me," Ludwina cried out to him, wringing her hands in despair and then hiding her tears in them.

"What did you say—Lili stolen—where was she?" asked Rudolph.

"In our yard, in front of the house. The tiger jumped over the fence and carried her off toward the hills," answered the distraught girl.

"There is no way to rescue the goat, but her murderer will bite the dust tomorrow. I will notify the director, and his hound will pick up the trail right away."

With these words, Rudolph dismounted and accompanied Ludwina back to her house, consoling her as he led his horse along.

"You must try to get hold of yourself, good Ludwina," he said soothingly. "The director will give you another nanny for sure; he has at least a dozen pastured behind his house, and he will give you the finest one he has."

"Poor Lili! She cried out so pathetically, as if pleading for my help, but I could do nothing for her," said Ludwina as she dried her tears. Rudolph laid the reins of his horse over the fence and accompanied his bride into the house to calm and console her for her loss.

"Listen, Rudolph," she continued, "you must teach me how to use a gun. I want to learn how to shoot so I can protect myself and what is dear to me. I see no reason why a woman can't make use of a weapon just as well as any man in an emergency; I will overcome the dumb fear of the noise soon enough."

"It pleases me to hear this request," answered Rudolph. "I have been meaning to suggest the same thing for a long time now."

"Very well then, tomorrow, during the day, you can give me lessons, and you will discover soon enough that Ludwina is up to the task," she assured him. Just then, the two became aware of approaching voices, and looking out the window they recognized in the moonlight the director with the major and the elder Wildhorst.

"My, that is a fine, fat buck," called out the director toward the window while halting at Rudolph's horse to examine the massive rack of the animal lying across the saddle.

But by this point Ludwina and Rudolph had reached the fence, and Nimanski had invited both his companions to come with him inside. Ludwina immediately related the tale of the loss of her beloved Lili, and in so doing, could not hold back the tears welling up in her eyes.

"We will replace the loss right away, *Fräulein*," the director said sympathetically. "Early tomorrow morning the unfortunate goat will be replaced with one just as nice, and perhaps even nicer." For this, Ludwina expressed her gratitude to the director.

"It is really an astounding impertinence on the part of this animal; he must be a full-grown lad to have jumped a five-foot fence with a heavy goat. Very well, early tomorrow we want to have a closer look at him for ourselves; he will not be far from here," remarked the director, as they all took seats on the porch. Ludwina disappeared into the house but quickly reemerged with a bottle and glasses, placing them on a table that Rudolph had set out for that purpose. She then fetched a bowl with cigars for the gentlemen.

"It is a genuine Hungarian wine that I brought over myself," noted Nimanski while filling the glasses. He then lifted his own in a toast, "Long live our beloved, old Germany!" At this there was a clear sound of glasses clinking as all seconded the toast.

While they were all sitting about so comfortably and congenially in the moonlight, full of nostalgia for the old homeland, things were livening up in the *Fandangohaus*, as the tavern where dances were held had been dubbed. In the narrow room which served as the dance hall, the young dancing pairs twirled around on the packed floor in dizzying waltzes, and whoever wanted to sit out a dance had to step out of the hall to get some rest.

It was a jovial collection of pretty young girls and ladies and strapping lads who were out on the dance floor, and occasionally an older lady would join in and brandish her skirts jauntily.

The dance hall was separated from the other room by a breezeway open to the front and back.[8] The whole was covered by a shingle roof. The breezeway served as a place to rest and cool off for the pairs who were not dancing. Besides these, many guests would stand around drinking and smoking or engaging in lively conversation. The second room served as the tavern.

The innkeeper had just recently received a barrel of an excellent Rhine wine, and his cognac and genver,[9] which was sipped diluted with water, according to the American custom, were both of excellent quality; consequently, the tavern was not empty this evening.

A regular guest in the tavern was *Herr* Weltge,[10] a well-to-do farmer from Nassau[11] who enjoyed an excellent reputation throughout the town, and a man often singled out by the director as an exemplary settler. He was the only one who had succeeded in cultivating a plot of land outside the city and putting in a corn crop; his garden, likewise, was the only one to yield a meaningful harvest, and his house, like the director's, was laid out in a sensible and practical manner. His wife, a good German *Hausfrau*, administered their household efficiently and economically, and his three stalwart sons and two grown daughters had been raised to know the meaning of work.

On this evening, Weltge sat together with several of his friends at a table opposite the large, open window in the back of the tavern. He had a flask of the new Rhine wine before him on the table, from which now and then he filled his glass contentedly, as if in remembrance of his life in Germany.

He was a stately man in his sixties, tall and broad shouldered, a man who gave the impression of being robust, energetic, and decisive.

He was speaking with his tablemates about the progress and prospects for Friedrichsburg, and complaining about the lack of willingness to work on the part of many of the town's inhabitants. He also stressed that it was a real blunder that the *Verein* had not located a single settlement between Friedrichsburg and Braunfels, and finally he came to what he considered to be the chief impediment to a rapid advance in prosperity for the colony: the Indians.

"What will become of our future herds of livestock if this rabble is allowed to roam freely? We do not have the time or energy, nor does it make any sense, to fatten livestock in stalls when there is so much pasturage out there free of cost and effort, where the animals can fatten themselves," said Weltge.

"Well, very soon peace is to be concluded with the Indians and then all the danger will be over," interjected another citizen.

"Peace," repeated Weltge. "That is so easy to say. Who will hold the bastards to account when they continue stealing and murdering? Will the peace treaty guarantee that you won't get an arrow through your body inside of your own four walls? There is no other solution for these vermin other than a war of extermination on the side of the government, and what a shame that it hasn't already . . ."

In just this moment, something came whizzing past the light and over the table, and with a horrible scream Weltge jerked back and grabbed with both hands the feathered end of an arrow, which had penetrated his chest. He tore at the projectile frantically, trying to pull it out, but his hands fell powerless at his sides, and he turned his gaze to his friends, who had sprung horrified to his side in the same moment in order to extract the arrow. But the arrow had embedded itself in the back of the oak chair so deeply that Weltge sat there as if nailed firmly to the chair. He struggled for breath; a violent shaking overcame him; the blood welled up over his lips; and his head sank to his breast.

One of the men had the presence of mind to slice off the feathered end of the arrow from Weltge's breast, pulling the dying man forward and away from the chair so that the bloody remnant of the projectile remained stuck in the back of the chair; with the help of others he laid the unfortunate man on the floor.

At almost the same instant from the dance hall across the way the cry arose: "Help! Murderer! Indians!" and in a wild throng the dancers came storming out of the door into the breezeway, carrying with them one of the female dancers with a splintered arrow sticking out of her shoulder. Behind her, confused and agitated, a young man with a long, wide cut on his cheek rushed out, indifferent to the blood that was streaming from his own wound.

Like a tornado, the throng of men rushed out into the moonlight and behind the building where the arrows must have originated; enraged and without weapons, they rushed up the hill toward the forest to try and catch a glimpse of the murderer—but nowhere was a sign of him to be seen.

In the dreadful uproar, swearing bloody revenge on the Indians, the men returned to the tavern. The director, who had heard the excitement while returning to his house, joined them in the breezeway of the building.

Weltge was dead, and the wounded young lady, Auguste Röder,[12] sat crying and whimpering in a chair. Nobody among those standing around had risked extracting the arrow from her shoulder. The pharmacist had warned them not to attempt it, insisting that they leave the job to the director.

Carefully but forcefully, Schubbert pulled out the projectile, the iron point of which had embedded firmly in the shoulder joint, and then quickly bandaged the wound while the young woman slipped in and out of consciousness.

For her partner, Carl Voss,[13] whose cheek had been opened up by the third arrow, he placed a temporary bandage and instructed the young man to come to his house later to get the wound properly cleaned and dressed. Everybody crowded around Schubbert in order to confer about what steps should be taken to improve the security of the settlement.

The talk went to and fro for a long time, but it was finally decided to place guards in listening posts around the city at night with orders to shoot down any approaching Indian. The director was acutely aware of the fact that these guards would most likely sit for months without ever seeing an Indian; nevertheless, he proposed these measures himself because the people would find some sense of security in them and also because he wanted to reduce the likelihood of any hostile action against friendly Indians, who would most likely only make an appearance during the light of day.

The morning came, but its light revealed no sign of the culprit: no footprint was to be seen either in soft or hard dirt; neither had his moccasin left a trace in the grass.

The director turned his interest to the less dangerous foe, but one still capable of much mischief, namely the jaguar which had killed Ludwina's goat and which certainly would not stray far from the vicinity as long as even one of these valuable animals was to be found within it.

Preparations were made to find the predator in its lair and, if possible, to bag it there. The director had not only Joe, but all his hounds tied together. All other useful hounds in the city, of which those of the butcher Kellner[14] stood out as the strongest and most spirited, were also put on leashes and brought before the director; the entire pack was turned over to young lads to manage.

In addition to Rudolph, eight members of the *Verein* militia were designated to ride along. All mounted their horses, and the director led them to the rise where Ludwina had last seen the jaguar with the goat.

They had scarcely reached the spot before Joe picked up the scent and came to a halt. He growled angrily while the hair stood straight up on his back. He cast an excited glance toward his master, as if to ask if he also realized to whom the scent belonged. The director praised him and waved him forward. Joe quickly took up the trail, but not so joyfully and eagerly as with other game. One could see in his whole demeanor that he anticipated a fight with a dangerous enemy.

Trying to be as quiet as possible, the hunters headed for the nearby hills. Now and then Joe stopped in order to point out a bloody spot where the jaguar had laid down its prey and briefly rested.

In a short while they had reached the barren, rocky heights over which several dome-shaped formations and ragged cliff faces arose. Here the predator had paused more often to rest. Soon thereafter, the director spotted the torn carcass of the goat as he rode along between the ragged cliff faces. One whole side had been eaten by the cat.

The men then held a short conference about how best to proceed with the hunt. They decided that the *Verein* riders should head around to the right and left of the closest domes and then post themselves at the passes. Only the director and Rudolph stayed behind in order to follow the trail of the jaguar up to its lair. After a wait sufficient to give the *Verein* men time to reach their positions, Schubbert signaled Joe to take up the trail again, but he had the boys with the pack of hounds, a good twenty in number, stay behind him a short distance.

He had hardly followed Joe fifty paces when suddenly from the side of the cliff wall a majestic, golden spotted animal came bounding forward in powerful strides toward the hound, with its tail in the air and uttering short, staccato squalls. Both riders took quick notice, pulled up short, and halted.

Simultaneously, Rudolph fired his rifle and the director his revolver at the marauder, who now took flight. In an instant, the riders were behind it, along with the entire pack of hounds, filling the hills with the sound of wild, frantic baying.

By the time they reached the plateau, the jaguar had gained a lead of a hundred paces. The animal was fired upon from four directions, where the guards had positioned themselves, but the nimble feline continued as if flying over the rocky ground. All eight of the *Verein*'s men then joined the chase in a thunderous charge, accompanied by the shouting of the hunters and the baying of the hounds.

The harried cat's strides soon began to shorten, though, and its pursuers quickly narrowed the gap. Joe led the hunt with powerful bounds and had caught up to within a few paces of the jaguar when it suddenly turned on him and attacked. But simultaneously a dozen or so of the following hounds fell upon it, and the cat disappeared in the swirling, battling mass. As soon as the riders neared, the cat shot out from between the hounds, taking flight once again.

With the now blood-stained Joe in the lead, the hounds stayed fast on his heels, and with bared fangs he glanced quickly to the left and then to the right at his determined pursuers, but did not risk further battle, for he saw the ten riders behind him, and so the procession continued ever forward over loose rocks, patches of grass, and thorn bushes.

Joe had just about caught up with him again when the cat suddenly sprang to the side and headed for a solitary live oak. Upon reaching it in a few quick bounds, he shot up the massive trunk and disappeared into the thick foliage of the tree's crown.

In wild, seething excitement, the dogs surrounded the tree, baying furiously; the riders soon arrived at the scene, and Rudolph asked permission from the director to bring down the jaguar.

"Very well, but you must shoot him in the head; otherwise, it will cost several dogs their lives," answered the director. Rudolph dismounted, approached the tree slowly, and peered up into the branches. Then he stopped, raised his double-barreled shotgun to his shoulder, and in the following instant fired. The report of the gun agitated the hounds even more, but everything remained still in the thick branches above.

In his death throes, the jaguar had grasped a branch with his forepaws and was hanging from it, dying. A good minute passed and then he fell with a mighty crash to the ground, dead. Immediately the dogs fell upon him to vent their wrath.

The massive goat killer was strapped to one of the horses of the *Verein* riders, who then led the horse by his reins behind him, and in triumph the hunters made their way back to the city, where they were received with cheers.

The director had the magnificent pelt of the animal tanned and presented it to Ludwina. He also replaced her white goat with an exceptionally beautiful one with black spots.

CHAPTER 8

Great Concern · The Old Peace Chief · The Wax Lanterns · Sudden Flight · The Mill
Springtime · The Flourishing City · The Grab · Munitions · The Cannons
The Night Music · The Old Friend · Coffee

*T*HE CHIEF OF THE DELAWARES showed up for lunch with the director,
who related to him the murderous events of the preceding night and
showed him the undamaged arrow which had grazed the cheek of the
young man and had been embedded in the wall.

Youngbear listened attentively and carefully examined the arrow. After the
director had finished, he spoke: "This is a Comanche arrow and no one other
than Kateumsi, your so-called friend, shot it. When the two-faced scoundrel
shows up again, kill him, because as long as his heart beats, the hatred he has
inside for whites cannot be taken out. I will inform all Comanche tribes that
have made peace with you of Kateumsi's treachery. They must become his enemies, too, and every Delaware will also mold a lead bullet especially for him."

The excitement, the consternation, and the longing for revenge were at
a fever pitch in Friedrichsburg. On every corner one heard threats expressed
against the first Indian who might dare show his face in the town. The director
had to muster all his powers of persuasion and employ all of his influence to
defuse the situation so that the prospects for peace with the Indians, which had
come so far, would not be undermined or discarded.

Several weeks passed without any disturbance to the peace, when one morning the Shawnee chief Kalhahi appeared before the director and reported to

Chief Old Owl, the mill, and the cannon. Drawing by James C. Kearney.

him that the old peace chief of the entire Comanche nation, Mopochocopie (Old Owl),[1] had arrived a mile outside of the city in order to pay him a visit and to conclude a pact of friendship with him. He was waiting for the director there to share a meal of friendship and then accompany him back into the city.[2]

The director had heard of this old Indian many times, a man who had served as the head war chieftain in his younger years, but now presided over the tribal councils of the whole nation.

It was a matter of high importance, then, for the director to win over this influential man as a friend. He quickly had his horse saddled and rode out with Kalhahi to the place where the old chief was waiting.

Mopochocopie was indeed a very old man, which his wrinkled skin and bent-over figure clearly betrayed, but his features were noble and his long hair, parted into two heavy braids, was still completely black. With him were two similarly old warriors and a granddaughter, a charming young maid of maybe twelve years. When the director walked up to them, they all arose from the buffalo hides and the chief strode forward in a friendly manner with open arms.

After three embraces, the old man led the director to his campsite, where the young Indian girl placed dried meat before him on a deerskin. Schubbert took his place beside the wild ones and partook in Indian fashion of the friendship meal laid out before him. Then he smoked the peace pipe with them, after which Mopochocopie began to speak, saying how glad he was that peace would finally come between the red and white children, and that his heart, now filled with joy, could have no rest until he hastened here to conclude friendship with the great captain.

The old man spoke tolerable English,[3] and the director did not fail to offer many assurances of his pleasure at now being able to greet him as a friend.

After a short consultation, they all mounted their horses and headed for town. Upon arriving at the *Verein* compound, the director asked him where he would like to stay and gave him a choice between the *Verein* house and another building directly across the street in a grove of live oaks which served as the apothecary for the city. This structure was a simple log cabin whose inside walls had been white-washed[4] as far up as the windows and door.

Mopochocopie opted for this house and together with his companions dismounted in front of it. The horses were hobbled in the grass field and the Indians carried their belongings into their abode for the evening.

On this day the table was twice set for the director's noon meal: first for the officials and then, after a short while, for his wild guests. The room had never seen such a large gathering of red children, because in addition to Kalhahi, Youngbear showed up, and his appearance was a pleasant surprise for the old chief.

The director had let it be known throughout the entire city that nobody could come near the house where his wild guests were quartered, neither by day nor night, because he feared this might make them uneasy.

Mopochocopie declared himself quite content after the meal and retired to the house with his companions, where they unrolled their buffalo hides on the floor in order to take an afternoon rest.

Before supper time, Youngbear paid him a visit in order to discuss the upcoming peace treaty and to keep the fires of interest stoked and burning. Before returning to his camp, he reported to the director that Mopochocopie's heart was filled with happiness and beating strong for peace.

It had already become rather dark outside. The Indians' fascination with candles was quite extraordinary; they lay in a circle around them and marveled at the flames. The director knew that he had entertained them well and that they had much to talk over before falling asleep. He had wished them all a good night and they had parted in an atmosphere of mutual affection and goodwill. But before the director lay down to take his own rest, he cast one more glance from afar through the open door over at the wild ones and saw that they were still lying contentedly around the candles, which by this point had burned down considerably.

The morning had scarcely arrived, however, when the quartermaster roused the director from his sleep with the news that the Indians had fled during the night in a panic, leaving behind all their things and riding away without even saddling their horses.[5] Bickel reported that Burg had followed the tracks a full mile outside the city, where the signs still indicated that their horses were at a full run.

Shocked, the director hurried over to the quarters of the wild ones, where he found their saddles, skins, food, cooking pans, and even the large silver medallions with the likenesses of several presidents on them, which had been sent to Mopochocopie as presents.[6]

What could be the cause of this sudden, wild flight? And what would the consequences be? These were the unsettling questions the hasty departure of the venerable old chief forced him to consider. In order to get some good advice about the matter, he rode immediately to the camp of the Delawares.

Youngbear was also troubled by the news, and after thinking about the situation for a short while, declared that he would send some of his people after the Comanches straightaway to return their effects and to ask them the cause of their sudden flight.

Thereafter, he accompanied the director back to Friedrichsburg and handed over the belongings to two of his men, which they packed on a mule. He then sent them off with instructions to catch up with the Indians as soon as possible and then bring back a report to the director here, since Youngbear had set his departure for the following day.

The next morning, Chief Youngbear joined the director and officials for breakfast and then, somewhat wistfully, took his leave from the gathering. He charged Rudolph with passing on the message to his bride that he would remain her best friend and then, with the promise to return the following spring, rode off to catch up with his band, which had already broken camp and traveled several miles ahead.

The sixth Monday had arrived since the appearance of the Mormons, and as the sun bent low, a wagon pulled by four oxen pulled up in front of the *Verein* compound. It contained a load of shingles and a sack of cornmeal, freshly ground at the new mill.

Schubbert was as surprised as he was pleased, especially since Strabbo, the bear hunter, had delivered the load. He offered him his best food and drink as refreshment and the following morning rode down to the Mormon settlement to have a look at the mill for himself and to place orders for lumber.

Mr. Grey, obviously quite satisfied with himself, received the director and led him over to the mill to show him how it had been constructed and equipped. It was a nice, tidy piece of work, the likes of which the director had never seen before—an incredible feat to have accomplished in so short a time.

After Schubbert had sufficiently admired this splendid bit of work, Mr. Grey led him to the enormous, completely enclosed field over which the emerging corn plants had spread a lovely, fresh-green luster.

As if by a stroke of magic these colossal projects had taken shape, and the director could not help but draw a comparison between the capacity for work of these people and the citizens of Friedrichsburg. The conviction also came home to him that no Indians would risk threatening such a company of determined individuals as these Americans. The director placed several large orders for wood products of various sorts. He then departed after once again voicing a sincere admiration for the accomplishments of the Mormons.

A few days later the two Delawares who had gone to find Mopochocopie returned to Friedrichsburg. They brought the answer that he had been an old wife: that he had had a nightmare in the enclosed space of the building, causing his heart to beat with fear, leading him to flee like a scared wife. He was ashamed to come back, but he would be present for the peace conference, and his heart was still filled with friendship for his white brothers.

As the date set for the peace conference in Friedrichsburg approached, interaction with the Indians increased as one new band after another made an appearance in order, so they said, to declare for the peace treaty, but really in order to get presents, because they knew the director let no band leave empty-handed.

If enough cattle were on hand, the director would have a steer driven over to the camp of the Indians and dispatched for their use; in general, he rewarded them richly while paying special attention to the chiefs.

So hardly a day passed without a band of wild guests setting up camp in the vicinity of the city and announcing themselves as friends of the director.

In vain, however, the director awaited the appearance of Santa Anna, the head chief of all the Comanches, with whom Schubbert earnestly desired to confer concerning the upcoming peace conference, but, more especially, to complain about Kateumsi, who had shot the unfortunate Weltge—about this he no longer had any doubts. Spring, however, was heading toward summer and Santa Anna had given no sign.

The city had in the meantime taken on a friendlier and more prosperous aspect. All the gardens around the houses were bursting in abundance. The director had distributed many seeds among the population, especially peas and beans, and had himself planted a large quantity of leafy vegetables in the communal garden, which he likewise handed out to the population as starts for their own gardens, so that these could yield a wealth of nutrition for the populace.

Contributing to this array, many people had transplanted flowering vines, shrubs, and trees from the nearby forests into their gardens and up against the houses. These did very well in the cultivated soil, filling with blooms and transforming the entire city into a large flower garden. The climbing roses, especially, had wound up and over many porches, causing them to look as if red clouds had settled over the houses.

With this change in exterior appearance, a new mood crept into the community: hope and confidence for a brighter future animated them, and the one impediment which stood in the way, the hostility of the Indians, now seemed about to be removed.

Among the most positive steps contributing to the self-sufficiency of the city was the arrival of a large number of cows and pigs, the pigs being delivered by Mr. Grey, head of the Mormons, and since the cornfield promised a rich harvest, all the needs of the population appeared to have been met.

Also, the amenities and comforts of the town were greatly enhanced by the Mormons' sawmill, since the people were now able to improve their houses with such things as wooden floors, and the cabinetmakers were able to build more refined furniture.

Several merchants also arrived to set up shop so that the people no longer had to depend exclusively on the supplies provided by the *Verein*, which were restricted to absolute essentials. In addition to all of this, a new tavern had arisen, which a *Herr* Freudleben[7] from Berlin had constructed in the Mexican fashion from blocks of clay. His talented young wife, who had exchanged the life of an actress in Berlin for "Paradise Texas," contributed in no small measure to imparting a cosmopolitan atmosphere to the establishment.

The slaughterhouse stayed busy now since large numbers of livestock had arrived, and two or three times a week fresh meat was made available.

In general, the women of the town, especially, gathered in the mornings in front of the *Verein* depot for the "grab,"[8] as the receiving of supplies from the *Verein* stores was termed, which was in part charged to individual accounts and in part distributed in payment for services rendered to the *Verein*, though such services were sometimes paid for in cash.[9]

Ludwina Nimanski also found herself with her basket under her arm from time to time among the "grabbers," even though she paid for everything in cash. Her appearance never failed to make a favorable and pleasant impression among the officials. She was universally adored, and they all strove to be helpful to her so as to garner a gracious thank-you or catch a friendly smile.

If, however, the quartermaster Bickel were present, none but him could serve her. And, truthfully, she preferred dealing with him because he was exceptionally good, obliging, and friendly, a man highly praised by all the citizens of Friedrichsburg.

One morning Ludwina showed up at the *Verein* depot to purchase a number of small necessities, and Bickel led her into the warehouse to take care of her needs personally. She picked out calico and other fabric, cotton and wool yarn, sewing silk, thread, and needles, and had packed it all in her basket. She then ordered coffee, sugar, and bear oil. The bear oil was used in cooking and also as fuel in lamps.

"Is there anything else I can help you with, *Fräulein* Ludwina?" asked Bickel in his usual friendly and attentive way.

"Well, you will probably laugh at me, but I would like some gunpowder, shot, and percussion caps," said Ludwina.

"Ammunition—what the devil—you intend to go hunting, then?" asked the quartermaster laughingly.

"Oh no, I couldn't bring myself to hurt some innocent creature," replied Ludwina. "But if it should occur to another jaguar to try to steal my goat, then I will know how to defend her. My husband-to-be has given me instructions in shooting, and I did so well at it, he couldn't praise me enough. But now I intend also to have my father's weapons ready for use. His pistols and shotgun are hanging there, but unloaded."

Bickel laughed out loud and said in a quasi-serious vein, "Yes, for sure, then I need to give you something else to put it in with—but the gun is going to make a loud noise, *Fräulein!*"

"No matter. I am no longer frightened by it, and just so that I can get better used to shooting, I intend to practice with my father's guns often," replied Ludwina smugly, while Bickel fetched the desired objects.

At this moment Rudolph entered the warehouse and said to his bride, "I had no idea that you were here, dear Ludwina," as he turned with a teasing reproach to the quartermaster. "And you, dastardly Bickel, said nothing to me about it."

"Yes, yes, my dear Wildhorst, this warehouse is my kingdom and I would deserve to be called dastardly if I did not attend personally to such charming clients as Ludwina."

"And what are you weighing out there—gunpowder and shot?" continued Rudolph, surprised.

"It is for me, Rudolph," replied Ludwina, as she chuckled out loud. "Don't look at me with such a worried expression. You will see soon enough how well I can shoot my father's guns."

"Yes, yes, you are something else; every day more delightful," interrupted Rudolph while kissing her hand.

"That's for certain!" rejoined Ludwina half seriously. "And every day you need to appreciate me more; otherwise, you will fall far behind me, and no man should allow that to be said about him."

"You are a lovely, delightful angel, and there's not another like you on this earth," replied Rudolph from the bottom of his heart, pressing his lips to the hand of the maiden. "Well, let me carry your basket," he continued. "For the moment I have nothing to do."

"Yes, certainly, you must carry the basket," answered Ludwina, assuming a very earnest expression on her face. "Do you think I would let the opportunity slip by to have you by my side? Take the basket, dear Rudolph, and you shall see with what pleasant company you will be rewarded."

Then she turned to the quartermaster with her natural charm and grace, gave him her hand in departure, and said, "I will always come to you when Rudolph is not here. You weigh the things out a lot better than he does." At this, she left the warehouse and stepped out into the street with Rudolph.

When they reached the end of the *Verein* buildings, Ludwina took notice of the cannon that had been set up there and remarked, "How does one fire the cannon, then?"

"I will show you," answered Rudolph as he walked over to the cannon and placed the basket on the ground, removed the leather covering from the flash hole, and took a fuse from the wooden box.

"Look, you light this fuse and place it here; that's all there is to it. It's just that you have to stand far enough to the side that you are out of the way of the wheel, because the cannon will recoil from the force of the shot." Rudolph then placed himself next to the cannon, bent over, and held out the fuse, as if he were about to fire it.

"I could do that," said Ludwina, and took the fuse from Rudolph and did exactly as he had shown her. "See? I could have fired it off," she said.

"And would have fallen down in fright," Rudolph answered, laughing.

"If it came to it, I would not be afraid to do it," Ludwina continued in a serious vein, while handing the fuse back to Rudolph. He carefully placed it in the box, quickly fastened the leather cover over the flash hole, and then, taking up the basket, continued down the street with Ludwina.

"When the cannon is fired, it is a signal for all the men to fetch their weapons, and Ludwina will also reach for her rifle, because now it is no longer going to hang there on the wall unloaded," she said as they walked along.

"Believe me, my dear, it is very reassuring to know that you now understand how to use a firearm, because with one shot you will be able to signal me to come over at any time in the night," replied Rudolph.

"It is also a great comfort for me; we live so far on the outskirts of town," added Ludwina. She then shared the news that her father had already drawn up a rough sketch of the house which the colonel and Rudolph intended to build and in which they all planned to live together.

"Oh, Rudolph, when I think about it, tears of happiness come to my eyes. I ask myself continually what I have done to deserve such happiness," Ludwina said, and laid her hand on the arm of the young man.

"With the joy, dear angel, which you bring to all of us, you have earned your own a thousand times over," answered Rudolph in a surfeit of emotion while gazing deep into her eyes and pressing her hand firmly to his heart.

"May the Almighty bless me with enough strength to bring happiness to your life; the will on my part is certainly there, my Rudolph," said Ludwina fervently as she snuggled close to him. In this spirit the pair strolled through the town and, as they did, received friendly greetings from all sides, which they returned heartily.

The director sat late with his officials this evening; and it was not until eleven o'clock that he walked over to his house and immediately went to bed, for the exertions of the day had left him very tired.

Heaven had blessed him with the ability to drift easily into deep sleep so that he needed only a few moments to pass into the realm of dreams. It did not matter whether he was lying in a bed or on the hard ground, in his room or under God's vast firmament; and this evening, as usual, he had fallen quickly asleep.

He had only been asleep a short while, however, when he was awakened by a racket, the cause of which he could not place in the first moments of awakening.

Quickly he sat up in his bed and listened in amazement. It was a buzzing, whistling, squeaking, beating, and screeching, such as he had never heard before in his life, and it appeared to be close to his house. He jumped up quickly and cracked the shutters open a little bit in order to have a look outside.

How surprised he was then when he spied in the bright moonlight a large mass of people in the sandy plaza in front of his house, who, all pressed together, were jumping in the air in beat with the heathenish noise of which they were the cause. In the next moment he realized that he was looking at a large group of Indians. Several warriors on horseback accompanied the dense throng, which was edging forward one step at a time.[10]

Schubert threw his clothes on as fast as he could and sprang outside to the wild guests. To his joy, he noticed that one of the riders was the chief of all the Comanches, Santa Anna, and his brother, Sanacho, a friend of longstanding.

Neither acted, however, as if they had seen him. They continued to keep beat even more enthusiastically with their outstretched arms as the noisy mob of humanity pressed forward, and then the full storm of music broke out in earnest.

It was several hundred men and women who held themselves so close together in formation that the back of the ones in front pressed against the chests of those behind, and all stood shoulder to shoulder. Keeping to the beat, the entire throng jumped in the air and advanced one step forward while emitting a song of sorts which descended into a deep thunder-like murmur and then rose back again quickly into a high-pitched squall.

In the middle of the group they carried a large deer hide stretched over a hoop, which served as a drum upon which four men gave full rein to their musical talents by means of clubs.

In addition, all the members of this singing society were armed with instruments which consisted of gourds and buffalo balloons filled with stones, of pipes and flutes of all calibers, and of trumpets crudely fashioned from muskets, and from these last especially they were able to conjure forth the most astonishing sounds.

The director recognized soon enough the somber seriousness with which this concert was being carried out to and fro in front of his house, and that it was all in his honor. Consequently, he endeavored to communicate his pleasure and satisfaction at this display by continually waving his hand at the Indians, since speech was out of the question in the presence of such an energetic orchestration.

He quickly discovered, however, that his acknowledgments of gratitude only served to heighten the intensity of the serenade, and he feared that the entire city would be startled out of their sleep and come running. Therefore, he chose a surer path to bring the racket to an end. He ran over to the *Verein* compound and knocked vigorously on the quartermaster Bickel's door.

"For God's sake, can you do something to put an end to this hellish spectacle, or the whole city will rise up in alarm," he called to the quartermaster through the window.

"I'll stop up their mouths soon enough," answered Bickel, and after a short while rolled a barrel of raw sugar out of the gate onto the plaza.

"Sugar, sugar!" he bellowed out in his lion's voice so that it drowned out the harmonious symphony. A moment later the last lingering tones of the concert died down.

The closely bundled square of humanity swarmed apart, and like flies around a honey pot, the children of the wilderness gathered around the quartermaster and his barrel of sugar.

Bickel then took his hands off the sugar barrel and held them high in the air so that he looked like a lighthouse rising above the waves of the sea. He then laughed out loud and called, "Coffee, coffee!" But then he set his big foot on the barrel, since the children of nature were showing signs of impatience as to when they might reach the sweet kernel so firmly encapsulated by the tough, hooped exterior.

Bickel signaled a guard who was coming out of the *Verein* compound to sit on the barrel and hurried over to the kitchen to have the portly *Verein*'s cook[11] prepare a large wash pot full of coffee.

Meanwhile, the two chiefs, the brothers Santa Anna and Sanacho, had received the welcome of the director and asked him with self-satisfied pride if it had not been beautiful music.

"The prettiest I have ever heard in my life," answered the director enthusiastically. Once again he thanked his friends for the great pleasure the music had brought to him. Both chiefs were delighted by this compliment. Santa Anna pointed with a smile at Sanacho and declared him to be the creator of this magnificent musical production.

Sanacho, the second most important war chief of the Comanches, was a completely noble human being, endowed with a generous spirit, a clear and perceptive intelligence, and a healthy attitude about life.

He had bestowed his friendship on Schubbert many years before; a friendship of a truer and nobler character one would never encounter in civilized society. With the most sincere inner joy he held the hand of the director in his own and said to him how happy it made him to see him again. Then he spoke of the good times they had once enjoyed together in Schubbert's wooden fort on the Leona.

During this, he entwined his arm in the director's and paced back and forth with the director in the moonlight. Schubbert quickly brought the conversation around to the upcoming peace conference and to the stubborn hostility of Kateumsi.

"After we have concluded a solid peace with the Comanches, you simply cannot allow this one tribe to remain at war with us; he belongs, after all, to your nation."

"We will do our best to fill his heart with friendship for you," answered Sanacho, visibly embarrassed.

"That will be useless. He has sworn his intention to take his hatred with him to his fathers," said the director.

"Then you must answer his arrows with your bullets," responded Sanacho evasively.

"But if he is treacherous and shoots his arrows from the dark, how can we punish him for his misdeeds?" asked the director, and since Sanacho gave no answer, he continued, "You are our friends now and will surely come to our aid against our enemies."

Sanacho fell silent for several moments, and then said resolutely: "That would mean to cut out our own insides. That is what has driven the red children from the shores of the big water all the way to these hills. That is what has broken their dominance and made small, helpless tribes out of once-powerful nations. You whites have divided us among ourselves and, in order to please you, we have taken up weapons against our own flesh and blood. Kateumsi is a Comanche and his brothers cannot redden their weapons with his blood. But Sanacho will speak with Kateumsi, and if he cannot turn his heart toward you whites at least he can unstring his bow against you."

The director could find nothing to object to in this declaration by his wild friend. On the contrary, he had to concede the correctness of Sanacho's attitude and basic principles, and so he replied, "You are probably right, Sanacho, but do your best to get Kateumsi to appear for the peace conference because, after all, one can live in peace with an enemy."

"Now your eye sees clearly," the wild one answered, relieved. "Let it always look friendly at Kateumsi and you will find his face pleasant enough even when his brow is furrowed. We were bitter enemies once and would not allow each other a peaceful night's rest by the fire, but see how you have comforted and pleased Sanacho's heart with your friendship? Only a few tribes of the Comanches will be missing at Friedrichsburg. In the large council, Sanacho spoke out loudly in favor of the whites, and the voice of your old friend Kiwakia[12] won many hearts among us. Also our cousins, the Mescaleros, want to come, among whom you have good friends: Wasa's heart beats strongly for you," Sanacho continued.

While the two walked back and forth over the grounds, deep in conversation, the portly Santa Anna was having a lively exchange with the quartermaster Bickel in front of the *Verein* compound, while around them the men and women were lying on the sandy soil around the barrel of sugar, keeping a steady eye on the gate where the promised coffee was expected.

Then two guards emerged with a large, steaming copper kettle, while another guard rolled out a barrel full of crackers behind them.

The Indians jumped and, grasping their drinking horns, shouted and danced with joy as the quartermaster opened the barrels of sugar and crackers and then gave the sign to the wild ones that they could serve themselves.

Santa Anna quickly exhorted them to be orderly, whereupon they began filling their horns with coffee and sweetening their drinks from the sugar barrel. They then retired a short distance away with a handful of crackers to sit down and enjoy their meal.

Santa Anna, however, after he had once again commanded his people to be quiet and orderly, accepted the director's invitation and accompanied him with Bickel and Sanacho into the *Verein* office, where the table had been laid with cold cuts and coffee.

Neither of the chiefs spoke during the meal. Later, though, after the director had handed them cigars, they began a lively conversation concerning the upcoming peace conference, and not until two o'clock did they emerge with Bickel and the director to walk back over to their people.

The kettle as well as both barrels had been completely emptied by this time, and the Indians sat and lay around the plaza in the moonlight waiting for their chiefs.

Santa Anna now asked the director if he would be pleased to hear a repeat performance of the night music, but the director politely refused this offer with the assertion that he hoped for a few hours of sleep.

With this, he and Bickel took their leave, and the Indians, extremely satisfied, retired to the camp they had made on the outskirts of the town.

The next morning the director had a fat steer driven to the camp and shot. Both chiefs, however, took all their meals with the director during their stay, which extended for several days.

Completely satisfied, they said farewell until they would meet again in August, and departed under the assurance of perpetual peace.

With the departure of the befriended Indians, a strange feeling overcame the director. They had disappeared like swallows into the distance without giving a hint of a direction, a trail, a destination; they drifted whither their spirits led them with their thoughts in tow; nowhere a permanent location; bound neither to time nor place; their homeland as far as the blue sky reached, without wish or deprivation; master of their happiness.

CHAPTER 9

The New City · Government Officials · Big Preparations · Day of Festivities
Grand Entrance of the Guests · The Proud Savage · The Parade
The Conclusion of Peace · The Feast · The Departure

*A*UGUST HAD ARRIVED, a month of great significance for the citizens of Friedrichsburg. The month not only promised peace and security, but also would bring in the first corn harvest for the town.

Only toward the end of the month would the full moon appear, the designated time for the signing of the peace treaty,[1] and it was important that the corn be harvested before large numbers of Indians appeared.

The entire town's manpower was directed toward first stripping the leaves as valuable fodder for horses. This was auctioned off to the highest bidders, and the money obtained was distributed equally among the workers, for not all families owned horses, so many had no use for the fodder. The corn itself was measured and then distributed proportionately among the participants.

It was a bountiful harvest of superior quality, and the future of the city was secured by means of it. Even if it would not supply enough breadstuff for a full year, the town would be able to easily satisfy any shortage in this regard from the Mormons. Their field was not yet ripe, but also promised a very rich yield.

Grand entry of Comanche chiefs. Drawing by James C. Kearney.

Since the Mormons were seldom seen or heard from except when they brought lumber or cornmeal into the city, the director wanted to see for himself the bounty which their harvest promised, and so he rode over to their settlement in the middle of August. As in his earlier visits, when he was continually astonished at the accomplishments of these industrious people, so too this time his first glance registered amazement, for the tent city had disappeared and in its place a new town had arisen.

The charming cottages, constructed partly from sawed lumber and partly from shaped logs, were laid out in rows on both sides of the road, and all included tidy gardens enclosed by decorated picket fences. In the middle of the village where Mr. Grey's tent once stood, a large building now rose above the other dwellings, a tabernacle where the Mormons could hold their religious services.

As he approached the settlement, the director noticed that the herds of livestock grazing in the surrounding pastures had increased substantially and that the number of oxen was especially conspicuous. He also noticed in the distance a dozen colossal cargo wagons, each hitched to six oxen, being driven around the prairie, apparently to no purpose. A single man walked along beside each wagon with a very long whip, while executing all sorts of turns and maneuvers with the vehicles.

Once he entered the town, Schubbert encountered a brisk, lively activity at every turn: over here, cartwrights busy with the construction of heavy wagons; over there, blacksmiths hard at work fastening iron rims onto wagon wheels or shoeing horses; to the side, next to the slaughterhouse, men engaged in fastening fresh ox hides to frames for drying; and in the gardens, many young women vigorously occupied with the many domestic chores attendant to housework.

In a most welcoming manner, Schubbert was directed to the house of Mr. Grey, where he was received in the usual calm and understated manner. Once again, Mr. Grey listened with quiet satisfaction to the words of praise from the director concerning the astonishing industriousness of his flock. Mr. Grey then offered to show him the furnishings in his house, which were all extremely tasteful and functional. Though constructed from the most basic materials, everything that one might need was present. It was all arranged to please the eye, and nowhere was anything superfluous to be seen. Except for those things which could be useful on a trip, there was, however, a noticeable dearth of furniture, something which the Americans prized highly. The stout wooden trunks served as bed supports and sofas, while the tables as well as the chairs were made to be easily disassembled.

The director also noticed as he rode through the town that no one had planted a tree next to a house or in a garden, something an American settler would be quick to do. When he expressed surprise at this, the remark seemed to catch Mr. Grey off guard, and he avoided a direct response with the reply that they had not yet found time to plant them.

"Since my last visit here, the number of oxen in your herd has increased substantially and, if I am not mistaken, as I rode up several of them were being trained to pull wagons. For what purpose do you need so many draft animals?" inquired the director.

This question also seemed to be unsettling to the leader of the Mormons, but he quickly parried, "One can't have too many of these useful animals." Mr. Grey then hurriedly changed the subject to the results of the corn harvest that had just been completed in Friedrichsburg.

"We are very satisfied with the yield, but we will probably have to turn to you for assistance next spring if it falls short of our needs," answered the director.

"It would be advisable to go ahead and purchase this year what you estimate to be your additional requirements. This is because we intend to use our surplus to fatten our many pigs. Once the acorns begin to fall, we will drive them into the oak forests, where they will fatten up nicely on the mast. Before we slaughter, however, we always finish them out with corn, which renders the bacon firmer and conditions the hams better for smoking," replied Mr. Grey, but once again in such a manner as if he were hiding the real reason for his suggestion.

Before the director took his leave from the settlement and in company with Mr. Grey, he had a close look at several of the cottages. At all turns he found the same tidiness and the same practical taste governing their appointments; still, everywhere he received the impression that in spite of the permanent housing they had constructed, these people were still on a journey, and no matter how expertly their dwellings had been built and how comfortably they had been outfitted, their inhabitants regarded them as no more than temporary abodes.

In every house he found the same scarcity of furniture. The trunks, which were all draped with spotlessly white, intricate crochet work, served as seats and places of repose. But what strengthened the director's conviction the most that the wanderings for these people had not yet come to an end was the absence of beehives, something that would never be missing in an American settlement.

Peace, harmony, and quiet contentment, however, filled every corner of the settlement and found expression in every house and on every face: not a loud word spoken nor vexed look seen. Everyone was industriously occupied. The men appeared to be self-motivated in their work, and happy, and the many wives were cheerfully going about their business and willingly assisting one another in their tasks.

Agreeably impressed by the spirit which animated these people, the director invited Mr. Grey to the upcoming peace ceremony in Friedrichsburg. Mr. Grey, however, did not want to give his promise to this since he did not want to be absent from his house too long while so many Indians were present in the neighborhood.

The month of August was coming to an end; the sliver of a moon began to wax, and for many miles around Friedrichsburg countless bands of Indians put up their tepees in the lush, watered valleys. These hills had most likely never seen so many human beings together at one time and so many campfires sending columns of smoke wending into the sky.[2]

Traffic with Braunfels had come to a complete halt since no one wanted to set out on the long, barren path at this time.

Though eagerly requested by the director, it had already been several weeks since any news had arrived in the city from the town below. Then one morning a long caravan of wagons arrived accompanied by a strong guard bringing valuable gifts for the Indians. They consisted of a large number of diverse trade goods suited to the Indians' needs. The main article, the one upon which the Indians placed the greatest value, was a rough, scarlet-red fabric woven especially for them, which the men wound around their bodies, and long, snow-white beads, also specially fabricated for them.

Along with the presents, the delegates of the government arrived. They brought the peace treaty, which had been drawn up on parchment paper. The officials consisted of Major Neighbors,[3] who already had been in the service of the U.S. government as Indian Agent for many years, and several subordinates, who were there to assist him.

With the approach of the predetermined time, excitement began to mount among the population, so much so that practically all work had ceased during the last few days. People everywhere were engaged in lively conversation about the upcoming festivities in a general atmosphere of anticipation and high suspense.

The preparations undertaken by the *Verein* contributed a lot to this because the designated spot where the ceremony was to take place, which was under the large live oaks opposite the *Verein* compound on the main plaza, had been decked out with wreaths in a festive way.

Only two days remained until the big peace-day and not an Indian had shown himself in Friedrichsburg. Then around sundown, Santa Anna and his brother Sanacho came riding up with the old chieftain Mopochocopie, who had earlier fled the city for no apparent reason.

"Mopochocopie, old wife," said Santa Anna to the director after the first greetings. He pointed, laughing, at the old Indian, who, likewise laughing, but somewhat ashamed, offered his hand to the director.

With his left hand, the old chief pointed to his heart, saying, "Mopochocopie no longer warrior; his heart like that of old wife which fills with fear after she dreams."

The faces of Santa Anna and Sanacho beamed with happiness and joy at the realization that they had finally achieved the long-wished-for goal, and now, for all time, peace and friendship would prevail between their people and the whites. They stayed for supper with the director and were very happy to visit with Major Neighbors, a man with whom they had been on friendly terms for many years.

As the morning of the festival dawned, the sky was bright and cloud-free, and the new light found the city already busily engaged in activity. Young and old, decked out in their best Sunday attire, were on the move. Most people had barely taken time to finish breakfast before they took to the streets in anticipation of the Indians streaming into the town from all sides. People gathered especially in the vicinity of the *Verein* compound and on the road to Braunfels, since most of the Indians were expected to arrive from the south and the east.

All the while, men were busy moving and arranging the gifts from the *Verein* compound according to the directives of Major Neighbors and stacking them under the oaks, where the ceremony was to take place.

The sun climbed over the hills and cast its golden light in the valley of Friedrichsburg, but still no Indians had appeared. Preparations at the ceremonial grounds for the reception of the guests had been completed, and from moment to moment excitement among the waiting guests was mounting, when out of the woods, toward which the road to Braunfels led, a glistening and sparkling became perceptible, and a procession of riders emerged at a walk.

It was Santa Anna, the war chief of all Comanches, together with the peace chiefs, the wisest and oldest warriors of the Nation. Slowly and solemnly, the procession approached, Santa Anna in the lead, mounted on a magnificent, milk-white stallion, his companions following him, two by two.

Devoid of clothing with the exception of the scarlet-red cloth wound around their bodies, the red-brown figures, manly and noble in appearance, sat tall and straight on their powerful and handsome steeds, and one could clearly see from their demeanor and bearing that they considered it to be a sacred obligation to secure peace and security for their people.

All were festooned in their finest jewelry and had woven into their own shiny black hair two long pigtails from the black beard[4] of the buffalo. These hung down on either side of their faces and across the breast as far as the underside of the horses, and to these braids were affixed rows of hand-sized, silver conchos, round and gleaming.

On their heads, they wore feathers from the golden eagle, while around their necks and over their chests lay strings of three-inch-long white beads. Shiny metal bracelets decorated their arms and colorfully stitched beadwork adorned the moccasins that clad their feet.

The most magnificently tanned animal skins served as saddles, while the bridles as well as the manes and tails of their horses were decorated with shiny, iridescent feathers.

Without a single weapon, these men, a thousand times over so unspeakably deceived, persecuted, and mistreated by the whites, rode into the German town in an attitude of unqualified trust and confidence in order to conclude peace and friendship with them—something that for twenty years the government of the United States had moved heaven and earth in vain to accomplish.

Major Neighbors, with his subordinates, and Director Schubbert, with his officials, stepped forward to warmly greet the approaching guests and then to accompany them into the town, past the *Verein* buildings, where they were received with jubilation by the crowds of Friedrichsburgers.

At the same time, cheers arose from the other end of the city as another band of riders approached from the far end of San Saba *Straße*, accompanied by an excited and happy throng of citizens.

It was Kiwakia,[5] the Comanche chief, and his brother, Ureumsi, and his senior warriors, festively adorned, without weapons, approaching on splendid mounts. In little time they arrived at the central square in front of the *Verein* buildings.

The reunion of these brothers with the director was a very happy event, and deeply moving, since many years before, each party had demonstrated their friendship to the other by rendering all-important, life-and-death assistance.[6] And now cries of joy by the populace resounded from just about every quarter of the town as tribe upon tribe, represented by their chiefs and senior warriors, paraded through the town toward the area of the *Verein* compound.

The Mescaleros also came decked out in their finery, and Chief Wasa, the old friend of the director, greeted him eagerly. And in such a manner, more and more of the wild guests arrived, until the count of chiefs exceeded fifty. But in vain one hoped for and awaited the appearance of Kateumsi; none of his red brothers would admit to having seen him and none could offer knowledge of his whereabouts.

"His heart is that of a panther; it cannot open to friendship; he will not come," Sanacho said to the director. "And because they listen to his insults and fear his anger, several Comanche bands will be missing."

"Well then, the frontier battalion of the government will treat him as an irreconcilable enemy and exterminate him and his entire band," inserted Major Neighbors harshly.

Sanacho cast a scornful, derisive look his way, and added, "Even if the horses of the frontier troopers were as fast as your tongue, their riders still would not have the eyes of a Comanche to find Kateumsi in the hills, nor the ears of the Indian to hear his approach before being awakened from their last sleep by his arrow! Fear of your frontier forces is not what brought us here today!"

"I know that, friend Sanacho," said the major quickly, in order to mollify the proud chief. "But precisely because we will now live in peace and friendship with all the Comanches, is it even more unpardonable that one small band continues to hold out and bear arms against us."

"Kateumsi has his own head and his own heart, and until now no Comanche has yielded to the power of another people," answered Sanacho, lifting himself to his full height and raising his voice so that the other red men in the vicinity would have to hear.

"Only under the power of friendship has Sanacho himself yielded," added the director quickly, holding out his hand to the chief, in whom anger, it was plain to see, was flaring up.

"And he will yield to this friendship as long as his heart beats," he replied gladly as he took Schubbert's hand in his own and a joyful contentment beamed once again from his large brown eyes.

The appointed time for the appearance of the Indians had long since elapsed when Santa Anna declared that no more Comanches would come. At this, he signaled Sanacho to order a move to the designated council grounds. In a loud voice Sanacho then relayed his brother's order to the other chiefs in the language of his people. Without another word, the chiefs and their warriors, assembled and arranged by twos, fell in behind their head chief, tribe by tribe, in a procession of solemn dignity.

Santa Anna, acting as if he were entering into the most sacred negotiations of his life, wheeled to the right and with his long column of riders in tow, described a large arc as he rode to the council ground. At the same time, Major Neighbors and his subordinates and the director and his officials strode toward the designated place.

Major Neighbors held high in his hand the roll of parchment with the peace treaty that had been approved and drawn up by the government as he stepped up to the table that had been placed under a magnificent oak. At the same moment, Santa Anna approached the table from the other side.

Major Neighbors laid the parchment on the table, extended his hand to Santa Anna, and greeted him in the name of the Great White Father, the President of the United States. Santa Anna returned the greeting in the name of all the Comanches. They then stepped forward and embraced three times.

After this, with an air of gravity befitting the situation, Major Neighbors took the parchment and unrolled it. At the same time, in order to translate the contents of the peace treaty, Sanacho mounted a small speaker's podium which had been placed near the table and decorated with wreathes of foliage.

By this time, the Indians had formed a broad circle around them, planted like bronze statues with their gazes fixed upon Major Neighbors.

A deep, serious hush befell the crowd. Then Major Neighbors began to read the contract slowly and in short sentences, which Sanacho immediately relayed from the stage in a loud, commanding voice in the tongue of his people.

Not a sound, not a whisper diminished the decorum of the presentation even as a growing expression of satisfaction became ever clearer and more noticeable in the dark faces of the wild ones. Finally, the major reached the end of the document and laid the parchment on the table. Then Santa Anna took his brother's place on the podium and made a forceful speech to his confederates in which he stressed the great advantages which the signing of this treaty would bring to his nation. He spoke at length and with an elevated and sincere enthusiasm, which stemmed from the depths of his soul, and which, by and by, began to have an effect on the otherwise stoic Indians, an effect which began to register in their countenances and gestures.

At the conclusion of his speech, Santa Anna left the podium and approached the table, where he declared himself ready to sign the treaty in the name of his people. The major entered the name of Santa Anna upon the parchment after the text of the treaty. He then handed the quill to the chief and helped guide his hand to place his mark next to his name. With a great sense of satisfaction, Santa Anna looked down upon this, his work, and then handed the quill back to the major.

The major then named Sanacho loudly and wrote his name down, and when the chief stepped forward, Neighbors likewise guided Sanacho's hand to set his mark in the correct place. Sanacho then called the chiefs forward to the table, one after the other, and each signed the treaty in a similar manner.

The work was finished and done in such a manner that the Indians had full confidence in the conviction that from now on peace and harmony would exist between them and the whites. And with this feeling alive in his heart, Santa Anna approached Major Neighbors and embraced him three times in his arms. Then he turned to Schubert and with a happy, beaming expression, embraced him with the words, "Old friendship once again young. Santa Anna happy!"

Caught up in the spirit of the moment, Sanacho emulated his brother in this ritual, and then all the other chiefs approached in order to seal the peace and friendship treaty through a threefold embrace.

Happiness and joy were reflected in all the Indians, and with growing anticipation they now directed their attention to the gifts. Major Neighbors had, in the meantime, walked over to the gifts and ceremoniously turned them over to Santa Anna with the request that he be allowed to personally distribute them among the various tribes on the spot. Santa Anna, however, asked that all the presents be transported to his camp on the Pedernales, where he would give each chief the part designated for his tribe the following morning. He said that the Indians would be happier with this arrangement and that they would thereby avoid any suspicion that favoritism played a role in the allocation.

The director summoned the necessary wagons and, as they were being loaded with the trunks and barrels, Santa Anna held a short address to his red brothers in which he relayed to them that the distribution would take place early the following morning at his camp.

Schubbert had already discussed with Santa Anna and Sanacho at their last meeting the manner in which he would entertain the Indians once the treaty was signed, and he had explained that it would be impossible to prepare a meal for so many people. The two chiefs suggested that they prepare coffee for all the Indians, including those who had never tasted the drink before, and that this would be a great treat for all. When Schubbert also mentioned that he intended to distribute cigars all around, they expressed the opinion that this would be the finest event that the Comanches had ever celebrated.

As soon as the gifts had been loaded and hauled away, accompanied by several of Santa Anna's old warriors, the chief bade his followers have a seat in a wide circle under the shade of the live oak tree. A large kettle of coffee was then brought to the circle, and several containers with raw sugar and crackers were set out.

In accordance with Santa Anna's instructions, the Indians had brought along their drinking horns, and the chief then bade them step forward to the kettle after his own example and help themselves to coffee, sugar, and crackers.

Major Neighbors and his people, as well as the director and his officials, followed suit and then seated themselves next to Santa Anna in the circle. Soon all the Indians were sitting in the grass, enjoying their unusual meal.

Their pleasure was soon greatly increased when the director had cigars passed all around. At this, the Indians stopped eating crackers but continued to fill their horns with coffee as long as the supply lasted.

The citizens of the town, who had viewed the proceedings from the beginning quietly and respectfully, but with the greatest interest, now joined in the circle with the Indians, sat and stood next to them, and made the effort to communicate and befriend them.

Ludwina was present among the townspeople, and many an "Ugh" of wonder came her way from the Indians.

As great as her hopes were for this gathering and as happy as she was to see the Indians and whites mixing in such a friendly way, still an uneasy wariness, which she could not overcome, held her back from their immediate vicinity, and in spite of many looks from Rudolph, who had seated himself in the middle of the circle, she remained standing with her father in the distance.

The Indians, however, showed not the least inclination to depart the banquet even after all the coffee was gone. They puffed furiously at their cigars, emitting clouds of smoke, so it seemed that they might be able to ask for another, and all the while they stroked themselves over the chest and body as a sign of utter contentment.

Santa Anna, above all others, appeared to be reveling in the moment. Happily, he let his glance pass back and forth across the faces of his red compatriots, and every now and then he muttered half audibly to himself, "Comanches happy!"

The white spectators, however, gradually began to disperse, as it was time for the noon meal, and in many kitchens throughout the town the fires had already been put out.

The time began to drag for the director as well, but, because of the other chiefs, he was not able to invite either Santa Anna or Sanacho to his table. He turned to Santa Anna and said, "I cannot invite either you or your brother to my table for lunch; my other friends would not take kindly to being excluded. So, why don't you ride out with them for a little ways and then both of you come back to dine with me?"

Santa Anna appeared very flattered by the invitation and nodded his acceptance furtively to the director. He then rose and declared the festivities ended. Now the chief urged the gathering to conclude the celebration. He extended his hand in farewell to both the Americans and the Germans. Sanacho did the same and all the chiefs followed suit. Then they hurried over to their horses under the trees, and before ten minutes had elapsed, all the Indians were gone.

As they departed, however, the director asked the chief Kiwakia and his brother Ureumsi, as well as the Mescalero chief Wasa, to pay him a personal visit before they took their leave of this region, so that they could renew their friendship and reminisce about old times. That all the tribes and bands would pull stakes as quickly as possible, of this the director was certain; otherwise, he would have grown anxious about the presence of so many new friends.

There was not food enough present in these hills to sustain such an enormous gathering of humanity. All the wild game had either fled or was already slain, and the buffalo only visited this hilly region occasionally and in much smaller numbers than on the prairies, where they could be found wandering by the thousands.

All mounted tribes of the southern plains lived almost exclusively from the buffalo, a fact underscored by the innumerable bones lying on the prairies, bleached white by the sun, which, from a distance, imparted to the trackless expanses a light sheen, as if covered by a white veil. The small amount of dried meat which these Indians had brought along with them on their journey to Friedrichsburg could not possibly satisfy their needs for any extended period of time, and thus after a few days not an Indian was to be seen in the area.

Kiwakia, his brother, and also Wasa kept their promise to call on the director before their departure. When they took their final leave, they assured the director that they would never pass through this region without paying him a visit.

After a few days, the lack of fresh meat also compelled Santa Anna and his band to head for the open grasslands to the northeast. Friedrichsburg found itself once again quiet and alone. With the conclusion of peace, a genuine sense of security and an absence of danger was shared among the inhabitants of the town. Almost no one was seen carrying weapons. As glad as he was to observe this new situation, the director continued to admonish the citizens to keep their guard up, pointing to the fact that Kateumsi and several other chiefs had not participated in the peace ceremony.

CHAPTER 10

The Vicious Foe · The Challenge · Defiance · Hostile Appearance · Warning Shot
Caution · Fall Day · Lottery · Pleasure Ride

*M*ANY WEEKS PASSED in undisturbed tranquility and with the usual hustle and bustle of productive activity. No one seemed to be thinking about the Indians anymore. One such afternoon Rudolph von Wildhorst could be seen sitting with his future bride on the veranda in front of her house. He had laid his arm over her shoulder and was discussing the happy event scheduled for the spring of the following year, when all their hopes and aspirations would find fulfillment in marriage.

"And then you will not leave me anymore, my dear Rudolph," said Ludwina, snuggling affectionately at his breast and looking up at him with an expressive intimacy.

"No, nothing will separate us then. I will plant cotton and raise livestock on my land outside of town on Walnut Creek, which the director has helped me obtain, and beyond that, only live for my Ludwina," replied the happy young man.

"You also need to acquire sheep. They offer lots of advantages, and it costs nothing to keep them," offered Ludwina.

Confrontation between Kateumsi and the director. Drawing by James C. Kearney.

"Nothing but to keep a close watch on them when they are out grazing; otherwise, the wolves won't waste any time dragging them off," replied Rudolph. "And as far as the Indians are concerned, we can raise as much livestock as we want."

"If only this Kateumsi and his followers don't stir up any more trouble. Most people believe he was the one who shot Weltge, and he didn't come to the peace conference."

"I don't blame the man and I don't know: if I were in his place, maybe I would have stayed away too. There is a pride, an unbending determination in that man that impresses me," remarked Rudolph.

"But to shoot poor Weltge in such an underhanded way," interjected Ludwina.

"This untamed Indian, powerless to stand in the way of what is happening, is simply trying to do what he can to avenge the injustices that the whites have foisted upon him. It really pained me to have to shoot him from his horse that time in order to save our own lives."

"You are too good, Rudolph, and I do believe you are being too generous with your excuses for his behavior," added Ludwina. "The whites haven't done him any harm."

"They are taking away the land that he now owns and that his fathers owned. The road to Austin is open now, and how long will it take before settlements spring up all along it? Soon all the pretty little valleys between the hills will be fenced and cultivated, and Kateumsi will have to leave the land of his forefathers and look for another place to live," answered Rudolph. Just then, the sound of approaching horses became noticeable behind the house of Nimanski, and in the next moment Kateumsi rode along the fence on his powerful black horse. As his gaze met Rudolph's, it was as if lightning shot from his dark eyes, but in the next instant, they fastened on Ludwina's and lit up brightly. Lifting himself high in the saddle, the wild one kept his gaze fixed on her until his path put the foliage of the arbor between them.

Directly behind the chief rode his warriors, outfitted in full war regalia: each had a quiver containing bows and arrows slung over his shoulder, a long lance decorated with colorful feathers, and long strips of leather in his right hand, a tomahawk placed in his belt, and a large, round leather shield held on the left arm. Silently they rode by on their magnificent horses, and following them came scores of wives and children on ponies and mules, driving a large number of heavily laden pack animals along with them.

Ludwina was taken aback by the intense gaze of the chief and, frightened, pressed tightly against Rudolph as he quietly said to her, "That is Kateumsi, about whom we were just speaking."

"I am afraid of him. That was not a friendly stare he gave us," she remarked, looking his way as he rode at the head of his band over the grassy field toward San Saba *Straße*.

"I believe he holds a grudge against me for shooting him off his horse; it appears that he recognized me," replied Rudolph. "But surely he must be here with peaceful intentions; otherwise, he wouldn't have the women and children along. I am really curious about what he is up to."

At this, Rudolph stood up, but Ludwina grasped his hand and begged, "Oh please do not go! The man means you no good, and he is probably looking for revenge."

"No, no, my best; he must surely be coming here to make peace. I will go quickly over to the *Verein* compound," answered the young man as he kissed Ludwina and, taking his hat, hurried away.

Ludwina called anxiously after him, "Come back quickly!"

The long train of Indians aroused much curiosity in the town. Everyone ran toward them to get a look, but the Indians looked neither to the left nor to the right as they continued their way along the street toward the *Verein* compound.

The officials and members of the militia had already emerged from the entrance. When Kateumsi brought his steed to a halt in front of the office, the quartermaster strode up to him and asked him in only a half-friendly tone what he wanted.

"Kateumsi wants to bury the weapons against you whites and make peace with you," answered the chief seriously.

"Why didn't you come to the peace conference?" Bickel persisted.

"Kateumsi was far away from here," continued the Indian, undisturbed and calm. "The moon is full once again; peace now just as good as with the last full moon."

The quartermaster did not know exactly what he ought to say and turned to consult with the other officials. At this point Burg stepped up to him and said, "Let me shoot the rascal down and then we will be rid of him."

"What are you thinking about, Burg?" replied Bickel in a vexed tone. "He has come here to make peace."

Then he turned back to Kateumsi and said, "The director is not here, but he will arrive soon. Ride out to the creek and make camp there. When the director returns, he will speak with you there."

Without another word, Kateumsi wheeled his horse back into the street, and soon he and his followers had disappeared from the view of those gathered in curiosity in front of the office.

"You should have let me shoot the scoundrel down; he and nobody else murdered Weltge," Burg said once again to the quartermaster.

"How can you be so sure of that, Burg?" replied Bickel in his usual calm manner. "First, it is only a supposition on our part that Kateumsi committed the murder, and second, think about it, what kind of bloodbath would his followers have loosed on the city?"

"That's what we wanted to prevent," interjected Kracke. "They would have been knocked from their horses before they knew what was happening."

"Look, I've heard enough of this stupid talk, Kracke—let's wait to see what the director has to say about it," replied Bickel. Looking down the street, he added, "It's really unfortunate that the director isn't here. I hope it won't be long till he returns."

"He couldn't be too far away because he didn't take his rifle along," observed Burg, but it was a good hour before the director returned. Schubbert had not even dismounted from his horse before Bickel announced the arrival of Kateumsi.

"Make peace?" repeated the director. "The scoundrel has heard that the bands were so richly rewarded with presents and now he is coming to get some for himself—you will see that I am right about this. In any case, we want to do whatever it takes to be done with him. Drive a fat steer over to his camp and shoot it. I will ride out later to hear what Kateumsi is up to."

The order was carried out immediately, and when the director arrived in the Indians' camp an hour later, they all sat by their fires, roasting and braising the meat and marrow of the steer. Schubbert stepped up to the fire of Kateumsi, who, without raising himself from his buffalo hide, signaled for the director to have a seat.

"Why didn't you come to the peace conference?" the director asked the chief.

"Far away!" he answered, gesturing with his hand to the north. Then he sat up straight, looked the director squarely in the eye, and said, "Kateumsi wants to make peace now and get his presents."

"The presents that were sent here for the peace conference have all been given away; Santa Anna undertook the distribution of them himself," answered the director. But when he noticed that this bit of news caused the brows of the chief to pull together in a dark expression, he continued, "But you shall not leave here without presents; I will send them over."

"Kateumsi demands just as nice and just as many presents as the other bands received," continued the wild one, looking firmly in the eyes of the director.[1]

"The United States government made the peace treaty with the Comanches, not I, and if I make an offering of presents to you, then I do it as a gesture of goodwill on our part; I am not obliged to give you anything. If you wanted to receive presents equal to the other Comanches, then you should have been here at the predetermined time. The Delawares delivered the invitation in plenty of time, but your answer to them was that you would not come." With these words the director looked Kateumsi in the eye just as firmly and resolutely as he had regarded the director.

"So, you will not give me any presents?" asked Kateumsi after a short pause and with a forced calm.

"If you have come as a sincere friend, yes—but if you have only come to get presents, no!" replied Schubbert emphatically.

At this, the chief once again fell silent, but then, as if he had come to a decision, he said, "Kateumsi has come to be a true friend and to get presents."

"Good, then you are welcome here, and tomorrow morning early I will have the presents brought over. Today it is already too late for it," said the director. He then rose, offered Kateumsi his hand, and departed the camp. Back in town, Schubbert made it known to the quartermaster which objects should be prepared as gifts for the unfriendly guests, and early the next morning Bickel sent the gifts to the camp of Kateumsi.

That morning, the town officials had just finished their breakfast and had headed over to the *Verein* compound. The director was standing in the gate with the quartermaster when Kateumsi approached with a steady, determined stride, followed by two seasoned warriors, his hands at his side and his body encased in an enormous buffalo robe whose ends dragged on the ground. When he neared the director, he said, "Kateumsi wants to speak with you."

"So speak," answered the director in the same unfriendly tone with which the wild one had addressed him.

"The presents that you sent are no good. There is no red cloth and there are no beads. They are not even enough for Kateumsi, and his men get nothing at all."

"As I have already told you, I am no longer in possession of those gifts which the government distributed among the Comanches and so cannot give you any, and if you are not satisfied with what I have offered you as a token of my own friendship, then I can't help you," answered the director, vexed at the insolence of the wild one.

"Then Kateumsi will make no peace and offer no friendship," he stated in an angry voice, looking at the director menacingly.

But the director's patience had come to an end, and he replied forcefully, "I am tired of trying to win your friendship. I will report your actions to the government and they will send the rangers[2] to punish you. Now do as you please, but don't show yourself here as an enemy again!"

At this, he turned his back to Kateumsi, who left but maintained a proud bearing to his gait.

"That is a miserable scoundrel," observed Bickel. "Maybe Burg's idea to blow him out of the saddle wasn't so dumb after all."

"No, no my dear Bickel," said the director. "When he sees that he can't accomplish anything by his scurrilous behavior, he will come around to a different point of view. You will see; in the end he will want peace." With this, the two moved over to the *Verein* office.

Hardly an hour had passed when Burg burst in and said, "Kateumsi is riding up with bags and packs." The director, along with his officials, stepped out of the gate, and also the militia had taken notice and assembled as Kateumsi approached with his warriors behind him, followed closely by the women, children, and pack animals. He rode up to the *Verein* compound, and his warriors formed up behind him while the others gathered in the plaza behind them.

"The scoundrels all have their bows strung," Burg called to the director.

"What do you mean coming here with strung bows?" the director yelled angrily at the chief, walking out close to Kateumsi's horse as warriors rode up closely on both sides of the director.

"I ask you once more, will you give me the good presents, or not?" Kateumsi answered harshly.

At this moment, Bickel grabbed the director by the arm and pulled him quickly from the midst of the Indians with the words, "Watch out, *Herr Direktor*, the scoundrels are up to no good." At this, the director took note of the gunner, Conrad Wissemann, who had hurried past him with the slow fuse, which had been lit.

"Don't load the shrapnel; fire off a blank, Conrad!"

"I ask once more, will you hand over the presents?" cried Kateumsi in an even more threatening voice, when, suddenly, fire shot out of the cannon near the *Verein* buildings; the concussion from its discharge shook the air, and clouds of smoke from the gunpowder rolled over the plaza among the Indians.

Startled out of their wits, the Indians scurried to and fro among themselves as if the earth had opened up to swallow them. The horses and mules began to pitch, knocking against one another and scattering their loads. Not wanting to be left behind, here a wife, there a child, clung desperately to the mane of their animal. All the while, a desperate outcry arose from the bewildered mass, as if Judgment Day had descended.

In a few short moments, the confused throng of terrified Indians emerged from the clouds of gun smoke and scattered headlong among the oaks without a backward glance—men, women, and children, and behind them the loose horses and mules—as if an evil spirit were hard on their heels.

"They won't be back soon," shouted Bickel, joining in the riotous laughter that had broken out among the men, drowning out all speech, until finally the director put an end to it with the remark: "I'm afraid we will see them again sooner than we might hope; we need to be on constant guard if we want to prevent a nasty incident."

The cannon shot had summoned all the men to their houses, and they soon came running up to the *Verein* compound, weapons in hand, where they were informed about what had happened. The director used the opportunity to make them aware of the danger now threatening the town, and he admonished them in the strongest terms not to venture from the town unarmed. He concluded by authorizing the militia to shoot Kateumsi on sight should they encounter him.

Neither hide nor hair was seen of Kateumsi, however. In fact, there was no sign of any Indian. It was if they had vanished from the whole region. Innumerable and immense herds of buffalo were now wandering the trackless prairies to the north. The southern bands had followed them there to live in plenty from their fat and meat and to store away winter provisions as well as to gather a supply of hides from which to make teepees and countless other items.

The citizens of Friedrichsburg, however, had grown more cautious and no longer left the city unarmed, and when they had to venture far out, as was often the case when their cows had strayed, they always traveled in parties. Everyone made sure to keep their weapons in serviceable condition and ready for use at a moment's notice. Moreover, they kept ample ammunition on hand.

The *Verein* militia also took measures to be more cautious. Instead of the usual practice of two men driving the horses out in the morning a mile or two to graze during the day, they now took eight or ten men with the animals. They were also much more diligent and punctual about keeping their nighttime watches.

In addition, the cannon was no longer loaded with a blank; it now had a full charge and was loaded with a canister of grapeshot.

But nothing happened to interfere with the quiet and security of the settlement. The town continued to grow; hardly a week passed without another party of new immigrants arriving from Braunfels, and the established settlers used this period after the harvest to improve their homes and gardens.

The fall had arrived, and it was time for the large communal field to be divided into individual plots among the settlers who had worked it. The director had the field surveyed into the appropriate number of portions, and the day arrived for those entitled to receive their shares by lottery.

It was one of those beautiful, southern fall mornings where all of creation appeared refreshed and recharged, and any man who sensed his own vitality flowing through his veins was drawn out into the open air, to the forest, and to the hills. The lush green fields were still gilded with blossoms; the rocky hilltops still adorned with colorful flowers, shimmering like precious stones, and the forests still had not yet been robbed of their thick foliage and their mysterious dark recesses. But the more tender species, the vines and climbing plants, had changed their leaf color, and these gracefully entwined garlands now hung weightlessly from branch to branch and from tree to tree, like gold and purple arabesques, swaying gently in the fresh morning air.

The sky had taken on its deepest, most transparent blue, and the rays of the sun no longer singed; instead, they cast a gentle golden glow upon the hills and valleys, forests and fields. It was a festival of creation and a festive day for the citizens of Friedrichsburg. Old and young alike had followed the director out to the communal cornfield in order to be present for the lottery, which involved most of the families in the town.

Also, Major Nimanski could resist neither the charm of the morning nor the persuasion of his friend Wildhorst, and, along with his long pipe, had hiked out arm in arm with the colonel to the field. The two had each taken their revolvers along.

"You should also come along, Ludwina; it is such a fine day outside," the major said to his daughter before he left to join his friend Wildhorst.

"The field is no longer pretty, dear father, and all the people will be thinking only about the lottery, which doesn't fit in somehow with Mother Nature's festive mood," answered Ludwina with an intense and happy expression. "I want to enjoy the morning to the fullest, especially from the hills, where you can look across our valley far out into the blue distance. It is so lovely up there, and it has been too long since I have been there."

"My dear girl, certainly you don't plan to go there by foot?" asked the major.

"No, dear father, I will let you in on a secret. I have already tied up your pony behind the house and intend to saddle and ride him. But please, don't say anything to Rudolph about it. You know how he is. He will see a thousand spooks."

With these words, Ludwina put her arms around her father's neck and offered her mouth tenderly for a kiss.

"Well then, ride in God's name. Be vigilant, my child, and don't stay away too long," replied Nimanski. Then he hurried off to the colonel, whom he joined on the way to the cornfield. He had hardly left the house before Ludwina latched the door, saddled the pony, and, accompanied by her large hound, rode away. Her destination was one of the highest points, barely a mile to the north of the town, from where one had an unrestricted panoramic view that encompassed not only the valley of Friedrichsburg to the south but also a similar valley lying farther to the north.

CHAPTER 11

The War Party • The Flight • The Storm • The Heroine • The Prisoner
The Honored One • The Triumphal Procession • The Grateful Indian
Undisturbed Tranquility • The Pleasure Trip • Good Advice
Freedom from Care • Charming Night Camp

*A*S LUDWINA SLOWLY followed the twisting path that led up the high hill, a large war party was on the move in the hills a few miles to the north. It was close to two hundred Indians, equipped for war. At their head rode Kateumsi on his black steed.

Silently they rode in single file along the narrow buffalo path into the valley below, and only after they had reached the lush, grass-covered banks of a meandering stream did Kateumsi rein in his horse and gather his warriors around him.

"Let your horses graze; the sun is not yet high enough," he said as he dismounted. Then he stretched out on the green bank and his men settled down around him.

After a while, he continued in a loud voice, "Only after the sun is high will the palefaces be at work, and many will leave the city. Then the time for our revenge will be at hand and also the time when we will take our presents for ourselves. Kateumsi knows where they are stored. In the house near where the whites have set up the big thunder gun that they use to put fear and anxiety in

Ludwina fires the cannon. Drawing by James C. Kearney.

the hearts of the Comanches with its great blast; there lie the presents we want. But the thunder gun will not put fear in our hearts anymore; it can't do us any harm since no ball comes flying out of it; it only thunders. Only old wives need be frightened by it."

At this, Kateumsi fell silent and let his gaze, keen as a falcon, wander across the valley. Then, after a short pause, he continued: "You will follow me to the house where the presents are stored and kill every white that your weapons can reach. The chiefs of the whites live in the house, and once we have taken their scalps and the presents we want, we will move from house to house, kill the men, and take the pretty white women with us. Kateumsi gives them all to you; only one he claims for himself. Her eye resembles the blue sky when it peers through the dark clouds, her skin is whiter than the snow on the mountains, she is lovelier than a moonlit night in the heat of summer, and prettier than the antelope on the prairie.

Once again the chief paused and withdrew into his thoughts. Then he looked around once more and up to the hills; after a while he continued: "You will receive richer presents than all the other Comanches put together because you will find them in every house. But the main thing is to kill the chiefs first. No more palefaces shall be allowed to live in these hills, and where their houses stand, the buffalo will graze once again. Kateumsi will also lead you to the other new American city and make a sacrifice of it to the Fire God. In that place, there are even more pretty women to warm your hearts."

Kateumsi continued to search the countryside as he spoke. Suddenly, as if shocked, he jumped up, and, shading his eyes with his hand, focused his gaze intently for several moments on the highest hill rising between this valley and Friedrichsburg.

All the warriors directed their looks to the hill, where a female figure appeared on horseback. "She has seen us—she is fleeing!" called out Kateumsi in a wild voice. "Forward! She can't reach the city before we do!" With this, he rushed to his horse and swung onto its back. All of his followers did the same, and as if carried by the winds of a storm, they sped off headlong in the direction of the high hill.

It was Ludwina who had reached the high point. Her first sight was of the Indians in the valley below, and she saw right away that they had spied her and were scurrying for their horses. Without a moment's hesitation, she wheeled her horse around and, filled with apprehension, forced him into a gallop down the hillside toward the town.

As soon as she reached the level plain, however, she gave her pony full rein and, urging him on with her quirt, brought him to a full run, storming past her house and into San Saba *Straße*.

"Indians—Indians!" she cried out with all the force of her voice at the houses to the left and to the right, and the people she encountered retreated quickly into their houses, locking doors and shutters.

In a couple of minutes, Ludwina reached the *Verein* compound, where she turned into the courtyard and yelled with all her might, "Indians—Indians!" But nobody came out to see what the commotion was about except the cook, the female servants, and a tailor by the name of Zinke, who, trembling, grabbed the reins of her horse as she sprang from the saddle.

"Where are the guards?" she cried out, horrified, looking around to see if she could find someone to help.

"They are all out at the field," answered the tailor with a quivering voice. At this, Ludwina did not hesitate a second longer. She rushed into the kitchen, grabbed a poker from the stove, and with her left hand grabbed the tailor by the shirt and jerked him out the door in the direction of the cannon with the words, "You are coming with me!"

"The cannon must be fired off as a signal for the men to come," she said to the tailor. "You have to fire it!"

"Not for the world, *Fräulein!* I wouldn't know how if my life depended on it," Zinke cried out, horror-struck. Ludwina, however, had quickly taken the slow fuse from the cannon box, ignited it with the red-hot poker, and removed the leather covering from the cannon. At this moment the blood-curdling war cry of the Indians sounded from the far end of San Saba *Straße* and a cloud of dust swirled up high in the air behind them.

Ludwina was just at the point of touching the slow fuse to the flash vent when she heard the wild war cry. She grabbed the tailor, who wanted to flee, by the shirt, and yelled at him in a commanding voice, "Turn the gun around quickly, point it down the street, and aim it at those charging Indians!"

Poised and firm, Ludwina remained standing alone next to the cannon, cold as ice but strong as iron, resolutely watching the frightful pack of approaching riders, who, pressed together horse on horse by the narrowness of the street, charged forward with a hellish howl.

Ludwina did not tremble. She held the smoldering fuse steady over the powder and stared with wide-open eyes at the onrushing barbarians until they were barely a hundred steps in the distance.

She recognized Kateumsi on the black stallion at the head of the charging mass. She glanced down at the cannon and touched the fuse to the powder vent, saw the flash, felt the blast, and fell unconscious to the ground.

The effect of the detonation was catastrophic: the grapeshot had spread out to cover the entire width of the street and had concentrated in the densely packed troop of riders whose entire forward row, both man and beast, struck full force by the iron hailstorm, fell crashing to the earth. But the iron shot had carried death and destruction through the whole throng as far as the last rider, so that a good fifty of the Indians had been killed, wounded, or robbed of their mounts.

Kateumsi's black stallion, struck in the forehead, tumbled head over heels into the dust, launching his rider over him into the dirt; but Kateumsi, also wounded and terrified, quickly gathered himself up and sprang into the confused mass of his companions, where he threw himself on the back of one of the riderless horses.

"Flee—flee—save yourselves!" he cried out with such desperation that it could be heard over the death cries and tumult of the Indians, while casting one last glance back at the cloud of smoke, which obscured the cannon.

"Away from the thunder gun!" he yelled again and spurred his horse into the milling swarm of riders whose horses were rearing, pitching, and running into one another, first this way and then that, so that for a moment the horde appeared to be wedged in the street.

But finally the last row had turned and the entire mob stormed back down the road in complete disorder at a full run in order to escape the killing field, even as from the left and right individual shots were fired off at them.

The cloud of smoke had drifted away; a deathly silence had descended over the area; and next to the lethal cannon, the virgin-heroine lay motionless on the ground.

The horseless Indians who were still ambulatory had scurried away, while the dead and severely wounded lay among the horses struck by the grapeshot, many of which were struggling in pain and seeking to right themselves.

No one, however, came to Ludwina's aid, for the women and the tailor had hidden themselves in the *Verein* office and expected at any moment to be discovered by the Indians.

Barely ten minutes had elapsed before the men of Friedrichsburg came storming back from the field with Rudolph at their head. He ran right past the gate of the *Verein* buildings on his way to Ludwina's house.

But making a sideward glance toward the cannon, he saw his bride lying senseless. With a cry of horror he rushed to her, threw himself down next to her, and took her frantically in his arms.

A deep sigh came from the breast of the senseless young woman, her pale lips moved, and from under her long, barely parted eyelashes, her eyes peered out with a faded gaze, as if awakening from a dream.

"Ludwina—my angel, Ludwina!" cried Rudolph, filled with fresh hope, and held her upright in his arms. Ludwina, however, buried her face in his breast and nestled in his arms, limp and depleted.

They still had not been noticed by anyone else, for the carnage in the street was the focus of attention. Pistol and rifle shots put merciful ends to the severely wounded Indians and horses that were still alive.

Without comprehending what had really taken place, the young people ran from the area to their homes. Then the old men came with their wives and children, and Rudolph stepped forward from around the *Verein* building to meet them, guiding Ludwina with his arms.

At this moment, the director hurried out of the gate with the tailor Zinke and exclaimed to Ludwina, "Is it possible, *Fräulein*? You—you have saved us; have saved the entire city?"

Ludwina, however, could not answer; a hint of a smile came over her pale features, and half-carried by Rudolph, she reached the dining hall.

The director was still occupied trying to revive her and get her strength back when her father came storming into the room, took his child in his arms, and gave free rein to his tears.

"Is it true, Ludwina? Did you save the city from these monsters? Did you fire off the cannon?" asked the old man, overcome by his own relief and happiness.

"I hardly know myself," replied Ludwina, as she began to come to her senses. "I found no one here willing to fire the cannon, so I had to do it myself. The charging Indians with Kateumsi at their head were already in sight and massed in front of me when I touched the fuse to the powder. I saw the flash but didn't hear the report.

"You, my brave child," her father said as he kissed and hugged her.

"Have the Indians run away, then?"

"In the face of such a fusillade, even the cavalry would have retreated," replied the overjoyed Colonel von Wildhorst, who had just stepped into the room and gripped Ludwina's hand. "I have never in my life seen grapeshot more deadly; the rascals and their horses are lying there by the row."

"My God, have I killed so many humans, then?" interjected Ludwina anxiously, folding her hands.

"And you have rescued us all by doing it," replied the colonel. "You have saved all of Friedrichsburg. The scoundrels would not have left a house standing."

After a short while, Ludwina had completely recovered and, to the astonishment of all, related the complete story of what had happened. The people were still questioning her about the chain of events when Burg opened the door and showed an Indian, whom he held firmly by the pigtails.

"Here, I bring you another one of the rascals, *Herr Direktor*," he said jubilantly. "Shall I put an end to him?"

"No, no, Burg, lock him up and put a watch over him so that nobody does him any harm. He will be of great value to me. Is he wounded?" asked Schubbert.

"Just a little," replied Burg. "He caught one in the hind leg, but the bone is intact. If he hadn't been wounded, I would never have caught him. The scoundrel can run like a rabbit." Then Burg turned to his captive and led him away by the pigtails with the words: "Come along, you red rascal!"

Before Ludwina could leave the *Verein* building, practically the whole population of Friedrichsburg had gathered at the door in order to catch a glimpse of their savior and express their appreciation. All her close acquaintances, however, pressed forward to her in the room, one after the next, to give heartfelt expression to their overflowing feelings of gratitude, while outside the hurrahs of the crowd continued.

The paleness had disappeared from the countenance of the young heroine, color had returned to her cheeks, and happiness and joy shone from her sparkling eyes as she arose to take the path to her home.

"I had your pony led to the gate, *Fräulein* Nimanski," the friendly quartermaster said to her, "because if you tried to go by foot, you wouldn't be able to make it in an hour; the people would never be done with you."

"Really, I prefer to walk," answered Ludwina, embarrassed.

"No, *Fräulein*, our dear *Herr* Bickel is right," the director interrupted. "Ride. You came by horse to save us all and the town, and by horse you ought to leave this place which bore witness to your courageous deed. Also Rudolph, and especially your father, insists that you should ride." Schubbert added enthusiastically, "It is an appropriate and just reward to hold a triumphal procession on horseback, and we shall serve as your honor guard."

Though reluctant to show herself to the persistent crowd, especially mounted, she finally acquiesced to the decision and was led outside and lifted up on her pony.

No sooner, however, had the people in the street caught sight of her than they broke out in a storm of hurrahs and crowded forward at the gate of the *Verein* compound. Each wanted to be the first to greet her and yell out his thanks.

Ludwina pulled up before the jubilant crowd. Words, she had none, but tears of joy aplenty; and as the tears streamed from beneath her long lashes like liquid pearls, she let her humbled gaze wander from eye to eye and with both hands waved greetings and returned thanks to her fellow citizens.

For a long time all efforts by the town officials to clear a path for her through the excited throng were in vain, until finally the director stepped forward and led the way, and she was able to resume her ride to her home accompanied by numerous and continuous cries of appreciation.

The street had been cleared of the bodies of the dead Indians, but their blood had stained the ground over which the heroine rode, and she looked sadly down at the scarlet traces and at the many dead horses through which her path wound.

The party moved up San Saba *Straße*. Old and young alike joined in the parade to be near the celebrated young woman, and with a thunderous farewell, took their leave when she finally entered her own house.

The tragic event was extremely important for Friedrichsburg because their dangerous enemy had been taught a lesson that he would not soon forget, and he would surely never attempt an open assault on the town again. Still, one could assume that the turn of events had inflamed his hatred to an even fiercer and deadlier pitch, so that individual townspeople had to be even more on their guard against him. The population as a whole, however, no longer felt a general existential threat from Kateumsi.

In order to make one more effort to soften the hostility of the renegade chief, the director decided to use their captive as a tool. Although he held him bound and closely guarded, still he took measures to ensure that his needs were fully satisfied and that he was treated kindly and humanely. He ordered ample food be sent over for his nourishment and undertook the treatment of his wound himself. The director spoke with the prisoner at length daily and attempted to assure him that he was a friend of all Comanches and that Kateumsi had no justification for remaining hostile to him.

The Indian, whose name was Potolick, grew friendlier and more trusting from day to day. After the director had completely restored him to health in a few weeks, he gave him a bow and arrows and also a tomahawk and knife from one of his dead comrades. He also outfitted him with provisions and some gifts and, finally, gave him a mule with which he could undertake the ride back to his tribe. Potolick took his leave with a heartfelt expression of gratitude, and with the assurance that he would never again take up weapons against the palefaces.

Peace and security now seemed to be assured for Friedrichsburg. Nothing was seen or heard of the Indians for several months. People freely traversed the road back and forth from Braunfels to Friedrichsburg by wagon, horse, or foot without encountering any problems. Nobody seemed concerned anymore, and the road to Austin grew livelier by the day. Goods of all sorts were now procured from there; cattle were driven up for slaughter, and it was no longer unusual to see single riders traveling the road.

Gradually, people became convinced that Kateumsi, through whose territory the road crossed, must have abandoned the region, or had decided to live in peace with the whites, because he allowed all riders to cross the area undisturbed. It was in the first days of December when the director gave Rudolph the job of delivering a timely and important dispatch to Braunfels, a task which he entrusted to no one else.

The anxiety which had overcome Ludwina on earlier occasions had now disappeared due to the constant, undisturbed intercourse with Braunfels. Since it was a beautiful morning when Rudolph started out on his ride, Ludwina and her father accompanied him as far as the Pedernales.

After lunch, Nimanski was sitting with his daughter on the veranda in front of the house with coffee and calculating how long it would be before Rudolph returned, when they saw his father walking toward them over the grassy field. Both went out to meet him, greeted him heartily, and invited him to share coffee with them. Ludwina quickly filled a cup and supplied him with a cigar.

"I come to entrust you with the oversight of my castle for a few days," continued the colonel, after he had securely lit his cigar. "I am riding to Austin for a few days and could pick up a few things for you there if you would like."

"To Austin?" asked the major, somewhat surprised. "What moved you to do that?"

"I just heard that former lieutenant Calden[1] from Hanover and the merchant Krebs[2] are riding there and intend to take along a *Verein* rifleman, and since I am in need of purchasing several things, especially sugar, coffee, cigars, and tobacco, I thought I might find a better selection and better prices in Austin. And now that Rudolph is away, you will need to take over the defense of my fortress should the Indians mount an attack," exclaimed the colonel cheerfully as he wiped his moustache to the side and shoved the cigar between his lips once again.

"My dear old comrade-in-arms, just be careful that the Indians don't mount an attack on you. They won't start anything here; that is out of the question now," continued Nimanski as he turned to Ludwina. "Isn't that the case, my dear? You took the wind from their sails in that regard."

"The road to Austin is traveled almost daily now, and for months now no one has been bothered," replied Wildhorst. "Besides, it is out of the question. There are four of us, and my scalp won't do them any good: there is hardly any hair left on it and they are supposed to be deferential to white hair."

"Well, I wouldn't want to entrust my fate to their opinions about hair. Tastes vary, and too much would be left to chance," the major replied light-heartedly. "But in all seriousness, Wildhorst, I wouldn't expose myself to any unnecessary danger. You could place your orders with Krebs, the merchant, and it would be worth it even if it costs you a few dollars more. It is a long, strenuous ride."

"That's just what I want. I need to feel horseflesh under me again; I need to keep up my equestrian skills. Also, the ride we made to Austin some time ago was such a pleasure that I have been looking for an opportunity to repeat it."

"Well, I have to say to you, old friend, I believe we both sleep a lot more comfortably in our own beds than on the ground out under God's open sky," remarked Nimanski with a smile. He continued in a serious tone, "You should follow my advice, Wildhorst, and stay here. That way you won't catch your death of cold and neither will you run the risk of losing your scalp."

"Nonsense—it's no longer dangerous and the ride will do me good. If I can get you something there I will be glad to do it."

"What do you think, Ludwina? We probably could use some coffee and sugar," said Nimanski to his daughter.

"Well, you think about what you might need and jot it down on a slip of paper," suggested the colonel. "That way, I won't forget anything. Bring it to me at my house in an hour or so. We are not departing until evening time, and I have several things to take care of before then."

With these words the colonel stood up, kissed Ludwina farewell, offered the major his hand, and headed off at a youthful gait down San Saba *Straße* in the direction of the *Verein* buildings.

When he arrived at the office, the director approached him with the words, "Is it really true, my dear *Herr Obrist*,[3] that you intend to ride to Austin?"

"Yes, I have decided on it, *Herr Direktor*; I enjoyed our last trip to Austin too much. If you have any kind of job for me, it would be my pleasure to oblige you," replied the colonel.

"The only thing I will burden you with is a couple of letters," replied Schubbert. He then continued, "As I hear, Calden and Krebs are riding along with you, and both have requested that I allow one of our riflemen to accompany them. Just make sure that you are well armed."

"I am taking both of my revolvers; hopefully, we will not need any more shots than that," remarked the colonel.

"And no rifle!" interjected the director, surprised.

"It is too uncomfortable to take along while riding," replied Wildhorst.

"What did you say, uncomfortable?" said Schubbert. "Truly, it seemed comfortable enough when Kateumsi and his band of warriors attacked us. Take your rifle along! You couldn't offer me enough to travel to Austin armed only with revolvers."

"Bah! Nobody is thinking about Indians anymore, so many people are coming and going over this road now," replied the colonel, and asked the director once again if he could do anything for him.

"We are riding around five o'clock so that we can spend the night with the Mormons," he said as he took his leave, and remarked that he would stop back by to pick up the letters and any other requests that the director might have.

In the company of Nimanski and his daughter, Colonel von Wildhorst arrived at the office of the *Verein* at the predetermined time, leading his horse behind him. His travel companions had already gathered there to await him and were engaged in conversation with the director and the quartermaster.

"Well then, no rifle after all!" Schubbert called out to the colonel. "I assure you in all seriousness that it is not a very prudent thing to do. I have never seen riders on the frontier more poorly armed. Lieutenant Calden has only a single-shot musket; Krebs is carrying a bird gun, as if he were going on a pheasant shoot; while you, my dear *Herr Obrist*, only have revolvers along, as if you were going out for target practice. Our militiaman, Kracke,[4] is the only one among you who is sufficiently armed."

"Do I not have twelve shots with which I can hit a target at fifty paces just as well as with a rifle?" replied the colonel, smiling.

"That is perhaps true when you are shooting at a target, *Herr Obrist*, but not necessarily the case if you should meet a savage who is keen on taking your scalp and who can easily put an arrow through your body at a hundred paces. Do me a favor and take along a double-barreled rifle from one of our rifle-men," replied the director in all seriousness.

"Truly, *Herr Direktor*, it is too much of a nuisance; I am willing to wager my scalp, and if push comes to shove, I will mount a full-fledged cavalry charge. You have not taken notice of my saber. It is never in need of reloading and it is always ready for service," answered Wildhorst with an air of youthful reckless-ness, tapping on the sword[5] which he had hung under his coat.

"Well, if you think you can deflect arrows with your sword, then I will let the matter drop, but just remember, any Indian would be more than happy to take on someone with a sword," remarked the director, who then handed over to the colonel a packet of letters for various merchants in Austin with the request to deliver them at their respective addresses.

Thereupon the colonel took his leave from his friend Nimanski and from Ludwina, bid farewell to the director and his officials, mounted his horse, and galloped off to catch up with his companions, who had already gained a lead of several hundred paces. It was already close to dark when the riders reached the Mormon settlement. Here they prepared to spend the night on the green, grassy bank of the Pedernales next to the mill, for the evening was mild and pleasant to such a degree that none would have exchanged the star-studded heavenly tent for a shelter made by the hand of man.

The crescent of the new moon had already begun to cast its dim light on the thunderous rapids streaming past them below, conjuring forth a magical spectacle of thousands of shimmering lights that seemed to be dancing on the wild and frothy surf. Meanwhile, their campfire glowed red, its flames dancing merrily over the embers, sizzling and popping, while spraying out a shower of sparks all around. After coffee had been boiled and the supper they had brought along consumed, each took out his pipe or cigar, as preferred, and found his place around the fire. A lively conversation added to their enjoyment of this magnificent night.

"An uninterrupted stay in the open air truly has a rejuvenating effect on an old body such as mine, a body worn down by too many stresses and strains," observed the colonel as he stretched out comfortably before the fire. "In the last years I spent in Germany, never did I feel so healthy and invigorated as I do here, where I am out of doors most of the time. It is really a magnificent land. The crowded housing in Germany robs people of health, deprives them of joy, and shortens their life spans from what they ought to be."

"With its ever-fluctuating cold and damp weather, how could people in Germany live in such open dwellings as are customary here, where the wind blows through the joints and cracks?" asked Lieutenant Calden, a handsome young man with a gentlemanly bearing.

"Certainly, it is this wonderfully mild climate that renders practically every house unnecessary here," observed the colonel as he looked around. "Such a night is unknown in Germany."

As he spoke, a gentle breeze seemed to be playing with the flames of the fire and whispering overhead through the leaves of the surrounding trees, and all the while the swooshing and roaring of the nearby waterfall provided an incessant counterpoint to the stillness of the moonlit night. The lights in the nearby Mormon settlement went out; the horses of the four denizens of Friedrichsburg bedded down in the lush grass; and the men themselves sank lower on their saddles and closed their eyes.

CHAPTER 12

Careless · Cry of Terror · Scalping · The Flight · Ruse · The Return
The Death Notice · Sympathy · Funeral Procession · Heavy Gait
Notification · Ill Foreboding · The Hearse · Composure

*N*OTHING DISTURBED THE delightful sleep of the wayfarers. They awoke refreshed and renewed with the first greying of the dawn. Breakfast was soon prepared and consumed and, even as a light rain began to fall, the four riders were already mounted and trotting happily along the valley floor between the high hills.

The men kept their horses to a lively gait for the whole morning but rested them in the heat of the afternoon under the shade of giant oak trees next to a clear stream. Thereafter, they continued their journey at a brisk pace in order to make evening camp in a timely fashion. The sun still stood over the high hills as they rode down the valley toward the wooded area where, when they were first surveying the road, Burg and Kracke had shot a couple of buffalo and where Colonel von Wildhorst had so wanted to set up camp.

The ambush. Drawing by James C. Kearney.

"Just for fun, this time let's stay here below and camp among these splendid oaks," said the colonel after they had reached the oak grove. "Earlier, the director was of the opinion that a party of Indians could be concealed in the nearby thicket waiting to ambush us."[1]

"Well, *Herr Obrist*, it wouldn't be impossible, and the oaks here are barely sixty paces distant from the thicket," interrupted Kracke cautiously.

"You, young man, are you also seeing spooks? I'll take full responsibility. Let's stay here, gentlemen. The grass is much better for our horses than on top of the hill up there," noted the colonel. He rode his horse under the oak canopy, where he pulled up and dismounted with the remark, "A nicer camping place I have never seen."

His companions followed his lead, albeit somewhat reluctantly. Only Kracke remained in his saddle.

"Hand me the reins of your horses, then. I will lead them to the stream and water them. I see a good place to do it below, at the edge of the woods."

"Good. In the meantime, we will start a fire," said the colonel to Calden and Krebs. All three handed the reins of their horses over to Kracke, who rode off with the weary animals in tow.

The three men placed their saddlebags, coats, and weapons at the foot of one of the oaks, and the colonel gathered some dry kindling with which to start a fire. He then took out his striker from his pocket and called to his companions, "Fetch some firewood, gentlemen; the kindling will soon be lit."

He had just knelt down by the fire, and Calden and Krebs had begun gathering dead limbs from the ground, when, suddenly, the dreaded war cry of the Indian pierced them to the core. Frightened out of their wits, they looked up to see a host of savages converging on them from the nearby thicket. They rushed for their weapons. The colonel attempted to aim a revolver at a charging foe, but before he could discharge his weapon, a shower of arrows came swishing swiftly in his direction. Three of the deadly shafts found their mark, penetrating deeply into his breast.

Simultaneously, Calden was able to fire off one shot from his rifle before he, too, collapsed, mortally wounded. Krebs attempted to flee, but he was also struck by arrows and fell to the earth.

Barely had the howl of the Indians reached the ears of Kracke, who was leading the horses toward water at a leisurely pace, when, startled, he turned around just in time to see the colonel lift his revolver, only to sink to the ground at practically the same instant as Calden.

He also saw Krebs collapse and quickly recognized Kateumsi, who, at the head of the wild troop, was rushing ferociously toward the fallen men like a tiger on his prey.

Kracke remained frozen for only a split second by the spectacle of his companions engulfed in the swarm of Indians before he dropped the reins of the horses he was leading and put the spurs and quirt to his mount, urging him forward at a full run toward the road and back down the same path they had just come.

Away he flew with such speed on the fleet-footed animal down the valley and up the next hill that rocks and sparks shot out from his hooves. Without a thought of resting him, he continued spurring his horse forward over hill and dale at a breakneck pace. His first thought had been that he could only save himself by the speed of his horse. That the Indians would be quick to follow him—of this, he was certain.

The added exertion, however, quickly sapped the animal's energy. Thoroughly winded, his mount was incapable of topping the next hill at a full gallop. The realization struck Kracke that with their fresh mounts the Indians would quickly overtake him. He had to abandon his horse; otherwise, he was lost.

At the same time, however, he had to divert the eagle eyes of the savages from his trail; while considering how best to do this, he topped the crest of the next hill.

He sprang quickly from his mount, untied his saddlebags, wound a rope around the middle of them, and tied to the short end of the rope two cooking pots and the small pan that he carried for drinking, boiling, and frying.

Then he bound the other end to the tail of his horse so that the leather bags and the metal containers would drag behind him on the ground. After removing bridle and saddle, he lashed his horse across the rump as hard as he could with his quirt, causing him to bolt forward in shocked surprise.

But no sooner had the noble animal heard the clattering of the containers and seen the saddlebags sailing behind him than he tore off for the road, leading downhill as if carried by the wind, continuing over the next rise, where he disappeared from view of his rider, who remained behind.

Kracke quickly gathered up his saddle and gear and hurried off in the direction of a thorn thicket, where he concealed himself in a pile of loosely strewn boulders.

He had scarcely reached his hideout and turned his ear in the direction of his expected pursuers when hoofbeats of running horses became audible. Seconds later, Kateumsi topped the rise at a full charge, followed closely by his fearful band, all hard on the trail of the riderless horse. As they sailed past, Kracke noticed that Kateumsi was riding the red stallion with white mane and tail which the director had persuaded the Delawares to return.

Kracke quickly climbed the highest rocky outcrop and, breathing heavily, watched for as long as they stayed in sight the dark figures of the Indians with long hair flying behind, cyclone-like, swiftly traversing the broken terrain that spread out below him.

Then he grabbed his weapons and hurried off in the direction of the adjoining valley, where he could find a stream that he knew would lead him to the Pedernales. The sun had disappeared and the light of the moon now assumed mastery over the earth.

Restlessly, Kracke wandered through the uncharted barrens, over loose stones and across swampy meadows, through thorny thickets and heavily wooded areas. More than once he was startled by fleeing game, or the sudden mocking cry of a hoot owl, or the howl of a pack of passing wolves on the hunt, but he continued pressing forward with his rifle cocked and ready to shoot, finally reaching the rocky channel of the Pedernales just as the last rays of the moon gave way to the approaching dawn. Exhausted by the effort, and even more so by the thought of the horrible fate of his companions, he sank down in a thicket under a tree and fell into a deep sleep. But shortly thereafter, a flock of wild turkeys that had found a roost in the tree over his head startled him awake. He bolted upright and reached for his rifle, but nothing but the wildly raging surf of the passing water disturbed the tranquility of the night.

Morning broke and the sun's light crept forward over the earth as Kracke resumed his journey upstream, following the bank of the river. As he traveled, he consumed all the food that he had brought along in his knapsack; he pressed forward without resting the whole day long, until the sun finally set, and once again he sought refuge in a thicket along the river, there to spend the night. Close by he shot a deer and prepared an evening meal from the venison, and then lay down to rest and await the new morning.

When morning came, without knowing for sure when he would come again into an area that he recognized, he trekked onward the whole day and as the sun began to bend low, he once again began looking around for a secure refuge to spend the night, when suddenly the channel of the river opened up to reveal the Mormon settlement in front of him. With renewed energy, he doubled his pace, reaching the house of Mr. Grey just as the sun was about to set. Mr. Grey listened to Kracke's account of the horrible turn of events with genuine sympathy and was more than willing to oblige his request for a mount with which to ride back to Friedrichsburg.

It was around nine o'clock when he arrived back in town and directed his horse through the gate into the courtyard of the *Verein* compound. The sentinels who were sitting around the campfire there had heard the approaching rider and were watching for him, but jumped up in shocked surprise when they saw that it was Kracke.

"My God, Kracke, is it you?" Burg called out to him, suspecting that something had gone terribly wrong.

"Where is the director?" asked Kracke urgently as he quickly dismounted.

"With *Herr* Bickel in the office," answered Burg as he grabbed Kracke by the arm. "So speak, Kracke! You look like you've just received a death sentence!"

Kracke, however, turned quickly away from him and his other comrades without replying and hurried into the house. When he opened the door, he saw the director and the quartermaster seated at a desk, both dumbfounded to see him and calling out as with one voice, "My God, Kracke!"

In the same instant, both jumped up to greet him, and the director asked in shocked surprise, "Has something bad happened, Kracke?"

"Something terrible, *Herr Direktor*," answered the rifleman, his voice trembling.

"For God's sake, tell me what happened—where are the others?"

"Dead!" replied Kracke.

"Dead?" repeated Schubbert and Bickel in shocked surprise, momentarily staring speechless and aghast at the bearer of the horrible news, as if their thoughts refused to comprehend the immensity of the calamity.

"Dead, did you say, Kracke?" the director finally muttered. "That is dreadful! For God's sake, how did it happen?"

At this, Kracke related the entire chain of events in detail. As he did, the director repeatedly called out "dreadful" or "terrible," but after Kracke had completed his report, he stood silently and motionless for a while, staring ahead as if searching for the best way to deal with the consequences of the disaster.

Then, wiping his forehead with the back of his hand, he turned to the rifleman and said, "Have you said anything to anyone else about this?"

"Not a word, *Herr Direktor*," answered Kracke.

"Good, then keep silent about it so that the terrible news will come to Nimanski's ears through no one else but me. I don't want to deprive him of his sleep and will go over to him first thing in the morning."

"And poor Rudolph!" he continued, turning to Bickel. "The blow, I fear, will be greater than he can bear with composure. What precautions can I take to prepare him for this horrific misfortune?"

"Perhaps if you send a messenger," suggested the deeply touched, goodhearted quartermaster, "you could write that his father has fallen seriously ill."

"Then he would drive himself and his horse to death trying to get back. No, I can't do that. He would spend so much time alone with the terrible uncertainty, alone with the pain and so long in despair—no, he needs to find out here, where a loving heart is close by to offer consolation. If I can only forestall the grim news spreading from here to Braunfels."

"Let me take care of that," interjected Bickel. "No one will leave here until I extract a promise of complete silence."

"He is due to return in a few days. See to it that no one allows him to ride past my house without referring him to me." After this, the director paced up and down his room a couple of times and then said to Bickel, "Get the small buckboard ready for travel; it needs to depart within the hour to fetch the corpses; Burg needs to accompany it with all the sentinels."

Then he turned to Kracke. "You need to stay behind Kracke; you are too exhausted and worn out!"

"Oh no, *Herr Direktor*, you must allow me to ride along. Truly, I feel strong enough," the rifleman implored.

"Very well then; if that's what you want, you can go along, but ask Burg to step in. He needs to know what has happened before you depart; the others can find out once you are under way."

Kracke left and Burg stepped into the room. He listened with growing horror to the report of the director and then, quite beside himself with anguish, remarked, "You see *Herr* Bickel, if you had let me shoot the scoundrel from his horse that time, then this disaster would not have taken place. May heaven grant me one more opportunity to lay eyes on him!"

"Quickly, then! Do what needs to be done so that you can depart as soon as possible," the director said, cutting him off. All then left the room in order to make the necessary preparations.

The moon was already high in the sky when the buckboard passed through the gate of the *Verein* compound, pulled by two powerful browns and followed by the entire home guard, commanded by Burg. The party stopped briefly in front of the director's house, who gave Burg more directives, and then the sad procession hastened off into the moonlit night.

The following morning the director took the path leading to Nimanski's house, with a heavy heart. The responsibility weighed heavily upon him, this sad task of delivering the grim news to the old friend of the colonel and to the fiancée of the colonel's son. But it was a task he had to perform to avoid an even more painful situation, for it surely would be even more devastating for them to discover the truth second-hand, through someone else. The closer he got to their house, the heavier his steps grew and the more anxious he became about the consequences of his task.

Ludwina had seen him coming and stepped out of the house with her father just as the director reached their gate. "Already out and about so early at this end of town, *Herr Direktor?*" Nimanski asked in greeting as he stepped out to welcome the director.

"You must be coming to bring some good news about Rudolph," added

Ludwina in anticipation, following her father out to greet the director with a broad smile.

"No, *Fräulein* Nimanski, I have heard nothing from the bridegroom; I hope he will be returning to you in a few days," the director replied, but in such a tone that his clouded spirit could not be concealed.

Ludwina looked at him with a surprised and quizzical expression on her face, but he avoided her gaze and said to the major, "I wanted to ask you a favor. Could you go down with me to the creek? I wanted to check out a possible home site. I would like to have your opinion about it."

"I'm glad to be of service," answered Nimanski as he stepped out to join the director.

Just as Schubbert turned to Ludwina to excuse himself with a slight bow, she looked him straight in the eye and asked earnestly, "It is really true then that you have received no word from Rudolph, *Herr Direktor?*"

"On my honor, *Fräulein*, I have no news at all about Rudolph," said the director as he said good-bye to the obviously concerned young lady. He then departed arm in arm with the major.

They had traversed a good hundred paces across the meadow without exchanging a word when Nimanski broke the silence. "You have something unpleasant to tell me, *Herr Direktor?* You are unusually serious and reticent this morning."

"Something very sad, *Herr* Major. Something so sad that you need to gather all your strength to hear about it."

"My God, you are frightening me," replied Nimanski as he took a quick step to the side, looking in dismay at the director. He then remarked, "Since you swore you have heard nothing from Rudolph, then the bad news must be about his father."

"I'm afraid so, honorable friend," replied the director as he fell silent once again.

"For God's sake, is Wildhorst dead?" the major cried out in horror.

"Yes, he is dead, *Herr* Major, and you must be the one to bear the news with fortitude in order to help Ludwina and Rudolph stand up to the new and terrible reality of his death," answered the director. He then proceeded to give a full account of the sad turn of events.

Nimanski was beside himself with despair, but the director admonished him about his duty toward the children, and with these words the old man began to regain his composure. His concern for the children's well-being quickly gained the upper hand over his own sense of loss and pain.

"I am not yet in a condition to stand before my child; she will be inconsolable, which would drain me to the point that I would most likely lose my self-control. Let me walk with you a little while, *Herr Direktor*, and try to digest this horrible calamity somewhat and let the reality sink in that Wildhorst, this brave and good man, is no longer alive," said Nimanski, shaken to the depths of his soul. Nimanski took Schubbert's arm again and the two walked slowly through the town toward the director's house.

Ludwina's premonition that something unpleasant, possibly something terrible, had taken place was not at all allayed by the director's assurances with respect to Rudolph. She had read his expression all too clearly. As the minutes passed by, she waited impatiently for the return of her father. Her unease and disquiet grew into a full-blown panic as the noon mealtime approached and her father still had not returned. What did the director have to say to him that was so serious?

Time and time again she ran to the window or to the door to peer out. Finally she spied him walking slowly down San Saba *Straße* in their direction. Yes, something very bad had happened—Ludwina could see it clearly in the demeanor of her father, could see by his measured and stooped gait that he was bringing news of a death.

Ludwina hurried out to meet him, wound her arm around him and asked, her voice trembling, "Tell me what has happened father. Say it straight out; the uncertainty is worse than the naked truth." The old man, however, wrapped his arm firmly around his child and continued walking with her silently through the gate and toward the house.

"For God's sake, father, the suspense is killing me! Tell me what has happened!" cried Ludwina, latching onto him with both hands and looking directly into his tear-reddened eyes.

"Nothing has happened to Rudolph," the major reassured her, regaining composure. He could not fail to notice that her lips formed a quick but silent, "Thanks be to God!"

"Thank God for that," she then cried out loud and with an audible sigh of relief. "But something bad has happened to someone. Who was it, father?" she continued, "Please tell me!"

"Next to Rudolph who stands closest to our hearts, my child?" continued the major in a soft and shaky voice.

"Oh—good God—Rudolph's father!" stammered Ludwina as a stream of tears flowed from her eyes. She cast her arms around her father's neck and, sobbing uncontrollably, buried her face in his breast. Nimanski, however, stood motionless and speechless. He held his daughter in his arms and quietly thanked the heavens for the gift of his daughter's tears, which would help her overcome her grief.

After a long pause, Ludwina unwound her arms from around her father, let her folded hands drop to her sides, and turned with a bowed head to withdraw to her room. The old man gripped her hand and restrained her with these words: "No, Ludwina, you must not be by yourself; I have to be here to speak words of encouragement because you alone are in a position to help Rudolph get past this. Only in you will he find strength and consolation sufficient to endure his pain. Otherwise, he will succumb to it. You know how moody he can be; he lives in opposites—either completely happy and carefree or thoroughly agitated and angry, and occasionally, even depressed to the point of despair. You, Ludwina—you need to stay strong. You need to be a pillar of stability for him to draw strength from; you need to prevent him from sinking into depression. Come here, my child, and sit next to me and let me tell you the whole, sad story; let us talk about it openly and you will be able to bear it easier."

With these words the major led his daughter to the bench on the porch, where they both sat down. He then related to her the major's fate, as the director had reported, but in a way that spared her the appalling details.

A mysterious silence lay over the population of Friedrichsburg. A returning hunter had passed the wagon with the home guards the previous night, and by the early morning the news had already spread through the town. The people were curious about the nocturnal expedition, and to this end found all sorts of excuses to stop by the *Verein* compound to make inquiries. A regimen of strict silence prevailed, however, which only fueled speculation and conjecture. A raft of unfounded rumors began to make the rounds.

The day, however, passed without the people receiving any explanation for the secret expedition; and then the next day had approached its conclusion without the wagon and the home guard returning.

The sun had set and a glow still hung over the western side of the town when the director stepped out from the porch of his house and looked impatiently down the road to the east. A solitary rider appeared on the road. Momentarily taken aback, Schubbert stared at him, for his first thought had been that it might be Rudolph. Soon thereafter, however, the wagon that had been dispatched emerged from the forest, followed closely by the contingent of home guards.

Burg rode ahead, and when he spotted the director he galloped forward to greet him. "We are bringing the three bodies, *Herr Direktor*," he said as he sprang from the saddle. "We saw neither hide nor hair of the Indians."

"In what condition were the corpses?" asked the director, deeply moved.

"Robbed of their clothing and horribly mutilated; all had been scalped," replied Burg.

"Tell the driver of the wagon that he should continue on without stopping to the house of Wildhorst. I will also go there right away. We will carry the colonel to his room. You stay with the home guards here and post one of them out on the street to watch for the young Wildhorst. If he should ride in, the guard is to instruct him to wait for me at my house and not to leave it before he has spoken with me."

Burg then rode back to the approaching caravan to relay the director's instructions. In the meantime, the director hurried into the *Verein* compound and reemerged with the quartermaster and several workers, just as the wagon with the bodies passed by. They all arrived together in front of the colonel's house. The two faithful servants emerged from the house, surprised and curious. The director then related to them the unfortunate story in as gentle a manner as possible. Accompanied by their weeping and wailing, their old master, whose soul had now departed him, was carried into his room and placed on his bed.

He presented a fearful sight: his scalp was missing, his skull was crushed, and his body revealed countless wounds from arrows and tomahawk blows.

The director ordered the body to be enclosed in a linen sack, had the door to the room sealed by the old servant, and enjoined the same to allow no one, whoever it might be, to pass.

The wagon had already departed to transport the other two bodies to their respective houses when the director left the house and hurried over to Nimanski to report the imminent arrival of the corpses.

He found the major composed. Ludwina, however, was bent over and tearful. They sat together in the gathering darkness of the room. The major arose to greet the director and quietly grasped his hand. After the director had explained the situation, the major spoke. "It was God's will and we should not demur. I thank you, *Herr Direktor*, for the solicitude you have shown the deceased."

At this, the director turned to Ludwina, took her hand in his own, and said in a voice that revealed the genuine depth of his concern, "You have to remain strong, *Fräulein*. Open your heart to poor Rudolph's distress and pain, so that he doesn't succumb. He might return at any moment, and he needs to hear the grim truth from your lips so that the promise of your love can offset the anguish of his loss. Be strong, *Fräulein* Ludwina, and come to the aid of your Rudolph."

With this, the young woman arose, dried her tears, pressed the hand of the director, and said after a short pause, "Yes, I will be strong and forget my own grief in the greater sorrow of Rudolph, and endeavor to replace with my love what a terrible fate has robbed from him."

With a heavy sigh, she then pressed both hands to her heart and raised her head, as if uttering a promise to the heavens. But then she continued with greater self-control, "If only Rudolph doesn't hear it first from someone else!"

"That, I will do everything in my power to prevent, *Fräulein*," the director said quickly. "Have no fear; he will come straightaway to you, because his suffering, if it comes from you, will only be a partial suffering." Then he left the bereaved and hurried toward San Saba *Straße*. When he reached it he turned around and saw that the windows had been illuminated in the Nimanski household.

CHAPTER 13

The Return Trip · Bad News · The Horror · Night of Love · Melancholy
Desire for Revenge · The Friendly Room · The Journey · The Delaware Chieftain

Rudolph views his dead father. Drawing by James C. Kearney.

*T*HE EVENING MEAL had just been set out when Schubbert returned
to the *Verein* compound. Before he entered the dining hall, however,
he reminded Burg once again that he wanted a guard posted outside
without fail until such time as the young Rudolph should return. During the
evening meal the director asked the quartermaster if he had heard of anyone
intending to travel to Braunfels. Bickel assured him that he had heard of no one
and that should anyone announce such intentions, he would be made aware of
the situation in a timely fashion.

Naturally the conversation focused almost exclusively on the tragic event.
Long after the supper dishes had been cleared, Schubbert and his officials sat
around the table absorbed in their discussions. Suddenly the director arose, listened intently a moment, and then sprang for the door with the words, "I hear
a horse!" He had not erred. He stepped out to see Rudolph riding forward,
accompanied by the sentinel who had been posted to intercept him.

The director walked toward him, and as they met in front of his house, Rudolph cheerfully announced, "Good evening, *Herr Direktor*. Does the sentinel posted to keep an eye out for me mean that you intend to have me taken prisoner?"

"My dear Wildhorst, I have something important to share with you," the director responded in a restrained but friendly tone. "Step down and come in for a minute."

Rudolph, somewhat taken aback by the unusual behavior of the director, quickly dismounted, wrapped the reins of his horse to a porch post, and followed the director inside.

There was an oil lamp on the table in Schubbert's room with the wick turned down low so that it cast a dim light over the room.

With a look of perplexed anticipation, Rudolph stood in front of the director, who placed two chairs at the table. Then, without looking up, he said to Rudolph, "Take a seat, my dear Wildhorst."

"Here are the letters from Braunfels," replied Rudolph, a bit ill at ease as he laid the dispatches down and took a seat.

The director pulled them over to his side of the table, and without opening a single one, began in a rather subdued voice, "I intended to speak with you before you rode into town because I hoped you would ride directly from here over to your fiancée's house without stopping."

"God almighty; she is not sick!" replied Rudolph apprehensively as he jumped up.

"No, my dear Wildhorst, she is not sick; she is, however, a little on the sad side and a bit out of sorts, and is anxiously awaiting your return," continued the director.

"You are giving me cause for concern, *Herr Direktor*," Rudolph responded in a quivering voice, as the color drained from his face. "May I have permission to go right away?"

"Yes, dear Wildhorst. I insist that you ride directly from here to the Nimanski household; you are urgently expected there."

"An unfortunate accident has not befallen the *Herr* Major, I hope?" Rudolph asked with growing concern, as he opened the door.

"No, Rudolph, you will find him with your future bride," said Schubbert. He took the hand of the young man and pressed it firmly and with feeling. Then he said, "The love of such a noble creature as your Ludwina is a rarity, a precious gift of the gods."

"For heaven's sake—what is going on?" Rudolph cried out, now beside himself with worry, as he rushed outside to his horse, threw himself in the saddle, and tore off at a run down San Saba *Straße*, his flight followed by the director's compassionate gaze.

He had reached the outskirts of the town. His eye searched for the house of his beloved across the grass meadow, but the reflection of the windows had faded in the moonlight. In a few short moments he spotted the trusted flicker shining across to him, and with one last mad dash his fleet-footed steed carried him to the Nimanski enclosure.

"Praise God, my Rudolph," came the precious, familiar voice of his beloved Ludwina from the porch, and, after throwing the reins over the palisade, he rushed into his beloved's arms.

"My Ludwina, thank God. I was so afraid that something had happened to you. Where is your father?" asked the young man, breathing a bit freer now, just as the major emerged from the house and stepped out on the porch, where he received Rudolph warmly and affectionately. Ludwina remained speechless but held Rudolph wrapped in her arms and led him into the house.

"You both are so quiet. What has happened, then?" Rudolph asked, his apprehension once again rising. He looked Ludwina squarely in the eyes. "You have been crying, Ludwina. Please tell me. What has happened to both of you?"

Ludwina, however, took him by the arm and led him to the sofa and then spoke to him, her whole soul in her countenance and gaze, "Will the love, the heartfelt, true love of your Ludwina suffice to help you bear the pain that has befallen you? Can it replace what you have lost?"

For only a split second Rudolph stared, paling, at the young woman; then he shook, folded his hands, and stammered through a stream of tears, "Oh my God—my poor father!" With this, he sank into himself, pressed his face in his hands, and began to weep like a child.

Ludwina also cried. She laid her arm on Rudolph's neck and pressed her cheek against his, and in this way they sat for a long time, yielding to the pain and surrendering to the beneficial and restorative power of tears.

"Oh, you good father!" Rudolph finally continued, the words spoken softly and sadly, "Why couldn't I have been by your side to close your precious eyes?"

Then he dried his eyes and made the effort to master his voice. He said to Ludwina as he drew her near, "He was so good, good to the bottom of his soul; this good, old man. And you, Ludwina; he thought so highly of you."

With this, the sobbing and tears welled up once again to drown his words; he struggled to regain composure and, after achieving it, resumed, "Has he been buried yet?"

"No, Rudolph, not yet," answered Ludwina with a quivering voice, and added softly, after a moment's silence, "It would be my hope that you could find the inner strength to resist the urge to see him one last time."

"I, not see him one last time!" cried Rudolph as another wave of tears overcame him. "Oh no! This loving, this good father. I must see him one last time."

"I'm afraid he is very changed, very disfigured," said Ludwina reluctantly.

"Death will have no power to make his cherished features any less precious to me. I must see him right away."

"Please, not tonight, Rudolph, wait until morning," begged Ludwina, even more urgently.

"My dear Ludwina, how would it be possible for me to pass the night without first visiting his deathbed, without first mourning him in his presence? No, Ludwina, it will be good for me; it will be a great consolation to have one last look at his beloved features even though death precludes him from looking back."

With these words, Rudolph intended to rise, but Ludwina, tortured by anxiety, held him back and said in a quivering voice, "He did not die here."

"Didn't die here—where, then?" asked Rudolph, taken aback.

"He was on a trip to Austin when his fate overcame him," continued Ludwina softly.

"So, he met with some bad luck—perhaps his horse fell with him? Oh, you good father, and I wasn't able to be with you," grieved Rudolph, once again succumbing to sobs and tears and covering his face with his hands.

"No, Rudolph; it was the Indians. It was Kateumsi who . . ."

"What did you say? Kateumsi?" yelled Rudolph, and flew from the couch as if yanked by the hand of evil. "Tell me again. Is it true? He was murdered? Murdered by this monster?"

"Please Rudolph, I beg of you, for my sake, stay calm," cried Ludwina, shaking and throwing herself at the chest of the young man. But he pushed her aside, wanting to rush out the door; Ludwina cast herself to the floor and latched onto his knee.

"Listen to me, Rudolph; listen to your Ludwina, I beseech you!"

In this moment the major stepped into the room and gripped the hand of the young man with the words, "It was God's will, Rudolph, and it is our duty to endure this tragedy that has befallen us without complaining and without turning our backs on His larger plan. How can you bear to see your bride, your Ludwina, at your feet, pleading, without heeding her request? Come, be our good Rudolph; we all share in your pain and grief completely."

Rudolph stood there, as if rooted to the floor, staring in front of him with a dark and unfocused gaze. As he did so, any possibility of calm acceptance of this deed lifted from his being. He stood there dumbfounded. But then he allowed himself to be led back to the sofa by Ludwina. He did not respond to her efforts to redirect his dark thoughts, efforts that sprang from her limitless, albeit anxious, devotion to him. Instead, he sat there for a long time, brooding, until finally he passed his hand over his forehead, arose, and in a flat voice announced, "I am going to my father now; I have to see him."

Ludwina sensed that any remonstrations would be useless and cast a help-less look in the direction of her father, who then stepped over to Rudolph and took him by the hand. "Then I will accompany you, Rudolph, but I would prefer if we waited for morning before we go."

Rudolph, however, grabbed his hat and his rifle and walked silently through the door and out to his horse. The major quickly followed him.

Ludwina hurriedly wrapped a scarf over her head, locked the house behind her, and joined Rudolph at his side as he took the reins of his horse and led him off.

"I am going with you, Rudolph. Just as there is no joy, so there is no pain that your Ludwina should not be allowed to share with you," she said some-what faint-heartedly as she put her arm in his. "And I am of the opinion that this is the way it has to be between two hearts who intend to belong to one an-other for a lifetime. If pain, or even happiness, has the ability to alienate these hearts, even for a short period, then their future happiness is hanging by a silk thread."

Rudolph sensed the wisdom in these words. He felt that without both of these true souls, between whom he now strode, he would find himself com-pletely alone and isolated in the world, and with this realization his heart, now afflicted with grief and despair, opened up once more to gentler and healthier thoughts. He reached out for both Ludwina's and the major's hands to signal through an affectionate grasp what he could not at this moment express in words, as he lowered his head and hat to conceal the tears that were welling up in his eyes once again.

In this way the three crossed the meadow and arrived at their destination. Rudolph looped the reins of his horse over the fence post, opened the garden door for his companions, and followed them, heavy of heart, to the house.

No light illuminated their way, but two dark figures righted themselves on the porch. It was the old servant and the old housemaid of the deceased. Ru-dolph stepped up to them and, shaken, reached out his hand to each. He felt his heart would surely burst.

He remained with them awhile; then, after regaining his composure, he asked the old man to tend to his horse. He then turned to the old woman and bade her, "Get us a light, good Liese!"

Liese led the way, weeping, into the house, and soon thereafter the room filled with the soft glow of a lamp which the old woman had lit. With tear-swollen eyes, Rudolph looked around the room and stood, hesitant, in front of the door through which he would need to pass to view his murdered father. Ludwina placed her arms around him gently and pressed herself against his breast.

"Come, children, let us go to our sleeping friend, and even if his earthly remains are terribly disfigured, what has happened to his mortal body is of no consequence to his departed soul. Come, Rudolph, be as strong as your second father," said Nimanski.

The major then took the light, opened the door, and stepped into the room of the colonel, followed by the others. They stood before the bier of their dearly departed, gazing at the linen shroud which cloaked him.

Nimanski, endeavoring to be strong, raised the lamp, grasped the upper end of the cloth, and pulled it back as far as the breast of the slain man.

With a cry of horror, all three started violently at the terrible sight of the bloody corpse. The lamp began to shake in the hand of the major, and he quickly pulled the cloth back over the head of the colonel with his other hand.

In the same moment, however, Rudolph tore loose from the arms of his beloved and threw himself in a fit of wild, uncontrollable grief over the body of his father.

He wailed, he cried out in his sorrow, and his plaintive cries, though only half-intelligible, sounded like vows of revenge. The major took him by the hand and led him back from the corpse, pulling him to his breast with these words: "Vengeance, sayeth the Lord, is mine. Find comfort and help in your second father and in the heart of a loving young woman, both of whom the Lord has given you in your moment of need."

Rudolph was overcome by his grief publicly on only one other occasion: it was at the burial of his father as the colonel was being lowered into the grave. But even in this moment of trial, true love and sympathy came to his aid and helped to still the wild waves of his anguish.

All of Friedrichsburg had accompanied the three murdered men to the burial ground to offer their final respects, and the bad feelings toward all the Indians in general, which the death of Weltge had engendered, were rekindled anew by the funeral procession. Within a relatively short period of time, however, the wheel of daily activity had begun to turn again routinely and the fate of Colonel Wildhorst and his companions had disappeared almost completely from the conversations and small talk of the town. Only Rudolph's totally altered appearance and demeanor, when one happened to encounter him on the street, invoked an involuntary reminder of the whole sad episode.

He was no longer the cheerful and carefree young man, happiness beaming from his large, clear eyes and pouring from his heart, fresh and open to the whole world. No longer did he walk with a light and elastic bounce in his stride, as if the earth were his for the taking as far as heaven's blue sky extended. No longer did he greet passers-by with a friendly word or witty comment, which seemed to issue from an abundant joie de vivre. No, his appearance was now earnest, thoughtful, withdrawn, his countenance gloomy. Whereas before he had gone out of his way to greet people, now he endeavored to avoid them. His steps were slower and firmer, as if more closely rooted to the earth, and his speech terser and more detached, as if his real thoughts were far, far away.

Wherever he went, wherever he stood, he could see the bloody, mutilated head of his father before him and, in the distance, the dark and devilish apparition of Kateumsi, who mocked him with the scalp of the old man, which he held by the locks of his silver-white hair.

An insistent, inescapable inner voice kept speaking within him: only one thing could bring his soul peace—death to his father's murderer by his own hand. When and where, he could not yet say, but Kateumsi's death was an imperative, even if the effort were to cost him his own life. From day to day the thought festered, growing into a clear and powerful obsession which displaced all other concerns and interests.

But where was he to find this monster, this Kateumsi, and how was he to get near him without being detected by his band of warriors and prevented from carrying out his purpose? It was not to be expected that he would show himself anytime soon in the vicinity of the settlement, but this seemed to Rudolph the only possibility of encountering him.

This hunt was now his only activity when he was not held back in town by official duties. Often he fetched his rifle and rode out to the nearby hills just as the sun was beginning to set. After taking his leave from Ludwina, he would spend entire nights on the outskirts of the settlement under the light of the moon rather than in the comfort of his house, hoping to catch a glimpse of his sworn enemy.

The change in Rudolph's behavior, in his thoughts and feelings, did not escape the loving eyes of Ludwina. In vain she offered up all her love, all the talents she could muster, in order to relieve his deep melancholy and banish from his soul the vision of his murdered father, which shadowed him like an evil spirit.

The major also made an attempt to influence Rudolph's attitude and actions, likewise in vain. When they found themselves alone, he would gently point out how Rudolph was undermining his own and Ludwina's happiness through his withdrawal and disengagement. Rudolph never disputed the truth of his words or denied the self-destructive nature of his behavior. He also readily acknowledged the pain he was causing Ludwina, which he regretted deeply. He promised change and was sincere in this resolve, but in short order the negative thoughts invariably regained ascendancy over his good intentions, and once again he fell under the powerful spell of the malignancy festering in his innermost being, which allowed him neither peace nor rest.

Nimanski was deeply moved by the fate of the young Wildhorst, since it affected the well-being of his beloved and only child so profoundly and his own equanimity as well. He cast about endlessly for ways and means to help the young man rediscover the happy, cheerful nature, which formerly was so much his.

Nimanski regarded Rudolph's solitary existence as one of the chief reasons for the persistence of his emotional preoccupation and self-absorption. Staying in the house of his father, he concluded, was constantly reminding him at every turn of the ghastly fate which had overtaken the venerable old man. To be united with Ludwina at the earliest possible date seemed to him to be the only sure way to restore Rudolph's peace of mind. His natural health and joy could find sustenance in their marriage, to the benefit of all.

The major quickly took steps to realize this goal and began to make the necessary alterations to his abode so that it would be possible for them all to live together. He had abandoned the idea of building a new and larger house, which the colonel and he had jointly planned. Instead, he determined it would be preferable to enlarge his existing homestead. He also decided to purchase two adjoining lots from the director to accommodate the increased size of his household. The wedding could then take place in the spring.

Winter had settled in. The fire in the chimney not only provided a cheerful diversion in the evenings, but also offered welcome warmth, for the thermometer often fell to zero. It was especially comfortable and cozy in the Nimanski living room. To be sure, the walls consisted only of bare logs that had been planed smooth and stacked on top of one another. The cracks, however, were filled with mortar and, over these, narrow strips of wood had been nailed so that, unlike in most other log houses, the wind could not blow freely through the house from any and all directions. The floor was made of stout, closely fitted planks over which a thick woolen rug had been laid. On the long trip from Europe to this place, the rug had often served the sojourners well as additional padding.

In its appointments the room exhibited a curious blend of European refinement and frontier coarseness. The large mirror, with its broad gilded frame, the beautiful oil paintings and copper plate engravings at either side, the red silk curtains—all stood in stark contrast to the crudely constructed table and rough benches. The sofa, however, joined elements of both the old and the new homeland. The red silk fabric with which it had been upholstered concealed a frame cobbled together from discarded pieces of wood by an unskilled hand and also wadding made from moss. In front of the spacious chimney stood a mahogany rocking chair representing American comfort, while small benches—thanks to the skilled handiwork of Rudolph—occupied a place to either side of the fireplace.[1] A fire crackling in the hearth, emitting myriad sparks while casting its light to play and dance throughout the room, completed the picture of a welcoming safe haven. And even with its abundance of refinements, no cozier and peaceful setting could be found in all of Old Europe.

Ludwina, mistress of this empire, sat in front of the fire in the rocking chair, dividing her charm and grace between the major sitting to her right and her heart's love resting on the bench to the left, and, in so doing, she appeared to be competing with the fire to provide the evening's entertainment.

Pecans and walnuts which she and Rudolph had gathered and put aside in the fall were brought out and roasted in the coals of the fire, after which the nuts were cracked. Occasionally Ludwina prepared *Glühwein*,[2] or punch, or baked a batch of sponge cakes, something she was quite good at. In this magical atmosphere the dark emotions haunting Rudolph were unable to prevail. He sensed here only the good things in his life: his revered Ludwina, the delight of her close presence, and the blessing of her love.

However, after she had accompanied him as far as the gate of her house and given him a last good-night kiss, Rudolph had to make the walk alone through the night to his house. In short order, the sinister thoughts would once again rise up in his being, pushing aside the image of his beloved Ludwina, who had just charmed him by her presence. The grieving servants, who received him silently at his house; all the objects in the room, which—illuminated by the soft glow of the oil lamp—appeared to be looking at him; his own solitude compounded by the stillness around him. All these factors rekindled his somber fantasies, and no matter where he looked, he saw his father and Kateumsi before him.

The director, whom Rudolph venerated, had also spoken repeatedly with him about his emotional well-being. He pointed out how the young man was undermining his own happiness, not to mention that of his future bride and father-in-law, by yielding in such an unmanly and powerless fashion to his sadness. He endeavored to keep Rudolph occupied with all sorts of tasks to distract his thoughts and divert his attention. He also frequently took him along when he went out to hunt.

The director welcomed an opportunity for Rudolph to deliver a packet of dispatches to Braunfels. He hoped a stay in that town among old friends and acquaintances would be good for his emotional condition. The same morning that Rudolph departed for Braunfels, the Delaware chief Youngbear appeared unexpectedly at the house of the director. He reported that he had arrived the previous evening on the banks of the Pedernales with his band and had set up camp there.

Youngbear related that he had just returned from his annual hunting expedition to the north, where he had spent a couple of months at the Delaware settlement on the Kansas River. According to his routine, he would be relocating farther south shortly to overwinter along the banks of the Medina, the place of "never-ending spring."

He was very sorry that he could not visit with Rudolph. He must have followed the road, while Youngbear took a shortcut though the woods, and so they missed each other in passing—so opined Youngbear. He said, "Young Eagle will see Delaware camp on the Pedernales and will return to visit his friend Youngbear."

The director then reported the sad story of the horrible fate of the colonel and the others at the hand of Kateumsi, and also related to him the unfortunate effect which this episode had had on Rudolph's state of mind.

Youngbear listened to the story intently while his countenance darkened. After the director had finished, he observed, "Who kills father must be killed by son, or kill him, too."

"Even though you are probably right in this, Youngbear, you cannot say it to Rudolph, because he would leave straightaway to look for Kateumsi and probably never return. And then what would become of Ludwina? She would not survive. And if you had given the advice, then you would bear the blame for the death of his bride," the director said in a very serious voice. The chief looked at him as if he sensed the truth of these words.

He stood for a few moments contemplating the situation and said, "Then friend of Young Eagle must avenge his father and stop the heart of Kateumsi from beating, once and for all. Youngbear is also friend of White Dove, who made present of silk scarf to Youngbear. Now I must protect her life. Youngbear will give to Young Eagle the scalp of his hated foe, the murderer of his father. But for now, Kateumsi is on the far reaches of the Brazos River where its waters fall over the high cliff[3] and where the roar of the crashing waves can be heard far away. There he hunts buffalo that migrate for the winter because there is not enough grass in these hills at this time of the year. When Youngbear returns here in the spring, however, to celebrate the wedding of Young Eagle and White Dove, then he will cast a bullet for Kateumsi."

"His death would be a blessing for our town because as long as he lives he will not leave us in peace," replied the director, who then related how Kateumsi had attacked the town and how Ludwina had defended it.

Youngbear's eyes lit up brighter and clearer with every word of the director until he burst out passionately: "The wings of White Dove are almost as strong as those of Young Eagle and her heart is as beautiful as her eyes. Youngbear is her best friend!"

After the two had spoken a good while, Youngbear said, "I have a request of you."

"Which I will gladly fulfill, if it is in my power," answered Schubbert.

I would like to take time out to do some bear hunting here in the neighborhood; I have seen several big tracks," Youngbear said.

"Hunt as much as you want," answered the director, "but with one condition: that you will sell us the bear oil, because our supply is about gone. Last winter, I had almost fifty deer hides full of bear oil in our warehouse, all of which weighed at least sixty pounds, and now only two or three remain. We have no other source of oil for frying and melting, for treating leather and for burning in our lamps. It's our good fortune that so many bears are here in the area and that the Indians are supplying us with oil. I can't remember going out on a bear hunt without having found at least one or more animals, but of course that does not mean that we were always able to bag one."

"I will put together a big hunt with all my people and you will not be lacking for bear oil."

"Good. I would like to ride with you; I haven't been outside the town for awhile," remarked the director. "When would you like to begin?"

"The day after tomorrow, early," answered the chief. "Today and tomorrow we need to rest our horses."

Youngbear stayed for the midday meal with the director. He was happy to see all the officials again, but especially his friend Bickel. After the meal, Schubbert accompanied Youngbear to camp, where all the Delawares welcomed him.

CHAPTER 14

The Bear Hunt • Indian Sign • Concern • On the Look-out • The Lovely Young Lady
The Deadly Enemy • Blood • Dismay • Chase

*T*HE SECOND MORNING AFTER Youngbear's visit, just at daybreak, some eighty Delawares, led by their chief, appeared before the director's house. About forty dogs followed the riders. All were mounted on their best horses and all were armed with long-barreled, single-shot muskets. They were also carrying bows and arrows. Quite a few women and children and several pack animals laden with frying pans and copper pots accompanied the hunting party.

The director was ready. His horse was led out, and Burg, who had asked permission to go along, presented himself front and center. The director left his own dogs at home because he feared they would not mix well with the other hounds.

The large hunting party, led by Schubbert and the chief, had to pass through the town along San Saba *Straße* and depart the valley of Friedrichsburg to the west, where the riders entered the hills through a narrow canyon.

Desire for revenge. Drawing by James C. Kearney.

It was a beautiful morning, the air cool and invigorating. The sky spread its deep blue tent, cloud-free, over the wild and hilly Texas landscape. The horses, as if sensing the hunt, pranced impatiently under tight rein, chomping at their bits and snorting incessantly. The Indians, however, sat quietly and intently on their powerful mounts, with not a word, not a sound passing over their lips.

The director, noticing this, remarked to Youngbear, "How is it that your people can remain so quiet? When so many whites are together, the talking, laughing, joking never ceases."

"Because the Indian only does one thing at a time, and when he does it, he does it totally, with his whole being," answered the chief. "You whites are interested in too many things, but can enjoy no one thing fully. Our joys are fewer, but deeper. You will see when the hunt begins how much pleasure we take in it."

Uphill, downhill, for a good hour the party rode onward in single-file along no discernible trail or path, when finally, they crested a rise and saw a long, narrow valley beneath them. The valley was no more than a thousand paces wide and was bounded on either side by high, steep cliffs. It extended to the southwest as far as the eye could see. It was watered by a creek, and lush grass grew in among the many large rocks, for the entire valley seemed to be populated with colossal boulders, scattered and tumbled next to and on top of one another, as if tossed by some giant hand. Here and there, ancient live oaks added to the charm of the vista, worthy of a painting.

The chief had brought his horse to a stop and, pointing to the valley below, said to the director, "Here many fat bears are sleeping and here the Delawares are going to have great fun. Previously, we held a good hunt here every year, but since you whites have settled in these hills, we have not wanted to hunt here, because we are friends and the hunting grounds belong to you. But you have not shot enough bears here."

"Not a single one," replied Schubbert. "I have never set foot in this valley before; it is totally unknown to me."

"Then your heart will be happy to see more bears together than you have ever seen before. Now, do you wish to ride with me and my men as we awaken the bears from their sleep, or do you prefer to stay with the others here below and wait for the bears fleeing from us and running in your direction? It will be a difficult ride among the rocks," Youngbear continued.

"In that case, I will take up a position below and wait for the bears to come," answered the director.

"You will have to wait a good while because we will be riding from this hill to the other end of the valley, which is over three miles long. From there, we will start our hunt back toward you. Don't grow impatient; it will take time," explained the chief.

With this, he gave Schubbert his hand as a way of saying the hunt had now commenced and rode off, followed by the larger part of his men and the whole pack of dogs. A good twenty Indians remained behind with the director and, together, they rode down a rather steep buffalo trail into the valley below. The women and children, however, remained with the pack animals at the top of the hill.

The men soon reached the area and spaced themselves at short intervals from one another in a straight line that stretched from one cliff face to the other across the whole width of the valley. All dismounted, tying their horses close by or between the boulders. The Indians then took out their pipes and tobacco and lay down in the grass to enjoy a smoke and await the bears.

The director had chosen a spot in the middle of the valley near the creek, where he could secure his horse behind two giant slabs of rock leaning together. He then followed the example of the Indians and took a seat on the bank of the flowing stream and lit a cigar.

The sun shone down warm and welcoming in the remote valley, whose peace was disturbed only by the happy twitter of birds, flitting about here and there in their colorful feathered suits while enjoying the warmth of the morning. Countless dark-feathered buzzards soared silently over the valley in wide circles; now and then a bald eagle let out a shrill cry from the top of the cliff face.

More than an hour had passed when suddenly in the far distance the faint hunting cry of the Delawares became audible and Schubbert saw the riflemen to either side of him spring for their muskets, as if touched by electric sparks. He called to the hunter to his right to ask why they were in such a hurry since, most likely, the bears would not be in too much of a rush and it would be a while before they arrived. The Indian waved back and yelled, "Panther and jaguar, quick!"

The director took up his rifle and waited. In short order, he spotted something shiny gliding among the rocks along the valley floor. Suddenly a magnificent, gold-spotted jaguar emerged, bounding forward in broad leaps, to escape the hunters below. The cat veered from the water and struck a path directly toward the Indian off to his right, who sank to his knee and aimed his musket at the cat. When it had approached to within forty steps, the Indian, remaining perfectly motionless, let out a short yell. At this, the jaguar stopped and looked around to locate the strange sound. In the same instant, the Indian took his shot and the splendid animal fell to the ground, writhing in its death throes.

A split second later, another shot cracked farther to the left, near the cliff wall. Another Indian had bagged the panther.

Next, a herd of deer came crashing forward in panicky flight and passed unharmed through the line of hunters without a single shot being fired at them.

The hunters now realized that the bears would be coming soon and that their guns had to be loaded and ready.

The sound of the hunt grew ever clearer, ever wilder, and the excited yapping and barking of the dogs, always music to the ear of a hunter, echoed up and down the valley. Now and then the crack of a hunter's musket reverberated like thunder among the hills.

Soon the dark, fleeting shapes of many bears appeared in the distance among the boulders. They scooted across the floor of the valley this way and that. One came bounding along the creek toward the director. Schubbert allowed him to get close enough to be shot in the head so that death was instantaneous; the animal, most likely, never even heard the report of the gun.

After this shot, the other bears who were visible immediately turned and fled back in the direction from which they had come only to encounter the guns of the Indians there. The closer the hunters approached, the more bears showed themselves, but with each shot they turned back from the line of riflemen.

A good twenty of these superb animals were now concentrated between the approaching riders and the stationary hunters. As long as they thought they could escape, they attempted to do so; but once they became aware that they were trapped, and with the dogs swarming among them, they turned to attack their tormentors, both to the front and to the rear.

The hunt reached its climax in wild confusion. The entire valley seemed to shake from the shouts of the hunters, the roar of the muskets, the baying of the hounds, and the snarling of the bears. The Indians rushed this way and that: over here to aid a comrade attacked by a bear; over there to chase a bear attempting to flee.

In short order, however, the action concluded and nine splendid bears lay stretched out in the same general area.

The riders had slain an additional four bears and another jaguar, so the entire kill amounted to thirteen bears, two jaguars, and a panther. Most likely, several other animals had been wounded and had carried death with them in their escape.

The wives and children quickly appeared on the scene and soon several fires were burning along the banks of the creek. The hard work of skinning and dressing the bears began. A large group of riders rode down the valley to drag back the animals slain farther off, using their horses and lassos.

By far the greater part of the bears had been slain with arrows, and some had received as many as twenty wounds.

While the women were busy stretching the pelts, laying out the meat to dry, and rendering the fat in the pots and pans which had been brought along for that purpose, the men set off in all directions to hunt deer so the women could fill their hides with bear oil.

Youngbear and the director stayed in camp and treated themselves to the delicacies that a bear offers to the hunter.[1] Once the sun started to set, however, the two returned with the majority of the Indians to Friedrichsburg. The other men stayed with the women and children since their labors would not be finished until the following day.

In all, the hunt yielded eighteen deerskins filled with bear oil—a welcome addition to the meager supply in the warehouse.

Youngbear only spent two more days at his camp in the neighborhood of the town and repeated his regret at not being able to see Rudolph. Moreover, his trek to the south toward the Medina River, where he intended to mount several more bear hunts, would take him farther to the west than the Braunfels road, so he was unlikely to encounter Rudolph along the way. Youngbear conveyed his warm greetings to Rudolph and asked the director to assure the young Wildhorst that as soon as the young leaves appeared on the trees, he would return for the wedding.

"Tell him that Youngbear is the friend of Young Eagle and also the friend of White Dove, which makes him the sworn enemy of Kateumsi, whose scalp he will bring to him." With these words, Youngbear bid farewell and took his leave until the following spring.

Rudolph returned several days after the departure of the Delawares, but his stay in Braunfels had brought about no favorable change in his outlook; on the contrary, he was even more withdrawn and beaten down than before. The one source of joy, the one thing that could help him reconcile with his fate, had been far away: Ludwina had not been there to keep his spirits up.

Consequently, the reunion with Ludwina was even more beneficial, the delight of her presence more enthralling than ever before, and for several weeks he seemed to have won a victory over the dark powers that had embittered his soul.

Still, when he stayed alone in his house, he continued to be reminded of the dreadful end of his father, and the memories left him little peace during the night. Consequently, even though the director had assured him that Kateumsi was now far away hunting on the upper reaches of the Brazos, his restlessness drove him to take his rifle and prowl the surrounding area while the town lay asleep, in the faint hope of meeting his enemy.

One morning, just at the break of day, as he was returning from one of his nighttime forays and approaching the Nimanski household, he was pleasantly surprised when Ludwina opened a window and waved eagerly at him. He quickly went over to her, and soon she came out on the porch to greet him with the entire magic of her unbounded love. Rudolph, however, was quite astonished to see her up so early, and when he asked her the cause, she replied, "The dog was really restless the whole night long; he was constantly running behind the house and growling and barking. He wouldn't quiet down even though I went to the window several times and fussed at him. Something was prowling around, and if another jaguar is in the neighborhood lusting after my nanny, he had better think twice. This time, as sure as I am alive, I will personally fill him full of lead. He can't harm her at night because she is shut up in the stall, but I have often wondered if such a predator might not even try to attack poor Leo and drag him off."

Rudolph had listened intently to what Ludwina had to say and, when she had finished, remarked, "Certainly a jaguar, or even a panther, would be capable of doing it; a dog would be easy prey for either of them. I have already lost a couple of good dogs in this way myself. I will have a look and see what it was. The dew is still on the grass and I should be able to pick up the tracks very easily."

With this, he passed through the fence and began intently searching the ground for some sign behind the house and in the meadow around the house. He walked in a wide circle in the direction of the hills, when suddenly he noticed a drag trail through the wet grass, which headed in the direction of the Nimanski dwelling. He followed the trail for some distance away from the enclosure. It led him in a wide bow around the house and then in the direction of the hills.

Rudolph's blood turned to ice water, because he had clearly seen right away that this was the sign of a human and could only be that of an Indian. Surely he was the only person in the city who had not spent the night in his own house.

He could not make out the imprint of a foot in the grass, so he quickly followed the trail to the first rise, where the grass gave way to dirt and gravel. It led in a straight line to the path which Kateumsi had used earlier to storm down from the hills when he pursued Ludwina with his wild band and attacked the city.

No sooner had Rudolph reached the foot of the hill where the path wound its way up than he spied the footprint of an Indian moccasin. The heavy dew had moistened the dry dirt and the wet soil had stuck to the bottom of the night wanderer's foot.

Rudolph now doubled his pace as he made his way up the hillside, following the path as far as possible before the sun's growing warmth blotted out the tracks. He hurried forward in double time: every sinew was tense; he sensed no fatigue. His gaze remained fixed on the tracks that were barely discernible. Breathless and sweating profusely, he arrived at the crest of the hill at the exact spot where Ludwina had been spotted by the Indians previously.

From this point the trail vanished from view. Rudolph avoided climbing to the very top, where he might be seen in silhouette by Indians below, but he was now totally consumed by the hope that he might come face to face with his arch-enemy.

He was certain that it had been Kateumsi who had left the trail, and the thought that he was now stalking his future bride and her father made the hair stand up on the back of his neck.

He was gripped by anxiety and rage alike. Shaking his rifle in a gesture of angered determination, he swore neither peace nor rest until he had killed this human predator. Rudolph understood Kateumsi's approach now and realized that, sooner or later, he would return. Of this he had no doubt.

Greatly agitated, he returned down the path, uncertain in his own mind about whether he should share his discovery and his suspicion with Ludwina and her father. It would surely upset them and disturb their nighttime rest. They would also be even more opposed to his own nighttime forays. On the other hand, it would be good for them to know that they were in danger and to be on their guard. It was also possible that Kateumsi might approach the town from the other side to carry out his evil intentions while Rudolph waited in hiding on the path in the hills.

To take up a night position in the vicinity of the house had disadvantages. It was certain that the Indian would wait for a dark night to carry out his plans. It would be much more difficult to get off a shot from the meadow than from the path in the hills, where Kateumsi would have to pass close by. It was also likely that he would use this approach again since he was familiar with it and there was no way for him to know that his tracks had been discovered.

Still considering the matter, Rudolph neared the Nimanski house and decided, finally, to conceal his suspicion that the nocturnal visitor had been Kateumsi, but to let them know that it had been the track of an Indian.

Ludwina sprang happily to meet him, and her father offered him a warm morning's greeting from the porch.

"Once again you have been roaming around at a very early hour, Rudolph," the old man remarked, a gentle reproach in his tone.

"I was hoping to shoot a deer but had no luck," answered the young man, trying hard to suppress his nervous excitement. Then he turned to Ludwina and said, "It was an Indian whom Leo caught scent of in the night. I clearly saw his tracks in the hills. You two need to be on your guard." After a short pause, he added, "Perhaps the scoundrel was just checking to see if there was something hereabouts easy to steal."

"An Indian?" started the major. "Are you mistaken?"

"No, there was no mistake. The outline of an Indian's foot was clear as day," replied Rudolph, "and he had some purpose in mind for sneaking up on the house in the night and then slipping back along the same path."

Ludwina's eyes had grown serious, and she said in an anxious tone, "What if he wasn't trying to avoid you, Rudolph? It worries me. Often you leave us late at night and usually without any kind of weapon."

"No, no, good Ludwina, don't worry," Rudolph quickly interrupted. "Why would an Indian be interested in stalking me of all people and taking such a roundabout path to do it? No, he just happened to be passing through the region and thought that he might be able to filch some clothes that had been laid out in the grass to air. Still, it's good to be on one's guard. We shouldn't forget what happened to Weltge."

"It's a real curse for the town, these Indians lurking around here," observed the major. "We just made peace and already these devils are up to mischief. For sure, the scoundrel was up to no good sneaking around the house like that."

They all fell momentarily silent, thinking about the seriousness of the situation. Finally the major broke the silence, laughing, with the comment: "Bring them on! Ludwina has the artillery in good shape and the both of us can raise such a racket with our guns that the entire city will come rushing to our aid."

"The first shot will bring me to your aid for sure," replied Rudolph. "And from now on, I will bring a weapon along when I come to visit you in the evenings. Ludwina will no longer have to worry about that."

True to his word, Rudolph showed up the following evening for supper with his double-barreled rifle and his hunting knife, as if he were about to go on a hunt. He seemed cheerful and carefree and stayed with his bride-to-be and her father until almost nine o'clock, sitting and chatting in front of the fireplace. Then he excused himself under the pretext that he needed to catch up on the sleep he had lost the previous night.

Ludwina accompanied him, as always, as far as the fence to their yard. From there he struck a path to his house, but as soon as he saw that she had gone back in the house, he changed his direction and hurried off for the trail leading to the hills that he had discovered in the morning.

It was rather dark, for the moon was in its last quarter, and it would be early morning before it rose. The night was still. Hardly a breeze stirred, and the slightest sound carried far in the distance.

With his rifle cocked under his arm, Rudolph eased up the path of the hill, listening intently and searching the darkness carefully with each step forward. He tried to avoid making any noise and would start when a stone under his foot made a soft sound or a twig snapped.

In this way, slowly and cautiously, he made his way to within twenty feet of the crown of the hill, where he took up position behind a large boulder that he had picked out that morning. It stood somewhat to the side of the path. He took a seat on a smaller rock which he had also seen earlier and rolled forward for that purpose. Thus situated, he kept his eyes fixed on the top of the rise, where he would be able to see any person silhouetted against the faint sky.

A deathly stillness lay over the area. Only the incessant howling of wolves on the hunt, which never seemed to let up—now far away, now closer by—and the solitary cry of the whip-poor-will[2] disturbed the serenity of the night, the latter calling out his own name in plaintive and haunting tones from a live oak tree not far away.

Rudolph sat motionless, listening and watching from his vantage point behind the large rock, but his foe did not appear. He felt for the hands of his watch to judge the hour; it was already past midnight. He felt certain Kateumsi would already have appeared by this time if he intended to come at all, because everyone in the town would be asleep and he would give himself plenty of time to make an escape, should that be necessary. "Nothing was holding him back from coming in the earlier part of the night, so why shouldn't he do it?" thought Rudolph to himself, as he arose from his seat. Still, after standing up, he listened intently once more and stared closely at the crest of the hill, as if it were possible that Kateumsi would materialize at just this instant.

He stood frozen for another quarter of an hour before taking the path leading back home. But once again he briefly hesitated, as if held back by invisible bonds; as if the arch-enemy had to make an appearance. He did not.

Rudolph now hurried quietly down the trail toward his house, where he arrived some fifteen minutes later. It was after one o'clock when he finally threw himself into bed and quickly fell into a deep sleep.

In this pattern, Rudolph slipped out night after night to take up his station behind the rock on the hill and lie in wait for his elusive foe, but his hopes and yearnings remained unfulfilled.

After several weeks had elapsed, Rudolph sat at his usual spot next to Ludwina by the fire. The young lady had taken pains to be especially cheerful and animated this evening. Rudolph stole several glances at his watch; the hill beckoned to him powerfully, but the charming young woman did not want to grant him his leave. She had roasted and cracked pecans and had filled three glasses with punch that could not have tasted better.

"I have no idea why you are so anxious to hurry home," she said with a threatening gesture of her finger. "It used to be twelve o'clock before papa would need to remind us of bedtime; now it seems like you are ready to head off to your evening's repose as soon as the chickens go to roost. Wait a little while longer. Have you grown tired of your Ludwina's company?" But with these words she let out a little laugh and, looking at Rudolph, slipped into his arms. Rudolph, overcome by the delight of the moment, momentarily forgot all his suffering as he pressed the enchanting young lady to his heart.

"Oh, my guardian angel," he said. "Is there anything else I would rather hear from now until the cows come home than your lovely, precious voice? But tomorrow I have to be at the *Verein* compound at the crack of dawn and I still have a letter to write for the Braunfels post, which is leaving early. I really have to say good-bye now, my good, sweet girl."

With this, Rudolph rose to take his leave and the major remarked, "Well then, if Rudolph has a letter to write, we had best let him go." The major shook his hand warmly in parting. The young man fetched his rifle and hat, and arm in arm with Ludwina, strode out to the front gate. Ludwina's parting kiss still burned on his lips as he ran toward the hill, for the clock had already struck ten. But once he reached the foot of the trail up the hill, he slackened his pace because it was possible he would meet Kateumsi on the trail, and then the outcome would depend entirely on who noticed the other first.

He had never been drawn so powerfully to the hilltop before—even so, the closer he got to the top, the slower and more cautiously he placed his steps. Finally he veered off the path and took his seat on the stone behind the boulder. Reassured that he had arrived in time, he took up his position with his rifle cocked and resting on the rock in front of him. But once again midnight came and went without a soul appearing on the trail.

The crest of the new moon had long since passed; the stars, however, sparkled and shone in their most glorious splendor. Despite the lack of any breeze, the night had turned quite cool on the hilltop and Rudolph had begun to shiver. In his haste, he had neglected to dress warmly and had been sitting motionless for several hours only lightly clad. It was a little past midnight, but still he did not want to abandon his post.

He listened and listened—not a sound from anywhere. He buttoned up his jacket but still the cold penetrated, and he grew more and more uncomfortable. Once again, he felt for the hands of his watch. It was almost one o'clock.

That was late enough. Kateumsi would not be coming this night. Rudolph withdrew the rifle from the boulder and put his right hand down on the stone on which he was sitting to help lift himself upright, but at the same moment he cast one last glance back toward the crest of the hill. Just then a dark figure emerged and a savage stood silhouetted against the starlit night.

It was Kateumsi for sure; his outline unmistakable. Rudolph's heart began to race; he gasped for breath and felt his hands shaking as he raised his rifle slowly to his shoulder and took aim at his deadly enemy.[3]

Cat-like, the savage eased down the trail toward Rudolph, his stout bow in his left hand and a bundle of arrows in his right. The rifle followed him, and less than ten paces lay between them when fire erupted from the barrel and a horrible shriek passed over the lips of the Indian. His bow fell to the ground, and with his right hand he grasped his left arm. In the same instant, he sprang back over the top of the hill in long strides, yelling loudly to his comrades below to come to his aid.

Rudolph, like a panther after his escaping prey, stormed after him, but had covered only a few paces when his feet became entangled, causing him to stumble and fall to the ground. He groped for the object around his foot; it was the Indian's bow which he had stepped through.

Then a wild war whoop answered from the other side of the valley, and Rudolph realized that he would not be able to follow the fleeing man any farther. Gnashing his teeth in fury that he had missed the monster, he was of half a mind to smash his rifle against the rocks. But it had happened, and now he had to think about his own safety, for the hellish war whoops of the savage horde were approaching ever nearer. He slung the bow over his shoulder and ran as fast as he was able in the darkness down the trail toward the town.

Once he reached the bottom of the hill, he paused to listen in the direction of the hills, but everything was quiet; the war cries had fallen silent.

How was it possible that his shot had missed—this, the most important shot that he had ever fired in his life? Distraught and beside himself with anger, he ran across the meadow to his house and into his room, where the lamp burned on the table. He took the bow from the table to examine it in the light and noticed that his hands were stained red. He quickly realized that the blood had come from the bow, and an inspection revealed that a good part of it was bloody.

He did not miss after all! He cried out in joy while studying the bow with a sense of satisfaction and pleasure. But how badly could the foe be wounded when he was still able to yell so loudly and run away so swiftly?

Then Rudolph recalled how Kateumsi had grabbed for his arm after the shot in the same instant that he dropped the bow. For sure, the shot had shattered his arm.

"Why couldn't I have hit him in the heart?" he cried out, disgusted with himself. With his gaze fixated on the bloody bow, the specter of his father's broken and mutilated head reappeared before his mind's eye. Oh, if he just had one more chance! For sure he would shoot him right through the heart.

Mumbling to himself words of regret and self-reproach, he strode back and forth across his room for a long time. He threw himself upon his bed several times but found no rest, and spent the rest of the night in a state of overwrought agitation. Nonetheless, with the first hint of dawn, he grabbed his rifle and hurried up the path again to look for the wounded Indian's bloody trail.

Breathless, he arrived at the spot where Kateumsi was standing when he had been shot. It was clearly marked by the blood on the ground while, close by, the arrows that Kateumsi had been holding in his hand lay scattered across the ground.

Rudolph gathered them up and followed the path over the hill and down the other side. He saw drops and splotches of blood, but the farther he went, the less blood he found. Soon he gave up the search; there was no sense in going any farther, and the desire to relate what had happened to Ludwina and her father, as well as the director, took hold of him.

He hurried back to his house and exchanged his rifle for the bow and arrows of the wild one. He walked up to the Nimanski household just as Ludwina was stepping out of the house to lead her nanny to fresh grass.

"Have you already delivered your letters?" she called cheerfully to Rudolph. She hastened to greet him, her arms open, but when she noticed the Indian weaponry she said, "My God, a bow! Where did you get that?"

"It's Kateumsi's bow. I took it from him myself last night. Unfortunately, I only wounded him in the arm," replied Rudolph, holding out the bow and arrow to Ludwina.

"For heaven's sake, Rudolph, you frighten me! How did you come to meet up with that monster Kateumsi?" exclaimed the young woman. Rudolph then explained the whole story.

"Oh, Rudolph, I am becoming more and more frightened of this horrible Indian. Now he is even more stirred up and he will do everything in his power to take revenge on you," continued Ludwina, her voice filled with anxiety.

"Or he will learn something from this episode, namely that we whites can be just as cunning as his people. And as far as his attitude is concerned, I don't see how it could get any worse than it already was. After all, what was his purpose in sneaking up here in the night? He was planning to murder again. But he won't be back anytime soon, that's for sure." After this exchange, Rudolph and Ludwina walked back into the house, where the major also heard the story with great consternation.

"If you had only been able to kill the scoundrel," he cried, shaking his head.

"It was too dark to take good aim, and I was really excited by his sudden appearance. I had not heard a sound from him," Rudolph explained, still overwrought.

"You couldn't get off a second shot, then?" asked the major.

"The smoke from the powder obscured my sight for a moment after the shot, and the rascal flew back over the hill so quickly that I had little time for a second shot," replied Rudolph. "Also, the director has stressed time and time again the importance of holding the second shot in reserve in an Indian fight, even in extreme situations, until the first barrel can be reloaded. Otherwise, the Indians, with their ability to fire off arrows so rapidly, will gain the upper hand."

They exchanged a few more words on the subject. Then Rudolph excused himself and hurried over to the house of the director, who, likewise, was astonished by Rudolph's tale and disappointed that his bullet, once again, had only wounded his prey. No sooner had Rudolph finished his report than the director summoned Burg and ordered him to get all the guards mounted and equipped to track Kateumsi. He ordered Burg to follow the trail without rest as long as the horses held out. Kateumsi, he pointed out, might not be able to ride very far due to his wound and probably was not expecting pursuit.

"If you don't catch up with him by sundown, turn around and take your time coming back in the morning. If you meet up with them today, however, shoot down as many of the scoundrels as you can," ordered the director.

Burg received the task eagerly. At a gallop and in less than an hour, he led his splendidly mounted and equipped troop out of the town in the direction of the hills. Rudolph, however, who wanted to ride along, was ordered by the director to stay behind.

CHAPTER 15

Much Excitement · Foundation Day · Hurried Preparations for the Festival
Morning of the Festival · Laying of the Cornerstone · Celebratory Feast · The Dance
The Promenade · Sitting at the Fireplace · Alone · The Frightful Face
The Abduction · Anxiety · Despair · The Wild Friend

O NCE THE NEWS ABOUT KATEUMSI spread, it caused much consternation among the citizens of Friedrichsburg. Once again, the young men
decided to man guard posts on the outskirts of the town.

The people eagerly awaited the return of the patrol sent out to pursue Kateumsi. The patrol, however, did not return until the third afternoon. The men
had followed the trail of the Indians without stopping on the first day until
darkness halted the chase. But the Indians had made their escape hastily and
had never paused to rest.

Laying the cornerstone and Ludwina's abduction. Drawing by James C. Kearney.

Weeks and months passed without an Indian showing his face. Even the friendly tribes seemed to avoid these hills in the winter. And, as had been the case previously, so it was now: over time, the danger of the renegade threat receded from public awareness.

With the approach of spring came a day of great significance for the citizens of Friedrichsburg, and everyone looked forward to the upcoming event joyfully and eagerly: it was the anniversary of the founding of Friedrichsburg.[1]

This time, a big celebration was planned.[2] The director decided it would be appropriate during the festivities to also dedicate the communal church,[3] the stone foundation of which had already been laid on a large plaza in the middle of town.

The shopkeepers and tavern owners in Friedrichsburg planned ahead for the upcoming events by ordering all the necessary items from Braunfels; the director also made sure that the *Verein* warehouse was fully stocked.

Similarly, individual households and families were caught up in a whirlwind of frantic activity. A lot had to be considered, but above all it seemed that the people regarded it of paramount importance to be appropriately dressed for the occasion. Due to the limitations of the frontier, however, this desire often met with frustrations—frustrations which, as might be expected, applied especially to the gentler sex. Their dilemma was compounded by the fact that they needed to arrive at a kind of consensus among themselves concerning appropriate dress. Friedrichsburg during these early years had evolved as an egalitarian society, without rank or privilege, and it was important that no one should be outfitted in a conspicuously better manner than others.

Ludwina was called upon for advice and assistance in this as in previous things. Luckily, several young ladies had arrived recently from Germany who were very accomplished seamstresses and also knowledgeable about cosmetics.

Needless to say, the new arrivals were very popular. They received commissions from all sides and wherever they appeared, the populace took pains to make their lives pleasant and cheerful.

Calico, though not the most refined weave of cloth, turned out to be the solution. But here on the frontier, far from the luxury of the civilized world, the quality of the cloth mattered less than an appropriate color and a comfortable fit. The material was readily available in all sorts of colors and prints, so that whatever one's individual tastes—whether flowered, striped or checkered, whether in dazzling sunny colors or pale tints—calico became the cloth of choice for the pretty ladies of Friedrichsburg.

The big event was still fifteen days away, and every household was busily at work in preparation. The young damsels visited one another constantly in order to inspect each other's wardrobes and to try out different coiffures.

They would do up one another's hair alternatively in a wild and coquettish style, and then they would try a more sophisticated look: combed back smooth from the forehead and with the strands allowed to hang down in long curls to the side and back. Artificial flowers and colorful ribbons alike, which had not been forgotten on the long journey over the ocean, were added to complete the masterpieces.

Also, several citizens had joined together to form a musical band, and they held practice daily.[4] The only instruments missing were the double-bass and a kettle drum. The last item, however, found a very satisfactory substitute in the form of a flour barrel over which deer hides had been stretched at either end, and, as it turned out, a not altogether unpleasant sound could be coaxed from this unwieldy contraption.

For a refined European ear, used to the very best, the local musical talent might not have measured up. For the robust citizens of Friedrichsburg, however, whose ears were more accustomed to the sounds of nature than the exquisite tones of a recital hall, it was all music, and all the more so because it was songs and melodies from the Old Country: waltzes, polkas (*Hopfer*), and *Galoppaden*. Here the old saying applied, namely: "It's easy to make music for those who like to dance!"

Behind the scenes, more serious preparations also were under way in order to lend the proper dignity and solemnity to the occasion. The pastor, especially, carried a heavy burden of responsibility. The significance of the day required first and foremost an inspired sermon during the religious service, and, thereafter, an appropriate and memorable blessing at the dedication of the cornerstone. The honest and upright man took his responsibilities to heart, daily retreating to the solitude of his study, where he gathered his thoughts and labored over his speech.

In addition to the pastor, nearly all the prominent men of Friedrichsburg felt obliged to have a few words prepared in advance to be held in reserve on the off chance that they might also be called upon to speak.

Next to these preparations, many found it necessary to insure that the libations on hand in the taverns for the upcoming festivities were of sufficient quality to match the gravity of the occasion. It was quite interesting to notice how the number of acolytes dedicated to this discipline proliferated in these establishments from day to day.

The most glorious arrangements, however, were undertaken by the *Verein* itself. The director ordered a colossal dance floor to be laid out in front of the *Verein* compound. The ground itself was raked smooth and tamped firm so that even the daintiest foot could glide over it easily and without hindrance. Round about the floor a row of benches were set up to accommodate the damsels not dancing as well as the couples worn out by their exertions.

The day before the festival the director had several small trees from the nearby woods cut down and brought into town. These were planted in the ground around the dancing space and decorated with spring greenery so that they would stand there fresh and welcoming for the occasion. The entrance to the dance floor led from the *Verein* compound. An exit graced the opposite side, leading to a grove of magnificent live oaks. The path also had been decorated with shrubbery in the same way as the dance area. A podium for the band was erected next to the dance floor, and a large number of tables and benches, roughly cobbled together from planks, were set up facing the stage for the benefit of the audience.

The evening before the long-awaited festivities finally arrived. Everywhere costumes were being inspected, speeches and toasts rehearsed, music practiced, and, of course, liquid refreshments sampled anew. It was late in the night before the last lights of Friedrichsburg went out, and many a pretty eye closed with the thought, "Only one more night to go!"

A cannonade started the citizens of Friedrichsburg from their sweet dreams of dancing and revelry and reminded them in dramatic fashion that The Day had finally arrived. Although not the customary hundred and one shots, twenty-five shots were fired off with even more powerful charges to make up for the reduced number. The day began to spread its light over the valley, and the town quickly resembled an ant hill; the people scurried busily to and fro, for nearly everyone had some last-minute task to complete.

Soon the women began appearing at their windows or in front of their houses in their Sunday best, which, due to the efforts and skill of the new seamstresses, had improved markedly in terms of beauty and adornment. The men emerged at the gates to their households in their best suits and, replete with long pipes, observed the comings and goings with interest.

The time for religious service had been set at an early hour, and at eight o'clock sharp the streets began filling with churchgoers. The house, which had served temporarily as a church, could not contain all the worshipers, so the door and windows were left open so that the people outside might be able to follow the pastor's edifying sermon and join their voices to the hymns that were being sung. This was not a problem, for the pastor had been blessed with a powerful voice.

Everyone was deeply affected, for the pastor's words conjured up vividly the entire catalog of dangers, deprivations, exertions, and sufferings that had attended the long journey from their quiet German fatherland. But all these travails had finally issued in this: Friedrichsburg, a safe harbor, a German refuge in the New World.

Many an eye filled with tears, looking back on the grave of a mother, a father, a child, a brother, a sister, or a loved one who had been left behind, buried in a shallow grave beside the lonely road on the long trek up-country from the steamy, sandy Gulf Coast below. But, at the conclusion of the service, all turned their heads upward to send prayers of thanks to Him who rules over our lives and fate, to Him whose rescuing hand had led them here and given to them the promise of a new homeland.

In a mood of great solemnity, the large throng dispersed from the House of God in silence, but soon turned their collective attention to the upcoming dedication of the *Vereinskirche*. But since the parade from the *Verein* compound to the construction site was not scheduled to depart until eleven o'clock, the people still had a good hour to wait—time they used to fortify themselves with a hearty breakfast, which would help them to better hold up to the exertions of the day.

As the eleventh hour approached, the population of Friedrichsburg assembled in front of the *Verein* compound and took their places in line for the parade.

The pastor, the schoolmaster, the head of the orphanage, and the orphans took the lead in the procession, followed by the director and his officials. Behind them came the mounted home guard. They were divided into two troops, with four mules pulling the cannon between them. Behind them, the male population of Friedrichsburg paraded two by two, while the female contingent watched from the side or rushed ahead to get a good vantage point for the upcoming dedication.

Everyone had taken his proper place and the director was just about to give the order for the parade to begin when suddenly a rider, whom people quickly recognized as the Delaware chief Youngbear, came tearing up the street on a swift horse.

Happy and excited, he jumped down from his horse and hurried along the parade line until he came to the director. He reached out his hand and announced, "Youngbear's heart wants to celebrate with yours."

"Welcome, friend," replied the director warmly. "You have arrived at a happy hour. I thought about you, but didn't really expect to see you here."

"The Delawares set up camp yesterday on the green banks of the Pedernales," the chief explained, happily moved. "When Youngbear's ear heard that you were going to celebrate a big day today, he ordered his Delawares to mount their horses. They didn't unfasten their spurs until they had reached the green grass of the Pedernales, where their teepees are now standing. Youngbear's horse, however, had to carry him here to his friends right away."

"Once again, a hearty welcome to you, Youngbear," replied the director. "Find a place in the parade and join right in!" The quartermaster waved for Youngbear to join him at his side. Youngbear, sensing the hushed seriousness of the occasion, crossed his arms in front of his chest, and the parade commenced.

Slowly and solemnly, the parade wound its way along San Saba *Straße* toward the large plaza in the middle of the town. The director had decided the church should be located here at the center of the plaza and the town. The men arranged themselves in a wide circle around the construction site, and the women and children found places among them in order to observe the ceremony.

The masons had already gathered at the trench along one part of the wall that had been left open to reveal the foundation layer of stone. Here a small hole had been left in the stonework in which to insert documents and plans for the church.

A hush fell over the crowd as the pastor stepped up to the trench and began his speech. His voice was loud and his tone was serious. First he reminded his audience how only shortly before, this land had been a wilderness where only wild Indians and wild animals had found a home and how, under the protection of the Almighty and the Christian Church, a thriving German town now stood here, as if by a stroke of magic—a town far removed from the civilized world, and a monument to German persistence and strength.

But the main anchor of stability for their collective life was missing, and that was a House of God. Founding this House was the solemn purpose of their gathering here today. His words were edifying and enthusiastic, and he closed his speech with a prayer to the Almighty, asking for His blessing on this work which had been undertaken in His name and for His glory. All joined in the prayer in an attitude of deep reverence.

Then the schoolteacher[5] led the assembled citizenry in a hymn of praise to God, and all joined in with uplifted voices. The pastor closed the ceremony with a solemn blessing for the building.

At this, the director stepped forward with an iron capsule in his hand wherein the documents had been sealed, and handed it to the masons. The master mason received the capsule with a short speech of acknowledgment. He then placed the capsule in the hole in the wall. After the capstone was lowered into the ditch, the master mason tied an apron onto the director and handed him a trowel with which to lay in the first mortar to seal the stone.[6]

After this, the director handed the trowel to the pastor so that he too could spread mortar and then, in a similar fashion, the officials of the *Verein* each took a turn with the trowel. The masons ended the project quickly and, once completed, one of their number delivered a final benediction. As soon as these words were spoken, the cannon, which had been placed to the side of the plaza, announced with its thunderous voice that the solemn ceremony was over.

The spectators then pressed forward, curious to view the stonework for themselves. Friends and family congregated here and there to discuss the day's happenings, and all slowly started to drift back to their houses, still engaged in conversation.

During the ceremony, workers had been very busy in front of the *Verein* compound because there, in the shadow of the buildings, a long table had been set up to accommodate fifty people. The director had invited the most distinguished persons of the town to a festive meal.

In addition to this gesture, a stand had been set up behind which stood several barrels of German wine and brandy, the contents of which the director intended to make available to the good citizens free of charge.

It was two o'clock before all of the invited guests, both ladies and gentlemen, had arrived at the compound. The director then led them out to take their seats at the table. At the same time, the musicians had climbed onto the podium next to the dance area and struck up a familiar air, an *Alter Dessauer*,[7] for the entertainment of the guests.

As soon as their vigorous notes, especially those of the horns and the improvised kettle drum, floated out over the town, people, now fully attired in their ballroom outfits, started streaming into the area of the dance floor and podium.

The happy throng milled back and forth along the outside circumference of the dance floor, the youths casting impatient glances at the festive table because only after the guests had eaten could the dance properly begin.

The table guests, however, were much too well mannered to consider excusing themselves prematurely. Besides, in addition to the portly lady who was employed full-time as the *Verein* cook, several other capable ladies had willingly volunteered to lend a hand in the preparation of the dishes, so that a multitude of culinary treats had been created.

Burg and several of his home guards had procured the requisite wild game for the feast, which consisted of roasted bear haunches and ribs as well as several colossal wild turkeys. An extraordinarily cheerful and relaxed atmosphere added the final spice to the meal, which was punctuated by myriad anecdotes and toasts.

All the while, the band continued to play along tirelessly, and their rousing melodies as well as the happy clamor of the crowd made it necessary for each guest at the dining table to speak in an increasingly loud voice so as to be understood by his neighbors.

The young people had crowded onto the dance floor and were growing increasingly impatient to begin. And since it appeared that the guests at the dinner table were in no mood to end their meal anytime soon, and since the band continued to play one dance tune after another, several of the youths decided that they could dance just as readily as the dignitaries could eat. Barely had one or two ventured to swing their partners in circles, than the whole crowd, like a dam bursting, poured onto the floor and everyone who had the slightest urge to dance soon was moving around the floor to the happy strains of the music. Pressed together tightly, the swirling pairs careened around the large circular enclosure, and one could clearly see that their joy in dance had been too long suppressed, and now nothing could stand in the way of a free release of their passion.

Instinctively, the musicians now directed their efforts toward the dancers. The trumpet players, especially, aimed their instruments at the whirling mass, and their loud and piercing tones only seemed to stoke the fires of enthusiasm among the dancers.

At this point the director arose from his seat and pointed to the dance floor. The whole party of assembled guests adjourned and followed him to the circle to join in the festivities. The director then called for the wine and brandy barrels to be set up and made available, and the attendants began dispensing the beverages to the people who had already lined up for the occasion.

As soon as the last strains of the gallopade[8] had faded, many of the young men and their pretty companions crowded around the beverage stand to sample the German wine. For the musicians, wine was brought in flasks onto the stage, which had the effect of reviving their flagging enthusiasm almost immediately.

In the meantime, the director had retired to his house, where he had invited several close friends to coffee. The entire festival could be viewed from the porch of his house. Ludwina stood at the side of her Rudolph among the ladies and gentlemen, but both were unusually quiet. Neither felt at home in this noisy and boisterous atmosphere. Rudolph was reminded by every happy face that a revered and beloved countenance was missing from among the guests, and the melancholy feeling which this memory produced left a mark on his features and was reflected in the soul of Ludwina.

Youngbear had accompanied the director to his home, where he had received a cigar to enjoy along with his coffee. But his attentions were drawn powerfully back to the festivities across the street, for he had been deeply affected by these strange new pleasures, especially the music and the dance. He stood next to one of the porch supports as if in a trance, gazing longingly at the dancers. Now and then he would cast a quick glance at the director, as if to ask whether or not it would be impolite to take his leave and rejoin the revelers.

Schubbert could clearly see by the chief's expression and demeanor how fascinated he was with the activities across the street, so the next time the chief looked his way, laughing and nodding and gesturing to the dance floor, the director happily gave him permission to leave: "Would you like to go back and watch our young ladies dance, Youngbear? Take a couple of cigars along!" The director handed him several with these last words.

"The nicest day of Youngbear's life," the chief replied, delighted. "His heart has never known so much happiness." At this, he glanced blissfully in Schubbert's direction, sprang over the railing, and in a few short seconds had disappeared in the crush of the merry crowd.

The sun disappeared behind the darkening hills of the valley of Friedrichs-burg, and dusk settled in even as the sky lit up in a fiery glow. The air was as warm as a summer evening. The leaves on the trees set up around the dance floor and along the pathway hung motionless from their branches. But no soon-er had the stars begun to shine than countless colorful paper lanterns which hung from the trees began casting their magical light over the throngs of mer-rymakers from Friedrichsburg, as if in a picture from a fairy tale.

The lights also hung along the promenade leading to the oak trees, and here and there a light shone forth from the dark interior of the grove. The joy, the happy mood seemed, if anything, to increase with nightfall: the voices of mer-riment grew louder, the shouting and cheering more raucous, the music ever livelier and more inspired.

The enthusiasm of the dancers, however, readily kept pace with the in-creased tempo of the band, and one could see in their faces that all the sorrows of the world had vanished from memory. Their faces beamed with joy as the young women threw themselves eagerly into the powerful arms of the young men, themselves intoxicated with pleasure, while they danced and twirled around the floor. And many a whispered exchange and fervent embrace ac-companied their movements.

The time was approaching nine o'clock when the ladies in the director's home rose to take their leave. They were mindful that the director had asked several of his friends, among them Major Nimanski, to join him for supper.

Accompanied by the gentlemen present, they walked across the street to be among the people and to take delight in their revelry. They watched the dancers for a while and then strolled in the direction of the oak grove, down the charm-ing promenade with its fairy-like illumination. In the mysterious darkness of the oak grove not a few couples had retreated to seek privacy behind a veil of dark-ness that was only slightly penetrated by one or two red lanterns. Thereafter, they bid adieu to the revelries and started on the paths to their homes.

Ludwina followed the party at some distance, arm in arm with her be-loved Rudolph, inspired and animated by her own thoughts and feelings, by the promise of the complete happiness which her upcoming marriage would bring in a few short weeks.

After the pair had said their good-byes to the various couples, they headed toward Ludwina's house and were glad once again to find themselves in the cozy security of the comfortable living room, the witness to their happiness. The fire in the fireplace had gone out even though part of a log remained. Rudolph set about reigniting the fire. Soon the flames were dancing happily again and the two lovers settled themselves next to its glow to discuss once again the approaching fulfillment of all their earthly wishes.

This peace and quiet did them well after the noisy excitement and raucous activity in front of the *Verein* compound. Only the faint sound of a trumpet or the beat of the kettle drum occasionally penetrated their sanctuary.

"Where is father?" she asked as she looked at the clock over the fireplace. "It is almost eleven o'clock."

"The director won't let him leave and, besides, the company is probably having such a good time that nobody wants to leave," observed Rudolph as he stoked the fire. "And they will probably continue dancing till the wee hours of the morn. It really pleased me to see how orderly and decently this whole event has proceeded. I didn't see one drunken person and I haven't heard one sour word."

"As little pleasure as I take in such merrymaking, I have to concede that it did me good to see the people enjoying themselves so thoroughly; it was truly a wonderful celebration," Ludwina observed as she looked at the clock once again. Then she added, "I just wish father were here."

"Yes, that would be better for me too because I need to go back to fetch Youngbear, who is supposed to sleep at my house tonight. I told him to wait for me at the dance."

"Well why don't you run back quickly and get Youngbear and father? Then I will get to see you once more before the evening is over," replied Ludwina.

"I don't want to leave you here alone, my angel," answered Rudolph while snuggling affectionately with his bride-to-be.

"Don't worry! I am often alone in the evening and you won't be gone long. Come! Hurry up! The sooner you leave the sooner you will get back!" said Ludwina as she arose. She gave him a kiss and an embrace. Then she handed him his hat and sent him off with the words: "Go—quickly!"

They stepped outside on the porch together, where Ludwina unfastened Leo from his chain. Ludwina gave one last adieu, then quickly retreated into the house and locked the door behind her.

Her heart buoyed with joy, Ludwina settled into the rocking chair by the fire. She tossed another stick on the fire and, rocking contentedly, took up a woolen shawl which she was knitting for her father. It was so still, so cozy, that the movement of the clock's pendulum and the gentle tapping of her knitting needles reverberated like loud noises.

Hardly a quarter-hour had elapsed since Rudolph had left when suddenly the hound began to bark in the yard. Ludwina lifted her head and listened, but Leo had fallen silent.

She started to knit again but Leo resumed his barking, this time more furiously, and it sounded as if he were trying to bite something through the staves of the fence. Ludwina jumped up, shocked, just as the hound let out a shrill cry of pain followed by a barely perceptible whimpering.

"For God's sake, what was that?" cried Ludwina, half-swallowing her words in horror. She stood motionless in the middle of the room with wide-open eyes, holding her hands before her as if in a posture of self-defense. But once again, everything was still.

She overcame the first, paralyzing fright, but for Ludwina, it was as if her hair were standing on end. She could feel that she was trembling and a cold shudder passed over her limbs. It turned quiet again and she began to regain her composure.

"What should I do?" she thought to herself, and her glance fell upon the guns on the wall. Just in that moment, however, as she turned to take a weapon from the wall, she was startled by a sound which appeared to be coming from the window, and once again she froze in her tracks to listen intently.

The sound continued as if someone were forcing the window from the outside, and Ludwina could clearly see that the frame and curtains were moving.

"God Almighty—help me!" she cried out in horror. She rushed to the wall and lifted the double-barreled shotgun from its rest, cocked both hammers, and aimed it at the window.

Just then, the window shattered into the room, a brown hand pushed aside the curtain, and Kateumsi's horrible features stared at her.

With a shrill cry she jumped back, but in the next instant she shouldered the weapon and fired at the spot where she had seen the savage, for the curtain had fallen back down over the window. No sooner had the detonation rocked the house than the steady beat of ax blows began to fall on the front door, shaking the whole house.

The paralyzing anxiety had now left Ludwina and a decisiveness born of despair took its place. Keeping her eye on the door, she lifted the rifle from the wall and set it next to the sofa. Then she fetched the pistols and laid them out in front of her. She stood there, pale as death, but resolute and calm.

"The stout door is still holding firm and soon Rudolph will come flying to my defense, for surely he heard my shot," thought Ludwina to herself. She stared at the door, which suddenly disintegrated in a shower of splinters as the devilish shapes of Indians came pouring into the room.

Ludwina managed to fire off one shot before she felt herself overwhelmed and restrained by powerful arms. A cry for help faded from her lips and she sank into unconsciousness.

Back at the dance floor, Rudolph, accompanied by the major, had just found Youngbear when he heard a sound. "Wasn't that a shot?" started Rudolph. He spun around, shocked.

"Your ear heard correctly. The shot was over there," and Youngbear pointed in the direction of the Nimanski homestead.

"Good God—Ludwina!" cried Rudolph, who, suddenly gripped by fear, lit off at a full run in the direction of the house. The chief ran after him and soon overtook him. "Youngbear, it was my bride who shot," he yelled as he ran.

"White Dove?" asked the chief.

"Yes, yes," answered Rudolph, almost out of breath. "God help us if Kateumsi . . ."

"In the name of the Great Spirit, we have to help her!" cried Youngbear as he ran alongside. He added, after taking a couple of quick breaths, "The Delawares are close by."

By this point they had raced past the end of San Saba *Straße* and were heading across the grassy meadow to the Nimanski household.

"Just God of the heavens, it has happened!" cried out Rudolph in heart-wrenching agony when he got close enough to see that the window and door stood open in the still, illuminated house.

As if carried by a storm, he raced past the gate, which stood open, and into the house. He rushed into the room, still brightened by the fire in the fireplace. He saw the splinters from the door, the shotgun on the floor, and on the rug by the door, a fresh pool of blood.

"Oh my God, oh my God!" he cried out in raving despair. He wrung his hands and pulled at his hair and ran up and down the room as if he were possessed.

Then Youngbear, who had been standing motionless, looking closely at the room, stepped forward and gripped Rudolph by the hand. He spoke to him in a firm and decisive voice. "Young Eagle cannot let his wings droop, because as long as Youngbear is friend of you and White Dove, then no Delaware's heart will be open to joy, no Delaware will lie down to rest without his weapons, no Delaware will look across the wide-open, flower-filled prairies again until White Dove is returned to Young Eagle and until Kateumsi's heart has ceased to beat. Now you must be calm and strong so that your eye is sharp and your hand is steady; your despair will not help White Dove. Go, saddle your horse, collect your weapons, and wait for Youngbear and his warriors here." Youngbear gave his hand to the unhappy man and headed in the dark for the *Verein* compound, where his horse was tethered.

The happy crowd continued to kick up their heels in a wild, unbridled dance across the wide circle of the dance floor. As if their instruments had grown warmer, the musicians played one of those lively gallopades that are often performed at the conclusion of public masquerade balls in Germany after the dust has obscured all the color of the costumes and the masks have begun to soften and disintegrate from the warm breath of their wearers. The dance seemed never to end. Each time the music began to trail off, the eager shouts and yells from the audience egged on the musicians to renew their efforts.

The wild dance continued on and on, when suddenly the words "Ludwina has been abducted!" reverberated across the floor. The music fell silent and the dancers stood still and petrified, as if they had been put under a spell.

Happiness, joy, and pleasure disappeared from the faces of the crowd and fright, horror, and anger took their places. The people crowded forward to the guards who had brought the news and heard that Youngbear had gone to summon his warriors and with them intended to pursue the bandit Kateumsi.

The festivities were forgotten; the women and young ladies hurried back to their houses, and the men came together in order to consider what they could quickly do to come to Ludwina's assistance. But they remained helpless and baffled. What could they do? How could they follow the bandits?

Before long, the entire male population of Friedrichsburg had assembled in front of the Nimanski household, where they found an inconsolable father wrestling with his grief. Rudolph soon appeared with his horse and his weapons and attempted to offer a few words of consolation and encouragement to the old man, but he quickly succumbed to his own sorrow in the effort. And all the men who approached them were likewise gripped by painful emotions.

A light was carried outside to check for signs of the break-in. In the yard they discovered the brave hound dead with an arrow in his breast. The strong blood trail out of the house and across the porch, however, revealed that the bandits had carried away someone who was severely wounded.

CHAPTER 16

The Warriors · On the Trail · The Bandits · Deception · The Valley · The Cave
The Prisoner · The Posse of Revenge · The Wounded · The Departure

THE NIGHT HAD BECOME unbearably long, and the people found it difficult to accept the new and harsh reality of what had happened. All anxiously awaited the appearance of the Delawares. The eastern sky had barely begun to redden when Youngbear came riding up San Saba *Straße* at the head of eighty warriors. He was greeted with a loud hurray by the assembled men in front of the Nimanski household.

Armed with muskets, bows, and arrows, the battle-ready troop pulled up in front of the house, and one could clearly see in the countenance of each of the riders that they were looking forward to the pursuit of a hated enemy.

Youngbear dismounted and followed the trail of the bandits for some distance from the house. He then returned, shook the hand of the major and the director and said, "Youngbear will bring back White Dove." He took the end of the silk scarf which was tied around his neck, held it up, and then called on Rudolph to mount his horse. He swung onto his own steed and in the next moment the entire war party took off in hot pursuit of the Comanche renegades.

Warriors on the trail. Drawing by James C. Kearney.

At the same time this was taking place, Kateumsi, followed by fifty of his warriors, was riding far to the north of Friedrichsburg along a buffalo path on the crest of a high hill. Seated in front of him on his horse was Ludwina, whom he held in his powerful arms. She was bound hand and foot.

His horse as well as those of his warriors was bathed in sweat, and it was easy to see that they had been ridden hard, almost to the limits of their endurance. In silence the riders followed the path in single file. Kateumsi kept his shining, uncannily glowing gaze fastened on the beautiful white girl caged in his arms.

"Have no fear of Kateumsi, you, the prettiest of all virgins. Kateumsi could do you no harm even if it were to cost him ten lives," he said while looking with hot passion into her half-closed eyes.

"You fiend! I am not afraid of you; there is nothing you can do to me. Death will be my savior and free me from your wicked hands," answered Ludwina, full of despair and closing her eyes again.

"You will not die; you will live. You will learn to love Kateumsi. He will be your slave. He will do everything to make your heart happy again and to turn your love toward him," continued the savage. His passion was even more inflamed by the words of Ludwina, and he pressed her forcefully to his colossal breast.

"Devil—predator—I hate you and I will continue to hate you as long as I live!" cried out Ludwina as if possessed, and with her arms she forced the chief away from her.

"Kateumsi will take the hate from your heart and fill it with love," he continued affectionately. He then added as he looked imploringly at Ludwina, "Kateumsi will do anything that you command him to do."

"Then take me back to my people and I will pardon you," said Ludwina with a pleading look on her face. "My poor old father and my Rudolph will both perish from grief and pain."

"Kateumsi doesn't know your father, but your Rudolph is his enemy. His bullet knocked him from his horse and he shattered the arm which now holds you tight. And also you, if it weren't for his love, Kateumsi ought to hate you, too, until his dying day since you killed his horse and over fifty of his warriors. But he can't hate you even if you had sent all the Comanches into the realm of their fathers with your thunder gun. You are too pretty. You are prettier than the moon, prettier than the magnolia blossoms, prettier than the sky when the red of the new day drives away the darkness of night. You are the prettiest thing in the world, and Kateumsi would not want to live if you were taken from him."

Ludwina did not answer him. She closed her eyes and sank into a dull, dejected exhaustion followed by a mood of total despair.

The top of the hill had been reached and Kateumsi stopped his horse and turned to his warriors, who quickly gathered around him. Several of the older men rode up to the chief. He spoke to them and said, "There below in the valley we will come to the creek where Kateumsi will part company with you. You will cross the creek and follow the buffalo path that leads over the next line of hills. The path will lead you to springs on the Llano[1] before the daylight is gone. There is plenty of grass for the horses there and you can rest by your fires. The whites will not be able to follow you so far today. The following day, follow the Llano till it meets the Colorado. You will not be far from your wives and children then, and also from Kateumsi's wives. You must see after their well-being and safety until Kateumsi returns. The cliffs are known to you where he will live with the pretty white girl and where he will be safe from every enemy's eye."

"Have you thought about the Delawares?" asked one of the older warriors. "They are your enemy; their eyes are as sharp as yours; their bullets reach farther than your arrows; and their horses are faster and have more breath than yours. The time has come for Youngbear to leave the banks of the gulf and come to these hills. You know he is a friend of the palefaces in Friedrichsburg."

"Youngbear is still hunting along the banks of the Medina, the Salado, and the Guadalupe, and by the time he puts up his tepees on the Pedernales, the dew of the night, the sun and wind will have erased the sign of your horses and he will never be able to pick up my trail," answered the chief. Just then the last of the warriors crested the hill. He was holding a dead comrade in his arms.

"Bring the dead one to the graves of our fathers. You will be there by tomorrow evening," Kateumsi added. Then he turned his horse and urged him down the path to the valley below, and his warriors fell in silently behind him in single file.

Soon they reached the valley floor, and the path which Kateumsi followed led across a meadow through which a fast-flowing stream meandered. Kateumsi stopped his horse at the bank of the stream, turned around, and addressed his warriors, "Send me messengers often and keep me informed about what is happening in our hills, and also, let me know if the Delawares appear. Should the palefaces dare to follow you so far, steal their horses when they are asleep, and when they find themselves on foot out in the tall dry grass, set it on fire on all sides and burn them up."

With this, Kateumsi parted from his warriors and headed his horse into the creek, where the water reached as high as the belly of his horse. The warriors, however, crossed the creek and continued along the trail leading to the hills.

Kateumsi intentionally kept his horse in the middle of the stream. He followed the creek for over a mile downstream until he reached a canyon with high walls where the water was forced to pass over and through many boulders and broken slabs that had fallen from the cliffs above. Here Kateumsi urged his horse out of the stream and up the steep bank. He then followed the canyon wall over the loose stones and rubble that formed the narrow bank of the stream.

It was difficult to believe that a horse could make his way here without losing his footing, but the big red horse of Kateumsi never stumbled. He carried his heavy burden sure-footedly through the narrow gorge, which soon opened up to reveal a lush, creek-bottom meadow adorned with small groves of trees here and there.

The valley was surrounded by tall, bare cliff walls on all sides and only on the far end where the creek flowed out of the valley did the hills incline toward the creek bed, whose course disappeared between them into a marshy and densely wooded area.

It was a lush valley, abundant with game, and seldom visited by the Indians because of its inaccessibility and the difficulty this presented for the horses. The swampy area at the other end was even more tricky and dangerous to navigate than the narrow pass that Kateumsi had chosen. Yes, this valley was probably unknown even to most other Indian tribes, and certainly no white man had ever set foot in it. Wherever one looked, small herds of deer and antelope[2] were feeding, totally unconcerned, as if in this sanctuary there could be nothing to fear. They grazed among the clusters of trees which lifted themselves like islands in painterly beauty from the fertile, flower-covered floor of the valley.

Kateumsi looked around, satisfied and victorious, like a predator about to carry his prey to his lair. He gazed again at the beautiful paleface who lay in his arms with closed eyes. He followed the cliff face to his left until he reached the middle of the valley to a point where a ravine with sheer walls opened into the valley. At its other end was a large cave. Many large boulders were strewn along the floor of the cut and several massive live oaks spread out their limbs to cover it in shade. A horse could only pick his way with difficulty through this maze. At its entrance, the chasm was a good forty paces across, but it narrowed considerably by the time it reached the cave. The floor of the ravine lifted as it receded, so that one could survey practically the whole valley once one had ascended to the cave.

When Kateumsi directed his horse into the gorge, four Indian women and one man emerged from among the boulders to greet him, as if they were expecting him. "Have you done what I told you to do?" the chief asked brusquely. "The cave is clean and tidy; your bed is soft; and the fire burns bright," replied the oldest of the women.

"And a haunch of venison is hanging on the limb in front of the cave," added the Indian man.

Hearing the strange voices, Ludwina opened her eyes and looked down at the Indians. She recognized right away that the man was none other than Potolick, the Indian that Burg had captured after the cannon had been fired and the man who had left the town seemingly so grateful to his captors and well disposed toward the whites. The recognition sent a shock wave of hope through her because she knew that he was especially friendly with Rudolph, who had taken an interest in his recuperation. Occasionally Ludwina had gone along to help and had had several friendly exchanges with the Indian. She could see right away that he also recognized her, but she also noticed that he held his gaze averted from her out of fear of Kateumsi.

The chief nodded to the man and then urged his horse forward through the maze of boulders into the gorge as far as the old oak tree which stood in front of the cave. Then he gave Potolick a sign. The Indian quickly sprang to the side of the horse and took Ludwina, whose feet were still bound, in his arms so that she could be lowered to the ground. Kateumsi then dismounted, took the prisoner in his arms, and carried her into the cave, "Come, pretty girl, the softest bed has been prepared for you so that rest will restore your spirits and renew your strength."

He then laid her down on tanned buffalo hides and placed another one that had been rolled up under her head as a pillow. Ludwina once again was overcome by a sense of utter helplessness and in her misery, which went beyond tears, she decided to end her existence by refusing all nourishment.

She had no way of knowing that her betrothed and her friends were already doing all they could to save her. Up and down the hills they rode on their hardy steeds, known for their endurance and accustomed to strenuous rides: Youngbear tenaciously on the trail of the Comanches with Rudolph at his side and his band of eager, battle-ready warriors in tow. Youngbear held his falcon eyes focused on the ground before him to see if one or more of the enemy had veered to the right or left from the main party. All of his warriors who followed him, one behind the next, were doing the same, but nowhere had they spotted a track leading away from the main party.

It was close to ten o'clock when the riders descended the high hill into the valley with the stream below, where Kateumsi had separated from his band of warriors. As soon as Youngbear reached the bank of the fast-flowing creek, he brought his steed to a halt and looked carefully upstream and down, sensing that this might be a juncture of significance.

He then called two of his men to come forward: "Follow the creek, one of you upstream, the other downstream, and look for a horse's hoof print where the water is shallow and the bottom is sandy. See whether such a print can be discovered on the bank of the creek. Follow the creek a long ways, for Kateumsi is as cautious as a beaver and as sly as a lynx. Either way, whether you find a track or not, come back and report to me."

Both scouts eagerly took up their task, because they knew it was an honor to be singled out by the chief, a sign of recognition of their ability and of the trust the chief placed in them. Youngbear then resumed following the trail of the main party of Comanches with his remaining men.

"The water is deep and well suited to hide the trail of his horse from you whites, if that is what Kateumsi intended. But he did not think about the eyes of the Delawares," said Youngbear as he rode forward.

"Wouldn't he want to stay with his warriors?" asked Rudolph, still plagued by anxiety.

"I think not. His horse, most likely, must carry both him and White Dove, and as good and noble as the animal is, his endurance is not enough to carry them much farther. Kateumsi is afraid of you and your home guard. The horses of his warriors can still carry them to safety," said the chief, his eyes still searching the trail in front of him.

They had not yet left the valley when Youngbear turned to Rudolph once again. "The horses of the Comanches are tired; their steps are shorter; they are not lifting their hooves as high off the ground. I believe Kateumsi has left his warriors. Also, they have ridden next to one another here and spoken with one another because their chief is no longer with them. When the tails and heads of the Comanche horses start to droop, that is when the horses of the Delaware become swifter."

With this, the chief spoke a word of encouragement to his horse. Energized by the sense that they were closing in on their prey, the troop continued on their way.

The sun had long since passed its high point when Youngbear followed the bend around a cliff face and followed the trail of the enemy up the slope of a hill. He had barely reached the half-way point when a shrill cry stopped him in his tracks and the chief spotted a head disappearing over the hill.

In the same instant Youngbear let out the war cry of the Delawares and with a storm of howls, the lips of his warriors picked up the cry. Burying their spurs in the flanks of their horses, the entire band stormed forward at a run over the hill and down into the valley on the other side.

Here the Comanches had made camp. At the first sound of alarm from their sentry, who had been posted on top of the hill to watch for enemies, the resting Indians had started up and rushed for their weapons. Their first impulse was to stand and fight the charging whites with their bows and arrows. But when they recognized the resounding war cries of Youngbear and the dreaded Delawares, who were now bearing down upon them at a full charge, they were seized with panic and took to their heels in the direction of the stream, there to seek safety in the woods on the other side.

The Delawares bore down upon them rapidly before they could reach their refuge. Once in range of their muskets, they quickly dismounted, took aim, and loosened a murderous fusillade into and among the fleeing Indians. A good twenty fell to the ground. In the next instant, the Delawares were again in their saddles, unlimbering their bows and withdrawing arrows from their quivers, intending to take up the pursuit and complete the slaughter. Youngbear, however, called to them, "Let them run, the old women; Kateumsi is not among them and it would be a waste if a single Delaware fell to their arrows. We have captured all their horses. They are all afoot now and not a one of them will be able to bring Kateumsi the news before the Delawares find him. Bring the wounded to the fire; Youngbear will see if there is a rascal among them who will betray his chief."

A dozen of the wounded Comanches were then brought to the campfire. Youngbear stepped in front of them and spoke. "You can save your life if you tell me where Kateumsi is; if not, Youngbear will order you shot straightaway." At this, he gestured his warriors forward and ordered them to shoot each in the head if he refused to disclose the whereabouts of Kateumsi.

An old warrior, struck in the leg, lay among the wounded Comanches. He lifted himself up on one arm and looked Youngbear straight in the eyes. "You have it wrong, Youngbear; you need to order your warriors to shoot any of us who would betray his chief. Let your men do their dirty work. There is no one among us so bad that he would betray our chief, just as there is none among the Delawares who would betray Youngbear." With this the old warrior sank back down on the buffalo hide in resignation and closed his eyes.

"Well said, old man, and you are right. Nevertheless, one of you will tell me where Kateumsi is. I have to know and I will know. All red men know Youngbear as a kind and peace-loving chief. But not today! He has vowed to the God of the Hunt that he will skin you alive and put live coals on your raw flesh if you don't tell him where Kateumsi's hideout is. Youngbear has to know—not for himself but for his friends, whom Kateumsi has robbed of all happiness in this life. Listen to my voice; I am not speaking with a forked tongue, and you, old man, shall be the first whom I will have skinned like an otter."

With these words, Youngbear's eyes lit in fiery anger and determination to follow through with his terrible threat. But just as he turned to give the order for the torture to begin, he spied the two scouts, whom he had ordered to explore the creek for signs, and who were now riding forward at a gallop.

He walked quickly to meet them. The first of the riders rode up and quietly reported, "The print of Kateumsi's horse is on the path in front of the narrow pass leading to the valley where Youngbear killed the grey bear two years ago. Kateumsi will be spending the night in the bear's cave—that is certain."

"Then he will die in the cave where Youngbear fought and slew the grey bear," replied Youngbear, his eyes lighting up with excitement. He then quickly added, regaining his composure, "Keep it quiet!"

Then he went back to the wounded and ordered his men to tie them up. He asked Rudolph to go back to the other fire with him, where they sat down in the grass. He took Rudolph's hand in his own and said, "Before the night is out, Youngbear will bring back White Dove to his friend, Young Eagle. But be careful that the Comanches cannot see into your heart. Kateumsi has picked out a hidden valley for his hideaway where only a few Indians might be able to find him. He is staying there in the cave of the grey bears. Youngbear slew one of them two years ago. Tonight, in this cave, Kateumsi will return to his fathers."

Tears of relief welled up in Rudolph's eyes. A faint smile of hope crossed his features and he began to shake with excitement; only the seriousness of Youngbear restrained him from giving full vent to his emotions.

Youngbear continued, "Our horses need to rest for a spell, and then, before the night is out, they will carry us to the cave where Kateumsi is hiding. He will be next to a bright fire so that we will be able to see him. The first shot must take away his life so that he cannot harm White Dove. He has the heart of the grey bear, who will kill his own cubs when he flies into a rage." Youngbear then had his people bring some dried meat, which he shared with Rudolph. His men hobbled the horses in the grass and then sat down to enjoy their meal.

Soon, however, all the warriors stretched out in the grass with their muskets in their arms to catch some sleep. The only exceptions were the guards posted to keep watch over the horses and the camp. Youngbear said to Rudolph, "Lie down and get some rest so that your hand will not shake as it did on the hill at Friedrichsburg when you aimed at Kateumsi's heart but your bullet flew through his arm. You whites think too much and your bodies become confused; we Indians think once and then let the body act. Moreover, our determination is stronger and our endurance greater. You must say to yourself, 'I must sleep,' and you will fall asleep. The Indian can sleep when and where he wants, even if an enemy's arrow is aimed at his heart. So sleep!"

With this, Youngbear placed his hands to his head as a sign that Rudolph should lie down, stretched out in the grass, and, in a few short minutes, had passed into the realm of dreams.

Rudolph did as he was bade. He lay down and closed his eyes, but his repose granted him little peace, for the terrible picture of his suffering Ludwina in the grasp and control of the fiend Kateumsi hovered before him like an apparition.

The sun bent low over the far-away hills when the guard roused the sleeping Indians. Silently, they all arose and hurried to their horses, and in a few short minutes they were saddled and mounted. Leading the captured horses, Youngbear turned to the wounded Indians and said, "Your comrades will return to help you and tend to the wounded as soon as the Delawares have departed. Tell them that Youngbear has spared your lives."

"You have given us our lives because you have found Kateumsi; may his arrow be quicker than your bullet," the old Comanche answered. Youngbear did not reply to this provocation, and as they departed the old man added one last expression of defiance: "May your horse stumble and fall along the steep path and crush you to death!"

"Good that the Comanches have lost their horses; otherwise, Kateumsi would soon get the news about the Delawares," Youngblood said to Rudolph. The party struck a fast trot back along the path whence they had come. Where the land was flat and smooth, they galloped, and in this way, rapidly put mile after mile behind them.

CHAPTER 17

The Enamored Savage · The Grey Bear · The Victor · The Friends
The Bound and Tied Captive · Passion · Horror · The Shot · Rescued
The News · The Return Trip

The cave, Grey Bear, Ludwina, and Kateumsi. Drawing by James C. Kearney.

*T*HE TWILIGHT OF EVENING had arrived in the valley which Kateumsi had chosen for his hideaway. The Indian women had gone out to bring back the horses which had been allowed to graze in the meadow in front of the gorge. Potolick, however, sat in the innermost recesses of the cave by a small fire, where he was adorning his lance with new feathers and ribbons.

Next to a large fire at the front of the cave, Ludwina lay bound by the feet on a large buffalo skin, with her head turned from her abductor, her face hidden behind her hands.

Kateumsi sat next to her lost in thought as he looked at his beautiful prey. "Shall Kateumsi not see the blue sky in your eyes, then?" he asked after a while in an embittered tone. "I ask little of you; only that you acknowledge my love."

Ludwina, however, remained silent and motionless. Only a quivering sigh arose from her breast from time to time.

"Kateumsi would gladly remove the ropes from your pretty feet," he continued after a short pause, still regarding her with an intense gaze, "if he knew that you would remain quiet and patient, because you cannot escape. My people would catch you right away and bring you back to me, even if Kateumsi has fallen asleep."

Again Ludwina refused to answer, but withdrew her feet and concealed them under her garment.

The Indian women returned with the horses and tied them to trees at the side of the cave; then they retired to the fire of Potolick in the interior.

As they passed, Kateumsi ordered, "Bring some tender roast so that your white mistress can enjoy something to eat." Then he turned once again to Ludwina and entreated her in an ever more insistent and passionate tone to allow him to look into her eyes, but in growing anxiety, she buried her face even deeper into the curly hair of the buffalo skin upon which she was lying.

Night had now embraced the valley completely so that the red glow of the fire danced even brighter along the rim of the giant circular opening of the cave. Its light reflected back as if trembling from the surfaces of the colossal stone blocks scattered around the entrance.

A deathly silence engulfed the valley; not even the solitary howl of a wolf interrupted the stillness, and like ghosts of darkness, the myriads bats[1] inhabiting the cave flitted nervously in and out of the glow of the firelight.

Kateumsi sat for a long time with knitted brow, his dark gaze fixed on Ludwina. Then he bent over her, laid an arm on her shoulder, and said, "Kateumsi will let his heart take pleasure in your beauty. He asks you to let him see your eyes because he will not force you to do it."

With his touch, Ludwina started, as if struck by a snake, and her body began to shake violently. "Oh God, let me die," she moaned plaintively and, in her horror, tried to draw herself into an even tighter ball.

Suddenly Kateumsi jerked around, for he had heard a strange sound that startled him. He looked toward the cave's opening, his gaze fixed intently at the space between the large boulders. Suddenly he jumped up and cried out, "Potolick, a grey bear!" The dim light of the fire outlined a colossal dark mass between the stones, a living and breathing behemoth, lumbering up the path, a low snarl rumbling in its throat. It was an enormous grey bear. With a start, Kateumsi reached for his bow and arrows and the heavy American ax he had acquired, and sprang for the oak tree in front of the cave.

The bear walked on all fours with his head lowered and had come to within twenty paces of the oak tree in front of the cave. Here he suddenly raised his huge form onto his hind legs, spread out his massive arms, let out a fearsome roar, and with his jaws wide open, started walking toward Kateumsi, who stood ready at the side of the oak with an arrow in his bow.

The enormous creature had not taken a second step when an arrow of the chief struck him in the left side and buried itself up to the feathers. With a thunderous protest, the enraged creature rushed for his enemy; but before he could reach the oak, a second arrow struck him in the breast. The furious bear clawed for Kateumsi around the trunk of the tree, but the chief was able to keep the tree between them and avoid his claws while sending another arrow into the body of the bear.

Unable to nab his prey, the bear, seething and snarling in anger, turned his attention from the chief to the cave entrance from where Ludwina, resting on one hand and holding the other outstretched, looked down in horror at the scene below. Instantly, Potolick jumped in front of her with his lance at the ready, the spear tip pointing toward the frenzied bear, which now attacked the Indian with a furious roar.

The moment the bear turned his back to Kateumsi, he grabbed the heavy ax and quickly sprang behind the monster. Just as the bear was about to throw himself upon Potolick, the chief delivered a mighty blow, practically burying the head of the ax in the skull of the bear.

As if struck by lightning, the bear collapsed to the ground, breaking the shaft of the lance which Potolick had thrust into his breast. Kateumsi let out a yell of victory that resounded through the cave and echoed back from the distant hills surrounding the valley.

At about this time, the Delawares, led by their chief with Rudolph at his side, had reached the grassy spot in front of the place where the canyon narrowed and the foaming stream carried its water through the constricted chute into the valley where Kateumsi was hiding. The riders dismounted and tied their horses to the branches of nearby bushes. They then lit several small fires.

Youngbear chose twenty of his best warriors. The others took up position next to the fires. It was very dark, but the sky was exceptionally clear, allowing the firmament to sparkle with such clarity that one could pick out any objects nearby.

"Follow me," Youngbear said to Rudolph as he strode toward the stream. "The eye of the Indian sees sharper in the dark than the eye of the white man."

His heart beating alternatively with fearful anxiety and soaring hope, Rudolph followed the chief while his warriors fell in behind in single file. Soon the last glimmering rays from the fire had disappeared behind the line of men. They reached the place where the canyon walls closed in and wound themselves silently along the treacherous, graveled trail. Not a word, not a sound passed their lips. Holding their rifles in their right hands, they carefully felt their way along the path to avoid stumbling. Without mishap, they reached the end of the canyon where it opened up into the valley.

Here Youngbear stopped and gathered his warriors around him, instructing them in a hushed voice, "Follow me into the ravine that leads to the cave, but stay behind me until my voice calls you to the fight. Let your foot tread silently like the panther, let your ear notice a leaf falling from the tree, your eye resemble the hawk. Do not shoot until I give the word, but then aim for the heart of your enemy and keep your bullets far from the White Dove, whom Kateumsi holds captive in the cave and whom the Delawares want to free. But Kateumsi will not have his warriors with him in the cave, so the bullets of Youngbear and his friend will likely do for the heart of Kateumsi."

Then Youngbear turned to Rudolph. "Give your boots to one of my warriors and take his moccasins so that your steps become as quiet as an Indian's." Rudolph quickly followed the directive of the chief, and as soon as he stood up in the soft and light footwear, Youngbear continued, "Youngbear will let you take the first shot at our enemy, but if the ball misses his heart, Kateumsi will soon hear the musket of a Delaware. If you make the slightest noise with your foot, remain still like a stone until the ear of Kateumsi is reassured. But it is harder to fool his eye; only a Delaware can do that. Now let's head for the cave. The Great Spirit will lead us."

The chief led the way through the grass, already softened with dew, followed by Rudolph and the warriors. They moved silently through the darkness, a line of shadowy, faintly outlined shapes, until they reached the opening of the gorge, whose walls seemed to flicker from the bright glow shining forth from the fire in the cave.

The chief bent over low and moved, ever so cautiously, sideways to the middle of the entrance of the ravine, where he could take cover in the long shadows of a large slab of rock that had fallen from the cliff above. Here he stopped once again, pulled Rudolph next to him, and whispered, "Do not try to pick out either Kateumsi or White Dove with your eye. Always keep the big rock between you and them, because as soon as your eye meets Kateumsi, his eye will also spot yours."

Then he gave the sign to follow, and the two began their stalk, creeping stealthily forward through the tall grass, crouching low to the ground, while making use of large rocks for cover. Foot by foot, inch by inch, they eased along the ravine toward the giant slab of stone that rose up barely thirty steps from the cave entrance and whose shadow stretched along the length of the middle of the ravine.

Terrified, Ludwina had witnessed the whole fight with the ferocious bear. She had not been able to turn her eyes away from the horrific scene. But after the fight was over and Potolick had been dismissed to the deep recesses of the cave, Kateumsi turned his attention to Ludwina; once again she withdrew into herself and kept her face hidden from his dreadful gaze.

She had not responded to any of his requests or words of enticement, and she adamantly refused to show her face. She sensed that the fight and victory over the bear had filled him with a new spirit, even wilder and less restrained.

With his arms folded, he paced back and forth across the opening of the cave, all the while gazing intently at Ludwina, a dark and sinister cast to his expression. Suddenly he broke out in wild, unrestrained laughter, while stamping his foot on the dead bear. Then he threw himself on the ground next to Ludwina and once again professed his love in a flood of passionate words.

Like the lamb awaiting the final pounce of the tiger, Ludwina sat curled in a ball, shielding herself as best she could. A cold shudder passed over her limbs. Why couldn't she will her own death as a final defense against this human monster?

The chief recognized clearly the disgust and revulsion in Ludwina, which incensed him even more. He suddenly stopped pacing, fixed his wild gaze upon Ludwina, and spoke out in exasperation, his forbearance plainly at an end. "You refuse to listen to Kateumsi's requests; you turn a deaf ear to his yearnings; you don't offer a word of thanks that he threw himself in the path of the bear and put his own life at risk in order to save yours; and you won't even reward the victor with as much as a gesture of gratitude. Kateumsi's patience has come to an end."

Ludwina felt unmistakably the storm in his inner being, which the measured and blunt tone of these last words could not conceal. Driven by the anxiety in her heart and the uncanny sensation that he had already taken hold of her bodily, she turned to face him.

Her gaze, though full of alarm and dismay, jolted the Indian like a bolt of lightning. The dark cloud lifted from his countenance, his eyes lit up with a mysterious glow, and, struggling to calm himself, he spoke. "Your eye is stronger than Kateumsi's anger, your gaze brighter than the anguish in his heart. It fills, once again, with love. I will untie your pretty feet now, so you can move free and unfettered around Kateumsi's dwelling. Your presence will add beauty and your nearness will bring joy to his heart and his poor soul, like the lark at break of day arising, will sing hymns at heaven's gate." His entire demeanor now betrayed the depth of the passion which had gained control of him; his friendly expression resembled more the smile of an evil spirit.

"Such a beautiful woman!" he uttered with a trembling voice as he went down on a knee in front of Ludwina, his gaze fixed at her feet with such intensity as though he meant to swallow them with his eyes. He leaned over and loosened the knot that bound them and then laid his hand around them.

"Oh God, help me!" cried out Ludwina at the touch of Kateumsi. She kicked reflexively with her foot, raised her body, and sought to hold him at bay with her hands. But Kateumsi held her foot firmly in his left hand and began to place his right hand gently toward her neck. At this, she gathered up all her strength and gave him such a kick that he flew backward on the floor.

Quick as a flash, she jumped to her feet, intending to flee, but Kateumsi grabbed her by her garment and pulled her back toward him with a fiendish laugh, crying out in a passion that now knew no restraint. "Come now, pretty paleface. The time has come for Kateumsi to take his pleasure: your blue eyes and white skin will be his." With this he grabbed her hand and pulled her toward the bed. In this very instant, a light flashed brilliantly from the large slab of rock and the thunderous report of a rifle shook the cave. Kateumsi jerked backward, grasping for his breast with his left hand, but with his right hand he reached for the knife in his belt. Crying out in fury, he sprang after Ludwina, who had fled screaming toward the back of the cave. At his second step, however, another shot rang out. Struck once again, he turned, and with a last surge of effort, he overtook Ludwina and attempted to plunge the knife into her breast. Potolick, however, jumped between the two and caught his hand.

An instant later, Rudolph reached the Comanche chief. Grabbing him by the hair, he flung him backward to the floor of the cave with such force that he rolled in his own blood.

With only a short cry of joy which emanated from the depths of her soul, Ludwina lay on the breast of her beloved. She had no words: crying and sobbing were words enough for the moment, and the two held each other in a tight and fervent embrace. The world around them was forgotten in the intensity of their joyful relief.

Youngbear stood there looking at the fortunate pair, an expanse of delight animating his features. He, too, appeared oblivious to everything around him as he allowed the joyful scene to sink into his being.

While they stood there so overcome with joy, the Delawares had silently approached. They looked approvingly first at their chief, then at the couple, and finally they turned their gazes triumphantly upon their hated enemy, Kateumsi, who was wrestling with death.

Like a dying predator, he rolled his bloody eyes toward the Delawares while babbling incoherent curses. But his life was rapidly departing him. A stream of blood had gushed from his wounds. One last shudder passed over his limbs, and Kateumsi was a corpse.

No sooner had Rudolph regained his composure than he threw himself on Youngblood's breast and stammered his heartfelt thanks for the rescue of his bride.

"Youngbear friend of Young Eagle and White Dove," replied the Delaware, still overflowing with feelings of happiness.

Then Ludwina stepped up to him, opened her arms, and threw them around the neck of the Indian. "Yes, you are the truest friend that this world has ever known, you good, dear Youngbear." With this, she pressed him to her breast and kissed him on the lips. "Thank you, thank you, forever thanks to you, best of all friends," was all that she could say, as she held out her hand, for her tears drowned her voice.

"Youngbear was in debt to you; Youngbear only did what your friend, your debtor, had to do," the chief said in a flurry of happiness, and pointed to the red silk scarf around his neck. The words came from deep within his soul, for the Indians know nothing lower, nothing more despicable and dishonorable, than to betray a friend.

Now Ludwina and Rudolph turned to Potolick, who stood off to the side at some distance, observing stoically the tearful reunion and rejoicing also in the favorable conclusion of this episode. The two poured out their thanks to him as well for grabbing the knife hand of Kateumsi, frustrating this, his dying act of evil. Both asked Potolick to accompany them back to Friedrichsburg so that they could reward him for his good deed. Potolick, however, pointed to his dead chief and said, "Kateumsi has to ride along with me so that I can bury him with his fathers. But Potolick will come to Friedrichsburg soon to be with his many white friends."

Only now did the reunited couple think about the bear lying close to the fire. Ludwina explained in a few short words how the frightful creature had come to be there.

Potolick had in the meantime fetched the venison ham from the oak tree and carried it to the fire. He called to the Indian women and instructed them to prepare a meal.

Ludwina then took a seat next to the fire, where shortly before she had wished for her own death. The waves of emotion which had rocked her so violently, first this way and then that, now subsided somewhat. Rudolph and Youngbear took a place on either side.

"Oh, if only my good father knew about my rescue," said Ludwina as she folded her hands. "His anxiety will be the death of the poor man."

"The best rider and the best horse shall take the worry from his heart," interposed Youngbear happily. He quickly walked over to his warriors, who had lit a fire in front of the cave. They had gathered around and also had begun to roast some venison. One of them immediately arose, grabbed his weapon, and hurried out of the ravine.

"We will reward him handsomely," said Rudolph and Ludwina at the same time to the chief, after he had returned and thanked him once again for his love and friendship, which seemed to be bottomless.

"Tomorrow, before the sun rises above us, your father's heart will beat with joy and relief," replied Youngbear. He took his place once again next to Ludwina, who began to relate the whole harrowing tale of her capture. The tears welled up in her eyes and many sighs came from her breast as she told her story.

But soon, an overpowering weariness overcame her, nature's remedy for the intense and extended emotional stress which had attended the whole affair. Ludwina was barely able to partake of the roasted venison before her eyes closed in exhaustion. Rudolph and Youngbear, with a smile of satisfaction, took her by the hands and led her to the bed, where she collapsed in sleep.

"Now, you must also get some sleep, and you will fall into a deep sleep even against your will," said Youngbear to Rudoph with a grin on his face. Both were soon fast asleep and wrapped in the world of dreams. The warriors were also fast asleep next to their fire; only one stayed awake to keep watch.

The sun's rays had already penetrated the cave before Ludwina opened her eyes for the first time to greet the morning. Her companions had allowed her to sleep until she awoke on her own. Breakfast was quickly prepared and consumed, and everyone made ready to depart.

Ludwina and Rudolph extracted one last promise from Potolick that he would come to visit them in Friedrichsburg as soon as possible. They then bid a last farewell, and the party struck out on the return path to the narrow cut in the canyon. They led Kateumsi's horse behind them for Ludwina to ride. By the light of day, the narrow pass presented few difficulties for the party, and they soon arrived at the camp of the other Delawares.

Camp was quickly broken and the necessary preparations made for the return trip. A buffalo hide was placed over the saddle of Kateumsi for additional padding, Ludwina was lifted up, and before a half-hour had elapsed, she was riding between Rudolph and Youngbear along the grassy bank of the creek. The warriors followed behind in a long parade with their captured horses. Before long, they reached the spot where Kateumsi, with his beautiful trophy, had parted company with his warriors. The three contented riders continued with all possible dispatch along their return route through the hills.

CHAPTER 18

Dismay · The Messenger of Glad Tidings · Jubilation · Yearning · Reunion
The Welcome · The Abandoned Town · The Wedding Day · Presentation of Gifts
The Polonaise · The Honored Guest · Merriment

HE HORRIBLE FATE OF LUDWINA had thrust the citizens of Friedrichsburg into deep sadness. Simultaneously, they had renewed concern and fear for their own safety, for who could lie down in his bed
with any confidence as long as this ferocious predator, this Kateumsi, and his
bloody band still roamed the countryside? No one could be sure that they
might not be the next to be attacked and murdered in their own beds before
their neighbors could come to their aid. And no one could be certain that their
house might not be set afire in the middle of the night and that they would be
awakened by the destructive flames.

Sadness, however, a deep and abiding sadness about the fate of Ludwina,
was the dominant emotion. The anxiety seemed to grow from hour to hour for
this beloved and venerated member of their community. Already a day and a
night had passed since Rudolph and the Delawares had set off in pursuit of her
captors, and still no news had arrived.

Youngbear and Ludwina at the dance. Drawing by James C. Kearney.

The Nimanski household was never lacking for friends and well-wishers seeking to offer words of solace and comfort to the distraught father. The director Schubbert was often among these friends. But what meaningful consolation could all the sincere words of concern, all the heartfelt testimonials, really offer? They could not restore the lost happiness; they could not bring back Ludwina.

This morning the tension increased with each passing hour; the desire for some word about the expedition rose to a fever pitch. The people began congregating first at the *Verein* compound and then at the Nimanski home, hoping for some news. Whenever people met, you would hear, "Any news about Ludwina yet?" But the question was always met with a dejected look and with words of regret.

The morning had edged toward noontime. The director had just come from the Nimanski household and was walking up San Saba *Straße*. One could clearly see in his outward bearing that he, too, was losing hope for the rescue of Ludwina. At almost every house along the way, people inquired about the fate of the captured girl. All he could do was shake his head and continue along his way.

It was twelve o'clock and most of the citizens of the town were at home taking their noon meal, when suddenly a commotion arose from the far end of San Saba *Straße*. Everyone began running to their windows and doors to see what was happening.

A Delaware Indian galloped past, his horse steamy from heat and covered in sweat. He offered neither word nor sign in reply to the questions hurled his way from both sides of the street. They all realized, however, that he must be bringing news, and, abandoning their food and drink, they hurried after him in the direction of the *Verein* compound.

Even before he reached the area, all the officials, guards, and servants had rushed out into the street to see what the cause of the disturbance was. When they saw that it was a Delaware, they all stood frozen in anticipation, for they knew this would be the news they were awaiting. And whether good or bad could not be read at first glance from the demeanor of the messenger.

The director also approached him in trepidation and asked even before he had dismounted whether or not he had good news to report. The warrior, however, refused to answer until he had dismounted and walked up to Schubbert and shook his hand. He then reported in a solemn tone, "Youngbear sends word that Ludwina is rescued and Kateumsi is dead."

As if from one mouth, a resounding cheer arose from the crowd that had gathered. The cries of joy were picked up by others up and down the street, and soon an answering cheer was heard from the far end of the town. There could only be one reason for jubilation: good news about Ludwina.

The Delaware was practically hauled bodily into the building. The crowd surged forward, curious to press him for more details and shake his hand. The director, however, took him by the hand and ushered him into the dining hall, where the noon meal was just being served. But before the Indian entered, he asked that his horse be led around for an hour, a request that Burg immediately asked one of the guards to perform.[1]

Schubbert sent a messenger straightaway to Nimanski's father to share the good news. The word, however, had spread rapidly from house to house and throughout the town so that the messenger had barely covered half the length of San Saba *Straße* before he met the major rushing up the street toward the *Verein* compound in a burst of excitement.

He was greeted with congratulations from all present when he entered the dining hall. Tears of joy and relief filled the old man's eyes as he took a seat at the table next to the director and opposite the messenger.

The Delaware now gave a full account of Ludwina's rescue and closed with the prediction that she would arrive back into town before the sun had set. Most likely never before had the entire population of a town participated so fully in such a shared moment of joy as the citizens of Friedrichsburg at this, the announcement that Ludwina had been rescued. Old and young alike were moved to tears, and all awaited with growing anticipation the moment the adored and respected friend to all could be welcomed back into the town.

Many of the men, driven by impatience, could not stand to wait until the rescued girl came back into town. They had to see her, had to go out to greet her, and so, some by foot, others on horseback, they rushed out of the town along the path in the direction of the hills. The director and the major hurriedly finished their noon meal and mounted swift horses, for they intended to be the first to be able to shout a hurrah of welcome.

It was very touching to see the old man: so eager—continually urging the horse that the director had lent him to an ever brisker gait—and so emotional, his countenance beaming with joy and tears of relief rolling down his cheeks. From tree to tree and hill to hill, he kept his eyes focused in the distance to espy the delight of his life, his Ludwina.

Up and down they continued along the trail, urging their horses ever forward, mindless to their needs. Mile after mile receded behind their fleet hooves when suddenly, as they climbed yet another hill, the forms of Ludwina, Rudolph, and Youngbear appeared above them.

"Great God Almighty! My child! I thank Thee!" cried out the major in a quivering voice, and spurred his horse into a gallop to cover the remaining interval, whereupon Ludwina received him with a cry of joy. The old man sprang from the saddle with a youthful quickness that belied his years. At the same time, Ludwina flew from the back of her horse to the ground and fell in the arms of her father.

It was a touching moment, the two both sobbing like babies, holding each other in a tight embrace, as if they never intended to separate. The director, Rudolph, and Youngbear stood nearby, deeply moved, sharing in this moment of blessed happiness.

After the first wave of turbulent emotion had passed, Nimanski turned to Rudolph and the chief as if he intended to embrace both at the same time in his arms. But Rudolph was the first to feel his embrace. Then the major pressed the chief to his heart and, choked with emotion, stammered a few words of thanks.

It was a long time before everyone fully regained their composure, but finally Rudolph lifted Ludwina back into the saddle, the men mounted their horses, and, in the highest spirits, they turned their horses in the direction of home.

Several miles from the town, in a large meadow, they came across the advance delegation from Friedrichsburg who, swinging their hats wildly in the air and voicing hurrahs of triumph, welcomed the captive with a thousand well-wishes. Soon thereafter they came upon the men on foot, who greeted them in a similar fashion.

The large column continued along the trail toward the town in the final light of the afternoon sky. The number of well-wishers swelled as ever more friends of Ludwina kept adding to the number. When the procession finally emerged from the hills into the valley of Friedrichsburg, the women and children of Friedrichsburg rushed forward, expressing their joy with shouts and hurrahs. But hardly had they given voice to their happiness than the thunderous boom of the cannon announced the town's welcome, echoing back and forth across the surrounding hills.

Surrounded by the milling throng of well-wishers, Ludwina arrived at her house, which had been festooned with wreaths of flowers and vines. Here she paused to express her gratitude for the outpouring of love and sympathy which had been shown to her, but the tears choked her words.

The crowd now turned their attention to the Delaware chief and his warriors, showering them with words of appreciation and thankfulness. They followed Youngbear and his men in triumph through the city to the *Verein* compound, where, accompanied by their hurrahs, the chief entered the building with the director.

The entire town of Friedrichsburg breathed a collective sigh of relief this evening. The threat which had hovered over them like a stubborn and persistent storm cloud had finally lifted: Kateumsi, the human monster, the bloodthirsty villain, was dead.

Tonight it would not be necessary to check the weapons and place them within reach before going to bed, and many a prayer of thanks was offered to the heavens for the liberation of Friedrichsburg from eternal worry and anxiety.

The relief was short-lived, however, for the following morning brought news which once again created consternation among the citizens of Friedrichsburg. A rider from Austin had arrived in the early hours with the report that the Mormons had disappeared and abandoned their town.[2]

People found it impossible to believe the news because just a few days prior, the Mormons had delivered a load of sawed lumber to the town. Immediately upon receipt of the information, the director mounted his horse to ride over to the settlement to see for himself the truth of the report. A number of curious citizens joined him for the ride.

What they saw confirmed the report: the town was abandoned and not a trace of the Mormons could be found. Using more than fifty colossal wagons, each pulled by six or eight oxen, this industrious, energetic people had pulled stakes completely in order to blaze a path through the wilderness to El Paso on the Rio Grande.[3] From there, they intended to follow the road to Santa Fe, and, thence, on through the Rocky Mountains to the Great Salt Lake, there to join their brothers who had established a New Jerusalem, a capital for the Mormon empire.

All the ironwork in the neat cottages had been removed; otherwise, they stood just as they had been when their owners lived in them. The mill, likewise, had been stripped of all its iron fittings and machinery, while the outsized smokehouses, where the people had cured the many hams and slabs of bacon from their large herd of swine, stood empty and forlorn, their doors swinging in the wind.

Gone they were, these Mormons, as suddenly and unexpectedly as they had arrived. Once again they found themselves on a long passage of many months' duration: a journey for the most part through uncharted territory, through trackless mountains, across barren plains, in a continual struggle with the elements and with hostile tribes, relying solely on their own wit and resourcefulness to overcome all obstacles, confront every danger, and endure continual deprivation and hardship.

The disappearance of the Mormons was a great loss for Friedrichsburg, and it rendered the new road to Austin of even greater significance. Now, at least, it would be possible to procure over this road the shingles, cornmeal, and many other things that the Mormons had been supplying to the town.

If it had been possible, the people would have picked up the abandoned houses and moved them intact to their own town. This was, of course, unworkable. Still, a good part of what was left behind eventually found its way into the city. The houses were cannibalized especially for their roofs and cedar shingles, which were highly prized.

Not everyone in Friedrichsburg, it must be said, was sad to see the Mormons depart. Unfortunately, a few shenanigans and fraudulent deals had clouded the overall favorable disposition of the townspeople. One of these episodes involved Mr. Grey himself. The esteemed and charismatic leader, it seems, had induced some citizens to lend him several thousand dollars in hard currency under false pretenses, and, in his haste to depart, he had neglected to repay his debts.[4] But now they were gone and there was nothing the citizens of Friedrichsburg could do to keep them from their wanderings. The memory of the Mormons was soon enough displaced by the upcoming marriage of Rudolph and Ludwina, a joyous event, which all the citizens of Friedrichsburg looked forward to with great anticipation.

In light of Ludwina's abduction and dramatic rescue, the whole town became involved in the preparations for the happy day more than they might have otherwise. The citizenry wanted to do justice to the significance of the event. So the houses in town were decorated with flowers and wreaths; the people were attired in their best suits and dresses; and, just as on the anniversary of the founding of the town, a dance floor was erected for the people's enjoyment. This time, however, it was placed in the shade of the oak trees near the *Verein* compound. Also, a booth was set up to serve the wine and brandy that the major had ordered from Neu Braunfels in sufficient quantity to satisfy the requirement for an appropriate round of toasts. Finally, the musicians in the community had reconstituted their orchestra in order to enhance both the solemnity and the gaiety of the occasion with their instrumental talents.

At the break of dawn, the cannon announced that the festive day had arrived. Soon, life began to stir in every household as the people busied themselves in final preparations so that they would have the rest of the day free to enjoy themselves. Then all hurried to the Nimanski home to accompany the bridal pair to the church for the commencement of the ceremony.

By ten o'clock the entire population of Friedrichsburg had assembled in front of the Nimanski household. Ludwina and Rudolph, in company with her father and the director, stepped out of the house to begin the walk to the church. The rest of the townspeople took their place behind them in a solemn procession.

As before, the House of God could not accommodate all the devout onlookers, this huge throng of happy well-wishers. Many had to find a place as best they could at the door or a window in order to catch a glimpse of the beloved and venerated bridal couple.

There they stood: Rudolph in the full vigor and vitality of youth, with an expression of complete earthly happiness on his handsome, masculine features;

Ludwina the perfect embodiment of female beauty, graciousness, and charm, the magic of the moment animating her angelic appearance.

The pastor was not lacking in material with which to embellish his sermon, and since he, too, was full of admiration for both the bride and the groom, his words flowed from the heart with a natural ease. When it came to the point in the ceremony where he placed their hands together and called on Heaven to bless their union, he could no longer hold back his tears, and in the whole assembled crowd one could not have found a single pair of dry eyes.

After the formalities were concluded, each wanted to be the first to offer congratulations. It took some time before the married couple could leave the church to receive the well-wishes of those standing outside. Then everyone adjourned to their respective households to make final preparations for the upcoming festivities, especially to change clothes and dress appropriately for the upcoming dance.

Rudolph and Ludwina, along with her father, had just arrived back at home when the Delaware chief Youngbear arrived with four young women bearing gifts with which to honor his friends.

All were true works of art. They consisted of a large number of beautifully worked and ornamented leather items for Ludwina's adornment. Additionally, there were several nicely tanned pelts for use as rugs, bed covers, and saddle blankets.

It was touching to see how the Indian observed Ludwina with a sense of deep satisfaction and joy. Ludwina received each of the presents, article by article, with words of admiration and a look of complete delight on her face. She showed each item in turn to her father and Rudolph. At the end, she reached out her hand in thanks to the chief and also spoke words, once again, of her profound gratitude for all he had done—for his friendship which seemed boundless.

These fresh acknowledgments brought tears of joy to the eyes of Youngbear and led him to say, "Youngbear's heart has beat in joy on many different occasions: when he emerged from the icy heights of the mountain into the bright sunshine to behold the full majestic panorama of the landscape spreading out before his feet and the awesome blue of the endless ocean beyond that; when he flew with the speed of the wind on his fleet-footed steed into the rows of the buffalo herd and emerged with a bountiful kill to carry back to his tent; when in the heat of the fight he gave the fearsome battle cry of the Delaware and then stood victorious over his vanquished enemies, who lay at his feet pleading for mercy—but none of these things has filled his heart with as much joy as the friendship of White Dove and Young Eagle."

After Ludwina once again had given thanks to her half-wild friend for the beautiful gifts, she looked into his dark eyes and, in her naturally charming manner, said, "Now, Youngbear, I have a present for you so that you can always remember your friend Ludwina. Today is the most beautiful day of my life, and without you and what you have done, I would never have been able to celebrate it." At this, she took a golden brooch set with precious stones from her breast and fastened it to the red scarf that was around Youngbear's neck. Then she said happily, "Now look in the mirror and see if that doesn't look pretty!"

Youngbear stood there in front of the glass, absolutely delighted at the lovely present from his dear friend, when the major stepped forward and handed him a magnificent pair of matched pistols, inlaid with silver, together with holsters made from softly tanned deerskin. "And so that you also have something to remember the father of your friend, to whom you have given back the joy of his life, please accept these pistols as a token of my deep gratitude. Perhaps someday, in a dangerous situation, they will stand you in good stead."

Youngbear was beside himself with joy and did not have a clue as to what he should do and how he ought to respond, but, in order to heighten his happiness even more, Rudolph then handed him a very large and exquisite music box, and said, "And so that you will also not forget Young Eagle, please take this device, a true product of German craftsmanship, to remember me every evening around your campfire." He then placed the music box on the table and wound the key, at which moment a beautiful German gallopade began to play, its tones flowing pure and true from the magic box.

Youngbear could no longer maintain his composure. He stood there in front of the little instrument as if bewitched, as if he could not trust his ears and eyes. After it had finished the song and the last note had sounded, he grabbed Rudolph's hand in a rush of enthusiasm and said, "You will really give Youngbear this magical thing which will obey him and give him music whenever he commands?"

"Yes indeed, my good friend, the box is now yours and must play for you whenever you desire," replied Rudolph, who was deeply touched by the elation the Indian felt.

Rudolph wound it once again, showing Youngbear how it must be done, and, as before, the little box tinkled its tunes, to the delight of the Delaware. Then Rudolph explained to him how he could amplify the sound by placing the device on an overturned pot or kettle.

Youngbear stood there in befuddled amazement, at a complete loss for words, as if his gaze could not absorb the extent of the treasures he had received. At this point, the guests invited to the noon meal, among them the director, began arriving to a hearty welcome.

The festive table had been placed on the porch, and Youngbear was seated next to Ludwina. Happiness and cheerfulness spiced the meal that the old servants of Rudolph had carefully and skillfully prepared. The major had supplied a strong Hungarian wine, which enhanced the mood even more. As usual, Ludwina's angelic presence worked its magic upon the assembled guests.

As they ate, the faint strains of dance music became perceptible from the festivities at the other end of the town. The director reminded the assembled guests that the young married couple would be expected to make an appearance before the happy citizens of Friedrichsburg, who were eagerly anticipating their presence.

The sun had gone down and dusk had descended over the land before the wedding party started on the path to the dance. Rudolph and Youngbear led the way, with Ludwina between them. When they reached the oak grove, the music fell silent and the happy crowd spilled out to greet the newly married couple. The trumpets sounded a fanfare as the crowd ushered them through a portal especially set up in their honor and festooned with flowers and greenery.

Once through the portal, the band struck up a lively polonaise. Ludwina threw a questioning glance at Rudolph, who swiftly nodded his approval. She then took Youngbear by the hand and led him into the circle with her right hand, proud and confident in her bearing.[5]

A thunderous "Hip, hip, hurrah for the Delawares!" resounded from a thousand throats, drowning out the music, and only now did it fully sink in to this son of the wilderness the extent to which he was being honored.

Anyone could clearly see that his emotions had gained the upper hand and were threatening to overpower him. His body shook; his eyes filled with tears. Still, he strode forward, upright and dignified, even aristocratic in bearing, confidently following the lead of his beautiful partner, as if he had been preparing his whole life for this hallowed moment, while behind them the rest of the gaily attired pairs fell in line.

The moment the polonaise began, the cannon sent forth a thunderous salute of greeting, and shot after shot continued to roll through the valley of Friedrichsburg during the course of the dance.

As soon as the music had ceased, Rudolph and Ludwina, together with the chief, were led to an ornately decorated throne at the side of the dance floor, where the young bride took her place between her husband and her friend.

This time, the celebration of the citizens of Friedrichsburg was not disturbed. And long after the young married couple had disappeared from the circle of revelers, a continuous round of "Long shall they live!" resounded from the happy crowd. Only after the stars in the sky had begun to fade did the music finally come to an end.

THE END

Notes

INTRODUCTION

1. For further discussion of the *Adelsverein*, see Kearney, *Nassau Plantation*, 10–21.
2. Koch, "Federal Indian Policy," 223, 224.
3. Biesele, *History*, 50.
4. Ibid., 69.
5. There is, for instance, not a single plaque to commemorate Dr. Schubbert at the Market Square, or central plaza, in Fredericksburg, even though the *Vereinskirche*, which was commissioned and built at the behest of Dr. Schubbert, has become the central symbol of the city.
6. Kitchen, *Political Economy*, 34.
7. Kiesewetter, *Industrieller Revolution*, 125.
8. Contributing technological factors were improved sanitation through the replacement of wool with factory-produced cotton, more readily washed than wool, and the introduction of vaccination in 1815, which reduced infant mortality rates (Kitchen, *Political Economy*, 44).

9. Kiesewetter, *Industrieller Revolution*, 141.
10. For a comprehensive discussion of the agricultural reforms that fundamentally changed the structure of land ownership and land use after 1815, see Abel, *Geschichte*.
11. Kitchen, *Political Economy*, 24.
12. Glaser, *Deutsche und Amerikaner*, 121.
13. Jordan, *German Seed in Texas Soil*, 50.
14. Translation by Anders Saustrup. The letter is reproduced in two early books about Texas: Dunt, *Reise nach Texas* (1834), 4–16, and Achenbach, *Reiseabentheuer und Begebenheiten in Nord-Amerika im Jahre 1833* (1835), 132–135.
15. Roeder, *Generations*, 12–20.
16. Stöhr, "Die erste deutsche Frau in Texas," 374.
17. Biesele, *History*, 43–49, 54–55.
18. Morgenthaler, *Promised Land*, 12.
19. Gammel, *Laws*, 2:777.
20. Bourgeoisie d'Orvanne, Henri Castro, and Henry Francis Fischer were the principals in three of these grants. The first two were French, and the third German, although all three enjoyed dual citizenship. They are often listed with others as d'Orvanne/Ducos, Fischer/Miller. This was a requirement of the law as written, but the other partner was merely titular. See Morgenthaler, *Promised Land*; Miller, *Bounty and Donation Land Grants of Texas*, 27.
21. Kearney, *Nassau Plantation*, 12.
22. When Napoleon put an end to the Holy Roman Empire with the *Reichsdeputationshauptschluß* [Imperial Decree] of 1803, reducing "Germany" from a collection of about three hundred states to a little more than thirty, a large number of German noblemen found themselves "mediatized," that is, placed under the sovereignty of other rulers. The kingdoms, dukedoms, and so on, over which they had formerly exercised sovereign status were merged with other states. Although still possessing wealth, prestige, and titles, they were now politically marginalized. These noblemen came to be termed the *Standesherren*, a classification of German nobility for which there is no English equivalent. For a fuller discussion of their role and importance, see Kearney, *Nassau Plantation*, 17–19.
23. Strubberg and several other contemporary writers preferred the term "*Fürstenverein*." A *Fürst* in the hierarchy of German noblemen ranked quite high, and the *Adelsverein* counted several among their ranks. There is no English equivalent of *Fürst*, which creates problems in translation. It is sometimes rendered as "prince," but this is not quite accurate.
24. Hawgood, *Tragedy*, 142.
25. Solon, "History," 5.
26. Meusebach, "An Answer," 12.
27. Roemer, *Texas*, 246.
28. Richardson, *Comanche Barrier to South Plains Settlement*; Roemer, *Texas*, 274.
29. Biesele, *History*, 83.
30. Tiling, *The History of the German Element in Texas*, 53.

31. "Solms Bericht," March 27, 1845, SBAt, XL, 87.
32. For a list of officials in New Braunfels, see "Texas *Verein* Account Books," *Verein* Collection, 3c32, Dolph Briscoe Center for American History, UT Austin.
33. Biesele, *History*, 123.
34. Solon, " History," 22.
35. Biesele, *History*, 139.
36. Sehm, *Armand*, 3; Barba, *Life and Works*, 29–31; Huber, "Frederic Armand Strubberg, Alias Dr. Shubbert," 38–40.
37. One biographer claims the shipwreck was near St. Louis, Missouri. See Huber, "Frederic Armand Strubberg, Alias Dr. Shubbert," 38.
38. See Losch, "Friedrich Armand Strubbergs fürstliche Abkunft."
39. Ulf Debelius to James C. Kearney, private letter, author's translation, January 26, 2011.
40. Hermann Seele, for instance, wrote: "At noon today the group from Hildsheim left by steamboat for Houston. From there they will travel up to the San Gabriel. Schubbert has acquired large parcels of land there, and they will have to work for him in exchange for the land he will make available to them" (Seele, *Diary*, February 10, 1845, 227). See also Meusebach an Castell, March 6, 1846, SBAt, LII, 138–142; Centralverwaltung, "Geschäftsbericht," November 4, 1846, SBAt, XXX, 1–4.
41. Biesele, "The San Saba Colonization Co.," 169–183.
42. In fact, the San Gabriel in Milam County would have been an ideal place to come into contact with many different tribes of Indians because it was the border zone between several different tribes. Also, the Torrey Trading Post, which held the licensed concession for trade with the Indians, was located only thirty to forty miles to the north near present-day Waco. The post was situated near the historic council grounds, where various tribes seasonally congregated, often in large numbers, to engage in trade and barter.
43. Strubberg's grandniece inherited his personal papers. Whether these papers might have thrown light on Strubberg's private life, we will never know. The papers, as well as Strubberg's grandniece, perished in the Battle of Berlin in 1945.
44. Meusebach an Castell, March 6, 1846, SBAt, LII, 138; see also Huber, "Frederic Armand Strubberg, Alias Dr. Shubbert," 4.
45. Kearney, *Nassau Plantation*, 130.
46. Seele, *Cypress*, 89.
47. Ibid.
48. Barba, *Life and Works*, 42.
49. See, for instance, Schubbert an Cappes, "Bericht über Friedrichsburg und Nassau Kolonie," January 29, 1847, SBAt, XLIII, 163. See also Seele, *Cypress*, 45.
50. Most commentators assume the epidemic was cholera, but others attribute it to meningitis (Biesele, *History*, 129–131; 142). Dr. Schubbert diagnosed it as scurvy and treated it accordingly. See Biesele, *History*, 142.
51. Seele, *Cypress*, 89.
52. "Bertram Bericht," June 1847, SBAt, XXVIII, 73.

53. *Vereinskirche* translates as Church of the *Verein*. This reflects the fact that it was a communal, nondenominational church, built at the *Verein*'s expense. Local residents referred to it as the *Kafeemühle* [coffee mill] because of its peculiar octagonal shape. The structure also served on occasion as a schoolhouse and a communal meeting house. The original church was torn down in 1898 because it stood in the middle of Main Street. The present replica was built in 1936 as a project of the Works Progress Administration and is situated slightly to the north of the original site.

54. Letter reproduced in Barba, *Life and Works*, 47, 48.

55. Von Coll to Meusebach, July 17, 1847, reproduced in Huber, "Frederic Armand Strubberg, Alias Dr. Shubbert," 61.

56. Penninger, *Festausgabe*.

57. As an example of this, see Barba, "Friedrich Armand Strubberg," 42.

58. "Aufruhr in Neu Braunfels gegen Meusebach," SBAt, XXVIII, 27.

59. Meusebach to Castell, February 2, 1847, reproduced in Huber, "Frederic Armand Strubberg, Alias Dr. Shubbert," 49, 50.

60. "Meusebach Bericht," January 19, 1847, SBAt, LXIII, 45.

61. In the spring of 1847 Meusebach wrote: "Der Verein lässt sich nicht von Anlage von Zwischen-Settlements ein, die nur Geld kosten, nichts einbringen und von den eigentlichen Zweck, möglich bald in den Grant zu gelangen . . . ableiten." [The Verein should refrain from the establishment of in-between settlements that would only cost money, not bring anything in, and divert from the main purpose, namely to get to the grant as soon as possible.] ("Meusebach Bericht," April 1, 1847, SBAt, XXXI, 66, 67).

62. Fischer-Miller Grant Transfers, GLOR. By the terms of the Fischer-Miller contract with the Republic of Texas, concluded June 7, 1842, and extended to September 1, 1843, each married settler was to receive a certificate from the republic for 640 acres of land and each unmarried settler for 320 acres. Fischer and Miller were to receive a bonus of 640 acres for every ten families introduced and 320 acres for each individual (see Solon, "History," 19). In addition to this, the emigrant families signed a document in Germany in which they promised to turn over one-half of their land to Fischer and Miller. The *Adelsverein* entered into association with Fischer and Miller in the summer of 1845 but bought out the contract and dissolved the association in December 1845. Eventually (a very complicated story), 4,200 certificates were issued by the state to the settlers for a total of 1,920,000 acres (see Fischer an die Aktionaere, May 31, 1855, SBAt, LIII, 165).

Unfortunately, many of these certificates ended up in the hands of unscrupulous speculators. Still, it must be said that the State of Texas kept faith with its side of the bargain in respect to the settlers. The *Adelsverein*, however, never received title to the premium lands to which it was entitled (192,000 acres) nor to the one-half of the land issued to the settlers, to which it was also entitled (960,000 acres). The *Adelverein*'s position in Texas had been prejudiced and compromised in every conceivable way over the years and, in the end, the company was forced to cede its claims to a consortium of creditors who had organized themselves in 1853 as the Texas and

German Emigration Co.—a sad outcome for such an ambitious and promising venture. For his part, Baron von Meusebach had served the *Adelsverein* only as a *Beamter*, a salaried official. He was not a significant stockholder in the corporation and not personally entitled to any land except as specified by the terms of his employment. In a fitting conclusion, however, he was appointed land commissioner in 1855 and ended up personally issuing land certificates to many of the German settlers who had come over under the auspices of the *Adelsverein*. One must assume that he found this to be deeply gratifying, for the certificates were a direct outcome of his stubborn perseverance in the years 1845, 1846, and 1847 (Solon, "History," 85).

63. Bené an den Grafen von Castell, "Finanzlage der Colonie," November 23, 1847, SBAt, XLIV, 2-11; Bené an den Grafen von Castell, "Colonie Bericht," January 9, 1848, SBAt, XLIV, 30; Bené an den Grafen von Castell, "Allgemeiner Bericht und Rechnungsabschluss," January 9, 1848, SBAt, XLIV, 119.

64. Schubbert an Meusebach, July 5, 1847, SBAt, LXI, 246–253.

65. Meusebach claimed that the "Fassungssystem" [Comprehensive system] that Dr. Schubbert had promoted in Friedrichsburg cost the Verein $8,000 a month to maintain ("Meusebach Bericht," April 1, 1847, SBAt, XXXI, 66, 67).

66. For those interested in following the controversy between Meusebach and Schubbert in the Solms-Braunfels Archives, the relevant passages are as follows: Schubbert an Cappes, "Bericht über Friedrichsburg und Nassau Kolonie," January 29, 1847, SBAt, XLIII, 83–86; Schubbert an Cappes, "Betr. Colonie," February 8, 1847, SBAt, XLIII, 120–121; Schubbert an Cappes, "Abänderung der Colonialverhältnisse dringend erforderlich," March 13, 1847, SBAt, XLIII, 131–141; Schubbert an Cappes, "Bericht über Colonialverhältnisse," March 28, 1847, SBAt, XLIII, 146–150.

Cappes replied on March 28, 1847: Cappes an Schubbert, "Antwort auf vorstehenden Bericht," March 28, 1847, SBAt, XLIII, 151.

Schubbert also wrote Meusebach on several occasions: Schubbert dem General Commissär von Meusebach, March 29, 1847, SBAt, XLI, 212–215; Schubbert an den Herrn General-Commissair von Meusebach in Neu-Braunfels, April 20, 1847, SBAt, XLI, 187–206; Schubbert an Meusebach, "Hülferuf!" May 26, 1847. SBAt, XLIII, 152–165; Schubbert an den Herrn General-Commissair von Meusebach in Neu-Braunfels, July 5, 1847, SBAt, XLI, 246–253.

Meusebach wrote Schubbert: Meusebach an die Direktion in Friedrichsburg, July 1, 1847, SBAt, LIV, 47–49; Meusebach an den Direktor Dr. Schubbert zu Friedrichsburg, July 12, 1847, SBAt, LIV, 123–126.

67. *Freidenker*, or freethinker: Many educated Germans of the period felt liberated and emboldened by the spirit of German critical philosophy that began with Immanuel Kant (1724–1804)and continued through Georg Wilhelm Friedrich Hegel (1770–1831). This spirit, as they understood it, was incompatible with traditional Christian assumptions, especially in respect to the divinity of Christ and the infallibility of the Bible. In the 1840s, many fell under the influence of the German philosopher Ludwig Feuerbach (1804–1872), himself a student of Hegel. In 1841 Feuerbach published a devastating attack on orthodox Christianity entitled *Das Wesen des Christentums* [The

Essence of Christianity]. Several of the prominent *"Freidenker"* who emigrated to Texas routinely referred to themselves as *"Feuerbachianer,"* or "Feuerbachytes" (see Sörgel, *Sojourn*, 92, 93). Added to this was the widespread conviction that the Christian church in Germany was a willing partner to the all-pervasive *"Obrigkeit"* [governmental authority] under which many chafed. German freethinkers are credited with establishing several "Lateiner" [educated] settlements in Texas, noted for the absence of churches. Meusebach did not conceal the fact that he was a *Freidenker*. See also Ransleben, *Hundred Years of Comfort*.

68. Schubbert an Cappes, "Bericht über Friedrichsburg und Nassau Kolonie," January 29, 1847, SBAt, XLIII, 85; Bené an Castell, February 22, 1848, SBAt, XLIV, 149.

69. Meusebach an den Direktor Dr. Schubbert zu Friedrichsburg, July 12, 1847, SBAt, LIV, 123.

70. Von Coll an Cappes, "Ausführliche Bericht über die elenden Zustände in der Colonie," February 2, 1847, SBAt, LXIII, 108.

71. German Emigration Co. and Frederic Schubbert, Lease on Nassau Plantation, Fayette County Deed Book D, 536–542.

72. The shoot-out was an extremely complicated affair. For a complete description, I refer the reader to chapter 10 in my book on Nassau Plantation. A shorthand version of the event would read as follows: Dr. Schubbert did not accept his dismissal graciously, and he refused to concede that his lease on Nassau Plantation was invalid. In the fall of 1847 he associated with several unsavory characters in La Grange, Texas, who were actually playing a double-game with him in an attempt to steal the Nassau slaves. These men helped him to wrest control of the plantation by force. The new commissioner-general of the German Emigration Company, Hermann Spiess, assembled a group of men in New Braunfels, and on October 20, 1847, attempted to take back the plantation at gunpoint. A gun battle erupted in which one man on each side was killed. Spiess and his consorts were charged with murder since they had initiated the fight. Although all were eventually acquitted, the legal costs were considerable and came at a time when the company was de facto bankrupt. Eventually Strubberg, who had removed to New Orleans, received compensation in the amount of $3,000 for breach of contract ("Dr. Schubbert soll in Galveston mit einer Entschädigung von $3000 abgefunden" [Dr. Schubbert is said to have settled in Galveston with a damage award for $3,000]; "Cappes Bericht," April 22, 1848, SBAt, LVI, 275).

73. Schubbert an Meusebach, May 1848, SBAt, LVI, 285.

74. Cappes an Graf von Castell, May 16, 1858, SBAt, XLI, 287.

75. Huber, "Frederic Armand Strubberg, Alias Dr. Shubbert," 69.

76. In a formal portrait taken years after Strubberg returned to Germany, he is shown without the patch.

77. Barba, *Life and Works*, 53.

78. Ibid., 65.

79. The original 1867 novel was issued as two separate books. The second volume begins at chapter 12, at which point the pagination restarts (see the appendix, "Chronological Bibliography of First Edition Books by Friedrich Armand Strubberg").

80. Johann Otfried *Freiherr* von Meusebach anglicized his name to John Meusebach in 1847.
81. *DTTR*, October 26, 1849.
82. Schilz, *Buffalo Hump*, 34.
83. Koepke, "Charles Sealsfield's Place in Literary History."
84. Ehrenberg, *Texas und Seine Revolution*. Subsequently published as *Der Freiheitskampf in Texas im Jahre 1836* (1844) and *Fahrten und Schicksale eines Deutschen in Texas* (1845).
85. It is beyond the scope of the present study to delve into the controversy surrounding Ehrenberg. For those interested, see Crisp, "Sam Houston's Speech Writers," or Crisp, *Sleuthing the Alamo*.
86. Sammons, *Ideology, Mimesis, Fantasy*, 105.
87. Barba, *Life and Works*, 106.
88. For a full discussion of these artists and their place in the Northern Romantic school, see Rosenberg, *Artists Who Painted Texas*; Newcomb, *German Artist on the Texas Frontier*; McQuire, "Views of Texas."
89. Ulf Debelius, *Friedrich Armand Strubberg*.
90. See "Michael Quast liest Friedrich Armand Strubberg," December 28, 2008, HR2 Sendung online, s.v. "Strubberg."

CHAPTER I

1. As the crow flies, Fredericksburg is located approximately seventy miles to the northwest of New Braunfels in the valley of the Pedernales River, but the route taken at the time covered over a hundred miles. The Fischer-Miller grant lay an additional forty-fives miles to the north. The established route followed the Pinta Trail, an ancient path used first by the Indians and later by the Spaniards as a military road between San Antonio and Santa Fe. From New Braunfels, one had to first travel southwest to Cibolo Creek and then turn north. Present-day Boerne, Sisterdale, and Cain City were on the trail. By connecting these points, one gains a rough idea of the lay of the ancient trail (Neighbors, "The German Comanche Treaty," 31). This is the path used by the young rider Wildhorst in the opening scene of the novel.
2. Throughout the novel, Strubberg refers to Native Americans as "die Wilden," or the "wild ones." This term is much less pejorative than the American term "savages." Therefore, I have avoided the use of "savage" except in those situations where the speaker was obviously hateful in his attitude toward Native Americans.
3. Lieutenant Bené led the first party to survey the site. He located the town between Bené Creek, which he obviously named after himself, and Baron Creek, about four miles north of the Pedernales River. Hermann Wilke, the *Adelverein*'s official surveyor, platted the town on a north/south axis. The town was laid out similar to a typical German village, long and narrow: it was thirteen blocks long (from north to south) and six blocks wide with a central plaza, or *Marktplaz* in the center. The two creeks merged at the southern entrance to the town (see "Karte von Friedrichsburg" [Map of Fredericksburg]).
4. The *Adelsverein* built and maintained several buildings, including, eventually, a slaughterhouse (*Schlachthaus*) and meat distribution house (*Fleischhalle*). The official

map of the *Verein* locates these just as Strubberg indicates, namely at the southern end of the town where Baron and Bené Creeks converged. The first structure built was a blockhouse that served as a fort in case of an Indian attack. Then a warehouse was constructed in July 1846 where provisions for the settlers and gifts for the Indians could be kept secure and dry (Penninger, *Festausgabe*, 68). Later a stable was added and the whole took on the aspect of a compound; Strubberg refers to it as the *Vereinlokal*, which I translate as "*Verein* compound." It was located in the first block into the town on the right of San Saba *Straße* [street].

5. The name was changed to Main Street from San Saba *Straße* at some point. The other streets mentioned retain their names to this day.

6. The director's house was across San Saba *Straße* from the *Verein* compound. In his novel Strubberg claims it was made of stone, but other sources describe it as a wooden structure (Penninger, *Festausgabe*, 68). Strubberg also had a kitchen and a communal dining room constructed where the officials of the *Verein* could take their meals communally.

7. Strubberg places himself in the novel using the name Dr. Schubbert, his assumed name at the time. Thus the novel has an autobiographical, or homodiegetic, contour.

8. Prince Solms-Braunfels ordered several cannons during his term as commissioner-general in 1844–1845. The Torrey Brothers of Galveston supplied them. A Houston newspaper of the period reported that the *Verein* owned eight field pieces varying in size from four to a formidable twenty-four pounds ("Description of New Braunfels and Fredericksburg," March 4, 1846). That one of these was located in the town of Fredericksburg as described by Strubberg can be documented from many different sources (e.g., Penninger, *Festausgabe*, 69, 70).

9. A *Marktplatz* [central market square] was (and is) a feature of German towns and cities. The *Marktplatz* of Fredericksburg (also known as the Adolph *Platz*, probably in honor of Adolph, Duke of Nassau) was centrally located on two full city blocks. It is probably the largest town square in Texas, having in total a size of nearly twenty acres. San Saba *Straße* went through the middle of it.

10. No person by the name of "von Wildhorst" can be documented as a settler in Fredericksburg. Rudolph von Wildhorst, his father, his betrothed, Ludwina Nimanski, and her father all appear to be literary creations of Strubberg. It can be documented that Strubberg/Schubbert was friends with a family by the name of von Zawitsch. When Dr. Schubbert was dismissed from his position by Meusebach in August 1847, the von Zawitsch family accompanied him to Fayette County. It is speculation, but the von Wildhorst family may be modeled on them.

11. The Society for the Protection of German Emigrants in Texas was contractually obligated to supply the emigrants under its control with food and other supplies until the first harvest was brought in (Biesele, *History*, 88). From May 1846, the date of its founding, through the spring and summer of 1847, the time frame of this novel, Fredericksburg depended utterly on food shipments as well as game provided by the Delawares and Shawnees for its existence. Most of these shipments originated in Fayette County and were organized by Otto von Roeder, an early Texas German

settler whose family had settled Cat Spring. The *Adelsverein*'s slaves at Nassau Plantation cut and split over twenty thousand fence rails, which were then shipped to the town (Dr. Smolka, "Bericht an die Aktionäre über den Stand in Texas," SBAt, LIV, 90). Otto von Roeder shipped more than ten thousand bushels of corn and also supplied beef, the cattle being driven to the colonies of New Braunfels and Fredericksburg from Fayette and surrounding counties as well (Kearney, *Nassau Plantation*, 153–164).

12. "The government of the United States wants to make peace with the Indians." This statement is accurate, but it leaves out two important facts. First, after Texas joined the Union in December 1845, the United States government attempted to continue and expand the peace initiative begun by Sam Houston during his second term as president of the Republic of Texas, 1842–1844. Second, the Comanches themselves desired peace, but were extremely wary, especially after the treachery of the Texans at the so-called Council House Fight, which occurred March 19, 1840, in San Antonio. It was an act of the utmost perfidy and treachery on the part of the Texans. The Comanches had sent word that they desired peace and would like a "big talk." Texas authorities responded positively, and thirty-three Comanche chiefs, along with some women and children, entered San Antonio under the white flag of truce. The prominent peace chief Mukwahruh, reputedly the father of the Comanche chiefs Santa Anna and Sanacho (both of whom appear in the novel), headed the delegation, which brought in several Mexican children and Matilda Lockhart, a sixteen-year-old white girl. Matilda, who had been captured with her sister in 1838, claimed that her captors had physically and sexually abused her. The Texans surrounded the chiefs with a contingent of soldiers in a very small house and demanded that the chiefs bring in more captives. Mukwahruh replied that these prisoners were held by Comanche bands beyond his authority. Failing to comprehend the diffuse nature of Comanche political authority, the commissioners rejected the chief's explanation and announced that they would be held hostage until all captives were released. In response to these threats, the Comanche chiefs attempted to escape, calling to fellow tribesmen outside the house for help. In the ensuing melee, Texans attacked several Indians while soldiers killed most of the Comanches who remained in the Council House courtyard. A single Comanche woman was freed by Texas authorities and ordered to secure the release of the white captives in exchange for twenty-seven Comanches captured in the fight. The Penateka leaders refused to respond to Texas demands; instead, they put most of their captives to death. In the meantime, most of the Texans' captives escaped. The Council House Fight outraged Comanche sensibilities, for they considered ambassadors immune from acts of war. Led by Buffalo Hump, the Penatekas retaliated by raiding deep into Texas. Comanche hatred of Texans, who were regarded as treacherous, continued throughout the warfare era and contributed much to the violence of the frontier.

13. Literally, "Fear protects the forest!" [Furcht hütet den Wald].

14. The Comanches were one of the last of the plains tribes to have any substantial contact with the Anglo-Americans, and many accounts confirm that, unlike (say)

the Delawares, they were reluctant to take up firearms. Ferdinad Roemer wrote, for example: "Die Waffen der Comanches sind noch immer Bogen und Pfeile und die lange Lanze" [The weapons of the Comanches are still the bow and arrow and the long lance] (Roemer, *Texas*, 333). They preferred their lances and bows, and, indeed, until the adoption of the revolver by John Hays and his Texas Rangers, these weapons actually gave them an advantage in a close fight. A Comanche warrior could fire twenty or more arrows in the space of time needed to reload a single-shot musket, and at close range the arrows were a deadly and accurate tool of death in the skilled hands of a seasoned Comanche warrior. In a typical fight, the Comanche warriors would feign an attack and try to get their Anglo opponents to discharge their weapons at a distance. Then they would swoop in with bow and lance for the kill. Strubberg describes this tactic wonderfully in the episode where Kateumsi and his warriors attack the men surveying the road to Austin. He also described the tactic in his first book, emphasizing how wedded the Comanches were to their horses in combat (Strubberg, *Amerikanische Jagd- und Reiseabenteuer*, 16).

15. The exact number of Comanches in Texas was debated at the time and is not known with any precision to this day. Dr. Schubbert estimated their number at between forty and sixty thousand in December 1846. This was a gross exaggeration and became the basis of the dispute with Meusebach, for the rumor created great consternation among the German settlers and was partially responsible for an uprising against Meusebach in New Braunfels on New Year's Day 1847 ("Aufruhr in Neu Braunfels gegen Meusebach," SBAt, XXVIII, 27).

Roemer estimated the total number of Comanches in Texas at about ten thousand in 1847 (Roemer, *Texas*, 331). In 1849, Major Neighbors, special agent to the Texas Indians, estimated their total number at twenty thousand, with four thousand warriors (Neighbors report no. 87, reproduced in Winfrey and Day, *Texas Indian Papers*, 3:108). On the other hand, Jack Harry, a Delaware scout, reported in July 1846 that he had just returned from Comanche Peak council grounds near the Canadian River, where a large number of Comanches had congregated; their numbers, according to Harry, were much larger than he ever imagined in his many years of contact with them (*NS*, July 1, 1846). Whatever their exact number might have been, it is clear that the Comanches were the largest and most formidable Indian tribe in Texas at the time and that their presence formed a barrier to Anglo expansion into the southern plains of Texas for many years. This fact was explored in depth by one of the most famous studies of the Comanches in Texas: Rupert N. Richardson's *The Comanche Barrier to South Plains Settlement*, originally published in 1933. It is also clear that if all the Comanches had united and directed their warriors in some sort of coordinated campaign, they could have easily swept the Hill Country clean of Anglo settlers and probably a good part of the rest of Texas as well.

16. White flag: I have found no other reference to the flag on the hill, but I suspect the claim is correct. It was probably put atop the so-called *Kreuzberg* [cross mountain], a bald hill to the north of the town where the Spanish had erected a large cross a century before. The cross had fallen down but reputedly still lay where it had fallen.

The town was located in a post oak forest and, until the trees had been sufficiently cleared, it was not easy to see the town from a distance. Thus, the placing of a large flag as a reference point from afar sounds practicable and reasonable.

17. The story of the communal cornfield as presented in the novel is factual and can be corroborated by many sources. It took nearly twenty-four thousand fence rails of split post oak to fence it. These were supplied in large part by the slaves at Nassau Plantation in northern Fayette County (Schubbert an Meusebach, March 29, 1847, SBAt, XLI, 214). By the end of April, the young corn plants had emerged strong and healthy, promising a bountiful harvest and insuring the survival of the city. The despair and disillusion in the town, which reached its high point in March 1847, gave way to a new optimism as winter turned to spring. The communal cornfield was an initiative of Dr. Schubbert, who should be credited for this crucial endeavor. On April 28, 1847, Dr. Schubbert wrote to his colleague Phillip Cappes:

> You will not recognize Fredericksburg any longer: all the yards have been fenced, the entire city is covered with vegetable gardens, the most charming buildings are rising up and it is a real pleasure to see from one day to the next the flowering of the town. The corn crop is excellent and I am no longer afraid for the future of the town. (Schubbert an Cappes, April 28, 1847, SBAt, XLI, 209, my translation)

A contemporary newspaper report confirms Schubbert's optimism:

> We learn from several gentlemen who recently arrived from Fredericksburg that this town is steadily improving, and already promises to outstrip any of our western towns, except Bexar [San Antonio]. There are already no less than fifteen stores opened at this place, and it is estimated that the population exceeds 2,000. The settlers have several large fields of corn under cultivation, and flourishing gardens are found in all parts of town, furnishing the settlers an abundance of excellent vegetables. (*DTTR*, June 28, 1847)

18. Lemberg was the capital of the Kingdom of Galicia in the Austro-Hungarian Empire. It was located in the western part of present-day Ukraine. Empress Maria Theresa began settling Germans in the area soon after the first division of Poland in 1774. The idea was that through their industriousness the area would become more productive and generate more tax revenue. Many thousands of German settlers made the 1,500-km move from (mainly) the impoverished and over-crowded Palatinate to relocate, and though the journey was long and difficult, many ultimately made a successful transition to a new home and community. The Nimanski family would have been part of this story. Almost no trace of the German presence remains. Many suffered horribly during the purges of Stalin and with the collapse of the *Wehrmacht* on the Eastern Front in World War II. Those who remained were either killed or forced to flee.

19. Texas fever: In its advertisements for emigrants in Germany, the *Adelsverein* portrayed Texas as a veritable Garden of Eden. The promise of free land, especially, proved to be a powerful inducement for many Germans. Some were so gripped by the idea

that their decision to emigrate was not wholly rational. Strubberg dealt with "Texas fever" extensively in his novel *Alte und Neue Heimath* (1859), where he follows the fortunes of a typical German emigrant family, the Werners, from Germany to Texas.

20. *Fürstenverein*: Strubberg's term is actually more accurate than *Adelsverein* [Society of Noblemen] as shorthand for the long and cumbersome official title: *Verein zum Schutze deutscher Einwanderer in Texas* [Society for the Protection of German Emigrants in Texas]. At the time, there were many associations of noblemen in Germany that could claim the appellation *Adelsverein*. The association that sponsored emigration to Texas was composed of the highest orders of German nobility, which *Fürstenverein* more clearly suggests. In the hierarchy of German nobility, a *Fürst* ranked very high, and there were several of these in the membership. There is no English equivalent for the term. Most of the German noblemen in the organization also belonged to the *Standesherren*. These were rulers of principalities, dukedoms, and so on, whose former sovereign status had been eliminated by the *Reichsdeputationshauptschluß* [Imperial Decree] of 1803, by which Napoleon put an end to the Holy Roman Empire. They nevertheless retained the prestige of their former status. The predominance of the *Standesherren* among the membership is important for understanding the organization (Kearney, *Nassau Plantation*, chapter 1).

21. The colonel is referring to the peace treaty of May 1846 between the United States government and the Comanches (Hoig, *White Man's Paper Trail*, 186, 187). With the election to his second term as president in 1841, Sam Houston immediately took steps to reverse the policy of extermination and expulsion of the Native Americans from Texas that his predecessor, Mirabeau Lamar, had pursued with diabolical vengeance and to establish peace between the Anglos and the hostile tribes (especially the Comanches). This policy enjoyed some temporary success, especially with respect to relations with the Lower Comanches, who were generally disposed toward peace with the Anglos as long as they were left a free hand to plunder northern Mexico, the chief target of their raids. When Texas became part of the Union in December 1845, the United States government attempted to build on the peace initiative of Houston. The major treaties with the Comanches up to the time of the German treaty were as follows:

> May 29, 1838, in Houston—Republic of Texas
> August 9, 1843, on Red River—Republic of Texas
> October 9, 1844, at Tehuacana Creek—Republic of Texas
> May 15, 1846, at Comanche Peak at Council Springs—U.S. government
> May 9, 1847, at Fredericksburg—Texas—German Emigration Co.

Referring to the 1838 treaty, President Houston said in council in 1844:

> Six years ago I made peace with the Comanches. The peace was kept until a bad chief [President Mirabeau B. Lamar] took my place. That chief made war on the Comanches and murdered them at San Antonio. He made war on the Cherokees, also, and drove them from the country. Now this has to be mended; war can do us no good. (Winfrey and Day, *Texas Indian Papers*, 2:195)

Because of President Houston's policy and its continuation by the U.S. government, a window of opportunity opened up in the latter half of the 1840s that enabled the Germans to settle the Hill Country. Without this window, the establishment of Fredericksburg, Meusebach's treaty with the Comanches, the surveying of the grant, and so on, would have been inconceivable. This fact has gone almost universally unrecognized. In the Texas Hill Country, the decade of the 1840s was, in fact, comparatively quieter and freer of Indian depredations than the following two decades.

22. The Comanches live disunited among themselves: This characterization is correct and was, in fact, the chief weakness of the Comanches in the face of encroaching Anglo settlers. The Comanches had no central authority or command structure that could bring them all together for a concentrated attack. They were organized into about four or five major groups with dozens of subgroups, or bands. Each group had a great amount of autonomy. Their organization was very democratic and admitted both war chiefs and peace chiefs. The peace chiefs were respected elders who were consulted for their advice on important issues, but acceptance of same was voluntary. The war chiefs, as the name implies, defended the bands, but also organized and launched raids. The famous war chief Potsanaquahip, or Buffalo Hump, as he was euphemistically called, for his name really meant something like "big buffalo balls," organized and led the most spectacular Indian raid during the years of the Republic of Texas. This was the famous raid on Victoria and the sacking of nearby Linnville in 1840 (Brice, *Great Comanche Raid*). Buffalo Hump was able to field upwards of five hundred warriors for this raid, hundreds of miles into Texan-controlled territory. The Comanches felt deeply tricked by the perfidy (as they saw it) of the Texans at the Council House Fight, and the widely felt need for revenge helped Buffalo Hump to gather such a large attack party.

23. Acquainted with these Indians: beginning with his first book, *Amerikanische Jagd- und Reiseabenteuer* (1858), and continuing through several of his other works, Strubberg consistently maintained that he spent a couple of years in a wooden fort on the headwaters of the Leona River in South Texas with three other companions. There, so he claimed, he first came into contact with many different tribes and chiefs, forging lasting friendships. The fort would have been located near present-day Uvalde, Texas. This is demonstrably a false claim, as discussed in the introduction. His description of the landscape does not match the region. His description does, more or less, fit the Devil's River, another fifty miles to the west, near where it empties into the Rio Grande. The Devil's River appears on maps of the period either as an unnamed river or as the Rio Puerco. It is in the realm of possibility that Strubberg had his fort on the Rio Puerco and mistook it somehow for the Leona. But the Leona does appear on maps of the period, so this is unlikely.

My own suspicion is that Strubberg was employed by Henry Francis Fischer and the San Saba Colonization Company for some period before he was engaged to be the colonial director of Fredericksburg. Fischer was keen to settle the area between the Llano and San Saba Rivers even before he was awarded a land grant to the same in February 1842. Several sources put Schubbert on the San Gabriel River during this period (e.g., Meusebach an Castell, March 6, 1846, SBAt, LII, 138; Centralverwaltung, Wiesbaden, "Geschäftsbericht," November 4, 1846, SBAt, XXX, 4; Huber, "Frederic Armand Strubberg, Alias Dr. Shubbert," 40, 41). Hermann Seele wrote: "At noon today the group from Hildsheim left by steamboat for Houston. From there they will travel up to the San Gabriel. Schubbert has acquired large parcels of land there, and they will have to work for him in exchange for the land he will make available to them" (Seele, *Cypress*, 227). Newspapers of the period also report that the first Anglo settlements on the San Gabriel River and Brushy Creek had been established in this time frame and that they were suffering from Indian depredations. Large herds of buffalo would migrate south and east from the High Plains in the winter and occupy the watershed of the San Gabriel, the Leon (not to be confused with the Leona), and other tributaries of the Little River. Comanches and other tribes would never be far behind the buffalo (see *DTTR*, May 22, 1844; July 17, 1844; January 22, 1845).

The San Gabriel River was in 1844–1845 "An der Indianergrenze" [On the Indian Frontier], to use the title of one of Strubberg's novels. Here, Strubberg might well have come in contact with the Indian tribes and chiefs he claims to have met on the Leona. It is also possible that Strubberg spent some time at the Torrey brothers' trading post near present-day Waco, Texas. Many different tribes would stop by seasonally to exchange furs and tanned leather for knives, cloth, pots, and other Anglo commodities. Also, several large council meetings between representatives of the Republic of Texas (and later, the United States government) and the Indians were held nearby at the traditional council grounds on Tehuacana Creek, also near Waco. These were large affairs. Many tribes congregated for these councils; the description given by Strubberg of the signing of the peace treaty in Fredericksburg more closely corresponds to a grand council that took place on Tehuacana Creek between Major Neighbors, as representative of the United States government, and many different tribes, including the Comanches and Lipan Apaches in September 1847.

CHAPTER 2

1. In August 1842, Count Ludwig Joseph of Boos-Waldeck and Count Victor August of Leiningen arrived in Texas as the first representatives of the *Adelsverein* (Kearney, *Nassau Plantation*, 25). Their instructions were to try to secure from the Texas government land for a colonization project and trade concessions to help defray the costs of such an undertaking. Count Boos-Waldeck strayed from his instructions and set up a slave plantation in northern Fayette County instead.

2. This statement alludes once again to the troubled period between 1839, when Mirabeau B. Lamar was elected president of the republic, and the second term of Sam Houston, which began in December 1841. Sam Houston once remarked that during this period, every pore in Texas bled. Lamar pursued a conscious policy of extermination and expulsion (Webb, "The Last Treaty," 152), which culminated in the infamous Council House Fight of March 18, 1840. The Penateka Comanche

war chief Buffalo Hump retaliated in a dramatic way for the perceived perfidy of the Texans with the massive raid on Victoria and Linnville in September 1840. This action, however, was preceded by many smaller hit-and-run raids where raiders crossed over the Colorado River and attacked settlements and settlers from Bastrop to San Antonio only to return unscathed to their sanctuaries in the Hill Country, just as Strubberg describes it (Schilz, *Buffalo Hump*, 21).

3. When Sam Houston assumed the presidency of the young republic for the second time in 1842, he needed to do three things: (1) protect the southern boundary from Mexican invasion, (2) reach some sort of peace or accommodation with the war-like tribes, and (3) bring some semblance of stability to the chaotic finances of the fledgling republic. He supported legislation to promote European settlers, which he hoped would help in at least two of these goals. On February 2, 1842, the legislature passed a colonization law to further this end. The Fischer-Miller land grant was one of four land grants issued under its terms (Solon, "Fischer-Miller," 11; Gammel, *Laws*, 2:777). The law reflected the empresario system, by which Moses Austin (and subsequently Stephen F. Austin) had established the original Anglo colony in Texas. Under this arrangement, empresarios entered into a contract with the Texas government to introduce certain numbers of settlers in a given period of time. The government issued land titles to the settlers directly and upon satisfaction of the terms of the contract rewarded the empresarios for their time, effort, and expense with enormous tracts of land proportionate to the number of settlers introduced. The signatories were Henry Francis Fischer, Burkhart Miller, and Joseph Baker, but only Fischer appears to have been active in promoting the grant. Fischer came to Texas originally in 1838 as consul of the Hanseatic League. He became a citizen, and in 1843 Sam Houston appointed him Texas consul to Bremen. He returned to Germany to fill the position and also to promote his colonization plans. The grant included more than 3 million acres between the Llano and Colorado Rivers. The original contract allowed the introduction of six hundred families and single men. Unsuccessful in settling the grant within the allotted time, Fischer and Miller took advantage of a legislative amendment passed on January 6, 1844, that extended the deadline. The amendment also increased the number of settlers to six thousand families and single men. On June 26, 1844, Fischer sold an interest in the contract to the *Adelsverein*. Later, in 1845, he relinquished executive rights, but retained an interest in the eventual profits. The thousands of immigrants introduced under the terms of this grant, as well as others, provided a valuable economic shot in the arm for the republic (*DTTR*, October 7, 1846). The new immigrants also helped to protect the southern border by populating vacant areas. But in respect to the indigenous Indians, the fresh immigrants provided a further irritant by accelerating the encroachments into traditional Indian hunting grounds.

4. For the sum of $200,000: This is not correct. The total cash consideration was about $8,000 (Biesele, *History*, 82). Fischer and Miller, however, were entitled to one-third of the eventual profits, which could easily have amounted to the larger sum. Thus, in a sense, Strubberg's assertion is not entirely incorrect.

5. Mission Santa Cruz de San Sabá was established in 1750 on the banks of the San Saba River near present-day Menard, Texas, by the Spanish authorities. The Lipan Apache Indians had requested the mission because they were under great pressure from Comanche intrusion into their former hunting grounds, and they looked to the Spanish for protection. On March 16, 1758, a large army of Comanche warriors appeared before the walls of the mission and, before the day was out, had destroyed it. Only one priest survived to tell the story. The episode sent shock waves throughout the Spanish colonies (Dunn, "Apache Mission," 403–411). The Spanish nobleman who was the principal benefactor of the mission later commissioned a painting commemorating its destruction. The painting is considered to be the first canvas depicting an event in Texas history (Ratcliffe, "Escenas de Martirio," 507).

6. The Comal River, said to be the shortest river in the United States, rises in a number of large springs in New Braunfels in southeastern Comal County and flows southeast for three miles to debouch in the Guadalupe River. The inexhaustible source of fresh, clean water and the general charm of the area produced one of the most beautiful natural parks in the state.

7. Eight thousand is the generally accepted figure for the total number of emigrants brought over under the sponsorship of the *Adelsverein.*

8. The best description of the horrors of the epidemic that broke out in the spring of 1846 and reached its high point that summer can be found in Seele, *Cypress,* in the chapter entitled "Shadows, Dark Days of Death and Sorrow in 1846," 85–92.

9. Several thousand . . . victims: This is an exaggeration on the part of Strubberg. The death rate was appalling enough, but it probably did not exceed seven hundred victims for all the settlements combined. In 1856, Frederick Law Olmsted, famous architect and designer of New York City's Central Park, traveled through New Braunfels. The Lutheran minister gave him the figure of 304 deaths in New Braunfels in 1846 and 71 in 1847 (Olmsted, *Journey through Texas,* 181).

10. Dr. Schubbert arrived with Commissioner-General von Meusebach in New Braunfels around July 14, 1846 (Seele, *Cypress,* 89). Dr. Schubbert organized the care of the sick and remained in New Braunfels until October 1846. Later, in a letter to Meusebach, Schubbert claimed that he had received inadequate thanks for

> working like a draft animal at that time, from six in the morning until one or two at night, for constantly moving from tent to tent, from hut to hut, and among the endless funeral processions in the heat of the day, and for endeavoring to make the unfortunate souls forget that the esteemed commissioner-general never once showed his face at these tents or huts, not to mention, enter one, in order to cheer up the people and offer some words of encouragement and consolation? Is this my thanks that, without any kind of pharmaceutical assistance, for two months, I prepared and dispensed by myself daily for over 400 people all the medicines that they received, and that, in the course of six months, spared perhaps 400 people from the grave? Is this my thanks that I did not shy away from being infected on five different occasions and was close to death myself, and still, as I lay sick in my bed, wrote up to eighty prescriptions a day? Is this my thanks that I hurried up to

Fredericksburg at your command when the news of seventy dead reached us in New Braunfels and that daily six or seven more corpses had to be carried away, and that the whole population wanted to abandon the colony and return to New Braunfels, and that with my appearance the epidemic was put to an end . . . over 200 people live here now who thankfully acknowledge that, next to God, they owe their lives to me. (Schubbert an Meusebach, April 20, 1847, SBAt, XLI, 198, 199)

11. This is an intriguing claim. There is no independent source, however, to corroborate it. An orphanage was established in New Braunfels that was administered by Louis Cachand Ervendberg for several years. For the best description of the orphanage and the role Ervendberg played, see chapter 6, "Louis Cachand Ervendberg," in Geiser, *Naturalists of the Frontier*, 95–131.

12. There is no independent verification for an orphanage in Fredericksburg.

13. Road to Austin: One of Dr. Schubbert's real accomplishments during his term as colonial director of Fredericksburg, which he undertook on his own initiative, was to scout a road from Fredericksburg to Austin. This achievement has not been recognized in the literature on the German settlements in Texas, and yet it was important. That Schubbert did in fact lay out the road can be corroborated from several sources. On March 13, 1847, Dr. Schubbert wrote to Phillip Cappes, special envoy of the *Adelsverein*, about the serious shortage of corn in Fredericksburg and the difficult, roundabout way in which the deliveries were being handled; corn originating in Fayette and Colorado Counties destined for Fredericksburg was being shipped first to New Braunfels. Schubbert mentions that he is planning to lay out a road directly to Austin, thereby cutting in half the time needed to ship corn (Direktor F. Schubbert an Cappes, "Abänderung der Colonialverhältnisse dringend erforderlich," March 13, 1847, SBAt, XLIII, 131–141). See the introduction, note 66, for more on the correspondence between Schubbert and Cappes and Meusebach. In a letter of April 20, 1847, Schubbert explains to Meusebach the need for the road (Schubbert an Meusebach, April 20, 1847, SBAt, XLI, 205). In April, Schubbert wrote to Cappes that he had just made the trip to Austin to scout the road: "Ich machte eine kleine Tour nach Austin gerade durch, um möglicherweise eine gute Straße dorthin zu machen." [I just finished a small exploratory trip all the way through to Austin to scout a possible route for a good road there.] (Schubbert an Cappes, April 20, 1847, SBAt, XLI, 207). He goes on to state that he started his trip on or about April 7, 1847, and that he found a good route. An article in a Houston newspaper confirms that by the summer of 1847 the road was open and in use:

A new road has recently been opened from Austin to Fredericksburg. The distance between these two places by this route is only seventy miles. The distance from New Braunfels, or San Antonio, to Fredericksburg is about seventy miles. It may be of some importance for our citizens to notice, that Fredericksburg is nearly in a straight line from Houston to Chihuahua. The German colonists expect that within a few months the road will extend from Fredericksburg to the old San Saba fort. . . . [a] portion of the valuable trade from Chihuahua will, at no distant date, be directed by this route to Houston. (*DTTR*, June 14, 1847)

Thus to Friedrich Armand Strubberg, alias Dr. Schubbert, must go the credit for establishing this most important link, which, more than anything else, secured an economic basis for the town. When gold was discovered in California in 1849, Fredericksburg found itself on the so-called "upper road" of the southern routes to California and the main staging center for the long, difficult journey across the Edwards Plateau and trans-Pecos to El Paso (see Martin, "California Emigrant Roads," 293, 294). Many trains passed through the town. As noted in the *Texas Democrat* (Austin),

> The town of Fredericksburg, like a flower, has sprung up and flourished in the wilderness, almost unnoticed by, and unknown to, the remainder of the world. Although a flourishing and populous place, being nearly a hundred miles in the advance of the settlements. . . . Fredericksburg is on the best route to the Pacific. (*TD*, April 28, 1849)

14. The story that follows about Herr Küster can be documented as largely factual. In March 1847 Philip Cappes wrote Count Castell in Germany: "Der Emigrant Küster aus Frankfurt ist hier wörtlich im Schmutz aus Geiz umgekommen, die Wechsel, welche derselbe in seinen Kleidern eingenäht, wurden bereits übermacht." [The emigrant Küster died here literally from filth caused by miserliness. The money found sewn in his clothes has been turned over.] (Cappes an Castell, March 9, 1847, SBAt, XLI, 171).

15. The discussion presented in this paragraph is historically relevant. Dr. Schubbert argues in effect that the whole idea of trying to move large numbers of settlers into the grant area, which lay a further forty-five miles to the north of Fredericksburg, should be abandoned. Instead, the society should concentrate on purchasing land outright along the numerous intervening rivers and creeks—land suitable for cultivation and settlements. As both Fredericksburg and New Braunfels began to prosper, astute American businessmen (the speculators to which Schubbert alludes) began to realize that the land in between was bound to rise in value. Sam Maverick, a storied Texas character of the period, was, in fact, heavily involved in such speculation.

   The disagreement gained a new dimension when Schubbert heard a rumor that Meusebach was actually involved in land speculation himself and had used some of the *Adelsverein*'s slaves from Nassau Plantation to develop some prime land that he had bought for himself (Schubbert an Cappes, April 28, 1847, SBAt, XLI, 208). Be this as it may, Meusebach was determined to see the terms of the Fischer-Miller land grant contract fulfilled, which called for the grant area to be surveyed by September 1, 1847, and for six hundred settlers to be located by January 1, 1848. A newspaper report of the period underscores Meusebach's determination:

> We learn from a gentleman who recently returned from New Braunfels that Mr. Meusebach, the agent of the colonists, has lately notified the emigrants at New Braunfels that the period designated in the colonial contract for the actual settlement of the colony will soon expire, and that it is necessary that a sufficient numbers of settlers should remove within the limits of the colony to secure the grant. The settlement at New Braunfels was intended *only as a temporary residence of the*

colonists, until their lands could be surveyed and the Indians induced to relinquish their claims on the soil. These objects have been so far effected that the colonists can at any time enter upon these lands and the agent is determined that those who refuse to comply with their contracts shall no longer be supported at the expense of the association. . . . It seems hard, indeed, that any portion of the emigrants, therefore, after being supplied with provisions at great expense for so long a period, should desert the association at the very moment when there is danger that the contract should be forfeited by their delinquency. (*DTTR*, June 14, 1847)

Meusebach's stubborn approach eventually paid off, at least in respect to the colonists. Over 1,500 headrights eventually were granted to the German emigrants who had come to Texas under the auspices of the *Adelsverein* in the grant area in the present-day counties of Llano, Mason, San Saba, McCulloch, Concho, Menard, Kimble, and Kerr (GLOR/GEC; Solon, "Fischer-Miller Grant").

16. There exists no documentary evidence to corroborate the claim that Schubert bought a herd of goats and had them driven to Fredericksburg, but I suspect that the claim is true.

17. Peter Bickel was quite a character and must have been very tall and imposing, but he was not universally respected. The faction in Fredericksburg that opposed Dr. Schubert considered Bickel to be Schubert's second in command and part of the tight-knit ruling cadre whom they despised. They referred to Bickel as "der lange Laster" [the tall vice] (Penninger, *Festausgabe*, 31). The Solms-Braunfels Archives contain twenty-seven references to Bickel that characterize him in more positive terms, however. The fact that Bickel was elected as the first justice of the peace of the precinct in Fredericksburg suggests that the majority of citizens considered him to be a competent and honest person.

18. The Shawnees, Delawares, and Cherokees made up the so-called immigrant tribes in Texas. The Shawnees and Delawares originally lived in the Northeast (as the name of the state of Delaware suggests) and were forced ever westward and southward with the encroachment of Anglo settlements. Several hundred settled in the northeast corner of Texas when Texas was still under Hispanic rule, while the majority of the tribe settled the junction of the Kansas and Missouri Rivers in what is now Kansas, a fact to which Strubberg alludes. The Shawnees were related linguistically and culturally to the Delawares and were often allied with them, as well as the Cherokees, whose ancestral home had been in Georgia. Though knowledgeable about farming, especially the cultivation of corn, squash, and beans, these groups also hunted seasonally, ranging widely across Texas, where deer and bear were plentiful. They seem to have been particularly fond of certain areas of the Hill Country. At all turns, the Delawares and Shawnees strove to remain on peaceful terms with the Anglos, and as intermediaries, scouts, and translators they served as the indispensable interface for a generation between the Texans and the "wild" tribes of the plains (Anderson, "The Delaware and Shawnee Indians and the Republic of Texas," 234).

Despite peaceful intentions and invaluable services performed (an effort scorned by Kateumsi in the novel), many Anglos resented their presence and sought to have them expelled. In 1839, under a trumped-up pretext and in a shameful chapter of Texas history, President Mirabeau B. Lamar ordered an attack on the Cherokees in Texas under the venerable Chief Bowles. The tribe put up a valiant fight, and the octogenarian chief died, sword in hand, defending his people at the Battle of Neches, July 16, 1839. The Texan forces prevailed and, in the end, the Cherokees were expelled from the republic (see Moore, *Last Stand*). President Lamar and his supporters had coveted their tribal lands in northeast Texas, which were extensive, covering most of the present-day county of Cherokee. The Delawares and Shawnees also came in for criticism, but were tolerated for the time being because they were more nomadic and had less land to confiscate.

Their position, however, remained precarious because many Texans suspected that the Delawares and Shawnees, especially, were middlemen in a vast, illicit trade in contraband, and thus complicit. This suspicion was plainly put forward in a long article that appeared in an Austin newspaper in 1851:

> These renegade and intruding bands of northern Indians . . . have kept up a constant trade with the wild tribes, trading for their stolen property, and giving in exchange, among other things, arms, ammunition, and whiskey. When these Indians have traded for as many horses and mules as they desire . . . they return to their homes and friends west of Arkansas and Missouri with their booty, which they have no difficulty disposing of to traders, merchants, and settlers stationed in that region . . . and this trade it is, I again affirm, that has prompted the wild tribes to raid and murder our frontier citizens. ("H. G. Catlett Reports," *TSG*, May 17, 1851)

The astounding range of the Comanche raids as well as the scope and sophistication of their trading arrangements with other tribes, especially the immigrant tribes, has been documented in the recent book *Comanche Empire*, by Pekka Hämäläinen. It is said that this illicit trade was so extensive that many of the mules working the plantations of the Deep South actually had their origins in Mexico.

It must be supposed that Jim Shaw, John Conner, Jack Harry, Segundae, and other notable Delawares of the period had actually honed their formidable linguistic skills while bargaining and trading with the Comanches and other plains tribes.

In the end the Anglos got their wish, for when Governor Hardin Runnels signed an order to remove all reservation Indians from Texas in June 1859, the order included the Delawares, Shawnees, and any other "immigrants" still residing in the state. Sadly, Jim Shaw's last official duty was to carry the news of the expulsion to his compatriots.

In respect to the German settlements, a lively and welcome trade had quickly developed with these tribes, who still roamed freely along the fringes of the Edwards Plateau when the Germans arrived. Julius Splittgerber described one of the first contacts, in June 1846, between the *Friedrichsburger* and the Delawares.

When we had come to the plateau between the so-called Dry Creek and the valley of the Salado, an Indian suddenly appeared before the wagon train who wanted to exchange some venison for powder and lead. Since it was a Delaware, the people gave him what he wanted, which made him very happy. This was to bear good fruit. The following day a young lady was wounded in the foot when a pistol was accidently discharged. They managed to stem the blood flow but the wound soon showed signs of becoming infected. The Delaware appeared again. He took a look at the wound, retrieved something from his pouch, and dressed the wound. He returned every day to do the same, and by the time the party reached the Pedernales, the infection had disappeared and the young lady was on the road to recovery. (Quoted in Penninger, *Festausgabe*, 66)

One of the indispensable items of trade provided by these tribes to the colonists in Fredericksburg, mentioned by Strubberg, was bear oil. Bear oil was used for cooking and also as fuel for lamps (Roemer, *Texas*, 232). They also were adept at tanning hides, especially deer hides, and doing intricate beadwork. The National Museum of the American Indian has several examples of Delaware hunting frocks. These coats, in addition to being very practical, were often stunningly beautiful in workmanship and beadwork design. They were a highly prized trade item. As luck would have it, such a frock is on display at the Texas Memorial Museum in Austin. Captain E. Krauskopf, a pioneer gunsmith in Fredericksburg, often traded with the Indians (see Biggers, *German Pioneers in Texas*, 98). In one of these trades he secured a hunting frock that the family later presented to the Texas Memorial Museum. The frock presents a beautiful piece of workmanship and conforms in every detail to the pattern of the Delaware frock.

Both Shawnees and Delawares were present when Commissioner-General Meusebach made contact with the Comanche chiefs near present-day San Saba, Texas, in February of 1847. The Shawnees served mainly as guides, mule skinners, and hunters, whereas the famous Delaware scout Jim Shaw, who appears in the book as Youngbear, served as an interpreter (see also Penninger, *Festausgabe*, 40–43; Roemer, *Texas*, 281; Neighbors, "The German Comanche Treaty of 1847," 312–322; "Expedition der deutschen Kolonisten nach dem San Saba in Texas," SBAt, LIV, 77–88). Both Jim Shaw and John Conner, as official interpreters, were signatories to the final treaty, which was signed May 9, 1847, in Fredericksburg.

The relationship between the Delawares and the German settlers, I would argue, is of equal importance with the Comanche connection. The Delaware connection, regrettably, has been largely forgotten. One of the accomplishments of Strubberg's *Friedrichsburg* is to vividly portray this relationship in all its scope and richness, albeit in fictionalized form.

19. Kalhahi: I can find no name to match this in documents from the period. This does not mean, however, that there was no one by this name.

20. Kateumsi, an important Penateka war chief, emerges as the chief antagonist of this novel, but Strubberg spins a role for him that has only a limited basis in fact. The

historical Kateumsi first made an appearance when Meusebach led an expedition across the Llano River in February 1847. The party was shadowed by Kateumsi and eight warriors for many miles ("Expedition der deutschen Kolonisten nach dem San Saba in Texas," SBAt, LIV, 77–88). The war party finally approached Meusebach and his caravan under the white flag of truce to inquire whether their purpose was peaceful or hostile. Many years later, in the 1880s, a town sprang up more or less at the site of this encounter. The town fathers, fittingly, adopted the name Katemcy [Kateumsi] for their new town in memory of this event.

The story of the historical Kateumsi is, in fact, quite complicated. The best exposition of his story is given in Hämäläinen, Comanche Empire, 308, 309. On the one hand, newspaper reports from the period corroborate that the real Kateumsi was a holdout among the Comanche war chiefs who did not agree with the concessions granted by Santa Anna and Sanacho to the Germans. He did not sign the Meusebach treaty of 1847. In 1849 a Texas newspaper reported that Kateumsi "is regarded by persons who are well-acquainted with the Comanches as the most faithless and perfidious of their chiefs" (DTTR, October 26, 1849). In July 1847 four of the American surveyors commissioned by Meusebach to survey the grant area were murdered by Indians. It was never determined for sure who the responsible Indians were, but the Delaware Indians suspected it was Kateumsi, who was dissatisfied with the presents he had received and did not agree that surveyors should be allowed into Comanche lands (DTTR, August 12, 1847). Kateumsi was also most likely the Indian chief who fired an arrow at Dr. Schubbert after his dissatisfaction with the gifts offered him, an event that Strubberg places at a later date in the novel. On the other hand, after an 1849 cholera epidemic carried away Mopochocopie (Old Owl) and Santa Anna, who both play prominent roles in the book, only Kateumsi and a band loyal to him remained in the south along the San Saba River. His name appears as a signatory to several treaties after 1849, such as the treaty of December 10, 1850, between U.S. Indian commissioners and representatives of the Comanches, Lipans, and other tribes. It was signed at Spring Creek on the San Saba River (treaty reproduced in full in TSG, December 28, 1850). These treaties promised gifts and friendship in exchange for stolen horses and captives, most from Mexico. According to Hämäläinen, Comanche Empire, 308, these later efforts on the part of Kateumsi to accommodate the Anglos infuriated Potsanaquahip (Buffalo Hump) and Pahayuko, who had moved further to the north to blend with the Tenewa band of Comanche. They were upset because the treaties implicitly acknowledged that the Anglos had rights over their lands and the authority to halt their raids into Mexico. They swore to kill Kateumsi on sight for his treachery.

21. Santa Anna (Santana) was an important Penateka Comanche chief of the mid-nineteenth century. He was initially a leader of Comanche resistance to Anglo settlement in Texas and later a proponent of accommodation and peace. Santa Anna, "a large, fine-looking man with an affable and lively countenance," rose to prominence in the years following the Texas Revolution. At that time conflicts between Comanches and migrating Anglo-Texans had become increasingly frequent. Santa Anna

advocated resistance to the white invasion of Comanche lands and gained prominence after the so-called Council House Fight in San Antonio in 1840. For the next five years he joined Buffalo Hump and a number of other war chiefs in conducting a series of raids on Anglo settlements. Though it is impossible to trace his movements with any sort of precision, Santa Anna probably took part in the raids on Linnville and Victoria in 1840 and may have been present at the battle of Plum Creek (see Brice, *Great Comanche Raid*). Before 1845 he was firmly identified with the faction of his tribe that opposed accommodation with whites. Indeed, there is no record of his ever meeting with officials representing the government of the Republic of Texas. In late 1845, however, he was persuaded to attend treaty negotiations conducted by United States officials, and by May 1846 he had agreed to a treaty promising peace between his people and American citizens in Texas. Santa Anna was invited to visit Washington, DC, and was the first of his tribe to make such a journey. He seems to have been overwhelmed by what he saw. In December 1846 he made the following speech at council:

> Last spring I followed your captains to see the great father [president of the United States] . . . when I came back I told the people what the great father had said. . . . What I say, I always do. My tongue is not forked. When I heard the talk the great father had sent my heart was glad. Many of my people when I came back would not believe the words my great father had sent by me were the words of truth. Now they have listened to his words and see the presents his captains have given them, their hearts are glad—they will go home and tell that my great father does not speak with a forked tongue. (*TD*, January 13, 1847)

This speech conveys simply but eloquently Santa Anna's desire for peace for his people. His subsequent signing of the Meusebach treaty in May 1847 underscored his sincerity. In November 1848 he traveled to San Antonio along with a Lipan chief to speak with Colonel Bell to reiterate his desire for friendship. A newspaper of the period reported the trip and recorded the impressions of a reporter who interviewed the chief while at the Llano camp:

> Yesterday Santa Anna, in company with the chief of the Lipans, and one other, arrived here *en route* to San Antonio, to have what they called a "big talk" with Col Bell. These two chiefs have given up the idea of further depredations on the Whites, and say that they are willing, as representatives of their two tribes, to enter into bonds of peace and harmony with us—Santa Anna is an intelligent Indian and a noble looking fellow. On his arrival he doffed his suit of buffalo skin, and put on his uniform. He reported himself to the commander of this post in a very formal but cordial manner. His uniform coat is that of a brigadier general in our regular army; his pantaloons of handsomely dressed buff buckskin, and when fully dressed he appears remarkably proud, though nothing like haughty, his deportment being really easy and graceful. Some of our regular gentry might take a lesson from this savage. (*CCS*, December 5, 1848)

It is interesting to compare his words and actions with the editorial view of an Austin newspaper, which echoed the opinion of many Texans of the period: "The Comanches in particular, have been remarkable for an almost total disregard of their promises. Treaties are for them mere preludes to aggression; they seem to view them as legitimate modes of obtaining advantages over those who are silly enough to believe in a single pledge they may have given of their sincerity" (*TD*, June 17, 1846). The historical record clearly shows that it was the other way around. Santa Anna perished in the cholera epidemic that raged through the Comanche camps in 1849.

22. Franz Wurzbach emigrated to Texas probably with this brother Jakob and family in 1844 from Mannheim, Baden province (Cappes an Meusebach, "Die Colonie betreffend," October 24, 1846, SBAt, XLI, 53). In 1846 the families moved to Fredericksburg. He was a *Mekaniker* [machinist] by trade and, as Strubberg relates, was engaged in building a mill for the *Verein* near Fredericksburg on Meusebach Creek. In a February 1847 report, we find the following: "Der Machinist Wurzbach ist hier [in Neu Braunfels] jetzt, um endlich die Reste der hierhergebrachten Mühle zu holen. Ein Teil liegt noch jenseits der Guadalupe; ein anderer sogar bei Lavaca." [The mechanic Wurzbach is here in New Braunfels to pick up parts of the mill works. Another piece is on the other side of the Guadalupe and still another is said to be in Lavaca.] (Cappes an Castell, February 2, 1847, SBAt, XXVIII, 140.)

The mill project was abandoned after the Mormon colony at Zodiac put up a mill in the spring of 1847. Franz Wurzbach apparently had a stormy relationship with the *Verein*. At a later point he sued to recover damages, possibly in connection with the mill. In 1850 he joined the Texas and German Emigration Co., which was in reality an association of creditors of the *Verein* in Texas, organized by Henry Francis Fischer. A nephew of Franz Wurzbach, Emil Friedrich (1838–1930), later became a well-known Texas Ranger and soldier. In 1915 he wrote a sketch of his adventures, published in 1937 by the Yanaguana Society as *Life and Memoirs of Emil Frederick Wurzbach*. He died on April 8, 1930, at San Antonio and was buried there in City Cemetery Six.

CHAPTER 3

1. Throughout the novel Strubberg refers to the Indians as "die Wilden," which translates literally as "the wild ones." The temptation was to always render this as the "savages." However, the English term is clearly pejorative whereas the German term is not; it suggests rather the Rousseauesque image of the noble child of nature. My solution was to use the term "savages" only in those situations where the speaker was clearly disparaging in his attitude; otherwise, I used the literal translation, "the wild ones."

2. Comanche men, like the men in most Native American cultures, often took more than one wife. A dozen wives, however, is most likely an exaggeration.

3. A Comanche's wives would typically be divided into principal and secondary wives. The principal wives slept with their overlord while the secondary wives spent most of their time performing the drudgery of camp life.

4. The Delawares had an uneasy relationship with the Comanches. On the one hand, they traded extensively with each other; on the other hand, they sometimes encroached on each other's territory, and the Comanches were leery of the Delawares because of their role as scouts for the whites. Because the Delawares combined proficiency in firearms with an intimate knowledge of Indian tactics, most tribes considered it prudent to leave them alone.

5. Strubberg's Youngbear is most assuredly based on the historical "Jim Shaw" (?–1858), to give his American name, though it is possible that Youngbear is a composite based on several of the famous Delaware scouts and interpreters, including John Conner. American reports usually translate Shaw's Indian name as Bear-Head, which is similar to Youngbear. Many contemporary accounts testify to Shaw's imposing presence: tall, strikingly handsome, and of superior intelligence. William Parker described him in 1854 in the following terms:

> He was the finest specimen of the Indian I saw during the trip, about fifty years old, full six feet six in height, as straight as an arrow, with a sinewy, muscular frame, large head, high cheek bones, wide mouth and eyes like an eagle—his countenance indicative of the true friend and dangerous enemy. (Parker, *Notes*, 214)

He could speak passable English and was fluent in several Indian languages as well as sign language. President Sam Houston relied on him and his fellow Delawares as translators, emissaries, and scouts during his repeated attempts to establish peace with "wild" tribes in Texas, which included the Lipans, Mescalero Apaches, Wacos, and others. Indeed, the Delawares served as the exclusive go-between for over a generation. Governor J. Pinckney Henderson wrote in 1847: "I would also suggest the propriety of giving him [Major Neighbors] power to employ Jim Shaw the Indian before referred to. He speaks the languages of most of the Indian tribes in the state and is known to them all" (Henderson to Marcy, January 12, 1847, Governor's Letters, Texas State Archives, Austin. Reproduced in Neighbors, "German Comanche Treaty of 1847," 313). For his service, among other things, the Texas Legislature awarded him a fine horse. One of the most poignant stories associated with his role as a translator and emissary to the Comanches is from the journal of General H. P. Bee. The general, along with another white man and his Delaware scouts, had been charged with making contact with Pahayuco, the head war chieftain over all the Penateka Comanche bands, for the purpose of inviting him to a peace conference. After weeks of travel on the plains, the party finally located the camp of Pahayuco and entered under the white flag of truce. Pahayuco and his sub-chiefs were not exactly pleased and held a lengthy pow-wow during which the lesser chiefs, remembering the treachery of the Texans that culminated in the Council House Fight, demanded that the white men be put to death in retaliation. Jim Shaw was present at these deliberations and had to bear the terrible news, but returned to the council to argue for the men's lives. His arguments must have been persuasive, for in the end Pahayuco overruled his underlings and ordered that the men's lives be spared (Wilbarger, *Indian Depredations in Texas*, 42–49). Thus, Strubberg's depiction is fairly accurate. Jim Shaw was also present and served as an interpreter when Johann *Freiherr* von Meusebach, Commissioner-General of the German Emigration Company, made contact with the Comanche chiefs in the winter/spring of 1847 near present-day San Saba and concluded a treaty of friendship with them (Penninger, *Festausgabe*, 40–43). Strubberg gives a much more complete description of Chief Youngbear and his band of Delawares in chapter 6. His depiction represents one of the most extensive characterizations of the Delawares that we have.

6. Mapotuska: Strubberg is probably referring to Mukwahruh, the head peace chief, who led a delegation of Comanche chiefs into San Antonio, which resulted in the infamous Council House Fight.

7. Sanacho was a historical Comanche chief. He is mentioned several times in the course of the novel. He was one of the signatories of the German Comanche treaty in May 1847. Kateumsi's claim that he was the sole surviving chief of the Council House Fight is incorrect. His father was killed there. John (Rip) Ford, storied character of the period, wrote about Sanacho, whom he met on an expedition to the San Saba River:

> Sanacho was a plain, matter of fact man. He was very kind to us, sending us venison, and doing us other favors. When he talked to a man he looked him in the face. He said at one time he thought he would never make peace with the Texians. "They killed my father. I did all I could to avenge him. I have buried the hatchet." Major Neighbors said Sanacho's father was killed at the affair in San Antonio [Council House Fight]. (Ford, *Rip Ford's Texas*, 119)

8. As noted earlier, the Comanches were understandably wary after the Council House Fight, which occurred in San Antonio on March 19, 1840.

9. Kateumsi's characterization of the fate of the Delawares is sadly correct. Allen Anderson summarizes their situation in the following terms:

> The Delawares sometimes took up the hatchet against white expansion, but to no avail, and over the years they were hounded, debauched, missionized and sometimes slaughtered by those with whom they collided. Uprooted and restless, they were well-suited for the role they would play. (Anderson, "The Delaware and Shawnee Indians," 232)

10. During its foundation year, the *Verein* maintained its own militia.

11. One of the provisions of Strubberg's contract entitled him to the right to appoint his own subalterns, and this he did. Peter Bickel, the quartermaster, was the most important of these.

12. In both the case of the Mormons at Zodiac and the German settlers in Fredericksburg, the leader was, in effect, a kind of pasha, whose word was law. This situation persisted in Fredericksburg for a full year and a half, until Gillespie County was organized in February 1848, when elected county officials took the place of the *Verein* administration, which disbanded in 1848.

13. The German emigrants were required to make a substantial deposit with the *Adelsverein* in Europe prior to sailing for Texas. Difficulty in redeeming these payments

became one of the sources of discontent among the settlers in Texas and was one of the underlying causes of the revolt in New Braunfels in January 1847 (von Iwonski, "Abschrift," December 31, 1846, SBAt, XLI, 107–111). Strubberg's explanation for the mechanics of the transactions is quite illuminating.

14. The uncanny ability of the Delaware and Shawnee Indian scouts to strike a course and find their way through country that was new even to them amazed many German commentators of the period. Dr. Ferdinand Roemer, for example, used almost exactly the same words as Strubberg in describing the ability of Jim Shaw to chart a sure path through unknown country: "When we started our return trip to Fredericksburg, we were at a loss which direction to go, but our interpreter, Jim Shaw, although he had never been over this route before, was at no time in doubt, and, as was proven, he was right. This appeared rather uncanny to the European" (Roemer, *Texas*, 281). Another commentator of the period, Captain Randolph B. Marcy, wrote:

> It is highly important that parties making expeditions through unexplored country should secure the services of the best guides and hunters, and I know none who are superior to the Delaware and Shawnee Indians. They have been with me upon several different occasions, and I have invariably found them intelligent, brave, reliable, and in every respect well-qualified to fill their positions. They are endowed with those keen and wonderful powers in woodcraft which can only be acquired by instinct, practice, and necessity, and which are possessed of no other people that I have heard of, unless it be the Khebirs or guides who escort the great caravans across the great desert of Sahara. (Marcy, *Prairie Traveler*, 167)

15. Strubberg's description of the battle strongly resembles a contemporary description of the Walker Creek battle, between Jack Hays and his small band of rangers and a larger band of Comanche warriors under chief Yellow Wolf. The battle took place June 8, 1844.

> The Indians had made their last rally, reduced in numbers to about thirty-five, were driven back with great loss, when the voice of their chief then rose high, exhorting them to turn once more, whilst he dashed backwards and forwards among his men to bring them back to the charge. The Texans had exhausted nearly all their shots. Hays called out to his men to know which one had a loaded gun. Gillespie rode forward and answered that he was charged—"Dismount and shoot the Chief was the order. At a distance of thirty steps the ball did its office; madly dashing a few yards, the gallant Indian fell to rise no more, and in wild fright at the loss of their leader, the others scattered in every direction." (*DTTR*, July 3, 1844)

16. The description of this area matches the site known as Live Oak Springs, which was located about twelve miles south of Austin within the city limits of present Kyle, Texas. In the fall of 1845, Friedrich von Wrede and Oscar von Claren, both officials of the *Adelsverein*, were murdered by a band of renegade Waco Indians (see Kearney, *Nassau Plantation*, 101, 102).

1. This episode appears to be based on a historical event that took place in June 1848 in Austin. A Houston newspaper reported the following: "A party, under the command of Santa Anna entered Austin so suddenly and unexpectedly that the citizens were thrown into such a state of alarm that they flew to arms and were all preparing for a deadly conflict until Santa Anna displayed the white flag, and by signs announced that his visit was of a friendly character" (*DTTR*, June 8, 1848). Strubberg apparently took this story, which was widely reported in the Texas newspapers of the day, and added pepper to it, as he would say.

2. *Portulacaceae*, a family of unusually succulent herbs (order *Chenopodiales*) having perfect, regular flowers. He is probably referring to "Moss-Rose" or "Flame-Flower," both of which are native to Central Texas. They are related to "Pulsey," a European herb often used in salads (Mills, *Roadside Flowers of Texas*, 109, 110).

3. The word Strubberg uses is "Mispelbaum," or "medlar tree." Medlars are not native to Texas, so it is not clear what tree Strubberg is referring to. He perhaps meant the prairie crabapple (*Malus ioensis*), a native of limestone ridges in Central Texas, which has a fruit somewhat similar to medlar. It could also have been buckeye (*Aesculus glabra*), which, likewise, produces a hard fruit.

4. The German word for silver nitrate is "Höllenstein." It had (and has) several medical applications. It was carried in crystalline form and when mixed with water formed a caustic soda that could be used to remove warts. It was also used as a disinfectant.

CHAPTER 5

1. John Grey is the name given by Strubberg to Lyman Wight (1796–1858), a historical Mormon leader. Why Strubberg used this name is intriguing: generally, he assigns authentic names to historical figures. No other corroboration exists, but perhaps Wight did, in fact, use this name with Strubberg. When Joseph Smith, the founder of Mormonism, was killed by a mob in Illinois in 1844, his followers split into two groups, one led by Brigham Young and the other by Lyman Wight. Young eventually led the majority to Utah territory, but Wight saw in the Republic of Texas the possibility of a new homeland, free of persecution and alive with opportunity. Thus, his followers shared with the German emigrants the vision of Texas as the promised land. In 1845, Wight and about 150 followers made the move to Texas, settling first at Webberville, east of Austin. Two observations stand out about Wight and his band: first, they were amazingly industrious, establishing gristmills and sawmills and hiring out as skilled carpenters and cabinetmakers wherever they settled; second, they were infected by an insatiable *Wanderlust* that led them to relocate every couple of years, abandoning the fruits of their collective labor to start anew. This restless spirit eventually led them to settle on the Pedernales River in the spring of 1847, about four miles below Fredericksburg. They named their new community Zodiac. On May 1, 1847, a suitable site for a saw- and gristmill on the Pedernales was located and, impressively, six weeks later the mill was in production. In addition to this, the fifty or so families set up a furniture shop, a shingle shop, a general store, a blacksmith shop,

and a wagon shop. They also planted a large cornfield in the fertile river bottom soil of the Pedernales. Richard Zelade, in his guidebook to the Hill Country, sums up their importance for the German settlers as follows:

> Wight's colony was a godsend to Fredericksburg; the Mormons supplied the Germans with seed, lumber and shingles from their mill, cornmeal from their gristmill, and furniture from their shops. The Mormons also helped the Germans adjust to the idiosyncrasies of farming on the edge of the desert. Many of the Germans were becoming farmers and herders for the first time here in Texas. (Zelade, *Hill Country*, 95)

At the 125th anniversary of the founding of Fredericksburg, celebrated May 7, 1971, the grateful descendants of the German pioneers recognized the invaluable assistance of the Mormon colony by dedicating a monument, a revolving replica of a mill wheel, in the Pioneer Garden Park ("Perpetual Gratitude Shown to Mormons," *Deseret News*, May, 8, 1971). In 1851, a disastrous flood destroyed the mill and most of the town of Zodiac. Rather than rebuild, Wight decided to relocate on Hamilton Creek, near present-day Burnet, Texas.

The relationship of Mormonism to the Texas Republic is a fascinating topic that has only recently received scholarly examination. See, for example, Johnson, *Polygamy on the Pedernales*, and Van Wagenen, *The Texas Republic and the Mormon Kingdom of God*. Several German writers of the period commented on the Mormons in Texas. Ferdinand Roemer, Alwin Sörgel, and Viktor Bracht all wrote about the sect (Roemer, *Texas*, 213, 214; Sörgel l, *Sojourn*, 72–75; Bracht, *Texas in 1845*, 75, 104, 185, 200). Apparently Mormonism had come in for vicious attack in the German press, and all were keen to judge for themselves. Roemer recounts the excellent relationship between the colonists and the settlers. Sörgel's account is especially entertaining. Like many German intellectuals on the Texas frontier, he was an avowed agnostic (a *Feuerbachianer*) and felt that the critical spirit of German philosophy offered a necessary antidote to those who would surrender their intellects to charismatic leaders and movements. Out of curiosity, he visited the Mormons when they were still located near Austin and wrote an amusing account of his visit. He pretended he was interested in converting and received a warm welcome. He found himself attracted to certain aspects of their communal life, especially the pretty young ladies, and did not know quite what was expected of him when he awoke one morning to find one in bed with him. But in the end, although praising their thrift and industriousness, he pronounced them a dangerous sect. Bracht's commentary followed the same line, minus the humor. Sörgel makes one intriguing observation: apparently, he maintained, the Mormons saw in the influx of German emigrants a fertile possibility for fresh converts and made at least one attempt to proselytize the German settlers in New Braunfels. This would help explain their move from Austin on the Pedernales River next to the new colony of Fredericksburg. They also could have been attracted to the fact that the Germans were not keen on slavery. The Mormons were decidedly anti-slavery. Taken together, the German writers offer the most extensive firsthand account of Lyman Wight and his followers that we have, and they do so from a completely different perspective from that of American commentators of the period.

2. The story about Wight coming to ask permission to start a colony is corroborated by Ferdinand Roemer, but Roemer places the initial meeting in November 1846 (Roemer, *Texas*, 213, 214).

3. The town of Zodiac was laid out along the Pedernales River about four miles to the southeast of Fredericksburg. There were between thirty-five and fifty families associated with the group, which would be consistent with several hundred horses and mules, and many head of cattle.

4. The Mormon settlements represent perhaps the largest and most successful experiment in communal living in Texas. Interestingly, Fredericksburg (at least in its first years) also represented a modified experiment in communal development, but it approached the idea from a completely different perspective; it built upon long-established traditions of cooperation and community involvement, a tradition especially strong in German village life. The *Verein* did subsidize one radical experiment in communal living at this same time, namely the settlement of Bettina on the north bank of the Llano River, across from Castell. Here forty or so intellectuals, loosely associated with the industrial school at Darmstadt, set up a short-lived communistic commune in 1847 (Fischer, *Marxists and Utopias in Texas*, 77–110).

5. Strubberg's detailed description of the Mormon village is the only one I have been able to locate.

6. Strubberg is unequivocal in stating that the Mormons under Lyman Wight were polygamists.

7. When Prince Solms-Braunfels established New Braunfels in 1845, he designated a nearby hill as a site for a fort, which he called the *Sophienburg* in honor of his fiancée. A real fort, as such, was never constructed, but the site did grow into a compound for the *Adelsverein* with a business office, stables, a wagon yard, and other structures. At present, a library and museum occupy the site.

CHAPTER 6

1. As noted, Strubberg's claim that he had built a fort on the Leona River on the southern declivity of the Edwards Plateau must be viewed with skepticism. But at some point, Strubberg had come into contact with the Delaware Indians, and they must have impressed him deeply, for they make an appearance in all his Texas novels and are invariably portrayed in a favorable, almost reverential way (see "Tiger" in *Amerikanische Jagd- und Reiseabenteuer*, or "die Delawaren" in *An der Indianergrenze*).

2. Medina, Nueces, and Frio Rivers: these three rivers all drain the Edwards Plateau region of Central Texas and flow generally in a south/southeasterly direction toward the Gulf of Mexico. Originating in the hilly plateau, they wend most of their courses through a flat landscape before emptying into the gulf. The Nueces joins with the Frio to empty into Nueces Bay near Corpus Christi. The Medina eventually flows into the Guadalupe, which empties into Lavaca Bay. The Frio and Medina Rivers are storied especially for their beauty and charm. With large spring inflows,

they usually run crystal clear and cold. Large, patriarchal stands of live oak, pecan, and cypress trees line their banks, adding to their charm. Prior to being settled, fenced, and grazed, the plains through which the rivers flowed formed vast mesquite grass prairies broken only by isolated tree islands and ribbon forests that followed the streams. Owing to the mildness of the climate, buffalo grazed these seas of grass year round, while an abundance of wildlife inhabited the hills of the plateau. It was a good place to overwinter, as Youngblood avers.

3. That the Delawares often camped close to Fredericksburg is corroborated by travelers and newspaper accounts of the period: "Taking leave of our Mormon friends, we rode on two miles, to an encampment of Delaware Indians. Stopped to see a chief, Jim Shaw, whom I was advised to employ to accompany us to El Paso, where he had been with other parties, and who, from his acquaintance and influence with the Indian tribes on our route, might be of great service. Unfortunately he was absent, and not expected to return for a week" (Bartlett, *Narrative*, 57). Delaware Creek in southwest Gillespie County also testifies to their presence.

4. The Apaches were divided into several groups. The Mescaleros generally lived in far West Texas along the Pecos River. They were not present for the signing of the German Comanche peace treaty in May 1847, but they had been invited to earlier peace councils. The Lipan Apaches, who are described by Strubberg in other works, were hereditary enemies of the Comanches and sought to ally themselves first with the Spaniards and then with the Texans as a means to protect themselves.

5. Once again, Strubberg alludes to his log fort on the Leona River. The opening scene of his first novel, *Amerikanische Jagd- und Reiseabenteuer*, describes the fort.

6. "Tiger" was a young Delaware warrior who decided to stay with "Armand," as Strubberg called himself in his first novel, *Amerikanische Jagd- und Reiseabenteuer* (1858), at his fort on the Leona; the two shared many adventures together in the book.

7. I have found no other mention of the name "Wasa."

8. All the chiefs mentioned are historical figures. Pahajuka is Strubberg's rendering of the Comanche name for Pahayuco.

9. In September 1852, the real Kateumsi made the following speech, recorded by the Indian agent Horace Capron:

> Over this vast country where for centuries our ancestors roamed in undisputed possession, free and happy, what have we left? The game, our main dependence, is killed and driven off, and we are forced into the most sterile and barren portions of it to starve. We see nothing but extermination left before us, which we await with stoic indifference. Give us a country we can call our own, where we may bury our people in quiet. (Horace Capron to Robert Howard, September 30, 1852, Commissioner of Indian Affairs, Letters Received, M234, Roll 858, Texas Agency, NA, reproduced in Schilz, *Buffalo Hump*)

10. "Hochzeitsfackel vor die Tür bringen" [Carry the marriage torch to the front door]. Strubberg uses this expression in several of his works. In *An der Indianergrenze*, he uses it in the context of a Lipan Apache village. I have found no other corroboration that this was a common ritual among plains Indians.

1. Strubberg quotes the well-known German saying "Aller Anfang ist schwer" [All be-
ginnings are difficult].
2. This is historically accurate. Herman Hale Smith wrote: "Six weeks after selecting
a mill site, the colony had a grist mill in operation, houses were built, shops erected
and crops planted" (Smith, "Lyman Wight Colony," 15).
3. Strubberg was obviously being facetious here. But it is interesting that we find two
settlements side by side that are organized and administered not according to the
laws of Texas, but rather according to their own private rules and administered
by an unelected bureaucracy. In both the case of the Mormons at Zodiac and the
German settlers in Fredericksburg, the leader did indeed function more or less as a
monarch whose word was law. As noted earlier, this situation persisted until Gillespie
County was organized in February 1848.
4. The building alluded to here was a precursor to the *Vereinskirche* (the nondenominational church built with *Verein* funds, at Dr. Schubbert's direction).
5. According to the Merriam-Webster's online dictionary, a "fandango" is a lively
Spanish or Spanish American dance in triple time that is usually performed by a
man and a woman to the accompaniment of guitar and castanets.
6. Galopp or gallop: name given to a lively German dance developed as a circle dance
for pairs in the nineteenth century. It is related to the polka and was danced in $^2/_4$
time. Today it is considered primarily a folk dance, but it is still danced at balls in
Austria and southern Germany.
7. The historic range of the jaguar included Central Texas. Strubberg was an avid
hunter from an early age, and all of his books include dramatic hunting scenes.
They have the ring of veracity and are probably based on real experiences. A jaguar
hunt appears in several novels (see, e.g., *Amerikanische Jagd- und Reiseabenteuer*, chapter
1, section 14).
8. This style of building was common to the Texas frontier and was universally referred to as a "dogtrot."
9. Genver is a kind of brandy made of grain, which some consider to be the national
drink of Holland. It is flavored with juniper and is similar to gin.
10. *Herr* Weltge: In June 1847, seventy leading citizens of Fredericksburg signed a pe-
tition expressing their support for Dr. Schubbert and urging him to continue as
colonial director. Among the signatories were Conrad Welge [Weltge?] and Jakob
Röder (letter reproduced in Barba, *Life and Works*," 47, 48). Another Welge, Heinrich
Friedrich, was one of the hearty pioneers who, rather than wait for transportation to
be provided in Indianola, walked the distance to New Braunfels, where he rested up
and then continued on to Fredericksburg. Eventually he settled in Cherry Springs,
where he established a large ranch that is in the family to this day (Mohon, *Gillespie
County*, 16). There is no record of either man being shot by an Indian in the town of
Fredericksburg.
11. The Duchy of Nassau, as it existed in the 1840s, was in effect a creation of Napoleon. It was located on the right bank of the Rhine and its capitol was Wiesbaden.

The *Adelsverein* was incorporated in the Duchy of Nassau, and Adolph, duke of Nassau, was a charter member of the organization. The *Adelsverein*'s slave plantation in northern Fayette County was named for the duke. The central square in Fredericksburg was labeled "Adolph's *Platz*" on maps of the period, probably also in honor of the duke.

12. There is a record of Jakob Röder, who arrived in October 1845 under the auspices of the *Adelsverein* (GLOR/GEC, 001553).

13. Carl Voss: There is a record of Johann Voss, who arrived in Texas September 25, 1846, under the auspices of the *Adelsverein* (GLOR/GEC, 000744).

14. Butcher Kellner: As part of the communal organization of Fredericksburg, a community slaughterhouse was located on Baron Creek where it was crossed by the Old San Antonio Road on the southeastern edge of town. The *Verein* apparently also had employed a full-time butcher. One Justus Kellner is recorded as having arrived under the auspices of the *Adelsverein* August 21, 1845 (GLOR/GEC, 002003).

CHAPTER 8

1. Mopochocopie, also known as Old Owl, was one of the historic peace, or civil, chiefs of the Penateka Comanches. We are indebted to Ferdinand Roemer for a precise description of him and several other chiefs:

> The three chiefs, who were at the head of all the bands of Comanches roaming the frontier of the settlements in Texas, looked very dignified and grave. They differed much in appearance. Old Owl, the political chief, was a small old man who looked very insignificant in his dirty cotton shirt, but was characterized by a cunning, diplomatic face. The war chief, Santa Anna, presented an altogether different appearance. He was a powerfully built man with a benevolent and lively countenance. The third, Buffalo Hump, was the genuine, unadulterated picture of a North American Indian. Unlike the majority of his tribe, he scorned all European dress. (Roemer, *Texas*, 269)

Mopochocopie was one of the principal Comanche chiefs who responded favorably to President Sam Houston's peace overtures in 1844. At a peace council at Tehuacana Creek December 19, 1846, he made the following speech:

> Our great father knows that I was the first Comanche who came to see Sam Houston and smoked the pipe of peace with him. I did not come just to see him and shake his hand in friendship, but I took him in my arms and told him his heart was mine. I made the treaty with Sam Houston to last as long as the sun would shine. I shall never break it. (*TD*, January 13, 1847)

2. While Meusebach was away on the expedition to the grant area, Comanches twice appeared in Fredericksburg, each time creating a fright. Strubberg has taken both of these events and used them in his novel. In the first situation, Old Owl and about sixty warriors appeared in Fredericksburg to ask the purpose of the expedition. Strubberg's characterization of Old Owl complements that of Roemer, given in the previous note, nicely.

3. Spoke tolerable English: Many of Strubberg's Indians (like those of Karl May at a later date) have mysteriously learned how to speak English to the point that they can express sophisticated thoughts with ease. In the case of the Comanches portrayed, this was patently not true. None of them could speak any English at all. Because of their long history of raiding deep into Mexico, many did have some rudimentary knowledge of Spanish, but beyond that, any communication between the Comanches and the Anglos required interpreters, and this job, for a full generation, fell to the Delawares.

4. White-washed: It was a common practice of the time and continued for many years thereafter to mix lime with water and "whitewash" buildings rather than paint them. The mixture had the effect of repelling insects and retarding rot. I have seen whitewash used on tree trunks both as insect repellent and as decoration.

5. The story of Old Owl can be corroborated from an eye-witness report from the period ("Expedition," SBAt, LIV, 74–88). After the Indians had been reassured, the chief, along with his wives and children, was quartered in a *Verein* building used as a pharmacy, while his warriors camped outside of town. A disturbance arose when a group of militia men arrived and settled in a room on the other side of the house. Fearing treachery, such as at the Council House Fight, the chief fled in such a panic that he left his weapons and clothes behind. He also discarded a peace medallion that he had received at a prior peace conference, probably at one of the Tehuacana Creek council meetings in either 1844 or 1846. Just as the novel relates, Youngbear [Jim Shaw] was sent after the chief to assure him that no treachery was intended.

6. By the 1840s a protocol had evolved for the numerous peace councils that took place between the plains Indians and the various representatives of Anglo government. This always included some sort of presentation of gifts, as well as medallions, which were commissioned especially for each event. These were usually highly prized by the Indians. (For a full description of one of these councils in Texas, see Hoig, "Sam Houston and the Indians," in *White Man's Paper Trail*, 57–68.)

7. Freudleben: No other source for this name has been identified, but I suspect that this is probably a true story since most of the other anecdotal accounts, which are not necessary for plot development per se, can be corroborated as factual. A man by a similar name, Friedrich August Freudenthal, arrived in Texas October 8, 1845, under the auspices of the *Verein* (GLOR/GEC, 002155).

8. The German word used was "fassen," to grab or take hold of.

9. For an accounting of the cost of supporting the town of Fredricksburg in the spring and summer of 1847, see Meusebach an die Direktion in Friedrichsburg, July 1, 1847, SBAt, LIV, 47–49.

10. The story of the Comanches entering Fredericksburg and staging an elaborate peace dance for the benefit of the citizens can be corroborated (Penninger, *Festausgabe*, 32, 33). Strubberg's depiction of the dance offers one of the ethnographic highlights of the book.

11. Just as the novel portrays, a full-time cook was employed at *Adelsverein* expense, and the officials took their meals together in a *Verein* mess.

12. Kiwakia: Once again Strubberg alludes to characters from his previous novels. We are left to wonder if such a chief existed, for no other source offers any insight into who Kiwakia might have been.

CHAPTER 9

1. Of the 367 Indian treaties in the history of the United States, the German Comanche treaty is often held up as one of the few successful ones. One source claims it as the most successful treaty in that its terms were never broken by either party (Kumanoff, "Born German"). That the treaty, once signed, was generally adhered to is confirmed by an article of July 14, 1847: "Mr. Giddings, one of the surveyors of the German colonial grant arrived in town a few days since and we were pleased to learn . . . the Comanches appear to be quite friendly and small parties of the Indians belonging to Santa Anna's band frequently visit the camps of the surveyors. They say: 'the Germans no hunt like Americans, and buffalo will be plenty where Germans build towns'" (*DTTR*, July 24, 1847).

The peace treaty was actually signed in Fredericksburg on May 9, 1847. Why Strubberg changed the date to August is not clear. The original treaty is now in the possession of the Texas State Library in Austin. It is a beautiful document with both German and English texts, side by side. It should be noted, however, that even though Major Neighbors, the official Indian agent representing the United States government in Texas, was a signatory to the agreement, it was not an official treaty between the United States government and the Comanche Nation. Such a treaty would have required ratification by the United States Senate. It was, rather, a private treaty between the commissioner-general of the German Emigration Co., John O. Meusebach, representing the German emigrants, and the Comanche bands under the leadership of Santa Anna and five other Comanche chiefs, to wit: Poohan Sanachgo'it (Sanacho?), Hoorahquitop, Hatisane (Santa Anna?), Toshawwhinesket (Buffalo Hump?), and Nokahwhoh. Noticeably absent as a signatory was Kateumsi, who was known to be in the area (Roemer, *Texas*, 287). On the German side there were three other signatories in addition to Meusebach: F. Schubert, colonial director of Fredericksburg; Hans von Coll, accountant of the Texas and German Emigration Co.; and Felix von Blücher, colonial director of New Braunfels. The two Delaware chiefs who served as interpreters, Jim Shaw and John Conner, also signed. For the Americans, Major Neighbors and John Torrey also signed. The Torrey Brothers were one of the largest merchants in Texas. They held the concession for trading with the Indians and maintained a large trading post near present-day Waco as well as a trading post in Fredericksburg. They also had extensive business dealings with the German Emigration Co., supplying, for instance, the wagons that transported the emigrants from the coast into the interior. Torrey no doubt supplied the $3,000 in gifts that were exchanged. The first thousand dollars had been given during the initial contact with the Comanches in March. The rest was distributed in May when the Comanches came to Fredericksburg to sign the treaty.

Newspaper reports of the period state that the Comanches had been very reluctant to grant surveyors permission to enter their lands, for they realized full well the significance of these "land thieves." One article stated that in the previous month a delegation of chiefs had entered Fredericksburg stating that they desired peace but that they would resist any attempts to survey their territory (*DTTR*, May 3, 1847). The Mexican War, it should be remembered, was in full swing during this period, and the Comanches followed the developments with keen interest. According to a subsequent newspaper report, they changed their minds after they heard news of the American victory at Buena Vista (*DTTR*, May 10, 1847).

In general, what emerges is a story of Comanche Indian chiefs who are fully aware of the existential threat posed by the ever-encroaching white settlements and the superior fire power of their soldiers. During a series of councils, first with Sam Houston and then with representatives of the United States after Texas entered the Union, the chiefs were always eager for some sort of comprehensive peace agreement, but one that would draw a clear line between what is ours and what is yours. Although Sam Houston promised such a treaty, he never delivered. Still, as noted earlier, President Houston's peace initiatives, starting with his second presidency in 1842, opened up a window of opportunity—a time frame between roughly 1843 and 1855 of more or less suspended hostility, which gave the German settlers in the Hill Country enough breathing room to establish themselves permanently.

2. In a contemporary newspaper report, we read:

> Large numbers of Comanches are concentrating around Fredericksburg to attend a council which is to be held on or about the 10th inst. Mr. Meusebach, the agent of the German colonists has invited them to attend this council for the purpose of forming a treaty with them on the part of the colonists. He proposes to purchase the privilege of surveying the lands of the colony on the San Saba, and the right to form a settlement on that river, allowing to them the right to hunt within the limits of the colony . . . They say they are more willing for the Germans to settle in their country than the Texians, for the former settle in towns and villages and do not scatter over the countryside and kill the game as the Texians do. They are very anxious that the encroachments of the eastern Texians on their hunting grounds may be checked, and repeatedly inquire when the "Great Father" will send an agent to treat with them and mark out a boundary that white men will respect. We have too much reason to fear that they are yet to learn by bitter experience that the "Great Spirit" alone can mark out a boundary that white men will never pass. (*DTTR*, May 10, 1847)

3. Major Neighbors: Major Robert Simpson Neighbors (1815–1859) is, in my opinion, a real Texas hero. He served as agent to the plains Indians during the waning years of the Republic of Texas and continued this role after Texas joined the Union in December 1845. He was appointed special agent to the plains Indians for the United States government in Texas. His appointment led to a smooth transition and a definite continuity in relations with the Texas Indians. Major Neighbors was truly

sympathetic to the plight of the Texas Indians, and most of the chiefs respected and trusted him. He advocated tirelessly and fearlessly on their behalf, often in the face of aggressive and bigoted opposition. His unpopular stance eventually led, in 1859, to his murder at the hands of a fanatical Indian hater whom he had never met.

4. Black beard of buffalo: the hair of the buffalo, in contrast to most domestic cattle, is exceedingly fine, soft, and pliant. This keeps the animals warm in the harsh winters of the High Plains. The bulls also have a beard that grows from underneath their throats. Because of its length, these strands were especially desirable to the plains Indians.

5. Kiwakia and Ureumsi: unlike most of the other Indians described in the novel, these chiefs cannot be corroborated from other sources. This does not necessarily mean they are creations of Strubberg's imagination. We simply do not know. They first appear in *Amerikanische Jagd- und Reiseabenteuer* (1858).

6. Once again Strubberg alludes to adventures he has described in previous novels.

CHAPTER 10

1. This story is a spiced-up version of two historically verifiable events. Two groups of Comanches appeared in Fredericksburg during the period that Meusebach was on the expedition to the grant area above the Llano River. The first was the arrival of Old Owl. In a second event, a Comanche chief who already knew about the signing of a peace treaty and the distribution of gifts appeared in Fredericksburg prior to the return of the Meusebach expedition and demanded gifts. Though unnamed in the sources of the period, this most likely was Kateumsi, for, as we know, he was the first to make contact with Meusebach after he crossed the Llano River, and he had already been informed that presents would be distributed in Fredericksburg at a later date. In the historical account, the chief was dissatisfied with the gifts Dr. Schubert offered him, gifts worth about $100. To express his displeasure, he fired three arrows at Schubert, which, fortuitously for Schubert, missed ("Expedition," SBAt, LIV, 81). Schubert kept these arrows and often showed them to his friends in Germany. After the treaty was signed, groups of Comanches would often come into Fredericksburg to trade. On one such occasion several of them showed curiosity about the cannon, and it was fired off as a demonstration. The Indians were apparently frightened out of their wits by the thunderous discharge. There is no record that the cannon was actually fired at Indians.

2. Strubberg uses the word "*Streifzug*," which usually translates as "patrol," but in this context, "ranger" makes more sense.

CHAPTER 11

1. Calden: This might be Friedrich Kahlden, who was awarded 320 acres of land in the Fischer-Miller land grant (General Land Office Records, 002215).

2. Krebs: This might be Georg Michael Krebs, who was granted 640 acres of land in the Fischer-Miller land grant (General Land Office Files, Bexar-3-005682).

3. *Obrist* means "colonel"; Schubert is showing the proper deference to the retired colonel by using his title.

4. Kracke: Friedrich Wilhelm Kracke arrived on the *Johann Dethardt* in Galveston from Bremen on November 23, 1844 (General Land Office Files, Bexar-3-3614).
5. Strubberg uses the word *"Pallasch,"* which was a straight-bladed sword used for both striking and thrusting; it was preferred by dragoons and other heavy cavalry throughout the nineteenth century.

CHAPTER 12

1. This whole episode of the ambush seems to be based loosely on a historical occurrence. In October 1845 Friedrich von Wrede, Sr., an official of the *Adelsverein*, rode to Austin on business and headed from there to New Braunfels accompanied by Oskar von Claren, another young aristocrat of the officer class, who had come into the service of the society. Unsuspecting, the two German officers made camp at Live Oak Springs near present-day Kyle, about twelve miles south of Austin, a well-known camping spot for sojourners of the day between Austin and San Antonio and also well known to Indians. Here they were surprised and overwhelmed by a party of renegade Indians, who scalped and killed them. Their bodies were discovered soon thereafter by a party of U.S. soldiers, who buried them with full military honors (Kearney, *Nassau Plantation*, 101). The news of the massacre created a sensation in Germany, where hundreds were preparing to depart for the New World. Many pointed out that the German immigrants would face the threat of hostile Indians, especially in the grant area.

CHAPTER 13

1. Rocking chairs are apparently an American invention. They were unknown in Germany, and many Germans found them fascinating as representative of American comfort. Count Ludwig Joseph of Boos-Waldeck, the first representative of the *Adelsverein* in Texas, also commented on them (Boos-Waldeck an den Herzog Nassau, July 31, 1842, SBAt, XXX, 208).
2. *Glühwein* is a popular and well-known German drink that is especially popular during the Christmas season. It is a combination of wine and spices and is served warm.
3. Falls on the Brazos: This probably refers to the falls on the Brazos near present-day Marlin in Falls County.

CHAPTER 14

1. The paws of the bear were considered to be one of the great delicacies of the hunt.
2. The whip-poor-will is a medium-sized nightjar common to the Hill Country of Texas, especially to areas where cedar grows. Their night cry is very distinctive and plaintive. A relative, the Chuck Will's Widow, utters a similar cry.
3. These are the classic signs of what is known as "buck fever." Anyone who has ever enjoyed the hunt will be familiar with this malady. In its worse form it leads to uncontrolled shaking, an elevated heart rate, and heavy panting. Once it takes hold, it cannot be willed away and renders an accurate shot almost impossible.

CHAPTER 15

1. This dates the event to May 6, 1848.
2. Strubberg maintains the fiction in the novel that he continued to serve as director beyond August 1847, when he was dismissed by Meusebach. The *Vereinskirche* was actually built and dedicated in 1847.
3. The so-called *Vereinskirche* has become the universally recognized symbol of Fredericksburg. It was originally designed and commissioned by Dr. Schubert and completed sometime in the spring/summer of 1847. The *Handbook of Texas* describes it as follows:

> It followed an ancient German style known as the "Carolingian octagon," exemplified by the original portion of the cathedral of Charlemagne at Aachen. Originally all the religious groups in Fredericksburg used the building, which stood in the middle of Main Street and was nicknamed the *Kaffeemühle* (coffee mill) for its octagonal shape. Each side of the Vereins-Kirche was eighteen feet long and eighteen feet high; an octagonal roof rose ten feet above the sides and formed the base of an octagonal cupola with ten-foot-square sides. The cupola was crowned by an octagonal roof about seven feet high. . . . The Vereins-Kirche was also used as Fredericksburg's first school, established under Leyendecker in 1847, and also as a town hall, a fortress, a sanctuary, and, in 1896, a pavilion for Fredericksburg's fiftieth anniversary celebration. In 1897, however, having fallen into disuse and disrepair and regarded as an obstruction to traffic on Main Street, the Vereins-Kirche was torn down. When the Gillespie County Historical Society was formed in 1934, its first goal was the construction of a replica of the old Vereins-Kirche, with the assistance of the Civil Works Administration, to be completed in time for the Texas Centennial celebration in 1936, in Fredericksburg's old market square. (*Handbook of Texas Online*, s.v. "Vereins-Kirche" http://www.tshaonline.org/handbook/online/articles/VV/ccvi.html [accessed October 14, 2010])

As an old picture clearly reveals, the original structure was of a *Fachwerk* [half-timbered] construction with stones laid in between the timbers and then plastered over. As far as I can ascertain, there is no other contemporary account of the laying of the cornerstone. The historical significance of Strubberg's account, therefore, is self-evident.

4. The German settlers in Texas were famous for their propensity to formalize their social life into *Vereine*, or clubs. Singing societies, choral groups, and bands were chief among these, so much so that in 1854 a state convention was held in San Antonio in which most of the German communities in Texas were represented.
5. The first schoolteacher in Fredericksburg was Johann Leyendecker (Biesele, *History*, 143). He arrived on the bark *Richard* from Antwerp. On January 20, 1848, he was awarded 320 acres in the Fischer-Miller grant (GLOR, Fisher-Miller Colony Transfers, 000517).
6. Interestingly, the ceremony for the laying of the cornerstone as described by Strubberg has all the earmarks of a Masonic ceremony.

7. *Alter Dessauer:* This was another popular dance tune of the period.
8. Gallopade: This refers to a choreographed sequence dance for a circle of couples that was popular in the mid-nineteenth century.

CHAPTER 16

1. Springs on the Llano: It is not clear what springs he is referring to. The Llano River is fed by hundreds of springs up and down its length, which contribute to its beautifully clear waters.
2. Antelope: It would have been extremely unlikely to encounter antelope in such a valley, even though their historic range did bring them into Central Texas. Antelope prefer open country.

CHAPTER 17

1. Bats: Mexican free-tailed bats are common in the Hill Country from April until the end of the summer. The railroad tunnel south of Fredericksburg, the Eckert Bat Cave on the James River south of Mason, Texas, and the Congress Avenue Bridge in Austin are three areas where the bats congregate at the present. Their nightly departures are spectacular events.

CHAPTER 18

1. Those familiar with horses will understand this request. Horses that have been subjected to strenuous and prolonged exertion need to cool down slowly, and the best way to do this is to walk them around for a spell.
2. The Mormons actually abandoned Zodiac in 1851 after a disastrous flood inundated their settlement and destroyed the mill. They then moved to Hamilton's Creek in Burnet County. Noah Smithwick, who subsequently bought their mill on Hamilton's after they moved from that location in 1853, related how after the flood, the all-important millstones were lost in the mud and sand. Lyman Wight prayed for guidance. He then walked to a sandbank and commanded his followers to dig; they recovered the stones. Thereafter the colony moved to Hamilton's Creek, where once again they built a mill and a complete settlement, just as at Zodiac (Smithwick, *Evolution of a State,* 297–302). They sold this site in 1853 and lived a nomadic life for several months before settling in 1854 in Mountain Valley, southeast of Medina in Bandera County, at a site now covered by Medina Lake. Wight died in 1858 while preparing to lead his followers back to Missouri. He was buried in the Mormon cemetery at Zodiac. His colony thereafter dispersed; a few remained in Texas, while others moved to Iowa, Indian territory, or Utah.
3. Road to El Paso: Strubberg did not get this part of the story correct. Some of Wight's followers apparently did make their way to Utah, but many stayed in and around Bandera, where their last settlement had been located.
4. Despite its industriousness, the Mormon settlement seems to have been plagued by a chronic shortage of money. Some members of the group apparently left unpaid debts in Fredericksburg.

5. In line with the pre-Freudian sensibilities of the day, "sex" is sublimated in *Fried-richsburg*. Still, the author has consciously woven sexual attractions and taboos into the story as unseen but powerful riptides that steer our emotional involvement to a greater degree, perhaps, than we are willing to admit. In the scene where Youngbear is invited to dance with Ludwina, the undercurrent rises to the surface. Youngbear is acknowledged by the German community as an equal, good enough hypothetically to mate with Ludwina, which the dance symbolizes. Clearly, Strubberg has inserted this scene as a balance and contrast to the near rape scene of Ludwina by Kateumsi, the horror of which is intensified by allusions to miscegenation by an "inferior."

Chronological Bibliography of First Edition Books by Friedrich Armand Strubberg

A complete and accurate bibliography of Strubberg's works, which would also include those works serialized in magazines, all subsequent editions, and all known translations, does not exist. Preston Barba's bibliography, the one usually cited, is deficient in many ways. Ulf Debelius, MA, of Marburg, Germany, is working on such a comprehensive bibliography for future publication. Among other sources, Herr Debelius has examined past issues of the *Börsenblatt für den deutschen Buchhandel* [Trade Publication of the German Book Trade], which has been published continually since 1834, to obtain precise dates of publication. Herr Debelius is also the editor of a new edition of the complete works of Friedrich Armand Strubberg. He has graciously shared his research with the author. I am confident, therefore, that the above limited bibliography (first edition books) is accurate. Its purpose is to provide the reader with a sense of the scope and thematic focus of Strubberg's oeuvre. It is interesting to note that although Strubberg released twenty-one separate titles, they appeared in fifty-two volumes, for many of the novels were quite lengthy. Of the twenty-one titles, ten take place in Texas.

Amerikanische Jagd- und Reiseabenteuer aus meinem Leben in den westlichen Indianergebieten [American Hunting and Travel Adventures from the Western Indian Regions]. 24 illustrations. Stuttgart and Augsburg: J. G. Cotta'scher Verlag, 1858.

Bis in die Wildniß [As Far as the Wilderness]. 4 vols. Breslau: Verlag von Eduard Trewendt, 1858.

Alte und Neue Heimath [Old and New Homeland]. Breslau: Verlag von Eduard Trewendt, 1859.

Scenen aus den Kämpfen der Mexicaner und Nordamerikaner [Scenes from Battles between the Mexicans and the North Americans]. Breslau: Verlag von Eduard Trewendt, 1859.

An der Indianergrenze [On the Indian Frontier]. 4 vols. Hanover: C. Rümpler, 1859.

Ralph Norwood. 5 vols. Hanover: C. Rümpler, 1860.

Sclaverei in Amerika oder Schwarzes Blut [Slavery in America or Black Blood]. 3 vols. Hanover: C. Rümpler, 1862.

Carl Scharnhorst: Abenteuer eines deutschen Knaben in Amerika. Mit 6 Bildern in Farbendruck, nach Zeichnungen von August Hengst [Carl Scharnhorst; Adventures of a German Boy in America. With Six Color Plates Based on Drawings by August Hengst]. Hanover: Carl Rümpler, 1863.

Der Sprung vom Niagarafalle [Leap from Niagara Falls]. 4 vols. Hanover: Schmorl und von Seefeld, 1864.

In Mexico [In Mexico]. 4 vols. Hanover: Schmorl und von Seefeld, 1865.

Saat und Ernte [Seed and Harvest]. 5 vols. Leipzig: Ernst Julius Müller, 1866.

Friedrichsburg: Die Colonie des deutschen Fürsten-Vereins in Texas [Fredericksburg: The Colony of the German Princes' Society]. 2 vols. Leipzig: F. Fleischer, 1867.

Aus Armand's Frontierleben [From Armand's Life on the Frontier]. 3 vols. Leipzig: J. Werner, 1868.

In Süd-Carolina und auf dem Schlachtfelde von Langensalza [In South Carolina and on the Battlefield of Langensalza]. 4 vols. Hanover: C. Rümpler, 1868.

Die Quadrone: Schauspiel in 3 Aufzügen [The Quadroon Lady: Play in Three Acts]. Cassel: Gotthelft, 1869.

Der Krösus von Philadelphia [The Croesus of Philadelphia]. 4 vols. Hanover: C. Rümpler, 1870.

Die alte spanische Urkunde [The old Spanish Document]. 2 vols. Hanover: C. Rümpler, 1872.

Die Fürstentochter [The Prince's Daughter]. 3 vols. Hanover: C. Rümpler, 1872.

Der Methodisten-Geistliche [The Methodist Preacher]. Prague: Druck und Verlag der Actiengesellschaft Bohemia, 1873.

Glossary

Adelsverein: Association of noblemen. See *Fürstenverein, Verein.*

Direktion: Used in the book to refer to the central bureaucracy of the *Adelsverein* in Texas, headquartered in the *Sophienburg* in New Braunfels.

Empresario system: The legal arrangement by which certain individual entrepreneurs (empresarios) entered into a contract with the Republic of Texas (continued after Texas entered the Union in 1845) to introduce certain numbers of settlers in a given period of time. The government issued land titles to the settlers directly and upon satisfaction of the terms of the contract rewarded the empresarios for their time, effort, and expense with enormous tracts of land (premium and bonus lands) proportionate to the number of settlers introduced. The law echoed the arrangement by which Moses Austin (and subsequently Stephen F. Austin) had established the original Anglo colony in Texas.

Fleischhalle: Meat distribution center.

Frau: Title of married woman.

Fräulein: Title of young, unmarried woman.

Freidenker: Freethinker.

Freiherr: Title reserved for members of the lesser nobility in Germany.

Friedrichsburg/Fredericksburg: Friedrichsburg was the original name of the town. The town was named for Friedrich, Prince of Prussia, one of the charter members of the *Adelsverein* in Germany. At some point the named was anglicized to Fredericksburg but the author has not been able to discover when this happened.

Fürstenverein: Strubberg and several other contemporary writers preferred the term "*Fürstenverein*" to "*Adelsverein.*" Both terms refer to the group of German noblemen who constituted the Society for the Protection of German Emigrants in Texas. A *Fürst* in the hierarchy of German noblemen ranked quite high, and the *Adelsverein* counted several among their ranks. There is no English equivalent of *Fürst*, which creates problems in translation. It is sometimes rendered as "prince," but this is not quite accurate. See *Adelsverein* and *Verein*.

Gemütlichkeit: There is no English equivalent; *Gemütlichkeit* suggests an ambience that is cozy, cheerful, and solid; an atmosphere conducive to good fellowship. A very Biedermeyer concept.

Glückskind: Darling of fortune.

Hausfrau: In the traditional Biedermeyer worldview of the mid-nineteenth century, which predominated in middle- and working-class families, the role of the German "*Hausfrau*" [housewife] was strictly defined: *Kinder, Küche, Kirche* [children, kitchen, church] were the watchwords. A good German *Hausfrau* fulfilled her role in respect to each of these things willingly and energetically.

Herr Direktor: Correct form of address for Dr. Schubbert as shorthand for his official title, "Colonial-Direktor." In German it is proper to place "Herr" in front of other titles.

Herr: Title of respect for an adult male akin to "Mr." in English; denotes respect.

Marktplatz: German towns and villages are typically laid out with a central market place. Friedrichsburg followed this plan and is said to have the largest town square in the State of Texas to this day.

Obrist: Colonel.

Schlachthaus: Communal slaughterhouse.

Sophienburg: When Carl, Prince of Solms-Braunfels, established New Braunfels, built a fort, which he named after his fiancée. It grew into a compound with little resemblance to a fort, instead housing offices, warehouses, and stables of the *Adelsverein* bureaucracy in Texas. Today it is the site of a museum and library.

Straße: Street.

Verein zum Schutze deutscher Einwanderer in Texas [Society for the Protection of German Emigrants in Texas]: Official name of the corporation of German noblemen (and one woman), chartered in the Duchy of Nassau in 1842. For a fuller discussion, see introduction.

Verein, Adelsverein, Fürstenverein: A *Verein* is an organization, club, or organization. *Adelsverein* means association of noblemen. *Fürstenverein* suggests that the members of the organization were of the highest order of German nobility. All these terms are used as shorthand to the long and cumbersome official title *Der Verein zum Schutze deutscher Einwanderer in Texas*.

Vereinskirche (Vereins-Kirche): Name given to the nondenominational church built in Fredericksburg at the expense of the *Verein* in 1847 on orders from Dr. Schubbert.

Works Cited

LIST OF ABBREVIATIONS

SBAt: Solms-Braunfels Archives, transcripts. Dolph Briscoe Center for American History, University of Texas at Austin
SWHQ: Southwestern Historical Quarterly
DTTR: Democratic Telegraph and Texas Register (Houston, TX)
TD: The Texas Democrat (Austin, TX)
CCS: Corpus Christi Star (Corpus Christi, TX)
TSG: Texas State Gazette (Austin, TX)
NS: The Northern Standard (Clarksville, TX)
GLOR/GEC: General Land Office Records, German Immigration Contracts

ARCHIVAL SOURCES

"Aufruhr in Neu Braunfels gegen Meusebach" [Revolt in New Braunfels against Meusebach]. SBAt XXVIII; 27.
Bené an Castell [Bené to Castell]. February 22, 1848. SBAt XLIV; 149.
Bené an den Grafen von Castell [Bené to Count Castell]. "Finanzlage der Colonie" [Financial Situation of the Colony]. November 23, 1847. SBAt XLIV; 2–11.

Bené an den Grafen von Castell [Bené to Count Castell]. "Allgemeiner Bericht und Rechnungsabschluss" [Comprehensive Report and Financial Accounting]. January 9, 1848. SBAt XLIV; 119.

Bené an den Grafen von Castell [Bené to Count Castell]. "Colonie Bericht" [Report on the Colony]. January 9, 1848. SBAt XLIV, 30.

"Bertram Bericht" [Bertram Report]. June 1847. SBAt XXVIII; 73.

Boos-Waldeck an den Herzog Nassau [Boos-Waldeck to the Duke of Nassau]. July 31, 1842. SBAt XXX; 208.

Cappes an Castell [Cappes to Castell]. February 2, 1847. SBAt XXVIII; 140.

Cappes an Castell [Cappes to Castell]. March 9, 1847. SBAt XLI; 171.

Cappes an Graf von Castell [Cappes to Count Castell]. May 16, 1858. SBAt XLI; 287.

Cappes an Meusebach [Cappes to Meusebach]. "Die Colonie betreffend" [Concerning the Colony]. October 24, 1846. SBAt XLI; 53.

Cappes an Schubbert [Cappes to Schubbert]. "Antwort auf vorstehenden Bericht" [Answer to the Report in Front of Me]. March 28, 1847. SBAt XLIII; 151.

"Cappes Bericht" [Cappes Report]. April 22, 1848. SBAt LVI; 275.

Centralverwaltung [Home Office]. Wiesbaden. "Geschäftsbericht" [Business Report]. November 4, 1846, SBAt XXX; 1–4.

Direktor F. Schubbert an Cappes [Director Schubbert to Cappes]. "Abänderung der Colonialverhältnisse dringend erforderlich" [A Change in the Arrangements of the the Society Urgently Needed]. March 13, 1847. SBAt XLIII; 131–141.

Dr. Smolka. "Bericht an die Aktionäre über den Stand in Texas" [Report to the Shareholders about the Situation in Texas]. SBAt LIV; 90.

"Expedition der deutschen Kolonisten nach dem San Saba in Texas" [Expedition of the German Colonists to the San Saba in Texas]. SBAt LIV; 74–82.

Fischer an die Aktionaere. May 31, 1855. SBAt LIII; 165.

"German Immigration Contracts." General Land Office, State of Texas. Austin, TX.

"Lease on Nassau Plantation: German Emigration Co. and Frederic Schubbert." Fayette County Deed Book D, 536–542.

Leopold von Iwonski. "Abschrift." December 31, 1846. SBAt XLI; 107–111.

Meusebach an Castell [Meusebach to Castell]. March 6, 1846. SBAt LII; 138–142.

Meusebach an den Direktor Dr. Schubbert zu Friedrichsburg [Meusebach to the Director, Dr. Schubbert in Fredericksburg]. July 12, 1847. SBAt LIV; 123–126.

Meusebach an die Direktion in Friedrichsburg [Meusebach to the Administrative Authority in Fredericksburg]. July 1, 1847. SBAt LIV; 47–49.

"Meusebach Bericht" [Meusebach Report]. January 19, 1847. SBAt LXIII; 45.

"Meusebach Bericht" [Meusebach Report]. April 1, 1847. SBAt XXXI; 66, 67.

"Meusebach/Comanche Treaty of May 7, 1847." Archives of the Texas State Library. Austin, TX.

Schubbert an Cappes [Schubbert to Cappes]. "Bericht über Friedrichsburg und Nassau Kolonie" [Report on Friedrichsburg and Nassau Colony]. January 29, 1847. SBAt XLIII; 83–86, 163.

Schubbert an Cappes [Schubbert to Cappes]. "Betr. Colonie" [Concerning Colony]. February 8, 1847. SBAt XLIII, 120–121.

Schubbert an Cappes [Schubbert to Cappes]. "Abänderung der Colonialverhältnisse dringend erforderlich" [A Change in the Arrangements of the Society Urgently Needed]. March 13, 1847. SBAt XLIII; 131–141.

Schubbert an Cappes [Schubbert to Cappes]. "Bericht über Colonialverhältnisse" [Report on the Condition of the Colony]. March 28, 1847. SBAt XLIII; 146–150.

Schubbert an Cappes [Schubbert to Cappes]. April 20, 1847. SBAt XLI; 207.

Schubbert an Cappes [Schubbert to Cappes]. April 28, 1847. SBAt XLI; 208, 209.

Schubbert an Coll [Schubbert to Coll]. March 13, 1847. SBAt XLIII; 84.

Schubbert an den Herrn General-Commissair von Meusebach in Neu-Braunfels [Schubbert to the Commissioner-General von Meusebach]. April 20, 1847. SBAt XLI; 187–206.

Schubbert an den Herrn General-Commissair von Meusebach in Neu-Braunfels [Schubbert to the Commissioner-General von Meusebach in New Braunfels]. July 5, 1847. SBAt XLI; 246–253.

Schubbert an Meusebach [Schubbert to Meusebach]. March 29, 1847. SBAt XLI; 214.

Schubbert an Meusebach [Schubbert to Meusebach]. April 20, 1847. SBAt XLI; 198, 199, 205.

Schubbert an Meusebach. [Schubbert to Meusebach]. "Hülferuf!" [Plea for Help!]. Neu Braunfels. May 26, 1847. SBAt. XLIII; 152–165.

Schubbert an Meusebach [Schubbert to Meusebach]. July 5, 1847. SBAt LXI; 246–253.

Schubbert an Meusebach [Schubbert to Meusebach]. May 1848. SBAt LVI; 285.

Schubbert dem General Commissär von Meusebach [Schubbert to the Commissioner-General von Meusebach]. March 29, 1847. SBAt XLI; 212–215.

Smith, Herman H. "The Lyman Wight Colony in Texas." MS. Dolph Briscoe Center for American History, University of Texas at Austin.

"Solms Bericht" [Solms Report]. March 27, 1845. SBAt XL; 87.

"Texas *Verein* Account Books," *Verein* Collection, 3c32, Dolph Briscoe Center for American History, University of Texas at Austin.

Von Coll an Cappes [Von Coll to Cappes]. February 2, 1847. "Ausführliche Bericht über die elenden Zustände in der Colonie" [Comprehensive Report on the Miserable Conditions in the Colony]. SBAt LXIII; 108.

"Wurzbach." SBAt XLI; 53.

BOOKS

Abel, Wilhelm. *Geschichte der deutschen Landwirtschaft vom frühen Mittelalter bis zum 19. Jahrhundert* [History of German Agriculture from the Early Middle Ages to the Nineteenth Century]. Stuttgart: Franz Steiner, 1978.

Achenbach, Hermann. *Reiseabentheuer und Begebenheiten in Nord-Amerika im Jahre 1833: Kein Roman, sondern ein Lehr- und Lesebuch für Auswanderungslustige und gemütliche Leser* [Travel Adventures and Incidents in North America in the Year 1833; not a Novel, but Rather a Reader and Textbook for Hopeful Readers Determined to Emigrate]. Düsseldorf: Gedrückt auf Kosten des Verfassers und in Kommission bei G. H. Beyer & Comp., 1835.

Barba, Preston A. *The Life and Works of Friedrich Armand Strubbert.* New York: D. Appleton, 1913.

Bartlett, John Russell. *Personal Narrative of Explorations and Incidents in Texas, New Mexico, California, Sonora, and Chihuahua Connected with the United States Boundary Commission during the Years 1850, '51, '52, '53, and '54 in Two Volumes with Maps and Illustrations.* New York: D. Appleton, 1854.

Benjamin, Gilbert Giddings. *The Germans in Texas: A Study in Immigration.* Austin: Jenkins Publishing, 1974.

Biesele, Rudolph Leopold. *The History of the German Settlements in Texas.* 1930. Repr., Ann Arbor: McNaughton & Gunn, 1987.

Biggers, Don H. *German Pioneers in Texas.* Fredericksburg, TX: Fredericksburg Publishing, 1925.

Bracht, Viktor. *Texas in 1848.* Trans. Charles Frank Schmidt. Introduction by Theodore G. Gisch. San Marcos, TX: German-Texan Heritage Society, 1991.

Brice, Donaly E. *The Great Comanche Raid.* Austin: Eakin Press, 1987.

Britten, Thomas A. *The Lipan Apaches: People of Wind and Lightning.* Albuquerque: University of New Mexico Press, 2010.

Crisp, James. *Sleuthing the Alamo: Davy Crockett's Last Stand and Other Mysteries of the Texas Revolution.* New York: Oxford University Press, 2005.

Debelius, Ulf. *Friedrich Armand Strubberg.* Marburger ed. Published and with a Supplement by Ulf Debelius, 2011.

Dunt, Detlef. *Reise nach Texas, nebst Nachrichten von diesem Lande: Für Deutsche, welche nach Amerika zu gehen beabsichtigen* [Journey to Texas along with Reports about This Country: For Germans who Intend to Emigrate to America]. Bremen: Carl W. Wiehe, 1834.

Ehrenberg, Hermann. *Texas und seine Revolution* [Texas and Its Revolution]. Leipzig: Otto Wigand, 1843.

Fehrenbach, T. R. *Comanches: The Destruction of a People.* New York: Knopf, 1974.

Fischer, Ernest G. *Marxists and Utopias in Texas.* Burnet, TX: Eakin Press, 1980.

Ford, John Salmon. *Rip Ford's Texas.* Ed. Stephen Oates. Austin: University of Texas Press, 2003.

Geiser, Samuel Woods. *Naturalists of the Frontier.* Dallas: Southern Methodist University Press, 1948.

Glaser, Wolfgang. *Deutsche und Amerikaner* [Germans and Americans]. Munich: Verlag Moos, 1984.

Hämäläinen, Pekka. *The Comanche Empire.* New Haven: Yale University Press, 2008.

Hawgood, John A. *The Tragedy of German-America: The Germans in the United States of America during the Nineteenth Century and After.* New York and London: G. P. Putnam's Sons, 1940.

Henning, Friedrich-W. *Landwirtschaft und ländliche Gesellschaft in Deutschland* [Agricultural Economics and Rural Society in Germany]. Vol. 2. 2nd ed. Stuttgart: Franz Steiner, 1988.

Hoig, Stan. *White Man's Paper Trail: Grand Councils and Treaty Making on the Central Plains.* Boulder: University Press of Colorado, 2006.

Hunter, Marvin J. *The Lyman Wight Colony of Texas*. Bandera, TX: The Bandera Bulletin, n.d.

Johnson, Melvin C. *Polygamy on the Pedernales: Lyman Wight's Mormon Villages in Antebellum Texas 1845–1858*. Logan: Utah State University Press, 2006.

Jordan, Terry G. *German Seed in Texas Soil: Immigrant Farmers in Nineteenth-Century Texas*. Austin: University of Texas Press, 1966.

Kearney, James C. *Nassau Plantation: The Evolution of a Texas German Slave Plantation*. Denton: University of North Texas Press, 2010.

Kiesewetter, Hubert. *Industieller Revolution in Deutschland: Regionen als Wachstummotoren* [Industrial Revolution in Germany: Regions as Engines of Growth]. Stuttgart: Franz Steiner Verlag, 2000.

Kitchen, Martin. *The Political Economy of Germany, 1815–1914*. London: Croom Helm.

Lich, Glen H., and Donna B. Reeves, eds. *German Culture in Texas. A Free Earth: Essays from the 1978 Southwest Symposium*. Boston: Twayne Publishers, 1978.

Marcy, Randolph Barnes. *The Prairie Traveler: A Handbook for Overland Expeditions with Maps, Illustrations and Itineraries of Principal Routes between the Mississippi and the Pacific*. New York: Harper and Brothers, 1859.

McQuire, Patrick. "Views of Texas: German Artists on the Frontier in the Mid-Nineteenth Century." In Glen Lich and Donna Reeves, *German Culture in Texas*, 104–121.

Meusebach, John O. *Answer to Interrogatories*. Austin: E. von Boeckmann, 1894.

Miller, Thomas Lloyd. *Bounty and Donation Land Grants of Texas, 1835–1888*. Norman: University of Oklahoma Press, 1972.

Mills, Mary Motz. *The Roadside Flowers of Texas*. Austin: University of Texas, 1961.

Mohon, Monty, and Michelle Mohon. *Gillespie County: A View of Its Past*. Virginia Beach: The Donning Company, 1996.

Moore, Stephen L. *Last Stand of the Texas Cherokees*. Garland, TX: Ram Books, 2009.

———. *Savage Frontier. Vol. 3, 1840–1841: Rangers, Riflemen, and Indian Wars in Texas*. Denton: University of North Texas Press, 2007.

Morgenthaler, Jefferson. *Promised Land: Solms, Castro, and Sam Houston's Colonization Contracts*. College Station: Texas A&M Press, 2009.

Neighbors, Kenneth F. *Robert Simpson Neighbors and the Texas Frontier, 1836–1859*. Waco: Texian Press, 1975.

Newcomb, William W. *German Artist on the Texas Frontier: Friedrich Richard Petri*. Austin: University of Texas Press, 1978.

Olmsted, Frederick Law. *Journey through Texas, or, a Saddle Trip on the Southwestern Frontier with Statistical Appendix*. New York: D. Edwards and Company, 1857.

Parker, William B. *Notes Taken during the Expedition through Unexplored Texas*. Hays and Zell: Philadelphia, 1856.

Penninger, Robert. *Festausgabe zum 50 jährigen Jubiläum der Gründung der Stadt Friedrichsburg [Commemorative Edition on the Occasion of the Fiftieth Anniversary of the Founding of Fredericksburg]*. Fredericksburg, TX: Robert Penninger, 1896. Repr. and trans. C. L. Wissemann under the title *Fredericksburg, Texas: The First Fifty Years*. Fredericksburg, TX: Fredericksburg Publishing, 1971.

Prucha, Francis Paul. *American Indian Treaties: The History of a Political Anomaly.* Berkeley: University of California Press, 1994.

Ransleben, Guido E. *A Hundred Years of Comfort in Texas.* San Antonio: Naylor, 1954; rev. ed. 1974.

Reichstein, Andreas. *German Pioneers on the American Frontier: The Wagners in Texas and Illinois.* Denton: University of North Texas Press, 2001.

Richardson, Rupert N. *The Comanche Barrier to South Plains Settlement.* 1933; repr. Austin: Eakin Press, 1996.

Roeder, Flora von. *These Are the Generations.* Houston: Baylor College of Medicine, 1978.

Roemer, Ferdinand. *Texas mit besonderer Rücksicht auf deutsche Auswanderung und die physischen Verhälnisse des Landes nach eigener Beobachtung geschildert* [Texas with Special Attention to German Emigration and the Physical Characteristics of the Country, Portrayed from Personal Observation]. Bonn: Adolph Marcus, 1849. Trans. Oswald Mueller, *Texas with Particular Reference to German Immigration and the Physical Appearance of the Country.* Repr. San Antonio: Texian Press, 1983.

Rosenberg, Marjorie von. *Artists Who Painted Texas.* Austin: Eakin, 1987.

Sammons, Jeffrey. *Ideology, Mimesis, Fantasy: Charles Sealsfield, Karl May, and Other German Novelists of America.* Chapel Hill: University of North Carolina Press, 1998.

Schilz, Jodye Lynn Dickson, and Thomas F. Schilz. *Buffalo Hump and the Penateka Comanches.* El Paso: Texas Western Press, 1989.

Sealsfield, Charles [Karl Postl]. *The Cabin Book.* 1841. Trans. Sarah Powell. Facsimile reproduction. Austin: Eakin Press, 1985.

Seele, Hermann. *The Cypress and Other Writings of a German Pioneer in Texas.* Trans. Edward C. Breitenkamp. Austin: University of Texas Press, 1979.

————. *The Diary of Hermann Seele and Seele's Sketches from Texas.* Trans. Theodore Gish. Austin: German-Texan Heritage Society, 1995.

Sehm, Gunter. *Armand: Biographie und Bibliographie* [Armand: Biography and Bibliography]. Vienna: Lauretum Verlag, 1972.

Smithwick, Noah. *The Evolution of a State, or Recollections of Old Texas Days.* Austin: Gammel, 1900; repr. Austin: University of Texas Press, 1983.

Sörgel, Alwin H. *A Sojourn in Texas, 1846–1847.* Trans. W. M. Von-Maszewski. San Marcos, TX: German-Texas Heritage Society, 1992.

Strubberg, Friedrich Armand. *Friedrichsburg: Die Colonie des deutschen Fuersten-Vereins in Texas* [Fredericksburg: The Colony of the German Society of Princes]. 2 vols. Leipzig: Friedrich Fleischer, 1867.

Tiling, Moritz. *The History of the German Element in Texas, 1820–1850.* Houston: M. Tilling, 1913.

Van Wagenen, Michael Scott. *The Texas Republic and the Mormon Kingdom of God,* College Station, TX: Texas A&M University Press, 2002.

Wilbarger, J. W. *Indian Depredations in Texas.* Austin: Hutchings Printing House, 1889. Repr. Austin: Eakins Press, 1989.

Zelade, Richard. *Hill Country.* Lanham, MD: Lone Star Books, 1999.

Anderson, Allen H. "The Delaware and Shawnee Indians and the Republic of Texas, 1820–1845." *SWHQ* 94, no. 2 (October 1990): 231–260.

Barba, Preston A. "Friedrich Armand Strubberg." *German American Annals* 14 (September–December 1912): 175–225; 15 (January–April 1913): 3–63; 15 (May–August 1913): 115–142.

Biesele, Rudolph Leopold. "The Relations between the German Settlers and the Indians in Texas, 1844–1860." *SWHQ* 31, no. 2 (October 1927): 116–129.

———. "The San Saba Colonization Co." *SWHQ* 23, no. 3 (January 1939): 169–183.

Crisp, James. "Sam Houston's Speech Writers: The Grad Student, the Teenagers, the Editors, and the Historians." *SWHQ* 97, no. 2, (October 1997): 203–237.

Dunn, William Edward. "The Apache Mission on the San Saba; Its Founding and Failure." *SWHQ* 17, no. 4 (April 1914): 379–414.

Hoerig, Karl A. "The Relationship between German Immigrants and the Native Peoples in Western Texas. *SWHQ* 97, no. 3 (January 1991): 423–431.

Huber, Arnim O. "Frederic Armand Strubberg, Alias Dr. Shubbert, Town-Builder, Physician, and Adventurer, 1806–1889." *West Texas Historical Association Yearbook* 38 (1962): 37–71.

Koch, Lena Clara. "The Federal Indian Policy of Texas, 1845–1860." *SWHQ* 28 (1925): 223–234.

Koepke, Wulf. "Charles Sealsfield's Place in Literary History," *South Central Review* (1984): 55–69.

Kumanoff, Nicholas. "Born German: Made American." *The Atlantic Times* (May 2006).

Losch, Phillip. "Friedrich Armand Strubbergs fürstliche Abkunft" [Friedrich Armand Strubberg's Noble Heritage] Heft 1 (1928): 19–20.

———. "Zum Stammbaum der Strubbergs" [On the Family Tree of the Strubbergs]. *Hessenland* 27, no. 11 (June 1913); 168.

Martin, Madelle Ephard. "California Emigrant Roads through Texas." *SWHQ* 28 (July 1924–April 1925): 287–301.

Muckleroy, Anna. "The Indian Policy of the Republic of Texas." *SWHQ* 25, no. 26 (April 1922–January 1923).

Neighbors, Kenneth F. "The German Comanche Treaty of 1847." *Texana* 2, no. 2 (Winter 1964): 312–322.

Ratcliffe, "Escenas de Martirio: Notes on the Destruction of Mission San Saba." *SWHQ* 44, no. 4 (April 1991): 507–534.

Richardson, Rupert N. "Jim Shaw the Delaware." *West Texas Historical Association Year Book* 3 (1927): 3–13.

Stöhr, Louise. "Die erste deutsche Frau in Texas" [The first German Wife in Texas]. *Der deutsche Pionier* 16, no. 9 (December 1884): 372–375.

Webb, W. P. "The Last Treaty of the Republic of Texas." *SWHQ* 25, no. 3 (January 1925): 151–173.

"American Victory at Buena Vista Causes Comanches to Change Their Minds." *Democratic Telegraph and Texas Register* (Houston). May 10, 1847.

"Comanches Appear to Be Friendly." *Democratic Telegraph and Texas Register* (Houston). July 24, 1847.

"Comanches Disregard Promises." *The Texas Democrat* (Austin). June 17, 1846.

"Comanches Gather Near Fredericksburg to Sign Treaty." *Democratic Telegraph and Texas Register* (Houston). May 10, 1847.

"Comanches Reluctant to Grant Surveyors Permission to Enter Their Lands." *Democratic Telegraph and Texas Register* (Houston). May 3, 1847.

"Description of Chief Santa Anna." *Corpus Christi Star* (Corpus Christi). December 5, 1848.

"Description of New Braunfels and Fredericksburg." *Telegraph and Texas Register* (Houston). March 4, 1846.

"Erlebnisse eines deutschen Pioners in Texas" [Experiences of a German Pioneer in Texas]. *La Grange Deutsche Zeitung*, August 19, 1915.

"Fredericksburg." *Democratic Telegraph and Texas Register* (Houston). June 28, 1847.

"H. G. Catlett Reports on Renegade and Intruding Bands." *Texas State Gazette* (Austin). May 17, 1851.

"Immigrants . . . an Economic Boost." *Democratic Telegraph and Texas Register* (Houston). October 7, 1846.

"Kateumsi Suspected in Surveyors' Murder." *Democratic Telegraph and Texas Register* (Houston). August 12, 1847.

"Key-tum-see Regarded . . . as the Most Faithless and Perfidious of Their Chiefs." *Democratic Telegraph and Texas Register* (Houston). October 26, 1849.

"Large Number of Comanches." *The Northern Standard* (Clarksville, TX). July 1, 1846.

"A New Road Opened." *Democratic Telegraph and Texas Register* (Houston). June 14, 1847.

"Perpetual Gratitude Shown to Mormons." *Deseret News*. May 8, 1971.

"Santa Anna Enters Austin Unexpectedly." *Democratic Telegraph and Texas Register* (Houston). June 8, 1848.

"Settlers on the San Gabriel." *Telegraph and Texas Register* (Houston). May 22, 1844; July 17, 1844; January 22, 1845.

"Speech by Comanche Chief Santa Anna." *The Texas Democrat* (Austin). January 13, 1847.

"Speech of Mapochocopie (Old Owl)." *The Texas Democrat* (Austin). January 13, 1847.

"Town of Fredericksburg." *The Texas Democrat* (Austin). April 28, 1849.

"Treaty of December 10, 1850 between U.S. Indian Commissioners and Representatives of the Comanches, Lipans, and Other Tribes." *Texas State Gazette* (Austin). December 28, 1850.

"Walker Creek Fight." *Telegraph and Texas Register* (Houston). July 3, 1844.

"We Learn from a Gentleman . . . New Braunfels." *Democratic Telegraph and Texas Register* (Houston). June 14, 1847.

REFERENCE WORKS

Gammel, H. P. N., ed. *The Laws of Texas, 1822–1897*. vol. 2. Austin: Gammel Book Co., 1898.

Handbook of Texas Online, s.v. "Vereins-Kirche." http://www.tshaonline.org/handbook /online/articles/VV/ccvi.html (accessed October 14, 2010).

Winfrey, Dorman H., and James M. Day, eds. *Texas Indian Papers*. 4 vols. Austin: Texas State Library, 1959–1961; repr. 5 vols. Austin: Pemberton Press, 1966.

THESES AND OTHER UNPUBLISHED PAPERS

Saustrup, Anders. Unpublished translation of *Reise nach Texas* [Journey to Texas] by Detlev Dunt.

Solon, Ollie Loving. "A History of the Fischer-Miller Land Grant from 1842–1860." Master's thesis. University of Texas at Austin, 1934.

Index

Page numbers in *italics* indicate photographs.